REVELATION

A Royally Forbidden Romance

Royally Forbidden

Book Two

CLEO WHITE

Contents

Isn't it cool when exactly the right person comes into your life at exactly the right time? This one's for you, Sarah. Happy wedding day!

(Don't worry, I also got you a vacuum cleaner.)

Author's Note

Some readers may find themes in this book triggering. For a complete list of content warnings, please see the list at the back of this book.

PORTER HEIRESS GONE WILD!

STELLAND'S RACE FOR PRIME MINISTER IS HEATING UP IN MORE WAYS THAN ONE

A scandalous set of photos has emerged of Blair Porter (26), daughter of the prominent businessman and Prime Ministerial hopeful, Lord Albert Porter. The images, captured over the weekend, show the young Porter heiress perched atop the shoulders of a mystery man at a popular Ibiza nightclub.

The pictures (*see above*) show Blair in high spirits, flashing a smile as she dances and celebrates along with the crowd, leaving little to the imagination, wearing only spandex shorts and quite a lot of body glitter. Originally shared by the club's social media, the photographs spread quickly, garnering many raised eyebrows, sending her father's high-profile campaign to become the next Prime Minister of Stelland into damage control.

Blair, who has long been known for her free-spirited personality and love of the nightlife, has not responded to requests for comment, but sources close to the young socialite suggest she is unfazed by the attention, reporting her as saying, "I am in my prime boob-flashing era. If not now, when?"

Unfortunately for Blair, many of Stelland's voters disagree.

For Lord Albert Porter, a billionaire businessman and philanthropist, the photos are a major distraction from his carefully curated image as an experienced, family-oriented leader. Critics of Porter didn't hesitate, seizing the opportunity to cast doubt on his leadership.

"How can Stelland trust a man who can't manage his own family?" questioned one member of the opposition party. "If he condones this behavior—which, let's face it, isn't what voters would like to see from their PM's daughter—what does it say about his judgement and values?"

The Porters have long been known as a family of privilege and influence in Stelland. Lord Porter (60) is known for modernizing and expanding the family's investment firm Porter Capital, and is considered a seasoned, respected leader in European business circles, while his wife, Lady Lydia Porter (54), is highly regarded for her philanthropic efforts. Their eldest children have also become great assets to the Porter empire. Cedric (33) has taken the reins of the family's financial holdings as his father's attention shifts to politics, while Alba (30) has focused on establishing herself as a practicing attorney and planning her wedding to His Grace, James, the Duke of Fairborne.

It seems clear to many political commentators that Blair's wild-child behavior has undoubtedly become a blemish on her father's polished, conservative public image.

"It's going to be a challenge for the Porter campaign to convince voters that his youngest daughter's behavior isn't relevant," offered *Stelland Says* political reporter, Ingrid MacCaul, in reference to the latest scandal. "While Lord Porter has spent decades carefully building a reputation as a statesman and a man of principle, scandals like this are what can undo all of that. When you're a public figure running for office, everything and anything is under scrutiny. While I wouldn't call this a major blow to his messaging, it's certainly a distraction."

Political analysts note that it remains to be seen whether the images will have any significant effect on Lord Porter's standing in the polls. Early reactions suggest the public is divided, with some viewing the photos as harmless youthful behavior and others questioning the impact on the Porter family's public image.

Whatever the case, in a tight race against an established, well-respected politician like Prime Minister Percy Worthinger, even Blair Porter's party girl antics could end up costing her father the election.

ONE

Blair

I've always thought that Thornhurst, my family's ancestral home, must have been constructed for the sake of sheer pride. No one—*and I mean no one*—would otherwise choose such a miserable location for an estate.

It isn't close to any major city, or even roads to comfortably take you into one. The wretched place stands alone on a thin strip of land between the mountains and the sea, a fortress of aging stone which is buffeted by icy ocean wind for one-half of the year, and torrential rain for the other. The rooms are too large to ever be properly warm, and no amount of maintenance or improvements ever quite shortens the list of repairs or updates needed.

Alas, even if it's impractical and undesirable and costs far more than is reasonable to maintain, generation after generation of Porter progeny have kept up the family's most noble tradition of fighting gravity to keep Thornhurst standing. It's a showpiece, one which tells the world *"we are far too rich, powerful, and important to trouble ourselves with such pedestrian matters as practicality.*"

This kind of behavior is how the upper classes end up at the business end of a guillotine. Yet still, we persist.

I can only assume that pride must be a genetic failing, because in the centuries since it was constructed, not one of my ancestors has been willing to admit that our birthright was built upon a foundation of flawed logic and leave it to crumble into the sea.

Somebody must have died.

Big family news is the only explanation for me being summoned back here because *no one* in the family actually *lives* at Thornhurst. Not full time, anyway. The house is mainly used for big events like weddings, Christmas, or the occasional fundraiser. It's a prop—an expensive, impractical one at that—and something dramatic must have occurred for my father to interrupt his polished, important life with a mandatory family trip to our ridiculous ancestral home.

It's hard not to be irritated as I step onto the tarmac at the tiny local airport, and my very first taste of "home" is an enormous gust of wind which nearly knocks me on my butt.

God, I hate it here.

Not even six hours ago, I was sitting poolside at my friend Chloe's penthouse in Sant Antoni. The primary topic of conversation was who to invite to her birthday party next month, whether her father would let her commandeer the family's yacht for the occasion, and how many cases of champagne would be considered excessive.

Admittedly, I'd been dodging my parents' calls for a few days, hoping their inevitable ire from the tabloid photographs would fade away by the time I plucked up the courage to speak to them. An incoming call from my father's full-time assistant—or part-time mistress, depending on who you ask—had seemed safe enough to answer, for Candice is also a frequent deliverer of parental bribery offerings. This optimism betrayed me, however, when she conveyed the most unwelcome of summons: Return to Thornhurst. Or else.

Dun. Dun. Dun.

It's September, but you'd never know by my current core body temperature. The two-minute walk across the landing strip has my teeth chattering as I slide into the back seat of a waiting Land Rover, cursing myself for not thinking to dress for the weather. A tank top and miniskirt might be appropriate for Sant Antoni this time of year, but Stelland's western coast is another beast entirely.

It's been ages since I was here. My most recent visit was Christmas the year before last, when my father announced he'd be making a play for PM, and delivered our assignments to support this "exciting" new endeavor.

My mother's was to stand behind him and smile.

My brother's was to keep a firm grasp on the family's many financial holdings.

My sister's was to flash her shiny law degree and marry well.

Mine was to stay out of the way.

If I were raised in a different family and needed my parents for emotional validation or whatever, being dismissed like that might have stung. Fortunately, I'm a Porter, and Porters are trained from an early age to view our parents more as distant, wealthy benefactors, rather than anyone we should expect love or affection from. As such, I wasn't sad about my dismissal from Stelland.

If anything, minimal campaign appearances and spending the next few years doing what I liked has been an ideal setup for me. I'd hoped that maybe they'd just forget about me if I stayed away long enough. Unfortunately, it seems the media actually cares about the PM election in a tiny, European country that's primarily known for our fishing exports and for having an American actress as queen.

Sighing, I lean forward as the car begins to move away from the airfield, holding my clammy hands in front of the heating vent. My temples throb. "Any chance someone has opened a coffee shop in this godforsaken place?" I ask the driver, without any real hope.

Sure enough, the man merely grunts. "Not that I'm aware of, Miss Porter."

Of course not.

If this were a warm, habitable environment, the Porters would have no interest in it.

It's so sparsely populated out here that as the minutes tick by, we only pass a handful of tiny dwellings and a single, minuscule fishing village.

The road to the estate winds right along the coast, bordered on one side by jagged cliffs and rocky beaches, and on the other by a distant line of misty mountains. Even if I have no desire to be here, I can appreciate the tragic, romantic beauty of this place. As a child, I'd imagined tiny, winged fae flitting between the trees, and that every glint of the sun off the churning ocean was something magical in its depths.

Now, at twenty-six, I'm too busy wondering whether my reception at home will be even more inhospitable than the environment.

The drive isn't nearly as endless as I'd like.

My head flops back against the seat as the nameless driver pulls off the road, stopping before a set of black iron gates, flanked on either side by a high stone wall. I wince at the blast of icy air that hits me as he rolls down the window and reaches out to enter a code into the little box. The gates sweep open, and we carry on, making our way along the long, winding drive that snakes through the forest before emerging at the edge of a vast stretch of open space.

The house itself is situated right in the middle of the sprawling lawn, surrounded by dense woods on three sides, and rocky coast on the fourth. The drive branches off, leading toward staff cottages and the house's utility buildings—all tastefully hidden from sight—but we continue, stopping at the base of the steps which lead up to the pair of ornately carved oak front doors.

"Can I pay you to drive in circles for another hour?" I muse aloud.

The driver, whom I have just now decided I don't like very much, ignores me. Leaving the engine running, he gets out, rounding the front of the car to open my door for me. When I still don't move, he eyes me expectantly.

I glare up at him, feeling like a gazelle must, when it wanders into a nice, open field for grazing, knowing there's a possibility it may soon be picked off and eaten for lunch by an emotionally constipated lion.

With great reluctance, and ignoring my innate sense of self-preservation, I uncross my legs at last, stepping out into the cold.

"Your breath smells like dog feces," I inform the driver as I pass.

It's a lie, I was never close enough to tell. Still, it's gratifying to pause at the top of the steps and glance back, only to see him heading back around the car with a hand hovering over his mouth. Checking.

Fighting a laugh, I pull open the door and step inside, closing it behind me with an echoing thud.

Thornhurst looks the same as it always has, from the polished, dark wood panels covering the walls, to the checkered, black-and-white marble tiles beneath my feet, to the massive iron-and-glass chandelier casting an insubstantial light over the familiar space.

None of it changes. Not really.

My mother might take it upon herself to have the wallpaper replaced in the formal dining room, or new drapes put in the guest bedrooms, but these alterations always fade into the general atmosphere and sheer magnitude of my family home.

A lump seems to be lodged in my throat as I take a cautious step forward, my heels echoing off the marble floor.

"Hello?" I call, trying to sound more confident and innocent than I really am. It's difficult when I don't know exactly what I'm walking into. Disclosing pertinent information isn't the Porter way, however, and I really should have known better than to ask Candice why I was being summoned when I took her call earlier. Sure enough, the question had barely left my mouth before she huffed, *"Lord Porter didn't share that information with me. I'm merely relaying the request for your presence and providing a travel itinerary."*

Sure thing, lady. Nothing says "request" quite like a chartered jet scheduled to touch down in less than an hour, and a driver already waiting to take you to the airfield.

Only to arrive at what appears to be an empty house. Has no one else arrived yet?

Edging toward the stairs, I cross my arms tightly over my chest and try again. "Hello?"

My optimism fails me yet again when, this time, my call is met with the sound of brisk footsteps from one of the side rooms. I turn in time to see my eternally serious brother Cedric emerging through a doorway, looking even more grim than usual.

He stops at the sight of me, his frown deepening. "Ah, Blair."

"Hello, Ced," I offer weakly. "How are you?"

"Well," he replies, and with an obviously forced attempt at brotherly familiarity, offers me a tight smile as he steps forward to press a perfunctory kiss to my cheek. "You look like you've had some sun?"

I glance down at myself. "Oh, some, I suppose. Do *you* know what's going on?" I ask a little desperately, careful to keep my voice low so it doesn't carry. "All Candice told me was that I need to get back here for a family meeting. Has someone died?"

Cedric's expression tightens. "Come through," he tells me by way of response. "Everyone is in the living room." And he turns, retreating through one of the neighboring doorways without a backward glance.

I let my head drop back, permitting myself a silent groan, before I follow.

The living room, which is smaller and less formal than the drawing room, is pretty much the only reliably warm room in the house, apart from enclosed spaces like the bedrooms or my father's study. As such, it's always been a bit of a gathering place for the family when we're here, allowing us to engage in the closest thing to bonding Porters ever do—sitting in silence while occupied by our own endeavors.

And that's exactly how I find them as I trail into the room after my brother.

My father, white-haired and stern, is sitting in the largest and most comfortable armchair by the fire with a computer resting in his lap. Across from him, my mother is posed on the end of the leather couch, absorbed in a book of sample fabric swatches, every one of which appears to be a subtle variation of ivory.

I've been told my entire life that I look like her, which is true enough, if you can overlook the decades of cosmetic procedures Mom has undergone to preserve that "natural glow." We have the same hair, which lies somewhere between red and blonde, the same green eyes and pointed chin.

Comments on our resemblance never fail to make Mom beam, and I consider a head transplant.

In the loveseat is my sister Alba–another lookalike of Mom's–who also has her laptop open. Unlike my father, she isn't looking at it. Instead, the whole of her attention is focused on the man sitting beside her, her fiancé, James—or, *His Grace, the Duke of Fairborne.* They only got engaged a few weeks ago, but neither of them looks especially joyful.

Everyone looks up as Ced and I enter the room. My brother crosses to sit beside our mother, but I hover in the doorway, even more unsettled than I was a minute ago. *What the hell happened?*

My father breaks the silence.

"Blair," he greets me, his tone grave, and his lips pulled into a flat, disapproving line. "Good. You're here." He closes his laptop and leans forward to set it on the table beside my mother's many booklets of fabric samples. "I trust your flight was comfortable?"

"Um. Yes. Thank you." I shift my weight, glancing around at everyone, hoping for a smile or any sign at all of welcome. My gaze flicks from person to person, and my heart falls further as I'm met with stony expression after stony expression. We haven't been all together like this for over a year. While no one could accuse my family of being a warm bunch, typically, there is *some* perfunctory display of affection. Not today.

Dad lifts his hand to indicate the last open seat: a straight-backed, wood chair that's situated between the couch and the loveseat. "Please. Sit."

I sit, wiping my clammy palms on my skirt.

"Now," Dad continues, calm and businesslike. "I trust you know why we've all come."

That brings me up short. "Um. No?" It comes out like a question. "Nobody told me."

Desperate for some guidance, I search their faces again, and my gaze catches on my sister's, which now appears a little less stern and a little more murderous. She doesn't speak, though, keeping her lips pinched together as she stares at our father, waiting for him to continue.

The fire rustles quietly in the hearth, and outside, wind buffets the side of the ancient house, rattling a window somewhere nearby.

Dad's lips curl in a slight, unamused smile. "Perhaps it would be clearer if you picked up your mother's or my calls from time to time."

"I didn't—"

"Oh, do us all a favor and *shut up*, Blair," snarls Alba unexpectedly.

My mouth falls open. While my sister and I are hardly what anyone would consider close, she's rarely outright nasty like this. "What is your problem?"

As if to further signal trouble approaching, at my sister's side, James winces.

"*My problem?*" Alba shrieks. "*My problem* is that I do everything I can to be an asset to this family, while you float through life doing whatever you like."

I open my mouth, a retort about her being a frigid little stick-in-the-mud on the tip of my tongue, but my father's cold, commanding voice silences the entire room with a single word.

"*Enough.*"

With a dark, warning look in my direction, Dad stands, crossing to the desk in the corner. Everyone is silent as he picks something up and returns to the circle of our seated family members, tossing it onto the table without further explanation.

My heart sinks into my belly as I stare down at the magazine cover.

The more sensitive areas of the image are blurred, but not so well that the casual observer would have any doubt what they were looking at. Which is me, dressed in nothing but a pair of tiny, neon-pink spandex shorts, sequins, and glittery body paint. I'm perched atop the shoulders of a man—also shirtless and adorned with glitter—with my lips pressed to a bottle of champagne. Technicolor lights and the blur of hundreds of people are framing us, but none are visible in the frame.

Probably because none of *them* is a Porter.

"Oh," I manage, sinking lower in my seat the longer I look at it.

My father's expression tightens. "Yes. *Oh*." As though unable to stand looking at it for even one more second, he reaches out to flip over the magazine. "What on earth were you thinking?" Every word is edged with incredulous disbelief.

My eyes burn. "I—"

"You *weren't* thinking," Dad continues, his jaw rigid. "If you'd exercised even the faintest shadow of judgement, you never would have..." He flicks his wrist toward the magazine, grimacing.

"It looks a lot worse than it is," I protest weakly, "I was wearing pasties!"

The room plunges into silence, yet again.

"Am I supposed to know what *pasties* are?" Dad demands incredulously, and with the way he's looking at me, anyone would think I've grown two heads.

Unhelpfully, Alba—who looks even more pissy than she did a moment ago—scoffs. "They're sticky patches that go over the nipples of idiotic, self-centered brats who go prancing around topless in public. To spare their *modesty*, allegedly," she informs him, before turning her glower onto me. "I truly believed you couldn't be any more selfish, but here you are, proving me wrong. Honestly, Blair, how could you do this to me?"

My mouth falls open. "Are you kidding me? How is me being photographed at a party about *you*, Alba?"

My sister looks as though she may actually throttle me. "*Stelland Says* was scheduled to run a two-page spread on our engagement, but decided to bump it, because *you* running around Ibiza half naked was more interesting." She tosses her hair over her shoulder and stands, storming from the room without a backward glance.

James, who couldn't appear less interested in the family drama, lets out a deep, resigned sigh and stands to follow her, leaving me alone with my parents and brother.

"Something needs to be done, Albert," my mother sniffs, peering frantically at my father. "We can't just allow her to embarrass the family like this. I don't know how I'll ever show my face at the Lady's Bridge Club again."

"It isn't good PR for Porter Capital," Ced adds gravely, lacing his fingers together as he surveys Dad. "Investors don't like to see frivolous spending and out-of-control behavior like this from a shareholder. We have a reputation to uphold."

There is a sinking sensation in the pit of my stomach, as if I'm driving at top speed, and suddenly realize the brakes don't work.

It's no use telling anyone this wasn't my fault, that I hadn't asked for the attention, or that I hadn't known about the article on Alba and James' engagement.

Something tells me they'd made up their minds before I even arrived.

My father turns his gaze to me, and I feel about six inches tall. "Go to your room, Blair. We'll discuss what happens next before I leave tomorrow."

Two

"You always were a terrible disappointment."

The parlor, which is situated along the eastern wall of my aunt's home, Willow Bend House, is luxuriously appointed in shades of cream and gold. Stiff, embroidered throw pillows are crammed into each corner of the armchair where Princess Araminta Ashwell is seated, her back straight and her nose wrinkled in distaste.

Having spent the better part of my adolescence as this woman's ward, it's an expression I'm familiar with. Araminta is perhaps the most fortunate woman who has ever lived and often finds herself devastated by anything less than utter perfection.

I smile vaguely, resigned to my fate. "Yes, I believe you settled on that opinion when I was about twelve. I seem to remember reading something to that effect in my birthday card."

Sniffing, my aunt lifts her gaze from the unsatisfactory

earrings I've just presented her with to glower at me. "I could do without the attitude, Damien. Why, I took you in out of the goodness of my heart—"

That has me laughing. "You took me in because the king ordered you to and doubled your allowance to compensate for the inconvenience." Last I heard, the fairly outrageous sum hasn't yet diminished, despite my being out from under her roof for several decades. I can only assume no one in the family has wanted to face the inevitable nightmare which would arise from informing Araminta she may need to compromise on her standard of living.

As if to illustrate the point, several of the estate's peacocks strut by the nearest window.

"Well, it wasn't nearly enough." She rattles the earrings in their box, as if this is irrefutable proof of this statement. "When have you ever seen me wear white gold?"

Sinking back in my chair, I permit myself a heavy sigh. It's difficult to be truly troubled by my aunt's disapproval when, according to her, everything I have ever done has been substandard in some way. If ever a day came when this woman told me she was satisfied with my gifts or expressed even a hint of fondness for me, I would rush her to the nearest hospital.

Even if I was prepared for it, my obligatory annual visit, which always takes place on her birthday, requires a higher level of emotional fortitude and patience than I have to spare at the moment. I've only just arrived and am already itching to leave.

"My mistake," I apologize calmly, watching as she sets the box amongst the dozens of other gifts mounded upon her parlor's coffee table.

I eye them, wondering whether these offerings are linked to her particularly sour mood. There are still more than any ordinary person could ever wish for, but I can't help noticing that the number seems to have diminished from last year.

While not royal by blood, Araminta Ashwell's ascension from the daughter of a high-ranking duke to princess by marriage wasn't exactly a Cinderella story. Her title served only as a way to cement her place in the highest echelons of Stelland's society, a status she clung to for decades after her husband's death.

Until recently, anyway.

At seventy-two, the spoiled old bat has seen a stinging fall in public popularity as of late. Nobody is interested in an out-of-touch relic when the new king has recently married, giving Stelland a queen who is young, pretty, and—heaven forbid—*relatable*. While she could hardly qualify as a victim, I can't help but feel a pinch of pity for the woman who saw me—with great reluctance and much complaining—through my adolescence.

At least until she opens her mouth again.

"I fired my cook," she informs me, lips pinched as she leans over to examine a tray of miniature pastries, which is balanced atop a spindly table beside her.

I don't bother to disguise my amusement. "Oh? Another one?"

Araminta doesn't require further encouragement to elaborate. Selecting a treat from the ones before her, she settles it atop a fussy, lace-trimmed napkin and rounds on me again, her eyes bright with outrage. "Yes. I told him to adhere to the diet my physician provided, not remove the taste from everything. The man was always *smiling* at me, too. It was quite unsettling."

"He sounds terrible."

My aunt finding universal agreement whenever she voices an opinion is undoubtedly how this monster was created.

If I weren't currently at the lowest point in my adult life—unemployed, burdened by inescapable guilt, and not speaking with the only living family members I care about—I might make more of an effort at reminding Araminta of reality. Unfortunately for us all, I'm not up to combating the conditioning provided by decades of sycophantic admirers.

I watch as she nibbles at the pastry, makes a face, and sets it down with a noise of disapproval. Experience has taught me that expression signals the verbal thrashing of a maid is imminent. Not quite having the spirit to witness it, I stand, fastening the button on my coat. "Well, I should go, I only wanted to stop in and wish you a happy birthday, Aunt."

Araminta accepts a kiss on her bony cheek without comment. Just as I'm turning toward the door, however, her weary voice calls out from behind me. "There is another matter that we should discuss."

I grimace reflexively but manage to school my expression into one of polite interest as I turn back to face her. "And what matter is that?"

The old woman stares back at me through narrowed eyes. "My funeral."

Oh, for fuck's sake.

I cross my arms, not bothering to disguise my impatience with her dramatics. "I know for a fact that there are members of the royal household in charge of making arrangements for such events. I'm hardly a party planner."

Disregarding the insinuation her funeral would be a party, Araminta tuts. "The logistical specifications have all been settled for many years. I've also arranged for my wishes to be made public, so *the king* isn't tempted to take any shortcuts." Her tone reflects what she thinks of the current head of the Ashwell royal family.

"That's very clever," I chuckle, filled with reluctant admiration for this plan. Having had quite a lot of experience with the king in question. I know that ignoring Araminta's undoubtedly outlandish last requests is precisely what he would do and can only hope I'm in the room to witness his reaction when he learns what she's done. "What do we need to discuss about it?"

The old woman shifts in her seat, her lined features tightening ever so slightly. "It's date. I thought it appropriate to inform you that the event will be occurring sooner rather than later."

For a moment, all I can do is stare at her, the meaning of her words sinking in with each tick of the grandfather clock on the far wall. "Are you telling me you're dying?" I ask, mustering up a feeble show of carefree bravado. It's hardly unlike Araminta to be melodramatic, and her version of death may be not receiving an invitation to the palace's annual Christmas party.

My aunt isn't pouting, though, or raging against the queen, or demanding I fix whatever it is that's displeased her. No, she merely sits before her disappointing array of birthday gifts, her nose wrinkled as if she's smelled something offensive. "Apparently. I've developed some ghastly mass. Not the sort they can remove."

My lungs are empty as I return to my seat, sinking slowly onto the rich, upholstered cushion. I'm hardly a stranger to loss. At forty-two, I've seen more death than anyone ought to, and yet the news that this woman—who was more of a disinterested teenage babysitter than anything resembling a mother—is dying, has knocked the wind right out of me.

I stare at her, watching as she selects another pastry from her tray, grappling with my shock and trying to think what on earth one could say in response to something like that.

"The doctors—" I begin, but Araminta brushes the question away with a flick of her thin wrist.

"There's nothing to be done," she assures me primly, abandoning her quest for another treat and folding her hands in her lap. "Don't force me to go into the specifics. It's terribly gruesome, and I would prefer to enjoy my last birthday, if it's quite alright with you."

I swallow back my questions and my natural response, which is to immediately enter problem-solving mode. As I really ought to have learned by now, life has a tendency to drum up situations that are beyond my personal control, and this is one of them.

Araminta Ashwell is dying, and there isn't a thing I can do about it.

"Is there anything you need from me?" I ask, a little desperately, because nothing will settle the familiar, gnawing pit of grief opening inside me except *action*.

Even shocked and reeling with the news, I have decades of experience with my aunt and certainly know when I'm being managed. Sure enough, Araminta sits up a little straighter, a flash of triumph in her pale eyes. "As a matter of fact, there is something which would put my mind at ease. Before the end."

I can't decide if I should feel annoyed or grief-stricken.

"What's that?" I ask, weary now.

Whatever request she is about to set before me will almost certainly be something I'd rather not do.

"You remember my goddaughter, Lady Porter, don't you?"

Already, I don't like where this is going. Lydia Porter, the daughter of Araminta's closest old-lady crony, was already engaged and well on her way to the life of a high-society wife by the time I came to live at Willow Bend House. We met a handful of times, but she had paid little attention to the "*child of a distant cousin*" her godmother was charitable enough to take in. In return, I—a grief-stricken eleven-year-old—could hardly have given less of a shit.

I haven't seen her since, or at least not in person. Admittedly, she appears on many screens or newspaper photographs in Stelland, usually smiling blandly beside her politician husband. Lady Porter is also one of my aunt's very favorite names to drop in conversation, a prestigious connection to reassert her relevance, if ever it's in question.

"Yes," I admit, eyeing the woman before me warily. "What about her?"

Pursing her lips, Araminta lets out a disapproving sigh. "She and her husband, Lord Porter—you remember Lord Porter, don't you?"

Dying or not, that question doesn't save her from my exasperated look. "*Yes.*"

Araminta isn't troubled by my attitude. "Well, I was invited to a dinner party there a few nights ago, and Lord Porter mentioned how they've found themselves in need of a new head of security for their home estate, Thornhurst. Apparently, the man they have has been asking to retire, and the computers and such need to be updated. Naturally, I suggested you. With your experience, they were *very* interested." She smiles triumphantly. "I told them you would be happy to help."

For fuck's sake.

"How very kind of you to volunteer me for a job I don't want."

The lack of enthusiasm has her attention. Frowning, she leans forward, glowering at me. "Why ever not? You've just told me you aren't employed. Surely such an opportunity would be quite beneficial to you."

It's exactly like Araminta Ashwell to assume I—as a non-royal, ordinary human being—would be beside myself for an opportunity such as this. While elections are nearly a year away, the polls appear promising for Lord Porter, which would make working for him excellent for my resume.

There's only one problem: I don't give a shit about my resume.

"I'm not unemployed, I'm taking leave. It's an intense job." And, more importantly, one that can't be done without a clear head. Not responsibly, anyway.

Araminta's answering stare is withering. "You never had problems with being in the guard before. Is it the queen?" An eager glint appears in her eyes as she poses the question. "I've wondered if she isn't quite as *sweet* as everyone makes her out to be. Tell me honestly, is she an opportunistic little harlot?"

How have we strayed so far from the point of this conversation in such a short period?

Willing my voice to remain steady, I attempt to get us back on track. "The queen is not an opportunistic little harlot, and I am very sorry you'll disappoint the Porters, however"—I fix her with a stern look—"I am not interested."

Silence.

"Haven't I just told you I'm dying?"

I lean back, crossing one leg over another. "Very sorry to hear. Happens to us all."

She tries again. "Lord Porter will very likely be elected Prime Minister."

"Good for Lord Porter."

Araminta splutters. "It's really quite important, Damien. Honestly, I'm surprised at you. They're practically family."

Though not for the reason she intended, this is the blow that lands the hardest, and my mouth is dry as I open it to voice my retort. "I have enough family."

Fucking *family*. With the complicated range of emotions I've associated with the word, it's a wonder it means anything at all to me anymore. This impression is solidified as Araminta's lips flatten into a line and she leans forward, obviously finished with my show of defiance.

"Well then," she declares. "If you're unwilling to take care of yourself, I'll have to do it for you."

This statement is a little ironic, considering it's issued by a woman who had the butler take me to the emergency room for stitches when I fell off my bike at age thirteen.

"Do tell," I counter, "how are you planning to do that?"

My aunt's lip curls. "By making you my heir."

I stare at her as the poorly veiled threat sets in, stretching this afternoon's range of emotions to include betrayal and fury as well. What she's saying... Of all the fucked-up fruit I've tasted from the Ashwell family tree thus far, this very well might be the worst of it all.

"I won't accept that," I spit, the words as meaningless as my aunt's facade of giving a damn about my welfare.

As she just told me she plans to make the whole thing public to prevent the king from pulling the plug on the lavish funeral arrangements, whether or not I accept the inheritance, the damage will be done. Princess Araminta leaving her fortune to an unknown, *former* member of the royal household would never go unnoticed.

The room swims around us as my vision narrows, closing in on the selfish woman sitting before me. "What you're doing is blackmail," I hiss. "You realize that, don't you? You are blackmailing me, Araminta."

Dismissing this with a scoff, she leans over to select another pastry. "Don't be so dramatic."

I let out a choking noise. "Dramatic? *You know*—" My voice has risen in my panic, and a warning glance from my aunt has me lowering it again, gritting out each word through bared teeth. "*You know* I've never wanted any part of it. I do not want to be an Ashwell."

And who, seeing this very scene, could blame me for it?

For so long, my anonymity was protected by the uniform I wore and the careful distance I kept from the spotlight. Now that I've taken it off, and with Araminta threatening to shed a bright light on me... It wouldn't hold up.

Secrets do not remain secrets when the entire country is

looking for them, and I, the illegitimate son of a long-dead king, would never know another moment's peace as long as I lived if anyone knew my true identity.

Settling back in her seat, my aunt gazes at me. "Well then," she says, lifting her bony chin. "I suggest you take the job."

THREE

In my experience, the best way to get through any Porter family gathering is to spend as much time sleeping as possible.

It's safer to be unconscious, and therefore blissfully unaware of whatever is underway elsewhere in the house, rather than being tempted to—god forbid—engage in it. I've employed this strategy since I was a teenager, and by now, my body seems to have developed a built-in trigger response: When exposed to Porter stress, *sleep*.

My brother thinks I'm a waste of space who isn't worth his energy? *Sleep.*

My sister thinks I'm an attention whore who would purposely ruin her engagement announcement by flashing my tits to half the world? *Sleep.*

My parents wish they'd stopped after two perfect children and not rolled the dice a third time? *Sleep.*

It works so well that, in the aftermath of the most half-hearted intervention ever recorded, I fall into bed and sleep for a record fourteen hours. There may have been one time I woke up to pee and down a glass of icy water in the darkened bathroom, but the memory is so hazy it might as well have been a dream.

By the time I (reluctantly) regain consciousness, my mouth feels as though it was stuffed with cotton balls, and my body aches from lying in one position for such a long time. I'm also starving. So, in the absence of emergency supplies—the maid must have taken the granola bars and fruit snacks out of the desk since I was last here—I'm forced to abandon the safety of my room.

The house is quiet and still as I slip downstairs, peering into every room I pass for signs of my siblings or parents. There's no hint of anyone, however, until I reach the ground floor hallway, which runs the length of the entire house and is the most direct route to the kitchens. It's there that I'm forced to come to an abrupt halt to avoid colliding with Candice—my father's mistress/assistant—whose nose is in her phone.

"Good, you're awake," she sneers, barely looking at me as her thumbs fly over the screen, composing a message that's far more deserving of her time than I am. "Lord Porter would like to see you."

My stomach twists. "Can it wait? I'd like to get some breakfast."

"It's one o'clock in the afternoon."

"Lunch, then," I counter, already moving past her.

God only knows what my father has to add to last night's discussion, but it won't be a loving heart-to-heart. As such, this *talk* isn't exactly at the top of my to-do list.

Apparently, the woman who spends her working hours with her nose up my father's ass and non-working ones probably doing more of the same, doesn't think much of my priorities. "Blair?" she calls after me, her tone sickly sweet and dripping with condescension.

God, if it wouldn't make my mother so happy, I'd do everything in my power to get her fired.

I halt and, baring my teeth into something resembling a smile, turn to look at her directly. "Surely you must mean, *Miss Porter*, Candy? The alternative would be quite disrespectful."

The smug, self-satisfied look on her face slips. "It's Candice, actually. And of course, *Miss Porter*." A vein in her forehead twitches. "I'm just letting you know that your father's car will be arriving in half an hour. I was actually on my way to wake you up. So, I'm afraid your *breakfast* will have to wait."

I let out a heavy sigh, more irritated that I have to do her bidding than at the prospect of putting off my meal. "Thank you so very much for your invaluable assistance, Candy. That will be all."

Without bothering to correct me, Candice strides off, shaking her head as though I'm the most unbelievable, audacious creature on the planet. I wait until she's gone before permitting my shoulders to drop and, recognizing defeat, abandon my path to the kitchen.

Thornhurst's staffing is typically pretty thin. My parents keep on just enough people to ensure the place remains in ship-shape: a maid or two, a maintenance man, and a groundskeeper. The staff, much like myself, see this place for the void of depression and futility it is, and don't usually last long.

The nearer I get to my father's study, however, the busier the house becomes. It's mostly Dad's staffers and a few campaign people I've never met before. I smile when I see Old Freddy stepping into the hall. "Howdy, Fred," I chirp in a fake American drawl, genuinely happy to see someone for the first time since I arrived.

Old Freddy, who lives in the nearest village with his wife,

has been the only consistent staff member as far as I can remember and has always been sweet to me. His job is technically only to coordinate personal security for the family and the house, but the remote geography of Thornhurst means it can take regular police hours to get here in an emergency. As the estate owns everything in the general vicinity, Freddy operates as sort of an unofficial sheriff, too.

Which must be why he wears the cowboy hat, despite having been born and raised in Stelland.

"Howdy to you, Miss Blair," counters Freddy, offering me a fond, if weary, smile as I approach. "You haven't been too good about staying out of trouble, eh?"

"Maybe next time."

His smile turns sad, but he doesn't respond or stop to chat more, carrying on down the hall as I pause before my father's office door with dread pooling in my gut. An indistinct male voice rumbles from beyond the fine, polished door, and god, I don't want to be here.

There's really no reason to be nervous. It's not like speaking to my parents has *ever* been easy or informal. I have no memory of my father coming to knock on my bedroom door, to sit at the end of my bed and discuss whatever I'd done, like in the movies.

It was always like this: me being summoned and sitting across a desk from him, usually in a seat that is shorter and less comfortable than his.

I should be used to it, and I am, but the familiarity of the routine doesn't make it pleasant.

Bracing myself for the inevitable ego-bruising to come, I lay my hand against the wood door and push it open.

The first thing I see is Lord Porter himself, who is standing behind the antique desk that is situated in the center of the stuffy room, arms crossed and frowning. He's silhouetted by the floor-to-ceiling bookshelves, which take up every wall in this room, each of them laden with rare books and legal tomes I've never seen him read.

My father's eyes find mine over the heads of the three aids sitting before his desk in wood chairs. All of whom are dressed in sleek office attire, a laughable contrast to my own sweat-pants and fluffy bunny slippers. They're speaking quickly, apparently mid-way through a debate on which polling is best to highlight in the meetings with donors next week, but fall silent when they realize Lord Porter is no longer paying attention.

All three turn, and, upon seeing who it is, just as quickly avert their eyes. As if having seen my tits in a magazine makes it indecent to look at me fully clothed.

My father sets down the paper in his hand and smiles grimly at his staffers as he sinks into the high-backed leather chair behind his desk. "Excuse us for a moment," he tells them. "I need to speak to my daughter before we leave for Wyngate."

I wrap my arms around my waist, stepping to the side as the three aids file out of the study, watching as my father leans back in his big leather chair, staring at me with a look I'm not sure I've ever seen him wear before.

My stomach twists as the last of them leaves. "Close the door, Blair."

I do as he says and turn back to take one of the empty chairs, folding my hands in my lap. Obviously, I knew I fucked up, but ordinarily I'm hit with a lecture and sent on my way. Out of the country and out of his hair is exactly how my father likes me.

Something is different this time, but I know better than to speak before I know what I'm up against, so I keep my lips pressed together, waiting for the ax to fall.

"I spoke with the family attorneys and my public relations team for the campaign this morning," Dad informs me conversationally after a pause, reclining in his richly upholstered chair and surveying me over the surface of the desk.

It's difficult to swallow past the lump in my throat. "Oh?" I manage, fiddling with the hem of my top.

He hums in acknowledgement, but doesn't reply, staring at me with an unsettling intensity that has me shifting in my seat. With every second of silence that passes, the desperation to know what he's thinking notches higher.

"I really am sorry, Dad," I blurt out after what feels like a full minute might have passed, unable to keep it bottled up any longer. "About the photographs, I mean. It won't happen again. Promise."

It's difficult to put my finger on what, but something in my father's energy seems to shift as I make my plea, like I've confirmed something for him without realizing.

"No," he agrees at last, his lips pressed into a flat line. "It won't." I watch as he leans down to pull open a drawer on the side of his desk. When he straightens up, there's a thick packet of paperwork in his hand, which he tosses onto the desk. "Do you know what this is?"

I glance down at the lines and lines of official-looking text, too edgy to even take a stab at decoding it, and shake my head.

Dad's weary, exasperated look makes me feel about five inches tall. "It is an emergency legal filing to freeze your access to your trust fund. My attorneys have expedited the process and have already submitted documentation and evidence to the presiding judge. You will receive the paperwork later today."

His words hit me squarely in the chest, pushing the oxygen from my lungs. It's so sudden and so intense that the room seems to swim in my periphery. Surely, what happened... it wasn't *that bad*, was it? I've fucked up before, and sure, the media caught wind of it this time, but to cut me off for it?

"Evidence?" I ask in a broken whisper, staring at the

packet of paperwork, which suddenly feels more like a bomb waiting to explode.

This can't be happening. It just can't.

"Evidence," my father confirms, his lips pulled into a grim, satisfied smile at my reaction. "That you are not of sound mind to make responsible, informed decisions with the money entrusted to you. The filing requests that an impartial trustee be appointed to handle any financial disbursements. For you to receive so much as a cent, you'll need to submit an official request. In short, Blair, you've been put on a very short leash."

Crying will not help me here. If anything, tears have been previously proven to make *Lord Porter* annoyed rather than sympathetic, but I can't help it. My eyes burn and I blink rapidly, scrambling for the correct thing to say, the precise sentiment he needs to get me out of this.

Even as I search for a way out, though, I know there isn't one. He might have forgiven me if I'd only embarrassed myself, but I didn't. This time, I embarrassed him *and* the family. He won't let that go.

Like he knows I'm beyond words, Dad continues, his lips pressed into a flat line. "The election is in eight months, and you have become a liability. Perception is vital, Blair, so until you have proven yourself capable of exercising restraint and managing your own affairs, it will be done for you."

My hands twist in my lap, and I stare at him, still mentally scrambling for a loophole, a way out. "What... what do you want me to do?"

"You will stay here, at Thornhurst, until the court order expires in May."

His words hit me squarely in the middle of my chest, so sharp and sudden and powerful that I can barely breathe. *Eight months.* I have to stay in this godforsaken place for *eight months.*

"None of your friends"—his mouth twists at the word, as

if the people I've spent my time with are too vile to mention with a straight face—"will be permitted onto the grounds. There will be no drugs and no alcohol."

I grit my teeth. "I don't do drugs."

Often, anyway.

Dad gives no indication he heard this. Lacing his fingers together atop the desk, he leans forward, cold eyes boring into mine. "Your mother and I think a little stability and routine will do wonders for your well-being. We've decided you're to use this time to focus on your health, committing to regular exercise and improving your diet."

Unthinking, I let out a sharp, disbelieving noise. "God, I haven't gained that much—"

Again, he continues as if I haven't spoken at all, his sharp, authoritative voice cutting over mine. "In addition, Candice has made arrangements for you to attend online intermediary classes, to brush up on your studies in preparation for the upcoming school year. Upon which time, you will enroll at Orwick University and earn a degree in something sensible. Something that can be leveraged to give you a position in the family firm once you've graduated. I've already pledged a sizable amount to the alumni association, and they've generously agreed to hold a place for you."

The noise I make in response is part cry, part laugh. "You can't just... decide all that. You can't make me stay here. I'm not a prisoner."

"No," he agrees. "You're more than welcome to make your own way in life, with no work history, no university education, and a proud history of displaying your breasts for half the world to see. Or you could enter a lengthy legal battle. Unfortunately, as you have already provided us with more than sufficient evidence of your erratic behavior, I can't see it going well for you."

My lungs ache as I sink back in my chair, staring at him as

I struggle to contain the panic swelling inside me. My father has never been soft with us, and while I've seen hints of his ruthlessness, it's never been directed toward me.

The phone sitting on his desk chimes, and Dad holds up a finger to stop my rebuttal, his eyes flying over the screen. When he looks up again and sees the tears streaming down both sides of my face, he merely sighs. "For Christ's sake, get yourself together, Blair."

My bottom lip trembles, and I shake my head bitterly. "I'm *so very sorry* that I have feelings."

"Perhaps that is another thing you can work on during your time here," he suggests blithely, rising from his chair. I watch, silently reeling, as he gathers up his phone and a few folders. Stepping out from behind the desk, he pauses, frowning down at me. "Think of this as an opportunity."

"An opportunity?" I echo shrilly, the words slanted in incredulous disbelief.

His mouth flattens into a grim line, once again. "To better yourself. Eight months to focus on finding some purpose in life, rather than fluttering around the globe like a lost bird. Doesn't that sound nice?"

And, obviously past caring whether or not I find it nice at all, my father pats me twice on the shoulder and continues toward the door.

An indistinct, meaningless chorus of murmuring voices carries back to me from the room beyond, but I stay where I am. I listen as they move farther and farther away, until all I hear is silence.

I'm alone.

Four

The call from Lord Porter's assistant comes not even a full day after I've returned home to Wyngate, cursing Araminta Ashwell and wracking my mind for a way around this ludicrous assignment she's pushed on me. Unfortunately, no obvious escape occurs to me, and I have little choice but to accept the man's invitation.

The location of this meeting, The Lord's Club, doesn't particularly surprise me.

The club is situated in one of the most expensive, exclusive neighborhoods in Wyngate, only a few blocks north of Ashwell Palace. It hides in plain sight, a historic marble structure which sits amongst a row of law offices and other upper-crust businesses that look just like it.

The only thing about the place that might hint at its purpose is a metal plaque set beside the front door, which is adorned by a coat of arms older than most family names.

If the rumors are to be believed, joining The Lord's requires a personal recommendation from a member and yearly six-figure fees. All so one has the honor of sitting amongst other men of a similar social and financial standing, smoking cigars and sipping overpriced drinks.

Even for a man who hasn't spent their entire life standing adjacent to great power, it would be impossible to miss the palpable *shift* which occurs when I step inside. The entryway is paneled in dark, rich oak and lit by a brass chandelier, which isn't nearly strong enough to truly break through the gloomy atmosphere. Through a door to the right, I hear a low rumble of male voices and find myself standing a little straighter as I give my name to the well-dressed hostess.

"I'm a guest of Lord Porter's," I tell her calmly, eyeing the portrait of an ugly old man which is hung just above her head.

She checks something in the book resting on her desk before offering me a bland smile, which doesn't reach her eyes. "Of course. Welcome, Mr. Mallory. Follow me, please."

I'd rather turn around and sprint from the building, but do as she requests, feeling the weight of dozens of sets of eyes as we move through the doorway and into The Lord's inner sanctum.

A gleaming bar stands along the wall to my right, but there are no stools, only leather chairs circling the glossy wood card tables stationed around the room. For a Monday morning, it's surprising how many of them are occupied, and how many of their occupants are holding tumblers of amber liquid. An acrid cloud of cigar smoke hangs in the air. That, coupled with the dim lighting, gives the entire space an unnatural, hazy glow.

If someone were to imagine "rich old man smoking club," this is what they would picture. To The Lords, it seems that sacrificing tradition isn't worth bucking the cliché of it all.

The hostess leads me through the labyrinth of tables and the appraising stares from their inhabitants, heading straight for the back of the room. Though he looks and dresses just like the rest of the men here, Lord Porter is easy enough to pick out from the crowd. A fit, white-haired man of about sixty, he's reclining casually in his club chair, listening to the small cluster of men who have paused to speak to him. As we approach, I watch him lift a tumbler of Scotch—which must cost more than many people's rent—to his lips.

He lowers it again when he sees me coming.

"You'll have to excuse us, gentlemen," Porter informs his companions, inclining his head toward me as he sets down his drink. He doesn't introduce me or give any indication as to what our business is, but I have no doubt that's by design.

As I come to a stop before him, the men eye me as they drift off into the murky room, leaving me alone with the man who will very likely be our next Prime Minister.

"Mr. Mallory, I presume?" Porter gestures to the chair across from him. "Please."

It's an invitation, but I don't discount the superiority behind the question as I take the offered seat. No doubt about it, this is a man accustomed to making the rules.

"Thank you for your invitation," I tell him politely, offering a tight, if unenthusiastic smile. Araminta might have cornered me into this, but I certainly won't bow and scrape for the job.

The corners of Porter's lips tug into the ghost of a smile. "Your relation, Princess Araminta, had quite positive things to say about your experience and expertise, but I did my own research. Of course."

"Of course," I agree coolly.

"Most impressive," Porter continues, reaching to pick up his tumbler again, never once breaking eye contact as he swirls the drink. Lifting one finger from the glass, he points at me. "Educated at Burgess, then served as an officer in the Royal Navy, with special training in the Intelligence Corps, before settling down to protect the crown itself. Is that right?"

I incline my head, my expression impassive. "It is."

Some might be intimidated by all this, but I have more than enough experience in dealing with powerful men to separate showmanship from genuine authority. I was never going to be one of them, and yet I was kept close, an outsider with a clear view in, and I learned how men such as Lord Porter operate.

Though their egos would be heartily offended by my conclusions, I know they are all more or less the same. He's counting on his reputation and on having something that I want to achieve the desired effect.

It won't work on me, as I care about neither.

Come to think of it, I care about very little these days. Guilt and regret have a way of draining one's priorities.

"The princess seemed to think you'd be an excellent fit for my household," Porter offers, after a long sip of Scotch. "I'm curious, though. Why leave the palace? This would be a step down for you, on paper, anyway." His lips curve, as if to say he might not have the title of King, but he sees himself as superior to the man who does.

Also not a surprise. Every man in this room thinks he would do a better job of it, and yet they would trip over themselves to kiss ass if my brother were to walk through that door.

I nod, arranging my expression into one which hopefully conveys how seriously I take the question. "My role as head of the royal guard was largely administrative. I did a great deal of scheduling, training, and management, but not much else. It was wearing on me, and my heart wasn't in it. Taking leave seemed the responsible thing to do, given the nature of my work."

Even the shadow of truth, hidden in those words, sends a vicious, shooting pain through my chest.

"Not one to sit behind a desk, then?"

"No, sir."

Porter chuckles. "I envy you. What I wouldn't give to be on my feet more, but that should improve as the election gets closer. Are you married?"

"No, sir."

"Children?"

"None."

This seems to satisfy him. "A man dedicated to his career. Admirable." He studies me, apparently making up his mind about something, before continuing. "While upgrading security on the estate prior to the election is a high priority, I'm afraid there is a bit more to the position than I disclosed to the princess. Aspects more sensitive than would be appropriate to discuss at a dinner party."

Despite my best efforts, he has my attention. "Oh?"

Another sip of his drink, and he sets down the empty glass, looking weary now. "My youngest daughter," he explains at last. "Blair."

Ah. I probably should have guessed she would have something to do with it.

While I would hardly call myself a rabid consumer of celebrity gossip, it's hard to escape learning about a scandal, especially one which involves the prospective PM's daughter being photographed dancing topless in Ibiza.

"Is this pertaining to... the news?" I have no idea how anyone could put it delicately.

"Yes," Lord Porter confirms, lifting his hand to signal another drink from the bar. When his gaze returns to me, he looks more composed. "There were threats against her personal safety following the publication of the images. My people investigated and found most of them to be baseless, but there were a few they thought credible."

For fuck's sake. Of course there were threats.

Just as I was familiar with the sort of powerful man sitting before me, without even laying eyes on her, I know exactly what sort of girl his daughter is. Spoiled, pampered little princesses who spend too much money and act out to get Daddy's attention are hardly uncommon in high society.

Porter continues, sounding a little weary now. "Frankly, the threats are only part of the problem. She's out of control. Partying, spending obscene amounts of money. There are drugs, alcohol..." He trails off, shaking his head. "Her behavior has become a liability. Your position would be as head of security for my home estate, yes. However, with my and my wife's protection handled by the National Protective Service, your chief priority will be upgrading the security systems we have in place in preparation for my appointment to PM, and to keep Blair safely out of the news for the duration of the campaign. For her own good, and mine."

My temples throb.

"Is she... on board with this?" I ask carefully, because I can't imagine the twenty-something Porter heiress would be content with setting aside her frivolous lifestyle for the sake of her father's image. While I'm confident I could secure the property, keeping Blair Porter inside could be edging perilously close to kidnapping, and I won't be a part of it.

Porter swipes his tongue over the front of his teeth, frowning slightly. "On board? No. She's hardly unreasonable, however, and understands that cooperating is in her best interest. My wife and I have made it clear that, should she not comply with the... *lifestyle adjustments,* then she's on her own. We've already obtained an emergency court order to limit her control of her trust fund, and it won't be returned until after the election. If she isn't cooperative, we'll consider more permanent measures."

In other words, Princess Porter has been put in time-out.

Considering her tits are on the front page of half the tabloids in Europe, and her primary accomplishments seem to pertain to binge drinking, I can't imagine she would fare well without an endless pile of money to play with. As far as plans to remediate the situation go, Porter's plan seems to be a decent one.

"Lifestyle adjustments?"

Porter heaves a sigh. "She's to remain in the grounds of the estate, apart from exceptions pre-approved by me or her mother. No alcohol, no drugs, no unapproved visitors." The bartender appears at his side, and Porter doesn't so much as glance at the man as he hands him a refilled glass and takes away the empty. Once he's gone, the lord continues. "We've instructed her to use the time to improve herself with exercise and online education. She needs structure, discipline, and someone professional to hold her accountable."

Fucking hell.

I would bet *"improving herself"* is the very last thing Blair Porter wants to do, but it seems she doesn't have a choice. After a lifetime of obscene privilege and being permitted to do whatever pleases her, she's finally stepped over the line.

And it's somehow become my job to rein her in.

It's difficult to bite my tongue and to not spit the truth right back in this man's self-important face. What I wouldn't give to tell him that I *despise* people like his daughter—People who have never known life outside their gleaming, golden bubble, or have any idea what true suffering is. I would bet she's never had to work hard, or exercise restraint, or *give a shit* about anything in her entire life.

Very like my own, dear aunt.

"We didn't feel it advisable to inform her of the threats," Porter continues airily, "my daughter is many things, but clear-headed isn't one of them. My advisors agreed, the less Blair knows on that front, the better. Whomever I select for this position will be expected to exercise discretion."

That gives me pause. While nothing he's told me thus far suggests his daughter is responsible, it seems ill-advised to *not* tell her something like this. Nowhere, not even her family's estate, is totally secure, and Blair's own ears and eyes are the most important line of defense. If she isn't aware of a potential risk, she won't be looking out for one. To me, it sounds like Porter is more concerned with keeping his reputation intact than his daughter's safety.

I shift uneasily in my seat, considering how best to put this, and coming up short. Even if I might not approve of these methods, is it really my place to question them? I'm an employee, not a member of the family.

Yet another adjustment for me to make.

"If you and your team think that's best," I say at last, hating it as I do.

Porter appears pleased, however. "There is a cottage on the grounds that would be for your private use, as part of your compensation package," he informs me, obviously eager to settle the matter. "I'll have my assistant reach out to you with a more comprehensive pay structure, employment contract, and a non-disclosure agreement. If I decide you're right for the job, of course."

The last bit almost makes me laugh. He may want to maintain the upper hand in this conversation, but it's fairly obvious to me that Lord Porter is desperate. Men like him never want to clean up their own mess.

Strangely, though, I don't hate the idea of this job quite as much as I thought I would.

For one thing, it might be good to be away from Wyngate with its many lingering reminders of my failures and the omnipresent shadow of my family. A chance to forget, and room to breathe.

For another, an unfortunate hazard of living as I have—adjacent to great power and privilege, but never a part of it—is that I have had to tolerate more people like Lord Porter and his bratty daughter than I'd care to.

How often does one have the opportunity to vent decades of resentment and frustration by reminding a pampered party princess that the world does not revolve around her?

This isn't a job I want, but, just maybe, it's the job I need.

For the first time since I entered this building, I feel myself smile. "When can I start?"

FIVE

BLAIR

By nightfall on Friday, barely twenty-four hours after I arrived at Thornhurst, everyone was gone, and an unnatural hush had settled over the great house.

It's my first time here alone, and at first, I could ignore the quiet. I occupied myself with perfecting a few new makeup looks, binging reality TV in the seldom-used media room, and exploring the house. It was lonely, sure, but lonely was better than my every move being scrutinized by my family.

Days passed, more days passed, and now, nearly a full week into my father's version of house arrest with only myself for company, I may actually be going mad.

It's been a long time since I was truly alone. In Paris, I lived with a pair of fashion influencers, Celine and Rachel, who kept our little townhouse full of their glamorous, interesting friends. In Amsterdam, there was Gabriel, and a coffee table full of drugs as a popular draw for glassy-eyed guests, here one day, then gone the next.

Wherever I went, I kept myself busy and surrounded by

people. There was music and laughter and *life*. My days were always different, and I did whatever pleased me, sampling every pleasure life had to offer. It was a hedonistic, bohemian existence, and I found it all very romantic.

Being shut off from that, plunged into the quiet, unearthly stillness of this place, is more than jarring. Within days, Thornhurst has begun to feel less like a house and more like a tomb.

Only seven months and three weeks to go.

Fan-tastic.

Despite spending every holiday here, for the life of me, I can't remember how I occupied myself as a child. I can only assume a highly paid nanny or two was available at all times to keep me entertained and prevent me from getting into too much mischief. A benefit which, unfortunately, isn't extended to adults.

The only visitor I've had is the housekeeper—who was sent by the agency my parents use for staffing, and speaks only Polish—and Old Freddy, who stops by the main house once or twice a day to check in on me, though I'm positive it's only on my father's orders. Even he won't be around for long, though, as the lord in question has allegedly secured his replacement, and Freddy will finally be allowed to retire in peace.

I'm not particularly looking forward to the arrival of this new entity, who is unlikely to be so benevolent. Whomever he is, and when he's going to arrive, however, hasn't been disclosed to me, and I'm not thinking about it when I wander downstairs on the sixth day of my entombment, dressed in nothing but one of Cedric's old football jerseys, panties, and fuzzy socks.

Though I know no one is here, I still find myself glancing through every doorway I pass, half expecting to find my father smoking a cigar in his study, or my brother pacing back and forth before the window in the dining room, barking orders into his phone.

Of course, I find nothing but dark rooms and more stillness.

When the phone in my hand vibrates for the first time in days, I stop dead in the middle of the downstairs hall, and my heart lifts when I see who it is.

"Antoinette!" I gasp, delighted, when my friend's face appears on the screen.

"Hello, darling!" coos Antoinette, and her voice, which is colored by a thick French accent, sounds unnaturally loud in the quiet of the house. "How are you holding up?"

I make a face as I start moving again, ducking into the formal dining room, which is only ever used to entertain important guests. "Oh, you know," I say vaguely, hurrying to open the heavy burgundy drapes which are drawn over the high, paned windows.

The view of the grounds, which is currently being lashed by freezing rain, is hardly more cheerful than darkness.

"We miss you! When are you coming back?" she asks brightly, holding the phone aloft so she can see me as she darts around her beautiful, sunlit apartment. I was there only last week, drinking a bellini at the end of her chic white couch, dressed in nothing but a bikini and a sarong. "There was talk of a trip to my parents' house in Saint-Tropez, and it wouldn't be the same without you."

I drag the chair out from the head of the long, formal table —my father's usual place— and drop down into it, propping my phone against a brass candelabra. Leaning forward to adjust the volume, I make a noncommittal noise. It seems pretty grim to say "never," but at this rate, it will be a miracle if my parents let me leave the estate without their permission again.

Rapunzel doesn't need to be locked in the tower when she

has no employment history, a shitty academic record, and her biggest accomplishment to date is a first-place trophy from a wet T-shirt contest in Miami.

God, my boobs get me into some *situations*, don't they?

"Next week?" Antoinette suggests, eyebrows raised.

"I'm not sure," I hedge, pulling my knees up to the troublesome boobs in question. "They're pissed about those pictures that landed in the tabloids. I'm probably going to have to hang out here for a while and make nice."

Admitting the truth to Antoinette—that I have basically been blackmailed into submission by my own parents—isn't going to happen. We might be friends, but it's decidedly of the *good time* variety. She isn't who I'd call if I were having a crisis, or relationship drama, or... well, anything other than fun.

My friend scoffs, waving her hand in a very dismissive, French way. "They're busy, *non*? Who cares? Alexei has been asking about you. We can invite him on our little getaway, too, if you'd like."

This information prompts a flicker of excitement that's extinguished almost immediately. "I'll let you know when I've booked my ticket," I assure her with a weak smile, watching as she moves around her apartment, gathering up things and shoving them in her purse. Her makeup is flawless, and her hair looks freshly blown out, ready for a day of fun.

I swallow my question of where she's going. It will only depress me.

"Alright, darling. We'll speak soon. *Bisous*," she tells me distractedly, and blows me a kiss before ending the call, leaving me staring at the lock screen of my phone with a hollow ache expanding inside me.

Despite myself, I'm already beginning to wonder... Would it even be the *biggest* deal if I snuck out for a few days? Maybe when Freddy is gone, the new guy won't even notice. Strong words with little thought to the actual, practical follow-through is exactly my parents' style. Which means, as long as I *appear* to follow their rules and *seem* to be a more responsible human being, all will be forgiven in no time.

Hopefully.

Letting my head drop back, I let out a theatrical groan, as if being dramatic will do anything at all when there is *no one here to hear it.*

Out of sheer boredom and filled with pent-up defiance which screams to be vented, I stand up on my chair. Taking a cautious step up onto the glossy wood tabletop, I pause, half expecting my mother to appear out of the woodwork and howl at me for befouling the priceless family heirloom with my fuzzy polka dot-clad feet. She doesn't, of course, and I smirk as I shuffle forward, picking up enough speed to go sliding a few feet over the varnished tabletop.

I saw this in a movie once. It's pointless, but so is my entire existence, so I lean into the fun of it. Back and forth I go, skating on the table that is so long, I can manage two or three decent kick-offs before having to turn around. I'm just concluding my fourth lap, and feeling cheerful for the first time in days, when a craggy male voice from the doorway makes my heart shoot into my throat.

"Miss Blair?"

With a squeak of surprise, I whip around—momentarily forgetting I'm standing on top of a slippery table—and my stomach swoops as my feet come out from under me. My butt hits the table, and I let out an unattractive *oof* noise before my gaze finds the two men standing just inside the room.

One of them is Old Freddy.

The other... isn't.

"Are you alright, Miss Blair?" asks Freddy in alarm, hurrying forward, his wiry brows furrowed in concern.

"Of course!" I attempt to play off my ridiculous behavior with an airy laugh as I scoot to the edge of the table. Sliding off and onto my feet, I offer him a reassuring smile, brushing off Ced's old jersey.

And, all the while, the stranger stands in the entrance to the room, watching us with a stern frown tugging at the corners of his mouth—*his hot mouth.*

Despite my fairly obvious daddy (and mommy) issues, older men have never really been on my radar. Maybe it was just a proximity thing, because the over-forty crowd doesn't typically attend all-Tuesday-night raves in abandoned warehouses. Or, more likely, Freddy's new friend is just ridiculously attractive.

He has to be about forty, but his medium brown hair is thick and a bit wavy. His square jaw is adorned with a low dusting of stubble, and if I'm not very much mistaken, he has dimples. It's hard to tell, considering he is currently doing whatever the opposite of smiling is.

He couldn't be Freddy's replacement... *could he?*

"Hi," I greet him breathlessly, not quite able to check my embarrassment at being caught in such a ridiculous predicament by the hottest man I've ever seen.

Apparently satisfied I haven't sustained some kind of injury on his watch, Freddy steps back, lifting his hand toward the silent stranger. "Miss Blair, I'd like to introduce you to Damien Mallory. He'll be taking over security here at Thornhurst until the election in May."

Oh my god. Never in my life have I been this excited about one of my parents' staffing changes.

Stomach swarming with butterflies, I smile at him—*really* smile at him, not the careful, seductive one I typically employ for men whose abs I fantasize about licking—and draw forward, holding out a hand for him to shake. "It's nice to meet you. Thank you so much for taking the job. I know poor Freddy's been begging my father for some peace for ages now."

Out of my direct line of sight, Freddy chuckles in agreement. Damien Mallory, however, doesn't so much as smile. His eyes drop to my offered hand, then up to my face, then over my shoulder toward the man whose job he's taking.

My hand falls, and my heart follows suit.

"You said something about a secondary basement access, Freddy?" he prompts, and I feel a dull stab of shame at the way his deep, melodic voice still makes my belly twist.

Freddy moves past me, saying words that don't really register. I stand right where Damien Mallory left me, watching the two men turn toward the door. He's an employee. I wasn't expecting him to flirt with me or anything, but basic professional courtesy would have been nice. Maybe he was just... nervous? I would be nervous if I were taking a job like he was, working for a man like my father.

At the thought of *Lord Porter*, my heart sinks—if possible —even further.

Without a doubt, Dad would have interviewed him personally before awarding him a position with basically unlimited access to our family home. Of course, he would have told the new security guy all about the house's one and only resident and probably filled him in on the finer points of why I'm here.

Worse yet, he's probably been put in charge of supervising me.

Even after all the past week has brought, none of it has made me feel lower than this.

Impatiently, I swipe away the tear that's escaped down the side of my cheek and let out a shallow breath.

If this guy, Mallory, is going to be my only company for months, I'll have to make nice with him and show him I'm not half as bad as my parents might have led him to believe. It would be shortsighted to write him off already. He probably felt the need to be firm with me in front of Freddy, to show he wasn't going to let me get away with anything. Maybe when the old man is gone—my lips twitch—well, I wouldn't mind if he still wanted to be firm with me. *Very* firm.

He wasn't wearing a wedding ring, and I can't imagine he has a girlfriend, either, if he's taken a job which means he has to live in a cottage in the middle of nowhere...

Realistically, I'm not getting out of this. I've been imprisoned here—in the most depressing, boring, inhospitable corner of Stelland my ancestors could have possibly chosen to build a house upon––whether I like it or not.

I can think of worse ways to kill eight months than in bed with my parents' new head of security.

Six

Damien

"What can you tell me about her?"

Freddy McKellen, Thornhurst Estate's long-suffering head of security, casts me a long, wary look, pausing in the act of gathering up the knick-knacks on his desk. The moment I walked into the office, it was clear my arrival had been highly anticipated. Though I'd only needed four days to close up my house in Wyngate and pack up a sparse collection of personal things for my time here, McKellen had already made a start on getting his own belongings into boxes.

"I can tell she liked the look of you. Lit up like Christmas came early when you walked in."

I laugh. Physically attractive she might be, but I'm confident Blair Porter won't be a temptation. Good looks can only take you so far when your personality is repellent. There are a lot of lines I'll cross if the situation calls for it, but *she* certainly isn't one of them.

Outside the window, the corner of the main house draws

my gaze through the trees, its many windows sparkling in the warm autumn light.

"You don't need to worry about that," I assure Freddy, crossing my arms as I return my gaze to the old man.

Freddy grunts. "She's not a bad kid. Never quite measured up, though. Don't get the sense she's very bright. Back in the day, Lord Porter had to make some *donations* to get her through school."

Not exactly a shock, given the shit situation she's landed herself in, and that Porter's parenting style seems to be: *throw money at it and hope for the best.* "Porter said something about drugs?"

"*Lord Porter—*" His lips press into a stern line, clearly not impressed by lack of formality, "Might be right. To be fair, we've never had any incidents here at the house, but she's never spent much time here, either. They sent her away to school when she was young, and then it was off to party afterward. No university. His Lordship's a busy man, don't think he cared much to try and rein her in, until she took it too far."

"Boyfriends?" I raise my eyebrows.

Freddy shrugs. "None she's ever brought around, and none that have turned up since she's been back. It's been quiet." He hesitates, a troubled look crossing his face. "His Lordship got some nasty communications after the whole business with Miss Porter's photographs in the papers."

"What kind of communications?" I press, because our employer had neglected to go into detail on such a small, inconsequential matter.

The question makes Freddy wince. "Emails to the campaign, a few letters, a package or two. There might have been more, but nobody tells me much. Above my pay grade."

I don't like the sound of any of that. "Was any of it delivered to the estate specifically?"

Considering Thornhurst is well known to belong to the Porter family, and has belonged to them for centuries, I'm not surprised when Freddy nods grimly. "Aye. It was turned over to the police, of course, but nothing came of it as far as I know."

"Did you take photographs? Any kind of documentation? I'd like to know what to look out for."

Freddy leans down to turn on his computer, and I move to his side, suppressing a wince at the jumbled assortment of out-of-date software and record keeping which appear on the old desktop.

My concerns about Thornhurst's security are doubled, however, when I see the scanned letters Freddy kept, some delivered as recently as a few days ago. After reading through the vile fantasies and seeing the array of equally disgusting photographs sent to the pretty, half-naked party princess these men saw in the papers, it's clear that *His Lordship* greatly understated the situation at hand.

Any one of the letters is enough to alarm me, and there are dozens.

"You'll look after her, yeah?" asks Freddy anxiously, peering sideways at me as we finally make it through the last of them. "She's not a bad girl, just a little lost."

"I'll look after her," I confirm grimly, and it's the truth, even if *'a little lost'* seems like a wildly generous overestimation of Blair Porter's character.

We move on. I listen patiently to Freddy's explanations of his systems and ask questions here and there, but I'm barely paying attention. My education in protecting high-profile families began at the very top of Stelland's social hierarchy, and managing an estate such as this won't be a challenge. Even with the recent threats against Blair, Thornhurst is located hours from any major city, and its only significant occupants currently live elsewhere. With any luck, the negative attention will die off as she stays out of the public eye, and we won't see any excitement.

Though the job itself might be quiet, I'll have work to do getting Porter's system up to date, because nearly everything Freddy has shown me so far is alarmingly antiquated. It's pure luck that they haven't had more issues with personal data being compromised, considering the internet password is *Thornhurst1*. Reporters or criminals don't have to pick through trash to find sensitive information anymore, and data security is as big a part of my job now as the physical.

Getting things locked down before the election, rather than scrambling afterward, is a smart move.

For a high-profile family like the Porters and an estate like this one, security is considerably more complicated than wiring in a few security cameras. The bespoke system will need to be as inobtrusive and infallible as possible, with multiple layers of protection for the family's data, as well as their physical safety and property.

The current systems might have been state-of-the-art at the turn of the century, but they're obsolete now, and seeing all the gaps that exist has me on edge, itching to get to work.

When Freddy is done with his rambling explanation of the software I'll be dispensing with at the earliest opportunity, the old man waves me into the estate's green utility truck and continues his tour of the property's many outbuildings and features.

Once, old European noble families all kept houses like this, until the astronomical cost of upkeep and shrinking pool of generational wealth made them too great a burden to carry on with. Now, places like this are nearly gone, converted into multi-use properties or broken up into condominiums. The Porters, who are one of the few families that managed to increase their wealth rather than see it drain away, seem to keep

Thornhurst as more of a showpiece than an actual place to live.

Not that I could blame anyone for not making this place their full-time home.

Purely from a practical standpoint, the estate isn't central to anything, apart from a smattering of minuscule local villages, and the craggy bluffs to the west are beautiful, but undoubtedly bring in a brutal wind during the winter months.

It's a lonely, desolate place, and I can't help feeling as though I've crash-landed at the very end of the earth.

As we drive, Freddy tells me about the skeleton staff kept on and the locals I'll need to watch out for. He's had problems with poaching in recent years, and the occasional hikers who wander into the area by accident.

"You'll do fine," the man assures me when we park back at the security office, which is a small brick structure, nestled beside the empty stables. "Not a lot you've gotta watch out for, to be honest. Things might heat up with His Lordship's election, but..." He shrugs, turning the keys to the truck and holding them out to me with a wry smile. "Nothing you can't handle. They tell me you worked for the Ashwells."

I take the keys, ignoring the ache which spreads through my chest at the mention of my former position. "Yes. I did."

"Why'd you leave a position like that? Must be more exciting than it is here," Freddy questions as we get out of the truck, pausing beside the hood with his hands on his hips, frowning at me.

This is the last thing I'd like to discuss right now, but I school my expression into an obliging smile. "Family trouble. I needed some space."

Freddy seems to accept this, nodding in understanding. "Yeah, I know all about that. My youngest isn't much better behaved than His Lordship's, and my wife," he scoffs, "well, don't get me started on my wife. I'll be on your doorstep, begging for my job back, just for a break from it all."

He carries on, talking about his family, wife, and the family fishing business he'll be helping more with in his retirement. It's explained that he lives in the neighboring village and never took advantage of the cottage set aside for my use.

Finally, when the sky is going dark, and the old man seems to remember supper time is approaching, he waves me off to find my new home with a rambling set of instructions, already halfway to his truck.

Even without his help, I find it without much trouble.

The structure is set out of view of the main house behind a copse of trees, composed of weather-beaten stone and a slate roof, which I can already foresee leaking in heavy storms. There are no lights on, and my shoulders are heavy with exhaustion as I grip the heavy brass key Freddy gave me and take my duffel bag from the passenger seat of my car, stepping out onto the dark drive.

Above me, the moon peeks from between the clouds, and somewhere in the dark trees surrounding the cottage, an owl hoots noisily. This place, which I will be calling home for the next eight months, is as far from my townhouse in Wyngate as I can imagine.

I am well and truly alone, and it unsettles me more than I'd like to admit.

My boots crunch over the packed-down gravel as I draw forward, making my way onto the porch and fitting the key into the old lock. It turns easily, the old hinges groaning noisily, as I reach inside, feeling blindly for a switch on the nearest wall.

It could be worse.

Undoubtedly, Porter's estate manager saw to it that the place was cleaned and updated a bit after going unused for who knows how long. The smell of fresh paint hangs in the air as I close the door behind myself, surveying the space wearily. A kitchenette is situated to my left, on the side of the house nearest the door, with a new stove and refrigerator standing amongst the old wood cabinets. The room is virtually empty, with no furniture apart from a little kitchen table, a single chair, and a cracked, ornate sideboard which looks as though it once belonged in the main house.

To the left, a combined living room and bedroom is furnished sparsely as well, but the mattress looks new, and the couch—another fancy, out-of-place relic of the Porters'—is clean. Beside the old iron bedframe, a darkened doorway stands open, likely leading to the bathroom. Someone, a housekeeper maybe, left a stack of sheets, blankets, and towels at the end of the bed.

Drawing forward, all the energy seems to go out of me, and I allow my bag to fall to the well-worn wood floor with a heavy thud.

The space is impersonal and cold. A fireplace stands ready on the back wall, logs stacked ready in the grate, but I make no move to light them as I sink into the single wooden chair at the kitchen table.

Being here feels like a punishment, one inflicted more on myself than by anyone else, even my wretched aunt. I want to go home, to be in the places I know, and amongst the people who matter to me. Right at this moment, dinner is being served at the palace, and if I were still there, I would be finishing up a full day's work in my office.

Maybe it would be one of the days when my sister-in-law would appear in the doorway, just as I was packing up my bag, and inform me—her smile bright and teasing—that my presence was *required* at dinner. Or, if I got off early enough, I might have gone in search of my brother and needled him into a game of squash.

Even if the way I did it was wrong, resigning had felt... It was right. Even now, with the ache of loneliness and homesickness opening up like a chasm inside me, I still believe that. In truth, I should never have been in that position to begin with, should never have agreed to take a job protecting the people I love. You can't be impartial or make clear, rational decisions when your family's lives are on the line.

Leaning back in the old wooden chair, I scrub my hands over my face, struggling to get a handle on my own misery. Before I can sink further into the familiar abyss, however, a knock on the cottage's door has me whipping around.

My first thought is that Freddy has returned, likely bearing some "critical" piece of information he forgot to mention earlier. When I force my weary body into a standing position again and cross to answer, it isn't an old man in a cowboy hat I find.

I blink, staring in surprise at the young woman on my doorstep, her lips curved in a hesitant smile. She's bundled up against the chilly evening, wrapped in a thick woolen sweater, and there's a picnic basket in her hands.

"Hi," Blair greets me breathlessly, glancing past me into the cottage, before returning her gaze to my face. "I'm so sorry to bother you, I just thought..." She trails off with an embarrassed little laugh, and I stare as she launches into a rambling explanation.

"To be honest, I have no idea where the nearest shops are, and I figured you wouldn't have had time to get there anyway. So I packed some things from the house for you. Nothing fancy, but, you know, edible. I think we might have gotten off on the wrong foot this morning, but since we're going to be neighbors and all." Her smile falters, obviously taken off guard by my lack of participation in this conversation.

For fuck's sake.

It really shouldn't have surprised me that she has the audacity to show up here, late at night, at the private residence of her family's employee, bearing a pretty smile and some scavenged food, obviously expecting me to thank her for it.

Under other circumstances, I might have thought this little visit was endearing, but I'm not foolish enough to take her behavior at face value.

I stare at her, my pulse thudding unevenly, as it registers that this is the moment to set the standard for the rest of our relationship. One which will not—under any circumstances—be a friendly one. This is a job, and the beautiful young woman who is smiling at me on my doorstep isn't being kind for the sake of it. She's trying to see if she'll be able to get what she wants from me, *and she won't.*

Silence stretches between us.

"Let's be clear," I tell her, my voice devoid of any semblance of warmth. "We are not neighbors. I am here to work for your father and make sure you don't do something monumentally stupid, like flash your tits for half the world to see. The only thing I need from you is your cooperation."

Something flares behind Blair's eyes as the hand gripping the basket falls to her side. "Wow. Okay, asshole. I'm just trying to be friendly, but—"

"You aren't trying to be friendly," I interject with a cold laugh, relishing the way her expression hardens at the sound. "You're trying to see how much you can get away with, am I right? Trying to see if I'll play your games? If you smile pretty enough, I'll let you do whatever you want?"

Bristling, Blair glares up at me. "It must be nice to be so unbelievably confident that you'll be a rude little turd face to a stranger, based on nothing but your own preconceived notions."

"I think the *whole flashing your tits for half the world to see* incident is fairly convincing evidence my preconceived notions were accurate, princess."

"Oh, yeah?" She's seething, and the basket falls to the

stoop beside her as she plants both hands on her hips. "What else have you concluded about me? I'd love to know."

I lean my shoulder against the doorframe, crossing my arms. "What I think or don't think is none of your concern."

A flush has risen on Blair's cheeks as we've spoken, and it glows brighter than ever at my refusal. "It is my concern when it's about *me*."

"*Me, me, me,*" I mock. "It must be very disappointing to find you aren't entitled to insight into my personal beliefs."

She lets out a high, disbelieving laugh. "My god, whatever unfortunate object is lodged up your ass must be sideways for you to be acting like such a crap stain."

"Just to clarify, am I a turd face or a crap stain?"

While obviously incredulous, Blair doesn't miss a beat. "*You* are the human equivalent of what would result from putting turnips and olives in a blender."

I have to hand it to her; the insults are creative.

"Go back to the house, you're wasting my time," I drawl, keeping my tone dull, flat, and convincingly bored. In reality, this is the least depressed I've been in months. I'm baffled how Freddy could have thought this woman wasn't very bright, when, in less than two minutes of speaking to her, I've found her to be quite the opposite.

Which, of course, makes her all the more disappointing.

Blair scoffs, peering over my shoulder into the sparse cottage, undoubtedly spotting the half-eaten protein bar on the kitchen table—my dinner. "Yeah, looks like you've got a lot on your plate," she sneers. "Not literally, of course. Since you're too good to accept food from me."

Heaving a sigh, I check my watch. "It's late. Go on home, princess, we have to be up early."

"Don't call me that. And *we* have to get up early?" she echoes in disbelief, raising her eyebrows. "No, *we* do not."

"Actually, *we* do. Your father has mandated you develop

some healthier living habits while you're here, ones that don't involve doing drugs or binge drinking. As I'm skeptical you're capable of exercising any sort of discipline unless forced, and in the interest of efficiency, you will be joining me on my morning runs. Indefinitely."

It was a spur-of-the-moment decision, but it makes sense. I certainly won't enjoy starting my day with her, but at least that part of my job description will be over before the sun has fully risen.

Blair obviously doesn't believe me. She scoffs, stooping to pick up the basket, and straightens up, glaring at me. "I hope you and the sideways object have a lovely evening." Without another word, she throws her shoulders back and turns on her heel, marching off down the drive.

"See you at six a.m.!" I call after her, and stand in the doorway, watching until the darkness swallows her up, and all I can hear is the rustling of wind through the surrounding trees and the distant crashing of the waves on the bluffs.

Filled with vindictive satisfaction, I go back inside.

Princess Porter will learn in the morning that I'm a man of my word.

SEVEN

BLAIR

I'm dreaming of my favorite flavor of macaron, from my favorite patisserie in Paris, when the noise begins.

I try to ignore it and hold on to this wonderful taste of paradise, but it never lets up.

Bang. Bang. Bang. Bang.

Sitting up, I stare blearily around my darkened bedroom. A slit of bluish light is poking through the gap in the curtains, and my confusion turns to anger.

Who—*what*?

Disoriented, I stumble out of bed and across the room to the door, which seems to be the source of the commotion. Tearing it open, the first thing I see is *chest*. Broad, well-muscled chest that is shown off by a black compression shirt stretched over it.

Blinking rapidly, I drag my reluctant eyeballs up to look at the head attached to the chest.

Him.

Our regrettably attractive new head of security is standing

in the darkened hallway outside my bedroom, a travel mug of coffee in one hand while the other is raised, obviously preparing to continue his assault on my poor door. The ends of his hair are damp, like he's already had a shower, and, considering the last time I was up at this hour was when I was a bit late going to sleep, the glint in his eye seems inhuman.

"Are you on drugs?" I snarl, shoving my tangled hair out of my face, to better facilitate glowering up at him.

The man actually has the audacity to look amused. "Get dressed," he tells me, maddeningly calm. "I have an appointment coming at nine, and I'd like to fit in a run beforehand."

What the actual fucking fuck does that have to do with me?

"So go run!" I jab my finger toward the long stretch of hall beyond his impressive shoulder breadth.

Mallory lifts his coffee to his lips and takes a long drink, the column of his throat working to swallow before he lowers it again and stares at me with a look of pitying exasperation. "We talked about this. Remember?"

Though I'd obviously heard it before, Mallory reciting my father's improvement plan last night when I brought him my peace offering was like a sharp jab to a still-tender bruise. I had no preconceived notions about this guy when he walked into the house with Freddy yesterday–God, I'd actually thought he was *cute*–but he must have decided I'm a waste of space before ever laying eyes on me.

My tongue feels heavy and dry as I force myself to speak. "I don't run," I spit, curling my arms around my torso.

Mallory actually laughs, taking a step back. "Well, how's this? If you're not on the front steps in five minutes, I'm turning off the internet for the next week. If that doesn't work, I'll call *Daddy* to tell him you're committed to remaining a useless embarrassment."

"I'm not doing it!" I squeak, conscious of the way my heart is beating faster and my palms have grown damp with sweat as panic clogs my throat. "It's the buttcrack of dawn, you ass! I thought you were kidding!"

In response, Mallory merely lifts his travel mug in a silent toast, and though he doesn't say a word, his meaning is perfectly clear: *On your own head be it.*

With that, he turns, strolling off toward the main staircase.

Dizzy with shock, I slam the door hard enough to upset the picture beside it and storm into my walk-in closet.

Row after row of designer labels hang, carefully ordered, and practically recoiling in horror as I move past them, going straight to the drawer containing my limited selection of athletic wear. Apart from a yoga class every month or two, working out has never been high on my priority list.

Objectively, I know it's healthy or whatever.

Realistically, I have better shit to do than jog in a circle for however long people do that garbage.

I breathe through my nose, trying to wrestle my temper into check as I shove my legs into a pair of leggings and my feet into the only pair of running shoes I own (purchased for their fluorescent pink qualities, rather than because I foresaw any practical application for them). Beyond that, there isn't time to do more than scrape my hair into a ponytail and brush my teeth before Mallory's deadline can't be put off another second.

God, I was asleep ten minutes ago and now... oh, fuck. This is going to suck so bad.

Even knowing I'm pushing it doesn't stop me from dragging my feet a little on the way downstairs, still reeling at the traumatic turn my morning has taken. However, the moment I step outside, my self-pitying spiral is briefly interrupted by two things: the freezing morning air, and Mallory's butt.

It, like the rest of him, is regrettably well-formed and accentuated by the bent-over, stretching position he's in. He straightens up at the sound of the door closing, turning to look at me with a cool smirk. "Good. You're not as stupid as I was led to believe." He bends one leg up at the knee and reaches down to catch the back of his foot. "Stretch."

I shake my head, the whole of my attention on the painful chasm his words opened up in my chest. "Let's just get this over with."

He lets the foot drop and moves on to the other one. "Stretch, or you'll hurt yourself."

I don't particularly care right now. The freedom to make any kind of meaningful decisions about my life seems to be in short supply these days, and I seize upon this sliver of control with a twisted, vindictive pleasure. Ignoring Mallory completely, I take off, sprinting over the pea gravel path which leads toward the nearest edge of the forest.

While it seemed inevitable he would follow, I hoped my pace would at least buy me some distance from him. Unfortunately, I hadn't taken the leg length discrepancy into account. The guy has to be almost a foot taller than me and is obviously well used to this kind of torture, because within sixty seconds, he's fallen into step beside me.

Determined not to look at him, I glare forward.

My lungs are tight, and my calves are burning before we reach the forest, but I hate the idea of showing any weakness in front of him, so I keep going anyway. The grounds of the estate are still in the early morning, and cold enough that vapor from my labored breathing curls through the frosty, early autumn air. Mallory doesn't say a word as we reach the edge of the polished grounds, plunging into the gloomy woods which surround most of the estate. There are trails here, albeit seldom used ones, and I keep my eyes on the ground, determined not to trip over a root or fallen branch.

While I haven't been back here for years, the forest is just as ominous as I remember.

A thick layer of fallen leaves covers the ground, limiting

the growth of brush and permitting fog to drift through the trunks of the great, mossy oaks which line the path. There are so many, growing so close together, that it's impossible to discern which branches belong to which tree when you look up.

The sensation of my lungs burning, and my present company, are enough to make me hate it here even more than I did as a child.

"Slow to a walk for two minutes." Mallory breaks the silence, not sounding winded in the slightest.

It's pretty hard to maintain any level of pride or defiance when your body is protesting every step, so I do as he says and stumble to a walk, sucking big gulps of air into my burning lungs. Meanwhile, Mallory—obnoxiously—jogs in place, inching forward beside me.

Glancing over, I see his eyes are scanning the surrounding forest, and my chest hardens as I return my own gaze to the path. Neither of us speaks. Just when I'm starting to stop wheezing, however, Mallory taps the screen on his watch.

"Run," he tells me, the word crisp.

Bizarrely, I want to laugh. *That's it? Run?* As if I've ever done anything resembling a run in my entire life, and he hasn't just thrown me in the deep end when all I've ever done is drink mojitos poolside.

I have to bite the inside of my cheek to prevent myself from wasting precious breath snapping at him as I force my weak limbs into motion again. The eerie, early morning stillness in the forest muffles everything except the pounding of my heart and the wet slap of my soles against the trail. We've barely made it another thirty seconds before each gasping breath is scraping my throat like sandpaper.

"I can't—" I pant, the edges of my vision blurring.

"You can," Mallory drawls, sounding bored now. "You just haven't had to. Stop whining, it's pathetic." Lengthening his stride, he gains a few yards on me, forcing me to pick up my pace to avoid being left behind.

I glare ahead because acknowledging this in any way, even with a denial, feels like it would be confirming something.

Last night, before walking through the cold, dark grounds to bring him food, I'd convinced myself to disregard his attitude when we first met. Maybe he hadn't wanted to be unprofessional in front of Freddy, or maybe he was just nervous about the new job. Even if my father *had* tipped him off about why I was there—which I learned later was most certainly the case—surely I could show him I was a decent person. There was no reason we couldn't at least be friendly during our shared time at Thornhurst.

Whatever I thought was dead wrong.

Damien Mallory had clearly made up his mind about me, and from what I've seen of his grotesque personality so far, he isn't big on change. Never in my life have I encountered someone who despised me so deeply, so quickly.

We round a bend in the path, and I glance over at him.

There isn't so much as a drip of sweat on his perfect, chiseled, possibly dimpled face. For god's sake, the prick doesn't even look winded.

Meanwhile, I can barely breathe, and my cotton T-shirt is sticking to my overheated skin from the amount of sweat I've already generated. My ponytail is coming undone, too, the loose strands sticking to the back of my neck, each one a humiliating reminder of just how weak I am—*and how right he was*.

Every wheezing breath, every stumble, every argument, only confirms I'm exactly what this horrible jerk expected me to be.

God, I hate that.

Every stretch of trail feels endless, and an agonizing stitch has appeared in my side as we round a dense clump of trees, revealing a fork in the trail. Mallory doesn't pause, taking the right.

I could cry when I see how much farther it goes on, and my distraction costs me. My foot hooks on a protruding root, and I stumble, only narrowly avoiding falling on my face. When I recover, straightening up, I'm infuriated to see the man beside me smirking.

"You really enjoy this, don't you?" I spit, hating how winded I sound.

He makes a noncommittal noise in response, eyes roaming over the forest. "Your father hired me to do a job. I'm doing the job."

"No," I snap back. "You're a sadistic, crusty turd who enjoys watching me suffer."

This time, he gives a tiny huff of a laugh. Not amused—just acknowledging the accuracy. "For what it's worth," he tells me, "this isn't personal. I assure you, neither of us wants to be here."

His words give me pause, but I have more pressing concerns before I begin wondering what or who brought Damien Mallory to Thornhurst. "It *feels* personal."

"That's because you're taking it personally, which isn't surprising."

I stop dead in my tracks.

He continues another two steps before realizing and turns back to face me, brows raised but otherwise unfazed. "Why are you stopping?"

My hands tighten into fists at my sides. "Because, just like last night, you're being an asshole for no reason!" I snarl. "You don't even know me! What the hell is your problem?"

His eyes flick over me—sweaty, gasping, probably more red-faced than I'd like to believe—and something in his expression shifts slightly, as if he's recalibrating. "If I wanted to be an asshole, you'd know it."

I blink, momentarily stunned. "Is... is that supposed to be *reassuring*?"

He merely lifts his wrist to examine his fitness watch, already jogging again. "Let's go. You have thirty seconds before the next interval starts."

The noise I make in response is somewhere between hysterical laugh and resigned groan as I force my unwilling limbs after him yet again.

We're moving deeper into the forest now, where the trees have grown closer together, and pale morning light barely manages to break through the dense canopy of branches overhead. Long, shimmering shoots of it cut across the path here and there, and the air smells like damp earth and cold leaves. The fog has thinned, and without it, it's almost peaceful back here. Yet with each step, a tangled mess of *something* keeps trying to crawl up my throat. It's painful, a horrible knot of shame, exhaustion, and resentment that is too big and too messy for me to properly untangle. Especially in the presence of my current company.

I hate that he thinks he knows me.

And, more than that, I hate that I can't point to a single thing I've ever done which would prove him wrong.

Another vague span of time passes in a painful blur of burning lungs and weakening muscles. Mallory moves confidently, like his joints are lubricated with decades of hard-earned superiority. Every time I glance at him, hoping to see some signs of fatigue, some signs of him being an actual human being, Mallory is still jogging at the same steady, effortless pace.

"Walk," he instructs again, after a while passes, and he can apparently sense I'm about to drop right onto the forest floor.

I practically collapse into the reprieve, bending forward to brace my hands on my knees, panting as my head swims and stars dance at the edges of my vision. My legs are actually shaking.

"Stand up straight," Mallory orders, his voice clipped, like he's annoyed at having to waste the words on me. "You'll breathe better."

"Please," I gasp, shaking my head. "Let me die in peace, Satan."

Mallory scoffs. "Dramatic, too, I see. For fuck's sake, princess. Straighten up. Now."

I groan but obey, lifting my torso with what feels like the very last of my body's strength. Unfortunately, he's right, and the difference is immediate.

I decide to resent him for that, too.

As I drag in greedy lungfuls of air, my eyes flick up the long line of Mallory's body, jogging in place beside me again. He isn't paying attention to my struggle for oxygen, too busy scanning the trees around us like he's expecting paparazzi to pop out from behind a nearby patch of ferns.

"What exactly are you looking for?" I manage to pant, following his gaze.

By way of a response, Mallory merely lifts his chin toward the path scrolled out before us. "If you can't run, walk. I have things to do and would rather not spend all morning watching you dry heave."

God forbid I interfere with his important freaking schedule.

Every muscle in my body seems to protest my compliance, but I manage it, stumbling into step beside him. I'm not sure if it's wishful thinking or not, but I could swear the forest is thinning a little up ahead, and in the distance, I can just make out the sound of waves crashing over a rocky beach.

Getting my hopes up has felt like a fool's errand lately, but to my intense relief, it isn't long before I get the first glimpse of the massive old house through the trees.

"I want you ready to go at six tomorrow," Mallory informs me when we emerge at the edge of the sprawling back lawn, not even bothering to look at me as he gives the order, too busy poking at the screen of his fitness watch.

"Yeah, well, I want you to get eaten by a bear," I bite back venomously as I force the weak, shaky muscles in my legs forward. "So, everyone's disappointed."

He ignores me. Again.

Maybe I deserve this after messing up Alba's engagement and giving the entire internet a front row seat to my boobs, but knowing it doesn't lessen the feelings of betrayal or resentment I have toward my parents and, by extension, Dad's pet asshole. Handing over my autonomy to people who have mostly ignored me my entire life, throwing money at my problems instead of teaching me how to handle them myself—god, is it any wonder I'm a useless, incompetent adult?

Mallory sees me all the way to the back kitchen door, but doesn't pause, diverting course and heading toward the estate's outbuildings. "Six o'clock, tomorrow!" he calls over his shoulder.

Woozy and weak-limbed, I pause with my hand on the doorknob, watching as he starts running again. His strides are long, effortless, and clearly experienced. The fucker probably runs every single morning, and now, he's expecting me to do the same?

Face hot and heart still racing, I tear my eyes from Mallory's retreating form and go inside.

I'm not going to take this—*him*—lying down. If there's one thing I'm unusually talented at, it's being difficult, and soon, my father's sucky new head of security is going to know it, too.

Eight

DAMIEN

"Anything to report?" Lord Porter asks, not bothering with preamble or pleasantries, when I answer his call—the first communication I've received from the man since I arrived at Thornhurst a full week ago.

"Nothing," I tell him honestly, closing the front door to my cottage behind myself and pausing just inside, lifting my running shirt away from my damp skin. "I sent your assistant a full report as well as a budget for the proposed security upgrades, and your daughter is... cooperating."

Barely. The attitude I got this morning from the daughter in question had taken on a particularly vicious edge when I attempted to get her up for our run. As far as I can tell, Blair's patience with me seems to be growing as thin as mine with her, and a more dramatic fallout seems inevitable. It's just a question of when.

Through the phone, I hear Porter's noise of amusement. "Well, I suppose *cooperating* is the best we can hope for. She hasn't responded to Candice's email with a link to her remedial studies program, has she mentioned starting it?"

Ha. Of course she hasn't. Thus far, Blair and I have had hardly anything to do with one another, apart from the runs. Even for those, most of our communication comes in the form of snapping or pointed silences, and she certainly hasn't told me about her coursework.

I pinch the bridge of my nose, annoyed with the entirety of the Porter family. "No. I'll follow up with her."

Though he and I touched upon the educational element of his grand plan to remake his daughter, it hadn't occurred to me that it would be down to me to—to what? Tutor her? Ensure she does her homework? The limited time we spend together has already made my temper shorter than usual. I'd rather not have anything more to do with her if I can help it.

There are more important matters to discuss, however. Yesterday morning, when the groundskeeper dropped the estate's mail delivery with me, there were three more of the disturbing letters to Blair. The same kind Freddy had shown me on my first day here.

"There's another matter I'd like to discuss, while I have you. There were more of the threats you mentioned, delivered over the last few days," I explain, glancing toward the drawer where I stashed them, uneasy. "Crude, threatening, sexually explicit communications, addressed to Blair. I'd like to request a copy of anything else that was delivered elsewhere, so I can compare them. We should be on top of this and looking out for signs that any of the senders might be becoming more persistent."

A stalker is the last thing I want to worry about on a property this big, especially before the security has been upgraded. Freddy's antique systems are peppered with holes, and I can't understand why Porter isn't more concerned.

A muffled voice sounds through the line, someone talking

to Porter. "Yes, I'll be there momentarily. Send my apologies," he tells them. Then, directed to me, "I'll have my people get in touch. In the meantime, make sure she's focusing on her academics. I'm sure she'll be resistant, but this is a priority. I want an update today, Mallory."

A tendon in my jaw twinges painfully, and I reach up, rubbing it. "Yes, sir. And the budget for the updates?"

"Pending further consideration." He hangs up without another word, and I shove the phone in my pocket, even more weary than I was a moment ago.

Freddy wasted no time clearing out his things from the office. Within forty-eight hours of my arrival, the former head of security had gone, leaving me with about a dozen filing cabinets filled with invoices older than I am, a leak in the roof of the office, and a desk chair that collapses in on itself at random intervals.

Even with the "upgrades" I was hired to facilitate—which are more like a complete overhaul—and the threats toward Princess Porter, it only took a few days for me to confirm this will be a long, tedious employment contract.

Outside, a distant rumble of thunder signals the approach of yet another storm, and I wander over to the cottage's window, staring miserably up at the graying sky.

In contrast to the hustle and bustle of Ashwell Palace— where we dealt with everything from unruly tourists to coordinating security for visiting global leaders on a daily basis—the quiet of the estate is unnerving. I find myself constantly on edge, waiting for *something* to happen.

A *something* which doesn't seem likely to come from Thornhurst's only other full-time resident.

Permitting myself a quiet groan, I turn away from the window and cross to turn on the shower in the cottage's small bathroom. As the hot water hits my back, and I move through the routine steps of cleaning myself, I find myself preoccupied —yet again—by Blair Porter.

Even as I go out of my way to avoid her, the interactions we do have leave me so irritated that I find myself reliving them over and over again like a masochistic skipping record. I ought to be savoring my time away from her and using it to focus on things that *don't* infuriate me beyond belief. Yet every time I've tried to turn my mind toward other, more important and relevant matters, there is something about her that snags my attention, pulling it back onto her.

The phenomenon is almost as frustrating as the woman herself, and I don't know what to make of it

Especially when my initial surveillance data has yielded few surprises about the spoiled socialite.

While I didn't particularly relish invading her privacy, decades of experience have taught me that failing to gather all the information about a job is opening yourself up to breaches. So, since my arrival, I've kept a close eye on her, interested in separating fact from fiction.

My first priority was getting a list of close associates. I wanted to know if we would have any problems from her friends trying to enter the property or sneaking in *substances,* which could undermine Porter's campaign. Blair getting caught with drugs at the family home would almost certainly be a massive scandal, and no one would escape the collateral damage. Including myself.

Having control of Thornhurst's internet servers makes my job almost effortless, but after days of searching fruitlessly for red flags or indications she was up to anything nefarious, I was almost disappointed in my preliminary conclusions.

Blair Porter may be impulsive, bratty, and turn her nose up at anything resembling discipline, but she isn't going to be a security concern.

She doesn't appear to have any close friends or lovers who

might come looking for her. She doesn't text at all, and the entirety of her communications seems to be through voice memo or video chat, with even those kept seldom and brief. Neither Lord nor Lady Porter nor any of Blair's siblings have attempted to contact her since I've begun monitoring her.

She hasn't tried to leave the property or let anyone onto it.

The alarm on the wine cellar hasn't been touched.

She spent a fairly disgusting amount of money on shoes, apparently not concerned that paying the credit card bill would be a problem with her funds frozen.

Everything I've learned should be enough for me to be reasonably confident Blair won't be a problem, but even though I can't put my finger on *what* exactly, something about the Porter heiress still isn't quite sitting right with me. I can only assume that my subconscious is picking up on *something,* and that's why she's dominated so much of my attention as of late.

After my shower, I'm keen to put off the inevitable rise in blood pressure which will come from "touching base" with Blair about her education, and choose to return to the office instead.

I spend the afternoon following up with a few of the contractors I'll be hiring once Porter gives me the green light. After that, I walk the edge of the grounds with a digital surveying software, marking off the tentative locations where motion sensors will be installed.

I make calls, check my email, and organize my top desk drawer.

I go back to the cottage to eat a late lunch and unpack my final suitcase.

I stall.

There is a long list of things I would rather do—among them wrestle a rabid weasel or attend one of Araminta's tea parties—before engaging in further communication with

Blair. Unfortunately, my work is slowing to a standstill until Porter approves the budget, and there is only so much I can do.

So, once I've checked my email another few times and can't justify putting it off any longer, I go in search of Blair.

I've been inside Thornhurst a lot, coming and going from the great house several times a day since I arrived. Still, it's strange to fit my master key into the lock on the back staff entrance and go inside without announcing myself.

The house is as quiet as it ever is when I close the door and pause, straining my ears for sounds of life. Just as always, though, there's nothing but silence. No footsteps. No murmured voices. Not even a television left running somewhere in the house.

I'm on the point of moving further inside when, unexpectedly, a soft sound breaks the silence.

My heart shoots into my throat. I freeze, not even breathing as I listen to the unmistakable noise drifting faintly back to me from a nearby room.

Singing.

It carries through the quiet halls, warm and slightly off tune, its singer unconcerned about being overheard.

Blair.

I should keep moving and go talk to her about the courses, but my feet don't move.

Instead, I stand in the entryway, my feet rooted to the stone floor. Listening.

She isn't performing for anyone but herself. Sometimes, the lyrics lapse mid-sentence, turning to a sweet, melodic hum. The song... For the life of me, I can't place it, and yet it's familiar in a way that raises goosebumps on the nape of my neck.

Without making the conscious decision to, I find myself moving forward, straining my hearing as though any moment now, a word will emerge that will remind me where I know it from. My boots are silent on the worn, flagstone floor as the sound of Blair's voice grows louder, and my heart lurches as I turn a corner and find myself staring into the house's cavernous kitchen. The space is lit by stormy daylight that drifts in from the large window above the sink, illuminating the rows of copper pots hanging from the rack on the wall, and the long marble-topped table standing in the center of the space.

And, at the end of it, is Blair.

She's dressed in an oversized sweater that's sliding off one shoulder, light red hair piled on top of her head in an untidy bun, and is too busy digging into a tub of ice cream to notice she's no longer alone.

My mouth is dry as I watch her sway her hips lazily, singing the same, hauntingly familiar song that pierces right through me for reasons I wish I could understand.

This woman could be an entirely different person from the wild-eyed creature who landed herself in half the tabloids in Europe, or the defiant little princess who flipped me off for reminding her to drink water this morning. I can't seem to look away, even when she pushes the top back on the ice cream and twirls across the room to put the carton back in the freezer, her feet bare on the checkered floor.

Dimly, I remember my purpose for being here, and that I should step into the kitchen and announce myself. Still, I stand there in the doorway, unmoving, as she hits a higher note—this one slightly flat—and laughs, shaking her head, before trying again.

Seeing her like this shouldn't affect me. And yet—*no*. Clamping down on the thought, I clear my throat loudly and step into the room.

Blair's head snaps up, eyes round with shock, and the spoon sticking out from between her lips.

"Ice cream for lunch?" I ask mildly, pushing my hands into my pockets. "Interesting choice."

Her cheeks go pink, and she hurriedly removes the spoon, sticking it back in the bowl. "What do you want? Shouldn't you be working?" she demands, recovering her sense of self-importance in an instant.

A nerve in my jaw twitches. "I *am* working. Believe it or not, I haven't come for the pleasure of your company."

"Of course. You don't do anything for pleasure, do you?" Blair scoffs, shaking her head. "Gosh, I bet *that's* why your face always looks all pinched and puckered up like a giant butthole. I'd probably get rectum face too if I slept in a coffin and subsisted exclusively on repression." And, raising her eyebrows challengingly, she helps herself to another spoonful of ice cream.

I have to actively remind myself that sinking to her level and engaging isn't going to help in the present situation. Steeling my features, I frown. "Your father wants to know when you'll be starting your remedial studies courses."

Blair does a poorer job of hiding her indignance than I do, and sets down the spoon with a noisy clatter, pursing her lips. "He could have called me for that."

"That's the advantage of having a great deal of money, you can pay people to take care of life's less enjoyable tasks for you," I point out, strolling further into the kitchen. "Well?"

She blinks, curling her arms around her middle, even as that pointed little chin lifts defiantly. "Well what?"

For fuck's sake.

I give her a pitying look that makes the color on the apples of her cheeks glow brighter. "When. Are. You. Starting. The. Courses? I can spell it for you, if you'd like."

Blair's head tilts to the side, looking a little bemused now. "Strange. I've never hit someone before, but I'm experiencing the strongest impulse to smack you in the face right now."

"You could try." I stop ten feet away from her, crossing my arms over my chest, and pointedly ignore the way her eyes dart to my biceps and away.

When she speaks again, her voice has taken on an edge. "Right. I suppose you would have a lot of practice in defending yourself against outbursts of physical aggression. It must be a bit of an occupational hazard, huh? From being such a terribly unpleasant person, and all."

It seems almost unbelievable that in the space of a three-minute conversation, this woman has told me I sleep in a coffin, provoke unprecedented acts of violence, subsist exclusively on repression, am a "terribly unpleasant person," and that my face looks like a butthole. And, what's worse, it isn't even close to the record number of insults she's managed to pack into a brief conversation with me in the week since we met.

"The courses, Blair," I remind her, dragging us back onto the topic at hand with a heavy sigh. "When are you starting them?"

Her answering smile is coy. "I'm not sure," she muses, turning the spoon between her fingers. "I'll *definitely* let you know, though."

There must be a long list of people before me who tried to get Blair Porter in line and caved from sheer exasperation. That evasiveness might have worked for her in the past, but it won't today. "Go get your computer. Now."

Gazing at me thoughtfully, Blair takes her time bringing another bite of ice cream to her mouth. The noise of pleasure she makes isn't obscene, and yet it has an immediate and powerful effect on my cock.

Fucking hell. Enough.

"Blair," I snap, more irritated with myself than her, now. "Let's get this over with. I have better things to do than watch you eat that."

Nevertheless, my eyes seem magnetized as the tip of her tongue darts out, licking away a tiny drop of cream that clings to her plump upper lip. After a sufficiently obnoxious amount of time has passed, she lets out a long, mournful sigh, pouting. "I lost it."

"No," I counter at once, "you didn't."

"I'll look for it! You know, at some point." She winks, scraping her spoon against the bottom of the bowl. "Pinky promise."

It hasn't escaped my awareness that, as this conversation has progressed, I've somehow lost the upper hand. I had her off balance with my unexpected arrival, but now she's flipped the script, toying with me for the sheer amusement of it.

Christ, she's impossible. I'm done playing her games.

Seething, I start moving, striding right past her and out into the hall, which runs the length of Thornhurst's ground floor. There are four sets of staircases in this house, and I make for the closest one, heart pounding as I jog up to the second floor. Emerging in the upstairs hall, I turn right, walking over the plush, carpeted runner toward Blair's bedroom.

Despite having been at the door every morning for a week, I've never actually entered Princess Porter's inner sanctum. The door is open, and I stride inside, pausing when I'm struck by the scent of apples and honey hanging in the air. It takes me by surprise, muddling my intention for being here, as—just as I did when listening to Blair's singing a moment ago—I find myself searching my memory for how I know it.

It takes a moment, but I manage to shake myself free from the state of déjà vu, looking around.

The space is just as I'd expect it to look: luxurious with minimal personal touches, just like the rest of the house. The bed is unmade, but apart from some clothes thrown over the back of a chair, the space is clean.

Her laptop is clearly visible and resting atop her desk, plugged into its charger beside a bottle of green nail polish.

Little brat.

Still holding my breath to avoid inhaling the intoxicating scent of whatever it is she's spraying in here, I stride toward the desk and snatch it up. Gritting my teeth, I leave the way I came, half expecting to encounter Blair in the hallway, on her way to stop me.

She isn't there, though, nor is she in the kitchens when I arrive back downstairs, setting the computer down on the counter beside her empty ice cream bowl.

"Blair!" I bark, striding over to the pantry and the adjacent bathroom, only to find both rooms dark and empty.

Is she fucking kidding me right now?

A few more minutes of fruitless searching of Thornhurst prove that Blair is most certainly not kidding. She's vanished, likely taking refuge in some unknown corner of the house, and my temples throb as I return to the kitchen, irritated beyond belief at being forced to engage in a game of hide and seek with a grown woman.

What am I supposed to tell Porter? That I couldn't speak to his daughter because she's hiding from me? For Christ's sake, that would make me look incompetent, and Blair probably knows it. My eyes find the laptop, resting innocently on the kitchen counter, and I feel my lips twist.

Fine. If she wants to play games, we'll play games.

Moving over to the device, I open it and stare down at the input field for a password. I frown, wondering what a self-centered, careless brat who has never had a true worry in her life would use to protect her sensitive information.

1-2-3-4

It's a shot in the dark, and I'm not actually expecting it to work. When the password screen vanishes, however, and I find myself looking at Blair's desktop—which is supremely cluttered—I scrub my hand over my face, almost overcome with exasperation. *Unbelievable.*

Her internet browser has no fewer than thirty tabs open, but it still takes me less than sixty seconds to find the email from Candice amidst a mountain of unread marketing for luxury clothing brands. The course offering is branded as a refresher for adult learners who are returning to their education after some time away. I scroll through the registration paperwork and overview, finding it to be all very reasonable and well laid out. There are weekly "support group" meetings offered with other students and courses dedicated to everything from developing effective study habits to technology usage. The program is part-time and only supposed to take a few hours a week.

As I read through it, I find myself more exasperated with Blair than ever before. For someone who didn't go to college, this is a good opportunity. Considering her daily schedule is wide open, and she spends her time doing absolutely nothing, I can't understand why on earth she's so opposed to it.

God forbid she improve herself.

Shaking my head, I move through the registration form, adding Blair's personal information, and requesting a start date of Monday. She's going to be furious with me when she realizes what I've done, but I couldn't care less. A part of me—one I pointedly refuse to examine very closely—even welcomes her inevitable fury.

When the course is confirmed, I straighten up, smiling grimly to myself as I head for the door.

"You start classes on Monday, Blair!" I call, raising my voice so it carries through the surrounding rooms, and hopefully into whatever corner of the house she's hiding. "I'll be sure to let your father know you're very excited for the opportunity!"

NINE

In the weeks since he arrived at Thornhurst, Damien Mallory has become my very least favorite person to ever step foot under its roof.

Which is saying quite a lot, considering the company my parents keep, and the endless parade of smug turds my sister dated before settling down and getting engaged to the biggest and turdiest of them all.

Those guests, however unpleasant, didn't often direct their unpleasantness toward me personally, and usually left after dinner. They certainly weren't granted authority over me in any way, or made it their personal mission to remind me what a loser I am at what is already the low point of my entire life.

No, the deep, undying type of *hate* I feel for the estate's new head of security is brand new and unprecedented.

I hate the way he has never once stumbled over a root or branch on our morning runs.

I hate how he is always wearing that stupid fitness watch

on his wrist and checks it like he's genuinely concerned about his freaking daily step count.

I hate his cold eyes and his patronizing smiles.

There are endless things I could add to my running list of reasons I hate Damien Mallory, but the biggest one, the one that takes my dislike of him to a whole new level, is that *my dumb vagina hasn't gotten the memo.*

It's actually becoming a problem. The man isn't *that* attractive—I've committed myself to repeating this lie until I believe it—so either the social isolation and its corresponding lack of potential sexual partners is driving me mad, or my self-esteem is worse than I thought. Regardless, the man has made his dislike for me abundantly clear, and there is no universe where I fuck someone who goes out of his way to treat me like the village idiot.

Unfortunately, there is a lot of room for error here, because the quiet of Thornhurst is starting to get to me a little. I haven't left the property in weeks now and keep having dreams of wandering aimlessly through the hallways like a ghost, as though my brain is incapable of imagining itself anywhere beyond these walls.

So, to keep myself in check and ensure I don't do something horrific, like throw myself at my jailer, I've decided to refer to him only as Satan (or names with similarly demonic associations) in conversation.

As an added precautionary measure, whenever I catch myself fantasizing about him pinning me against a tree and fucking me senseless during one of our runs—which has happened *way* more than is healthy—I force myself to go down the list of times he called me an idiot, or useless, or lazy.

A list which, most helpfully, grows longer by the day.

Mallory's attitude is the part I recount to my sister, leaving out how hot his arms are.

"Well, I hardly know what you expected." Alba purses her

lips as she takes another garment bag from her closet and lays it over the end of her old bed.

I hadn't known she was coming. She arrived half an hour ago, shortly after I finished my morning exercise/torture session with His Royal Evilness, brushing past me with an airy explanation of needing some things from her closet. I followed, peppering her with complaints about our parents and the demonic turd they selected to mind me.

Predictably, she isn't sympathetic.

I curl my legs up beside me on the armchair in the corner of her room, my heart in my stomach. "I wouldn't have minded if he were an actual trainer or professional or whatever, but he is such a jerk. It's like they went out of their way to pick the meanest ass kisser Dad has on staff." This is a lie. I would have *minded* having my free will stripped away by pretty much anyone, but coming from Damien Mallory, it's especially terrible.

Alba gives me a look which plainly says she knows I'm full of shit. "I don't feel sorry for you. They've been telling you to get it together for years." Unzipping the topmost garment bag on the stack she's laid over her bed, my sister frowns critically at the contents. "Damn, I thought this was more polished than it is. What do you think?" She holds it up so I can see the dress inside, which is pretty enough, but at least three years out of fashion.

My judgement must not be entirely worthless, because my thumbs down earns the dress a one-way trip to the crumpled pile of discarded garments on the other end of the bed.

"What's this for, anyway?" I ask as she moves on to the next option.

A line appears between Alba's meticulously plucked brows as this one is promptly discarded as well. "James has business in New York. They're a newer client, and the company is very *trendy*. I thought something vintage would be appropriate."

My chest aches. "I haven't been to New York in ages," I murmur, dragging my thumbnail over a seam on the chair's upholstered arm. "Can I come with you? We can go shopping when he's doing his boring business things. I know this great place that sells curated vintage in the East Village."

I have limited hope of her agreeing, but I'm willing to take the chance of rejection if it gets me out of this stupid house, even if it's only for a few days. The company isn't ideal, but being with Alba and James is pretty much the only arrangement I can imagine our parents agreeing to, securing my release.

Sure enough, Alba scoffs. "We didn't do that sort of thing when you *weren't* on house arrest. I don't see why we should start now."

Pulling my legs to my chest, I let my chin rest atop my knees, watching as she disappears into the closet and returns, bearing another prospective dress, before I speak again. "Dad wants me to start taking courses online while I'm here. *Prep courses. For university.*"

My sister's hand stills on a zipper for a fraction of a second before she begins moving again, casting me a wary look. "Oh?"

"Can you talk to him?" I plead, my voice wavering just a little. "*Please*, Alba. I'll owe you the favor of all favors if you can get him to drop it. You know I'm too stupid for all that."

The attempt at humor falls flat, and for a moment, Alba only stares down at the final dress remaining, expressionless. Finally, she lifts her head to look at me directly, a pinch of regret in her beautiful face. "It may seem cruel, but Dad has your best interests at heart, Blair," she tells me, her voice determinedly measured. "I know school has always been a bit of a challenge for you, but honestly, what are you going to do without a degree of some sort? You can't avoid it forever. It's time to grow up."

I can't decide if her words make me want to scream or cry.

A bit of a challenge? *A bit of a challenge?* Running is a bit of a challenge. Being here all by myself is a bit of a challenge. Knowing every single person in my family is annoyed by my existence is a bit of a challenge.

School... School is torture compared to all that.

Alba casts one last lingering look at the pile of discarded dresses. "Do you want any of these?" I shake my head miserably, and she nods distractedly, clearly going out of her way to avoid looking at me directly. "Toss them in the donation bin for me, would you? I need to get going."

As she's starting toward the door, I unfold my legs to stand, too. "Just a second, I might have something," I tell her quietly, brushing past into the hall and down two doors to my own bedroom. The remainder of my belongings were delivered yesterday from the apartment I'd been renting in London, and I go straight to the corner of the closet where I hung them.

My sister is waiting when I emerge, holding out a dress that makes her eyes go round. "It's a favorite of mine. Be kind to her," I explain, offering a weak smile. "Consider it an apology. For the thing with your engagement."

Alba takes it without hesitation, her lips parted as she examines the deep red velvet skirt, which is draped artfully around the waist of a sheer, corseted bodice. "Oh, wow. Where on Earth did you get this?"

"A little shop that sells curated vintage in the East Village."

My sister's eyes zoom to meet mine. "Thank you," she tells me, her tone cautious, as if waiting for me to ask for something in return. When I don't, she drapes the dress carefully over her arm. "I'll have it returned when we're back next week."

I smile wryly. "No rush. The only person I'll be seeing anytime soon is Dad's meanest lap dog, and I wouldn't waste it on him."

To my surprise, Alba purses her lips. "He isn't."

"Isn't?"

"Dad's lap dog," she clarifies. "I mean, Dad hired him, but it's a recent thing. Apparently, he was recommended to them by Princess Araminta. He worked for the Ashwells for years and years."

That's... surprising. "*The* Ashwells?" I clarify, because after weeks of thinking of him as one of Dad's besuited security personnel—obviously selected for this position by being the least friendly of them all—it's hard to imagine Satan wearing a uniform for the royal guard and standing at attention for the King of Stelland.

Alba hums in confirmation. "Yes. Apparently he'd taken a leave of absence, and Dad snatched him up. I'm sure he thought it would be prestigious to employ one of the king's men. Or, at least, it's very good for their relationship with Araminta. A show of trust, don't you think?"

Personally, I don't think Mom being the goddaughter and on good terms with the oldest, most irrelevant, and least popular member of the royal family is going to do anything for Dad's election campaign, but I have to admire the commitment.

Araminta Ashwell is a relic of a bygone era of royalty and a notorious snob. Having weathered multiple dinner parties sitting beside the old bat, I know firsthand how difficult it is to keep yourself from wincing every time she voices her disappointment in how "the old ways" are dying off and how nobody does anything properly anymore. Which makes it a little surprising she would be aware of Damien Mallory's existence at all, never mind recommending him for a position in our household.

I don't have time to ask any follow-ups, though, because with a final, obligatory smile, Alba is striding off toward the stairs, leaving me alone once again.

Frowning, I wander back up to my room and pause, hovering in the doorway to stare at the laptop on my desk. After putting it off for as long as possible, I started the first of the remedial courses only last night. Within thirty minutes, I was tearful and defeated, spiraling until grasping even the most basic of concepts was beyond me. There's a lot more work for me to do, hours and hours of it, but the longer I stand looking at the damned computer, the more hopeless the whole thing feels.

What is the point?

Turning away, I wander out of my room and back into Alba's to retrieve the clothes she asked me to donate. It's hardly more pressing than my school stuff, but any excuse to put it off a little while longer is impossible to resist, so I head downstairs, intending to put them away in the laundry room donation bin before resuming the demoralizing task of talking myself into doing my coursework.

As I trudge downstairs, however, my mind isn't on school at all.

Alba's information about Mallory—which I'm certain is accurate, considering her golden-child status—has piqued my attention. I mull it over as I traipse into the laundry room and dump Alba's discarded clothes in the donation bin. As I straighten up, movement in the corner of my eye makes me stop, turning to look out the window. It's a nice day for once, and the grounds look warm and inviting, with nothing but blue skies overhead. From the laundry room, there's a clear view of the staff parking area, where the two men are conversing beside a white utility van and the estate's green truck.

The first is the evil butthole himself, dressed in his usual black pants and a matching zip-up. The second, who I can only assume is a contractor of some sort, is wearing a blue jumpsuit, adorned with a logo I can't make out from here.

As I watch, Mallory laughs—*actually laughs*—and claps the man on the shoulder, dimpled grin visible even from here. The expression is so foreign to me that I actually find myself recoiling a little, startled by how different he looks. Smiling, Satan could be someone else entirely, someone friendly and warm.

My heart sinks.

Other than our brief introduction by Freddy, this is the first time I've actually seen the man interact with anyone other than me. I hadn't stopped to think much about it, but if I had, I probably would have assumed he was a prickly asshole to everyone.

Apparently not.

Pursing my lips, I allow my head to fall to the side, watching the interaction curiously as I remember what Alba told me about Satan's background. It presents questions about my newly established nemesis, ones that might have answers that could get rid of him once and for all.

Turning away from the two men at last, I make my way slowly back up to my bedroom, thinking it all over.

Why would Princess Araminta—who I can't see being aware of much outside her self-important bubble—know that a member of the royal household had taken leave, and go so far as to recommend him for this job to my father?

I also have to wonder why Mallory would take this job to begin with—which he clearly hates—when his old one was undeniably more prestigious. Why would he want to spend his time ordering new security cameras in this miserable corner of the world when he could be living in the capital city of Wyngate and working for the Ashwells?

It's beyond strange to think that, if Satan worked for the family for years and years like Alba said, he would have met at least two kings.

Stellanders' relationship with our royal family has seen its fair share of ups and downs. In my lifetime alone, I've had three kings, and each of them came with their own unique set of trials and tribulations.

First, there was King Fabian, who died when I was only ten or eleven. While at the time I hadn't thought much about the man, I learned later that his reign was plagued by rumors of infidelity and a general unpopularity amongst the people.

Then came his oldest son, Arthur, who did well enough, but I always suspected much of the show of relatability was for the benefit of the press. Admittedly, my opinion may have been colored by his sons, who weren't much younger than me. They'd attended the same middle grades academy as I did, and if the rumor mill was to be believed, they were monstrous little beasts who loved to pick on the scholarship students.

King Arthur wasn't an old man, and likely would have reigned over Stelland for a long time, had it not been for the plane crash which took the lives of his entire family, only a few years ago. It was a great tragedy, and one that further complicated the nation's relationship with our monarchy, when the crown landed squarely on the head of Arthur's wildly unpopular younger brother, Benedict.

The second Ashwell son was recently divorced and had the reputation of being a bit of a stick-in-the-mud. *Nobody* was happy about it, but my father, predictably, found an opportunity in Benedict's unexpected accession to the throne. I certainly wasn't party to any of the discussions, but it wasn't a secret that he and my mother did everything they could to thrust my sister under the single, childless king's nose.

Even if Benedict wasn't popular, having a queen for a daughter—or, better yet, grandchildren in line for the throne—could only do good things for the family, and my parents pulled every single string they had, determined to get a crown on Alba's head.

It came to nothing.

As far as I'm aware, King Benedict didn't so much as glance in my sister's direction. Before anyone knew what had happened, he'd already been caught up in a whirlwind, highly publicized romance with an American movie star, Zelda Flowers.

I remember sitting at the dinner table on one of my rare visits to Wyngate last summer, listening to my father assure my pouting mother that *"the American"* was merely a fling, and it was only a matter of time before the king decided to settle down with someone more *appropriate*.

It wasn't a fling.

In a matter of months, they'd gotten married, and if the way the king looked at his new queen wasn't convincing enough evidence of Zelda's permanence, the announcement they were expecting their first child sealed the deal. King Benedict might not be a charmer, but honestly, he doesn't need to be after marrying a woman with charm enough for the both of them. Zelda Flowers might not have been a traditional choice for queen, but she was a good one.

I reach my bedroom and sink down on the edge of my bed. Lifting my phone, I open the internet browser. "Search: *Ashwell Palace Royal Guard*," I say clearly, and the device produces results immediately. There are websites and other listings, but I ignore them, clicking right to the page of images. Most of them are of the men who stand outside the gates, taken by tourists or news sources, but—my heart leaps into my throat.

The familiar profile of my least favorite person is unmistakable.

Satan is dressed in the same dark blue uniform as the other members of the guard, but judging from his position— standing before a line of straight-backed men in the palace courtyard—he was in a position of authority.

I scroll through more and find him again, this time

standing beside two other guards, barely discernible behind the late King Arthur, who appears to be mid-speech. In the next one I find, he's one of a line of other uniformed officers on horseback, riding behind the newly crowned King Benedict and Queen Zelda, as they complete their coronation procession.

Holy shit.

Reeling, I set down my phone, suspended in a state of incredulous disbelief.

Mallory didn't just work for the royal family as some ordinary guard; he was a high-ranking officer. The man I've called a "turd face" at least three times was present at significant, historical moments, and knew the family well enough that even Princess Araminta cared when he quit.

Damien Mallory was *important*. Which, naturally, leads to the question: Why is he *here*?

And, more importantly... How can I get him to leave?

Ten

I brace my hands on my knees, struggling to steady my breathing as waves crash against the rocks far below the bluffs where I'm standing. It's early, not even eight, but I'm already exhausted.

Blair Porter has that effect on me.

We've been at it for weeks now, but much to my annoyance, this morning she failed to get up on time yet again. Routine and structure are clearly unfamiliar to her, but my patience—which is quickly exhausted by banging on her door until she can't ignore me any longer—is coming to an end.

I've dealt with disrespectful little shits in the Navy, and trained plenty of young, immature royal guards. None of it fazed me. After all, I was the one holding the reins. They could buck against my authority all they liked, but in the end, they either fell in line or met the consequences.

Lord Porter's bratty daughter should be no different, and yet there seems little point in denying there is *something* about her that gets under my skin. Every time she mouths off, sneers, or insults my face, I'm tempted to do the same right back, which is the very opposite of how I should respond.

After our run this morning, I left her at Thornhurst's kitchen door with a reminder to drink some water and stretch—this was met by a thoughtful suggestion on how best to drown myself—before heading off on a second run at a less glacial pace. I needed to vent some of this frustration, to clear my head, but it's clear I overdid it.

Straightening up with a groan, I let my head drop back, staring at the sky as ocean wind nips at my face and hands. It's not often that I feel my age, but the last few months have taken their toll. The stress, the corrosive, bitter guilt, and worst of all, missing the only family I have left.

As if determined to make myself feel worse, I think of the dozen or so calls I've received from Leo, and four from Zelda, in the past week alone. Calls I haven't returned, because I'm too cowardly to face their questions, or to admit I don't have any of the answers.

The radio silence from Ben is somehow more difficult to stomach.

My brother has come a long way, but old habits die hard, and he's always put up walls when he's hurt. The decision to leave my position in the guard was as sudden to me as it was to him, but at least I knew why. My brother had no such luxury. From his perspective, he was abandoned by one of the few people in his life whom he had always trusted implicitly.

Objectively, I know what I'm doing—pushing away the people who love me in my guilt—but even recognizing my behavior for what it is isn't enough to break free from the vicious cycle.

I stare out at the churning sea for a while longer, allowing my breathing to slow, and watch as a fishing boat drifts slowly across the horizon. Finally, when I can't stand being left alone with my thoughts any longer, I turn back toward the security office.

I don't make it to the door.

An alert chimes loudly on my phone as I approach the building, and I take it out, frowning down at the notification from the ancient, front gate buzz-in system—another improvement that will be made as soon as possible. There is no microphone or camera, just an alert that someone requested entry, or that one of the employee codes had been entered. I suspect Freddy had the habit of letting guests in without bothering to drive down and check, but I divert course without a second thought, heading toward the estate's truck.

There have been a handful of newcomers since I arrived, mostly contractors, but nobody who stopped by unexpectedly. Considering it's a Saturday, and I have no work on the schedule until Tuesday, whoever this is wasn't invited.

As I drive down the long road leading into the estate and finally set eyes on the high black gates which separate Thornhurst from the outside world, I'm glad I did.

An unfamiliar, plain white sedan is parked outside, with a man leaning against the side, arms crossed and staring off into the distance. He turns at the sound of the truck and watches as I approach. When I come to a stop, leaving twenty yards between myself and him, the man pushes off the car, smiling politely.

"Can I help you?" I call as I get out, my suspicions heightened now that he's close enough to see properly.

"Good afternoon," the stranger replies cheerfully, strolling forward until he comes to a stop just on the other side of the gate.

I don't move closer, looking him up and down.

Everything about this man's appearance, from his white running shoes to his zippered windbreaker, is nondescript.

Even the car is an ordinary, mass-produced white sedan, the kind you wouldn't look twice at if it parked on your street.

There is nothing about him which suggests he's up to anything nefarious, but in my experience, people who go out of their way to fly under the radar are the ones you've got to watch the closest. That and the fact that he's Thornhurst's first unannounced visitor since I arrived, raises more than a few red flags.

"Can I help you?" I repeat, suspicion prickling at the back of my neck.

The man doesn't appear to be put off by my lack of manners. "I'm here to meet with Blair Porter," he tells me, pushing his hands into his pockets.

Ice spreads through my chest. "Blair Porter?" I repeat, raising my eyebrows skeptically. "Lord Porter's youngest?"

"That's the one." His eyes search my face, waiting for me to give some indication that whatever hunch brought him back here is correct.

He'll be waiting a long time. "You're going to have to look elsewhere, then."

This doesn't faze him in the slightest, which only heightens my suspicions. When ordinary people, ones who aren't sniffing around for something, are met with a brick wall, their first reaction is to check themselves. Maybe he would pull out his phone to verify the address he was given is correct, or ask me if there were any other properties nearby.

This man—a reporter, if I had to guess—does none of that. If anything, he looks pleased. "So, you're telling me she isn't here?" he asks, tilting his head quizzically.

"I'm telling you this is private property, and you're trespassing. I can call the police, or, if you'd like, I can take your contact details and do what I can to get you in touch with Miss Porter."

He only smiles. "That won't be necessary. Though I

wonder if *you* might be able to help me." Pausing, he seems to consider the best approach to ask for whatever it is he wants, before deciding to throw caution to the wind. My stomach hardens as the man reaches into his pocket to produce a white identification card, hanging at the end of a blue lanyard. Press credentials. He's a reporter.

My lip curls. "Fuck off."

"We can speak off the record," he assures me, grinning now. "Nothing needs to get back to your boss. Come on, working for a man like Porter has to be frustrating. I bet you've got some real dirt on that asshole. The better the information, the better we pay for it."

I let out an incredulous bark of laughter and lean closer, trying to make out the logo on the lanyard as he tucks it away. The bold red font is, unfortunately, too familiar to mistake. "Jesus, man. Get the hell out of here."

This fuck isn't even a real reporter; he's a gossip-mongering paparazzi. He isn't trying to uncover political corruption or serious news, he wants a quick, dirty story, and is sniffing around in the hopes of finding Blair. I'm betting the prospective PM's young, beautiful daughter, partying topless on the front page of his magazine, was very good for sales. No doubt he's trying to publish a follow-up and keep the money rolling in. Typical.

"Alright, I'm going." The man chuckles, obviously used to being shut down, and backs toward his car. "You might want to tell Porter's little wild card that if she wants to keep a low profile, she might want to avoid tagging her location in her selfies."

My blood runs cold.

Is she insane?

Numb with furious disbelief, it takes all the willpower I possess to keep myself from reacting to this as I stand my ground, making sure the fuck actually leaves. This is exactly the sort of thing I was worried about when Porter mandated that Blair should be kept in the dark about the threats against her. If you don't give a careless, entitled person a good fucking reason to be cautious, *they won't be.*

Seething, I watch as he pulls out onto the street and drives out of sight. Finally, after a few minutes have passed and I'm reasonably confident he won't be making a second attempt, I rip open the door of the truck, all but throwing myself into the driver's seat.

Even when the vehicle rumbles back to life, however, I don't drive off. My chest burns as I take out my phone, and it's the work of about thirty seconds to find Blair's social media profiles. I'd checked them when I took the job, and her accounts are just as I remember: riddled with images of her in sparse, metallic clothing, usually with a drink in her hand and an effortless smile on her face, accompanied by a rotating cast of well-dressed socialites.

According to the date on her latest post, she hasn't put up anything new since she arrived back in Stelland. The only indication she's been active on the account is a status update at the top of the account, which is simply a cookie emoji. When I press it, a picture comes up of Blair—standing in what I recognize as Thornhurst's sprawling kitchen—biting playfully into a cookie.

My stomach hardens as I see the text at the top corner, which dates the image to last night and has an actual geotag for nearly right where I'm currently standing. Providing her exact location to her twenty-five thousand followers, and anyone with a search engine.

Even not knowing about the disgusting communications sent her way after those topless pictures hit the press, it defies all common sense for her to do such a thing.

Disgusted, I toss my phone onto the seat beside me and

throw the truck into drive, tearing down the road toward the main house.

I have no idea who I'm angrier at: her for being so careless, Porter for not allowing me to give his daughter important information about her physical safety, or myself for not seeing this coming. I ought to have made sure her location services were dismantled before anything else, but I didn't think to, because typically the people I work for aren't reckless little fools.

All for a picture of her biting into a fucking cookie. *Christ*.

The truck groans loudly as I slam on the brakes outside Thornhurst's kitchen, blood rushing in my ears.

"Blair!" I bellow the moment I step inside, shoving the door closed behind myself. Nobody is in the kitchen when I enter, but when I reach the back hall, opening my mouth to yell for her again, the woman I'm here for appears from a side room.

And, just like that, I'm brought up short.

It's the same oversized sweater I'd seen her wearing the day I caught her eating ice cream for lunch, which should be innocent enough, but there's something about how the neckline slips from her shoulder, exposing the elegant curve of her collarbone—absent the strap of a shirt or bra—that makes my mouth go dry.

I'm still struggling to regroup when she plants her hands on her hips, frowning at me. "What do you want, demon?"

The bratty, impatient tone is enough to reignite my ire. Blowing out a heavy lungful of air, I glare back at her. "I was just down at the gates, speaking to an unexpected visitor. A reporter, actually."

Blair's lips twitch. "*Ooooo*, are you going to be on the cover of *Stelland Says*? Is it their least eligible bachelor edition?"

I scrub both hands over my face, almost beyond words in

my frustration. "What on earth were you thinking, tagging your physical location on social media?"

She stares back at me, utterly bemused. "I didn't do that."

It's unbelievable she thinks she can lie about something like this. I glower at her. "You did. I saw it. Give me your phone."

"Yes, but are you *sure* it was me?" Her eyes sparkle, like she's *enjoying* my anger. "Could it have been a *different* Blair Porter? One to whom I bear a striking resemblance?"

I let out a hard, disbelieving laugh. If ever I was actually in the mood to deal with her nonsense, today would most certainly not be the day. "We are not doing this. Hand it over."

"No!" Blair objects, lifting her chin. "It's my personal property, and I have nudes on there that you don't deserve to see."

Being furious and turned on at the same time is fairly disorienting, but the mention of her naked body alone is enough to have heat spreading through my groin. I can't decide what's more infuriating: the woman's attitude or the fact that it makes my dick hard.

I grit my teeth against the flurry of questions which instantly arise—mainly pertaining to who she *did* deem worthy of seeing them—and hold out my hand, palm up. "I am not fucking around. Give it to me. Now."

As if determined to send my blood pressure into the stratosphere, Blair's lips curve into a self-satisfied smile. "Or what?"

I imagine putting her over my knee and bringing my hand down on her bare ass. Hard enough to leave a mark. Hard enough to make her remember.

In truth, I don't have any real recourse here. It's not as if I can tackle her to the ground and take it, but the alternative of having to go through her father—or, more likely, his obnoxious, self-important assistant—seems like an easy way to strip myself of whatever shred of actual authority I have over this woman.

I allow my hand to fall back to my side. "Or I will make your life even more unpleasant than it already is. I mean it, Blair. This isn't a fucking suggestion."

For a moment, I think she's actually considering it.

Very slowly, Blair reaches into the side pocket of her leggings and produces her phone, staring at me thoughtfully as she turns the device between her fingers. "So, I totally get you could turn off the internet or make me run in circles for hours, or whatever. That all sounds super unpleasant, don't get me wrong. But the thing is," she sighs, putting the phone away again. "The thing is, you are *so mean*, and *superior*, and just generally *the worst*. So it makes me want to do what you want even less than I want those unpleasant things. Does that make any sense?"

In other words, she wants to spite me, even if it's at her own expense. How the fuck are you supposed to reason with someone who knows she's being unreasonable, but is committed to doing it anyway?

For the first time in my life, I truly appreciate the need for the expression: *pull your hair out.*

"Thornhurst has security measures for a reason, princess," I grit out, conscious that I'm so tense, I'm barely moving my jaw as I speak. "Your daddy is a very important man, and, as you certainly know, has lots and lots of money. Broadcasting your personal location, after those photographs were published, is not a good idea. Believe it or not, I am acting in your best interest here."

It's the closest way I can think of to tell her she could be in danger, without outright saying it.

Unfortunately, it seems that subtlety isn't a language that Blair Porter speaks.

She hums, tapping her finger on the side of the device in

her hand. Taunting me. "This may be a challenging concept for you, oh Lord of Darkness, but maybe you should try asking nicely every once in a while," she suggests sweetly. "I've heard you catch more flies with honey than vinegar."

"You're comparing yourself to an insect whose entire purpose in life is to shit and die."

This statement is met with a withering look.

"Fine. Let's try it your way." I bare my teeth into something resembling a smile. "Would you *please* be kind enough to show me your phone, so I can disable location services, thereby preventing your ungrateful, spoiled ass from being kidnapped and held for ransom."

The infuriating creature before me actually laughs, wholly unconcerned with this very real threat to her personal safety. "Gosh, you're a charmer. Consider my panties melted, Satan. I'm starting to see how you landed yourself on the least eligible bachelor list!"

"Blair."

She claps her hands together, her expression bright with false encouragement. "Come on, pal! You can do this! Just ask yourself, how would a *normal* person who *isn't terrible* approach this conversation?"

It's futile to try and wrap my mind around the ludicrous situation I've found myself in. Christ, even allowing Araminta to take the equivalent of a flamethrower to my life is beginning to seem preferable to prolonged exposure to this woman who may actually drive me out of my mind.

"Blair," I try again, forcing a deep breath in and out through my nose. "Please let me see the phone. You are welcome to supervise and ensure I do not invade your privacy in any way, but this is important." There. I was polite. Calm. She has absolutely no reason to object.

I realize too late—as her smile widens ominously—that my logic was faulty. You cannot reason with someone who is unreasonable, and if I've learned anything about the woman standing before me, it's that she is exactly that. Unreasonable.

To a casual observer, it might appear that she's thinking my words over, but I know better.

Sure enough, after whatever she deems a sufficiently dramatic pause, Blair beams. "No thanks." And, without another word, she turns, flouncing off in the opposite direction with an extra spring in her step from the batshit crazy victory.

As I stare at her, my ears ringing, and completely lost for words, I experience a strange moment of clarity.

There is no possible way we're making it through another seven months of this.

ELEVEN

BLAIR

For someone who is so obsessed with security, it's weird that Satan didn't think to lock his door.

Maybe he believed the lack of anything or anyone for miles around meant the chances of break-ins were low, and perhaps that I—the estate's only other full-time resident—wouldn't have the audacity to go snooping through his things.

If that's the case, he was *wrong*.

I'm utterly delighted with myself as I stroll down the gravel drive toward Damien Mallory's inner sanctum. I'd been careful, first waiting to make sure he was occupied with yet another clipboard-wielding man in a jumpsuit, before hurrying out the back door on my mission.

There were holes in this plan, unfortunately, and the biggest of them was that I hadn't been able to find a key to the back cottage anywhere. After cursing my parents for their lack of hands-on landlording, I decided to wing it, and the fates must have thought my determination should be rewarded with an unlocked door.

Now that I've gained entry with practically no effort, my top priority is understanding the enemy, so I might use my ill-gained knowledge to destroy him.

"How irresponsible can you get, leaving your door unlocked, princess?" I ask the open air in a deep-voiced imitation of Mallory, pausing in the little entryway with my hands on my hips, looking around. *"Are you an idiot, princess?"*

Admittedly, I'm a little more wary now that I'm actually standing here. He wouldn't actually hurt me, but the truth is, I have absolutely no idea how His Royal Evilness would react to finding me here. Certainly, he wouldn't pour me a cup of tea or roll out the welcome mat. In all likelihood, he would be furious, and it would make our already combative relationship about ten times worse.

I *was* horribly bored at the house, though, so I might as well go through with it.

Humming cheerfully to myself, I venture further into the cottage, eyeing the scrupulously clean space with interest. Mallory hasn't bothered to do much in the way of decoration —not a single moat of brimstone or burning cross to be seen —but there are a few personal belongings left out, and he's dressed the bed in plain white linens.

The zip-up I've seen him wear a few times is hanging on the old wooden hook beside the door, and his running shoes are resting beneath them, with those little odor-reducing balls inside.

I cross the room and pull open the fridge, leaning down to examine its contents. Gross. Who eats this many vegetables when nobody is around? Disappointed, I turn, examining the room more pragmatically.

If I were a bossy, pompous, fart face, where would I hide something?

My eyes fall upon the bedside table, and I stride across the cottage to pull open the drawer. The only contents, a bottle of lotion and half-used pack of tissues, make me laugh. Even if the objects immediately inspire a very enjoyable fantasy of Mallory using them.

God, he's so hot. It's such a shame about the personality.

Pointedly ignoring the heat that's settled in my core at the mental image of the worst person in the world masturbating, I carry on. His clothes are all obsessively neat and folded in the drawers, and the only books on the shelf are a collection of old mystery novels that may or may not be left from the cottage's last inhabitant. Everything about the space is impersonal and sparse, like Mallory isn't bothered with creature comforts or sentimentality.

I poke through a few more cabinets and flip open a notebook left out on the table—which is filled entirely with notes about work—but nothing at all stands out to me as potential blackmail material.

Still, determined to make the most of this opportunity, I head for the last unexplored space: the bathroom.

Like the rest of the cottage, there isn't a single thing out of place, though I do learn more here. Satan must have some level of vanity, because he actually bothers to moisturize—a rarity among men—and uses nearly as many hair products as I do. Not that his grooming habits are particularly useful to me.

I pretend I don't enjoy the way the room smells, fresh and masculine, clean without being sterile.

Huffing, I pull the shower curtain closed again and turn my attention to the glass-fronted medicine cabinet hanging above the pedestal sink. Inside, there is a disappointing lack of boner pills or anti-psychotics, but on the top shelf, the edge of something gold glimmers just out of my view.

Reaching up, I close my fingers around the cold metal and take it down. A gold wristwatch.

For a moment, I stare at it, struggling to pinpoint why the

hair has lifted on my arms, and my heart is beating faster than it was a moment ago.

The watch is nice… very nice. Its strap is made of a fine, polished leather that has gone buttery and soft with age. The face, which is set into a gold frame, is alive and ticking, its tiny dials moving in an elegant choreography around a familiar logo at the very center.

This isn't an ordinary watch. It was made by one of the most well-known luxury makers in the world and would undoubtedly fetch tens of thousands of dollars at auction. It's the sort of piece my father, brother, or future brother-in-law would wear, an heirloom dripping in old money.

Swallowing, I drag my finger over the crystal face, captivated by the tiny mechanical movements beneath its surface. I may be wrong, but I don't think this is the type of watch that uses a battery. It needs to be reset every single day, and I can't imagine why Satan would bother, as I've only ever seen him wearing his fitness tracker.

Slowly, I turn it over to check, and my breath catches as I make out the coat of arms engraved into the back metal plate.

A coat of arms that would be instantly recognizable to any native Stellander, because it belongs to our royal family.

With difficulty, I swallow and put it back where I found it. Closing the medicine cabinet with no further exploration, I stare at my pale, shocked expression in the mirror.

Why on Earth would a royal guard have something like that?

If he'd stolen it—which is the most logical explanation— surely he would have dispensed with the thing at the earliest possible opportunity. It wouldn't be difficult to have that engraving buffed out, reducing it from royal heirloom to vintage luxury showpiece.

Mallory didn't get rid of it, though. He kept it in his bathroom cabinet and appears to have made a habit of setting the time every day, despite never wearing it. That doesn't suggest a former employee of the royal family looking to make some quick money; it suggests the item is precious to him. Sentimental.

I'm not sure how much time has passed since I got here, but it seems unwise to linger for too long.

Deciding I've seen enough, I flip the lights off in the bathroom and step out into the main living area, surveying the space to ensure I haven't left any indication I was here. All is as I found it—sparse, boring, and devoid of any personality—so, satisfied, I start toward the door.

Which is when I hear it.

Heavy footfalls outside on the wooden porch.

Holy ever-loving shit.

My heart rockets into my throat, and I turn, diving back into the dark bathroom. The shower curtain is still swaying gently from me hurrying behind it, when I hear the sound of the cottage's door opening and closing.

I clap my hand over my nose and mouth, conscious of how loud my breathing sounds in the dimly lit, enclosed space, as footsteps move in the direction of the kitchen. A faucet is turned on and off, and something hard is set down on a wooden surface.

Every nerve in my body is lit up, buzzing with awareness of my surroundings as I listen to him walking around just one room over, oblivious to my presence.

The water runs again, longer, followed by the distinct sound of a zipper being pulled down, and the rustle of fabric being set aside.

Footsteps draw closer, until he's in the bathroom, standing just feet away from me with only a flimsy plastic barrier separating him from the intruder in his home. The medicine cabinet opens and then, after a long moment, closes.

Silence falls, and my heart is slamming so hard against my

ribcage that I swear he must be able to hear it. Squeezing my eyes shut, I will my pulse to slow, my lungs burning with lack of oxygen because I don't even dare to breathe right now.

Then, Mallory's voice comes, quiet and far too controlled. "Did you find what you were looking for, princess?"

It's all I can do to stop myself from squealing as the shower curtain is yanked back and light floods the bathroom, sudden and blinding. I blink rapidly, as I find myself staring at Mallory, his body blocking the narrow exit to the shower. He's not wearing the jacket I saw him in earlier, and his sleeves are rolled up over his corded forearms, looking infuriatingly composed, given the circumstances.

One dark brow lifts, as if he's caught a child with her hand in the biscuit tin rather than a trespasser in his home.

I recover my bravado and lift my chin, glaring right back at him. "You should probably consider locking your door, Satan."

His inky gaze drops—slow and deliberate—taking me in, before lifting back to my eyes, darker and sharper than before. "You should probably consider staying out of places you don't belong."

The words settle heavily between us.

"It's my property. I can go where I like on it."

Mallory lifts a hand to grip the edge of the shower harder, the muscles in his forearm standing out as he boxes me in. We're close enough now that I can smell him, and I swallow, wishing I could ignore the hot, tight feeling which has settled low in my belly. The one asking—no, begging—for whatever consequences he sees fit to deliver.

"It's your father's property, not yours," he murmurs, every word still infuriatingly calm. "Boundaries are important, Blair. You need to learn to respect them. For your own good."

This should not be turning me on, but with every second

that passes, the hot ball of desire in the pit of my stomach grows a little heavier and a little harder to ignore.

My tongue darts out, wetting my lips, and his eyes track the movement, lingering too long. "And is this typically how you enforce personal boundaries?" I ask, my voice sweet and coy. "Shower imprisonment?"

His mouth flattens into a hard line. "No," he admits. "But in this case, the punishment fits the crime, wouldn't you say?"

No. Not really. As a traitorous, undeniable slickness spreads over my panties, and I have to remind myself not to squirm, I can think of better ways for him to punish me for this particular crime.

I exhale, attempting to regather my scrambled thoughts. "One might say the same about your unlocked door. Very careless, for a man in your profession. I'm surprised at you."

A tendon in Mallory's neck leaps as he braces a hand on the tile wall beside my head and leans forward, reducing the distance between us to inches. "I never want to see you in here again," he murmurs, the words a low, dangerous purr. "And I promise you, I won't be so patient a second time."

For a moment, I think he's actually going to do something. I'm ready for it, my entire body poised at the edge of a cliff, waiting desperately for the fall. All I see is him, all I smell is him, and every cell in my body is begging me to give in.

Never in my memory can I recall wanting a man as deeply as I want him.

But then, something hardens in Satan's handsomely carved features, and it's all I can do to stop myself from crying out in disappointment when he leans away. Stepping to the side, he fixes me with that same intensely irritated look I've come to associate with him, the one which makes me feel like an unimportant and unappealing bug stuck to his windshield

"Get out."

The two words are enough to get me moving. As I brush

past him, my shoulder grazes his chest, a brief, accidental contact. He inhales once, sharp and contained, and the sound sends a thrill through me. I don't stop, though. I keep moving toward the door of the cottage and only pause to look back when my hand is resting on the cold knob.

Mallory is standing in the bathroom doorway, his arms folded over that very impressive chest. "I mean it, princess. Don't come back."

With a rush of daring, I allow myself to smile, full and wild and alive for the first time in weeks. "What if you invite me?"

His features harden. "I won't." There is no doubt in the words, like he still believes wholly in the strength of his self-control, even after I saw it splintering before my eyes only a moment ago.

Still smiling, I open the front door and step outside, calling back over my shoulder, "We'll see!"

TWELVE

DAMIEN

I've suspected since we met that Blair Porter must have sprung into existence as a twisted form of karmic retribution.

Lately, however, I've begun to wonder whether I've unknowingly done more damage than previously believed.

On Monday of this week, she produced a vial of fake holy water from her sports bra during our run and proceeded to flick it at me with fake hissing noises until I snatched the thing away and tossed it into the forest. After which, I endured a lecture from her on the evils of littering—in between much panting and complaining—while I tried not to imagine fucking her plump tits.

On Tuesday, I spent hours of my day troubleshooting why the floodlights on the grounds weren't working, only to discover Blair had been turning the electrical breakers on and off at random when I wasn't looking. After realizing what was going on, I yelled at her while she ate grapes, and had a hard-on the entire time.

On Wednesday, she pretended to sprain her ankle while running and was in "such excruciating pain" that I relented to giving her a piggyback ride back to the house. This endeavor wasn't exactly easy, with my hands on her thighs and the warmth of her body bleeding into mine. When I deposited her in a kitchen chair—intending to call for Porter's personal on-call physician—Blair sprang up, thanked me for the ride, and skipped off toward her rooms.

Every fucking day, she finds a fresh, inventive way to drive me mad, and it may actually be working. Because, just as my irritation with the woman seems to grow more potent by the day, so does my attraction to her.

It's perverse to find myself fantasizing about fucking the woman one minute and pushing her off a cliff the next. The two feelings—desire and loathing—shouldn't be compatible and haven't been in my experience. That is, until I wandered into the eye of the mad hurricane that is Princess Porter.

Through it all, though, I've kept myself together and have neither fucked her, pushed her off a cliff, nor worked my cock to the fantasy of doing either. I might not be able to help the intrusive thoughts and my body's reaction to her, but I can certainly stop myself from acting on them.

I don't know how long I can keep it up.

"Would you prefer *Beelzebub* or *Bringer of Darkness* on your tombstone? Just trying to plan ahead for when you're inevitably struck down in the battle between good and evil."

I pause, staring straight ahead at the *Private Property: No Trespassing* sign I'm attempting to nail into a tree, then down at the hammer I'm holding. "Are you at all concerned about the advisability of provoking someone who is holding a blunt instrument?"

Leaning against a nearby trunk, Blair merely sighs, her eyes in the sky.

We're standing along the quiet country road which

borders the estate's eastern property line. Behind us, hidden beyond the tree line, is a ten-foot-tall, barbed wire fence. One which is now practically useless, thanks to the hundred-year-old sycamore which fell over it, somewhere between last week and now. I'd spotted it on my run with Blair this morning and made a call to the groundskeeper when I returned to my cottage.

As the man hadn't gotten back to me hours later, I decided that replacing the faded and rusted old warning signs would be today's task. I'd only been at it for half an hour before Blair appeared from out of the woods, apparently bored enough to seek me out and engage in her favorite hobby: instigating mental anguish.

I'm wary of having her out here, especially following the cookie picture incident. The estate hasn't received any more of the threatening letters, but I know better than to let my guard down. Now that she's appeared, I'm doubly distracted, listening for traffic and prepared to obscure her from the view of a passing car.

"If you aren't going to leave, at least make yourself useful," I tell her, after I've hung another sign, and it becomes clear Blair isn't going anywhere. "Grab the crowbar over there and start pulling down the old signs."

I don't look at her, but after a pause, I hear her footsteps crunching over fallen leaves and debris as she moves toward the place where I left the tool. "Does it seem advisable to give *me* a blunt instrument?" she asks as she brushes past, and I catch a faint hint of the scent of apples and honey that washed over me that day in her bedroom.

The weight of the hammer in my hand is satisfying as it comes down on a fresh nail, driving it into the tree. "Yes, actually. I'm hoping you'll put me out of my misery."

Blair lets out a bright, tinkling laugh, obviously delighted. "Oh, you really would love that, wouldn't you? Retake your rightful throne in the underworld? An unlimited supply of souls to torture, instead of just me?"

"I would argue that I'm the only one being tortured here. Don't you have anything better to do?" Unable to help myself, I glance over and see her frowning in concentration, trying to notch the tool over the rusted old nail without success.

"Nope," she supplies, eyes narrowed on the offending nail. Her handling of the bar is poor and inexperienced, as I would expect from someone who hasn't had to do manual labor before in her life. I don't waste my breath attempting to offer advice, hoping her incompetence will get her frustrated enough to leave me in peace.

Of their own accord, my eyes drop to the curve of her ass through the petal-pink leggings she's wearing.

"What about your schoolwork?" I ask, dragging my reluctant gaze away, and move past her to the next tree.

I've learned that bringing up the courses she's being forced to take seems to be one of the only reliable ways to put Blair on edge, and my only truly effective weapon against the brat's attitude. "If you're out here, you must be finished with everything."

Far down the road, I hear the distinct sound of an engine moving toward us. Without hesitating, I let the hammer fall to the ground. Stepping over to where Blair is struggling with the nail—her expression now scrunched up and indignant—I block her from view of the road with my own body.

"You're doing it wrong," I offer in explanation, reaching over her shoulder to take hold of the crowbar. She huffs but allows me to guide it to the appropriate place, and heat spreads through my chest as her back brushes my front.

All I can smell is apples and honey as, behind us, a freight truck rumbles past without slowing.

"You'll have an easier time getting it under the sign itself. See?" My forearm brushes hers, and I pretend not to notice the tiny hitch of her breath, or the way the sound makes my abdomen go hard, desire pooling in my groin.

Fucking hell.

I draw away from her, returning to my own work, as with a groan, the aging sign falls onto the ground at Blair's feet. "Ha!" she hisses, victorious, and from the corner of my vision, I watch her lean down to pick it up, examining the metal with interest.

Pinning a new sign to a neighboring tree, I feel my lips twist bitterly. "You never answered my question. About your courses."

"They're fine," she answers too quickly.

Letting out a hard laugh, I bring the hammer down on the nail. "Why do I doubt that?"

Though I don't look at her, I feel the weight of Blair's gaze on my profile. "Oh, I don't know," she muses, an edge to her voice now. "Probably because you're committed to thinking I'm an idiot."

I don't, actually. If anything, I'm disappointed in how her obvious intellect has largely been put to use looking for ways to avoid doing anything with it.

"An idiot? No." I shoot her a nasty, scathing look. "Even idiots know how to use a crowbar without assistance."

She glares at me, the bar hanging at her side in one hand, and the sign in the other. "Most people would say thank you for the help. This is your job, not mine."

"What do you know about jobs, princess?" I sneer, savoring the savage, vindictive impulse to wound, a welcome alternative to the near-constant desire to fuck her senseless. "Right now, your only job is to do as your daddy says, stay out of trouble, and complete your coursework like a good girl. How would you say you're doing in that *very difficult* career path?"

I'm only beginning to realize that as deeply as she seems to want to get a reaction from me, I crave the same from her. My chest expands, filling with a dark, twisted triumph as Blair's expression flickers, registering that my hit landed.

She recovers in seconds, however, sneering as she allows the crowbar to fall to the ground at her feet and planting her hands on her hips. "How would you say you're doing with *yours*? You hate me. You hate this place. Why not quit?"

Fuck, I can't stand the sight of her. What I wouldn't give to do just that: quit, leave, and never look back.

My answering smile is mocking. "I'm doing what suits me, and believe it or not, it has nothing to do with how unbelievably fucking insufferable you are. The world does not revolve around you, princess, and you're flattering yourself if you think a spoiled, immature *child* has any kind of power over me, never mind my career."

Blair takes a single step toward me, her features ridged with fury. "I might be a spoiled, immature child, but you're a cruel, bitter asshole. Who hurt you? Who made you like this?" She scoffs, "Whatever. It doesn't matter. Just do me a favor and stop acting like it was *me*."

"Go." I point up the hill toward the house, my lungs burning. "I'm done. Get the hell out of my face."

For once, she doesn't need to be told twice. "It would be my pleasure, you massive chunky shit," Blair sneers, stepping over the fallen tool and up the embankment toward the opening in the fence, hands balled into fists at her sides.

I watch her go, my chest rising and falling heavily, still half expecting her to turn back and start shit up again. She doesn't, though. Blair doesn't say a single word as she makes it to the top of the hill and pauses with one foot on the trunk of the fallen tree. She shoots one brief look back at me, her features schooled into an expression of pure loathing, before she lifts herself up onto the trunk, walking over the crushed fence and vanishing from sight.

Seconds pass, and still, I can't quite breathe as I should.

Adrenaline is still coursing through my body, and after it becomes clear Blair won't be returning, I gather up the tools and the remaining signs to be put up, following her path up the embankment.

As I stride through the forest, I can't hear the distant crash of the waves onto the rocky beach, or the wind coming off the sea, or anything beyond the blood rushing in my ears.

I can't remember what we were arguing about or what was said, all I register is the furious heat which has roared to life beneath my skin. The heat that will not loosen its hold on me. If anything, it tightens, growing more unbearable as I emerge from the forest onto the section of utility road, where I'd parked the truck less than an hour ago.

Except, *there is no truck.*

There is no truck, and there is only one person who could have taken it.

The many metal objects in my arms fall to the ground with a noisy clatter, and I shove my hand through my hair, almost shaking in my fury. Desperate for some way to vent the feeling, I reach down and pick up the hammer, hurling the tool into the nearest tree.

It doesn't help.

"*Fuck!*" The single, bellowed word echoes through the empty forest, scattering a pair of birds from their perch somewhere above.

Without bothering to retrieve any of the tools, I leave, striding down the utility road in the direction of my cottage. Even in a life that has been rife with injustices and mistakes and problems much bigger than myself, never have I been angrier than I am right now. It defies reason how any person could have the power to do this to me, that *Blair-fucking-Porter* could drive me so out of my mind I'm reduced to this.

I don't recognize myself.

I don't like myself.

Yet as I approach the familiar structure of my temporary home, I'm still caught in the tailwind of whatever storm Blair unleashed. The front door of the cottage has barely slammed shut behind me before I'm wrestling my belt open and shoving the garments out of the way with shaking hands. No sooner have I managed to free my engorged, throbbing dick than I've seized it. I'm so fucking turned on that precum is already dripping from my slit as I begin to work myself, hard and fast.

My lungs burn as I brace one hand on the door, filling the room with the sound of my ragged breathing, and I squeeze my eyes shut, mentally scrolling down the list of fantasies I default to when I'm jerking off.

None of them work.

All I can see, all I *want* to see... *Goddamn it*. I'm fucking helpless to do anything but sink into it, and as the fantasy blooms in my mind's eye, my grip tightens to the edge of pain.

Blair sprawled out on her bed atop crumpled sheets. She's naked, and her knees are bent and parted, one hand between her thighs as the other teases the tips of her plump breasts. From my place in the doorway, I can't see what she's doing to herself, but I want to. My cock grows harder, longer as I watch the sensual roll of her hips and the way her chest rises and falls in breathy pants.

Every inch of her is fucking ripe.

She turns her head, her heavily lidded eyes meeting mine where I'm standing in the doorway. Her lips curl.

"Am I breaking the rules?" she asks with a breathless laugh, even as the muscles in her thighs and abdomen begin to tremble.

No, she isn't breaking any rules, but I will be soon.

I draw forward, approaching the bed in slow, measured steps. As I round the end of the mattress, I stop, staring down at the exquisite creature sprawled out before me. From this angle, I can clearly see the pink, rose-shaped vibrator she's got pressed to her clit. I can also see the bare lips of her cunt, and the slickness leaking from her entrance.

What a fucking waste.

She's so goddamn gorgeous. There's nothing I want more than to throw that fucking toy on the floor and put my mouth to work on that horny little cunt.

I palm my cock through the thick material of my pants, watching. "I'm afraid there will be consequences for this behavior, Blair." *The words come in a low, threatening purr.* "You're not supposed to make me hard."

My entire body shudders as I work myself faster, filling the cottage with a low, pained groan of longing. What I would do to the little brat if I had her in front of me now…

She moans, the muscles in her forearm straining with how hard she's holding the little device. "I'm prepared for the consequences. I can take it."

I almost laugh.

"Is that right?" *I round the side of the bed, stopping inches from where she's lying. Keeping my eyes locked with hers, I watch them widen in panic as I reach down, plucking the vibrator from between her fingers.*

"Shit," I snarl, slowing the pace of my hand, because— fuck me—I'm not ready for this to be over yet. I'm already going to hell, I can let this play out a little longer.

"Damien," *she whines, watching as I lift the vibrator, inspecting the arousal coating the device.*

I press my thumb to it, feeling the vibrations and the pressure of the suction… Jesus. I can do better than that.

Lifting my gaze to meet hers again, I turn the device off and toss it onto the bed. "You don't need that thing," *I growl as I grip the hem of my T-shirt, yanking it off over my head.*

Blair's pupils dilate as they drop to my chest, then lower to the unmistakable bulge of my cock straining against my pants. "I definitely do," *she giggles, glancing up at me and catching her bottom lip between her teeth. "Unless you have an alternative in mind."*

In response, I reach down, and Blair inhales sharply as I cup her warm, supple breast in my palm, drawing my thumb back and forth over her tightened nipple. I've never considered myself a particularly imaginative man, but as I look down at this woman—naked and wet and horny—suddenly I have an endless list of fucking alternatives.

The thought of them alone is erotic enough to make me groan, the noise punctuating the harsh, slapping noise of my hand working my dick.

"Yes. I do." My chest burns as I allow my hand to fall away from her breast. "Did you leave that door open so I'd see you like this?"

Blair nods, almost panting as I bring my hands to my belt.

"That's what I thought." I shove down my trousers and briefs, leaving me as naked as she is, and Blair whimpers when her eyes find my cock. Without another word, I climb into the bed, kneeling between her soft thighs. "Actions have consequences, princess, and you need to clean up your own messes. You'll learn that in a moment, when I'm pounding this wet little cunt, giving you the rough fuck you deserve."

My eyes flick up to hers, suddenly worried I've gone too far, but all I see there is desire.

I grip my base, smacking my cock against her wet slit.

There's nothing I want more than to see that, but I'm too fucking far gone, and I can't hold it back. My orgasm tears through me, sudden and violent, filling the cottage with my roar of pleasure. My release leaves me in long, heavy spurts, covering my hand, the ground, even the fucking door. I can't remember the last time I came so hard, or so much, and my knees almost collapse under me when it's finally over.

I stand there panting, my eyes screwed shut and my ears ringing, as the shame and self-loathing seep in.

What the fuck have I done?

Gritting my teeth, I push away from the door and cross to snatch a hand towel from beside the sink, wiping up my mess.

I'm disgusted with myself. Even if I'm physically attracted to her—because Blair Porter is, objectively, attractive—that doesn't change that *I don't like her*. I don't enjoy her company, and I certainly don't want to see any more of her.

Clothed or otherwise.

Thirteen

Blair

The day after I steal the truck belonging to Evil Incarnate himself, I wake up screaming.

Which, honestly, is a pretty understandable reaction to being torn from sleep by a large amount of ice-cold water hitting your body. Gasping and disoriented, I sit bolt upright, staring down at my bare legs and the sodden white T-shirt clinging to my body.

I don't need to look far for the source.

"I warned you. Six o'clock," Mallory barks over his shoulder, already marching back toward the bedroom door, a bucket swinging from one hand. "Get your ass downstairs."

This fucker.

With a screech of pure rage, I scramble to the edge of the mattress and seize the closest object I can find—a box of tissues—and hurl it at his retreating form. It misses and hits the doorframe instead, tumbling to the floor with a dull thud. The antichrist definitely sees, but doesn't acknowledge my escalation to attempted physical violence, his pace not even faltering as he steps over it and rounds the corner.

The lack of reaction is even more infuriating than not hitting him.

"I hate you!" I yell, already struggling to rid myself of my soaking wet pajamas. Satan must have gotten quite the view, because the cheeky panties and oversized T-shirt I like to sleep in leave little to the imagination when they're dry.

A laugh echoes back to me from somewhere down the hall.

My teeth are chattering as I finally rid myself of the shirt and let it drop with a wet splat. Cursing under my breath and wondering how on earth you're supposed to dry out a mattress, I glance toward the bed. This turns to a double take, however, when my gaze catches on something glistening on the sheets. When I lean in to get a closer look... *ice cubes.* Mallory didn't just dump some cold water in a bucket and call it a day, *he took the time to add ice.*

Holy shit.

That is so messed up.

Though certainly not his intention, Demonic Damien probably did me a favor with the ice. I don't know whether it's the horrific wake-up call, or my underlying frustrations about my situation, or I'm just worn down from *his* bullshit. Whatever the cause, every muscle in my body aches, protesting painfully as I pull on my leggings, sports bra, and running shoes.

Even lifting my arm to open the door requires a Herculean effort, and the muscles in my legs are weak and shaky, threatening to give out on every single step downstairs. I find Satan in our usual meeting place out front, too busy scrolling on his stupid fitness tracking watch to spare me a glance as I close the front door behind myself.

Is there a social media app specifically for sociopaths? I bet

Thornhurst's resident monster would pay a lot of money to brag about his accomplishments to his fellows.

I bend over and grip the back of my calves, attempting to stretch out the tight, abused muscles.

"Stretch," barks Mallory without looking up, not realizing I'm already doing exactly that.

God, I hate him so much.

There was a storm last night, and the grounds are an absolute mess. Muddy puddles line the front drive, and I know the path out back will be a million times worse. By the time we make it back to the house, my pink running shoes will be brown, but by now I know better than to ask for a day off.

After all, ironically, the Harbinger of Misery enjoys his morning routine. I imagine that after we finish our run through the freezing rain, he'll round it off with a bowl of unsweetened porridge and cup of lukewarm black coffee while watching a compilation of nature documentary footage, which is just orcas eating baby seals.

We set off without exchanging a single word.

My hair is still fairly wet, and the damp ends slap against my neck every time my feet hit the soft ground, reminding me of how it got that way. I didn't think I was the type to hold a grudge. When my childhood friends and I would fight, I was always the first to break the silence and beg them to play with me again. Even then, my pride wasn't worth being alone.

Now, I would light my pride on fire if it would get rid of this man.

We jog over the forest's edge. I've noticed Satan extending my running periods and shortening my walking periods, but today, I'm too sore and exhausted to make it as far as I did yesterday. My pace slows.

"Keep going," Mallory barks, without even looking at me. "You made it to that big log yesterday."

That big log is just barely visible at the end of this stretch of trail.

I grit my teeth, forcing myself forward. There are things I'd like to say—like how the only big log I see out here is him—but it seems ill-advised to waste the tiny amount of air I have left for a pretty lackluster insult.

My legs are burning by the time he lets me walk again. I should be used to his callous, shitty attitude by now, but maybe somewhere in the back of my mind, I thought I kind of deserved his ire. This morning's ice water seems to have been the last straw to disabuse me of that notion.

God, I've just had enough. Damien Mallory is an *actual sack of shit*, and I refuse to be *treated like shit* by *shit*.

Exhaustion temporarily outweighed by righteous indignation, I start moving faster as we approach the place where I know he'll tell me to run again, getting a few yards ahead of him. My heart is hammering, and for once, it isn't from the cardio. As we get closer, moving along a narrower part of the forest trail, I wipe sweat from my forehead and glance behind me to find Mallory frowning at his fitness watch.

Which means he definitely won't notice my foot hooking under a nice, chunky glob of mud at the trail's edge.

I kick it backward and for once—*for freaking once*—the universe is on my side. The mud arcs through the air in a glorious, sloppy curve and hits its target, splattering right across the front of his pristine white compression shirt.

Mallory stops dead in the middle of the trail, hands held aloft like he's been shot, and stares down at his filthy chest. I keep moving, whipping back around to pretend I didn't notice, even as I'm mentally composing my own obituary.

"Are you serious?" comes the disbelieving bark from behind me, and I turn, blinking in (hopefully) innocent surprise at the mess on his shirt.

"What happened?"

Satan's nostrils flare, and there's a nerve pulsing ominously in his forehead as he gestures to the muddy front of his shirt. "You can't be this immature."

Oh, I absolutely can be. Desperate times call for desperate measures, and if my current situation has taught me anything, it's that sometimes I need to work with what I've got. In this case, I've got mud.

I throw him a megawatt smile that isn't even a little genuine. "Was that me? *So* sorry! The risk of running after a rainstorm, I guess!"

"That was intentional." His voice has dropped several degrees. "You moved in front of me."

My laugh startles a bird somewhere in the dense canopy above us, and it takes flight with a disgruntled caw. Neither Satan nor I breaks eye contact, though, staring each other down from ten yards apart. "I thought you'd be pleased." My smile is maniacal. "*That I'm improving.*"

A muscle in his cheek jumps, and I can tell it's taking him a lot to stay calm and not react to my childish behavior. "If you're improving, maybe we should extend the run," he counters thoughtfully, a demonic glint in his eyes now. "Let's take the left trail at the fork up ahead, it takes us through the woods for an extra half mile."

That has my glee fading, not that I'll let him see it. "No thanks. I have *lots* of very important coursework to get to! That's my job, right? I seem to remember you saying something to that effect."

He ignores this, advancing on me in calm, measured steps until there's less than a foot between us, and I have to tilt my head back to meet his death stare. "It's a bit late to backpedal, princess. Get moving."

God, he's terrible.

So am I, though, because the muscles below my belly

button have gone warm and tight as this exchange progressed. Seriously, *what is wrong with me?*

"Do you get off on being a smug, controlling prick?" I spit, abandoning my act.

He doesn't react, not even a twitch, but something seems to darken in those cold, impenetrable eyes. "Get. Moving." He repeats the words low and calm, edged with mocking superiority. Right at this moment, he thinks he's backed me into a corner, and I have no choice but to comply

Unfortunately for Mallory, he's wrong.

Keeping my eyes trained on his, I sink slowly down, ignoring the burning protest of the muscles in my legs. His jaw tightens as he watches my tongue dart out to wet my lips. My hand closes around a cold, slimy clump of mud.

There's no way he's missed what I'm doing, but Satan makes no move to stop me as I rise to my full height again. He only breaks eye contact, squeezing his eyes shut, when I lift the mud and smack it into the side of his face.

It's so gratifying that I'm actually turned on as I smear it down his stupid, perfectly square jaw and up into his hair. Then—because I know I'm about to pay for this and might as well make the most of it—I crouch down and grab some more. I don't stop until most of his face and all of his hair is caked in the slimy earth, and some of the frustration built up inside me has been released.

"Okay," I tell him when I'm finally done, allowing my dirty hand to fall back to my side. "Let's move."

Retaliation seems inevitable, but I kind of assumed it would come in the form of an extra-long run, or something equally painful. Mallory is too mature to reduce himself to my level... or so I believed. I must be rubbing off on him, however, because I barely make it three steps away before something cold and wet hits the back of my head.

I know instantly what he's done.

Whipping around, I stare at him, lifting one hand to touch the mud dripping from my hair. Mallory looks back at me, lips curled in a smug, satisfied smile. Seething, I crouch down, retrieving yet another handful of muck. Again, he doesn't try to stop me as, careful not to lower my eyes, I stop right in front of him and slip one finger beneath the waistband of his running pants, pulling them away from his body.

At that moment, something in the air seems to shift. It's both inside me and out, tightening and tugging against the space between us. The forest goes quiet, and I'm so aware of him, of the tension in his body and the look on his face which couldn't be mistaken for anything less than *want*.

Before I drop the mud, anyway.

The spell is broken. Mallory curses, springing back, and—knowing I'm about to pay dearly for that one—I turn, sprinting off down the trail.

Unfortunately, despite his advanced, borderline geriatric age, my adversary has focused a lot more on his cardiovascular health than I have. I squeal as a large, warm, muddy weight hits me from behind, an arm looping around my waist to seal my body against his, as we tumble onto the ground in an uncoordinated mess of limbs.

Apparently keen on avoiding the awkward questions that would arise from his crushing me to death, Mallory manages to turn us, so his back hits the dirt instead of mine.

Disoriented, I squirm against his hold and, with a well-aimed kick to his shin, manage to get free. I roll onto the ground, but escape doesn't seem to be in the cards for me, because seconds later, Satan's hand has closed like a vise around my ankle. Before I can even think about how to get free, he's yanked me back toward him, and I find myself flat on my back as Mallory swings a leg over my torso.

The canopy of branches and leaves is obscured, as I find myself staring up at his muddy, seething expression.

"Let me go!" I snarl, thrashing.

With frightening ease, Mallory gathers my wrists in one of his massive hands, pinning them over my head. "Let's see here." He smirks, an unhinged glint in his eye as he reaches over to retrieve another handful of mud from the side of the trail.

I barely have time to squeeze my eyes shut before he's dragging it over the side of my face, exactly as I did to him. "You're such a freaking ass!" I screech, but press my lips together tightly as I realize how perilously close the mud is to the corner of my mouth.

"And you're a brat," Mallory counters, reaching over to give the other side of my face the same treatment. It's cold and gritty, and somehow slimy, too. Nothing about this is even remotely like the mud masks I had at that spa in Barcelona, an experience I absolutely will *not* be repeating again with the image of the real thing seared into my memory until the end of time.

"Now, listen up," he seethes, leaning in to look me directly in the eyes. "Like it or not, I'm in charge. The sooner you accept it, the less miserable this *experience* will be for both of us." The weight on my chest increases as I try to buck against his hold, and the asshole growls in frustration.

My temper overrides my concern for getting mud in my mouth. "Screw you, you oversized, sadistic turd canoe!"

He lets out a bark of laughter. "Screw you right back, you spoiled, entitled little shit."

"Poop-themed insults are my thing! Get your own!"

"*Little shit* is not a poop-themed insult!"

This pisses me off even more, and I'm only grateful there is no one to witness the way my legs flail, trying and failing to land a kick against his broad back. Finally giving up with a noise of frustration, I glower up at him, panting. "Get. Off. Me."

Mallory leans in, not stopping until our muddy faces are inches apart, and I can smell the peppermint from his toothpaste. Time shudders to a stop as we stare at each other, and the sounds of the forest seem to fade away, leaving only our panting and the violent pounding of my own heart.

Despite being cold, dirty, and completely furious with the man looming over me, heat floods my core as his lips curve in a wicked smile. "I was advised you catch more flies with honey than vinegar, princess."

So, I'm not the only one who can hold a grudge.

I glare at him, squirming half-heartedly, and as I do... *Oh.*

My head spins as I stare into those dark eyes, dizzy with the rush of feeling so many things at once. Finally—*finally*—a flaw has appeared in the seemingly impenetrable armor of Damien Mallory, giving away that the controlled, smug asshole on top of me isn't as perfect as he'd like everyone to believe.

Because, even with no less than three layers of clothing between us, there's no mistaking what's pressed against my stomach.

The urgency to get back to my feet is forgotten as I look into his eyes. "Is that what you want? To catch me?" Winded as I am, the murmured words come out soft and breathy. My voice sounds like it would if he were pressing me into a mattress instead of the cold ground, and I was preparing to beg for his long, hard cock, instead of relief from this battle of wills.

Mallory's hand tightens on my wrist, and I see his throat working to swallow as his gaze drops briefly to my lips. "What?" he manages, his chest heaving.

Oh my god.

Feeling bolder than I ever have in my life, I arch my back, pressing myself harder against his erection as I respond coyly. "Do you have me right where you want me, right now?" It sends a thrill through my entire body as I see his pupils dilate and feel his cock twitch, betraying the effect these words have on him. The effect I know—I just *know*—he can't stand.

I see it in his eyes when he realizes what he's done.

Mallory recoils, pushing himself off me and back to his feet in a rush, dripping bits of mud and forest debris as he turns away. I stumble to my feet and stand there, watching as he gets himself together, gathering up all the armor he dropped until he's fully guarded and ready to face me.

Even then, I see far more gaps in its gleaming facade than I did before.

Panting, cold, wet, and caked in mud from head to foot, we stare at one another from opposite sides of the trail.

"Let's make one thing very clear," he begins, every syllable quiet, dangerous, and laced with poorly concealed fury. "If you break into my home, or steal my truck, or pull a stunt like this again, you're done."

Wind whispers through the branches above our heads, a peaceful soundtrack to the battle underway down here.

He's threatening to tell my father I'm a hopeless case, to strip me of the money that's my only hope of a comfortable life, and I couldn't care less. Possessed by the rush of understanding which swept over me a moment ago, my mud-caked face splits in a smile. "Can't wait."

FROM PARTY TO BLACKOUT: PORTER HEIRESS DISAPPEARS

Out of Sight, Out of Mind? Not for the Porter Campaign.

With the general election only seven months away, Lord Albert Porter, Prime Ministerial hopeful, has bigger problems than his narrow lead over opponent Percy Worthinger. The Porter family's once-immaculate public image is showing its first cracks as voters in Stelland and beyond ask the same question: *Where is Blair Porter?*

The Prime Ministerial frontrunner's daughter has not been seen in public for over a month, following the explosive circulation of photographs taken in Ibiza that appear to show the twenty-six year old socialite dancing topless at a private beach party. The images, obtained by multiple outlets, spread rapidly.

Neither Lord Porter nor his campaign has addressed the incident directly, issuing only a brief statement insisting that "Miss Porter is a private citizen and entitled to her privacy." And that this is a "family matter." But the lack of follow-up has only fueled speculation.

Political insiders whisper that Blair Porter was swiftly ushered out of the public eye to avoid further embarrassment during her father's tightly managed campaign. Others claim she has been sent abroad, while more sensational rumors suggest a discreet stay at an exclusive rehabilitation facility.

The Porter campaign has firmly refused to confirm or deny these claims. However, Lord Porter, who has long been celebrated for his traditional family values, now finds himself navigating uncomfortable questions at campaign events, where reporters repeatedly try and fail to get answers about his daughter's whereabouts.

Opposition figures have been quick to pounce, suggesting hypocrisy, while supporters argue the attack is unfair and irrelevant. "This is a political smear dressed up as concern," said one senior campaign aide. "Lord Porter's family should not be dragged into this."

Still, the optics are difficult to ignore. As Stelland prepares to choose its next leader, voters are left wondering whether this sudden family scandal will remain contained—or if more revelations are waiting just out of sight.

For now, Blair Porter remains unseen, and the questions keep coming.

Fourteen

Damien

Following the events of yesterday, I can't think of anything less advisable than spending six hours in an enclosed space with Blair Porter.

After my last, feeble threat, neither of us exchanged a single word as we strode, side by side, out of the woods and back toward the house. I'm not sure I even could have spoken, too shocked and horrified by what transpired to enter one of the verbal sparring matches that communicating with Blair so often leads to.

Since it happened, I've gone over the incident too many times to count, hardly able to recognize myself in my behavior. This isn't like me. None of it. I could sooner understand the motivations behind a stranger's actions than my own since I arrived at Thornhurst, and every day I spend here only seems to muddle things more.

Or, more likely, it's *her*.

Even if she drives me mad, even if I find her attractive, I'm a grown man. A professional.

In theory, I should have no problem controlling myself in her presence. In reality... well. Spending the better part of an hour in the shower yesterday, scrubbing mud from my body and beating off to the memory of her warm body pressed against mine, doesn't exactly speak to my possessing much in the way of self-control.

It was all getting to be too much. I needed time—*space*—and resolved to find ways to minimize our interactions over the next week.

Unfortunately, I won't be getting either. Not today, anyway.

When the email came in, I stared at it for an entire minute, reading and rereading the brief message at least four times, searching for some way out of it, while battling the impulse to quit on the spot.

Mr. Mallory,

I apologize for the last-minute notice, but Miss Porter is needed at a campaign event in Wyngate City tomorrow, October 22nd. Below, please find a full itinerary for your day's travel. Be advised, Lord Porter has requested Blair not be left unattended at any point during the day.

Best Regards,

Candice McCauliffe

Executive Assistant to Lord Albert Porter

- 6:30 A.M. - Depart Thornhurst Estate
  - *Approx travel time: 3.5 hours*

- 10:15 A.M. to 12:15 P.M. - Blair @ LaBelle Ette Salon (199 High Street, Wyngate)
  - *Appt with Stephanie for makeup, haircut and color touchup*

- 12:45 P.M. to 1:45 P.M. - Blair @ Century Boutique (2769 2nd Street, Wyngate)
    - *Appt with personal styling department*
    - *Pre-approved wardrobe selection will be pulled*

- 2:30 P.M. to 3:00 P.M. - Blair @ Porter Campaign Headquarters (52 Gate Street, Wyngate)
    - *Brief meeting, to provide details and guidance for event*

- 3:30 P.M. to 5:30 P.M. - Blair @ Wyngate Women's Shelter
    - *Meet & greet between Porter family and shelter leadership*
    - *Alba & Blair to assist staff in nursery while Lord & Lady Porter engage in more serious sit-down with leadership and Cedric assists building new bunkbeds with volunteers.*
    - *Entire family to help serve dinner*
    - *Photo-op with staff and residents*

- 6:00 P.M. to 7:00 P.M. - Porter family dinner @ Rose Hill House (3909 S. Williams Avenue, Wyngate)

My being at the receiving end of some twisted form of karmic justice is beginning to seem more likely by the day.

No matter how I thought about it, I couldn't find a way around a direct order from my employer and spent most of the night tossing and turning, dreading what the morning would bring.

Having nearly a month's worth of experience in the challenges associated with getting Blair out of bed before the sun rises, I'd hoped her laziness would be the downfall of the whole thing. It wouldn't be *my fault* if she overslept by three hours and missed half the day's appointments.

It was a futile hope, and one that is crushed nearly the moment I pull the estate's Land Rover up to the front door of Thornhurst at exactly the time Porter's assistant specified. A day at the spa, shopping, and smiling pretty for the camera must be much more appealing than running, because I've barely stepped out onto the drive—intending to knock as quietly as possible—before the front door bursts open.

"Road trip!" Blair sings, all but skipping toward me with a tumbler of iced coffee in one hand and a large purse swinging from the other.

She's dressed up for the occasion and looks more polished than I've seen. Her hair, which ordinarily has a slight wave to it, has been straightened. My mouth goes dry when I lower my gaze and see that she's swapped out her typical ensemble of loungewear with a short, black velvet dress. She was even up early enough to put on a full face of makeup, and her green eyes look wider than usual.

Questioning Blair's choice of attire might be pushing it a little, but I still find myself frowning as she draws closer, far more focused on the unnecessary length of her stocking-clad legs on display than I ought to be.

For fuck's sake.

The purpose of this visit is to visit *a homeless shelter*. I read the schedule over enough to remember the Porters will be spending the afternoon in clear view of the press, serving hot meals to some of Stelland's least fortunate.

What is she thinking, dressing like that?

It's safe to say her wardrobe for the event falls firmly under the umbrella of *none of my god damn business*, however, and my renewed resolution to keep things between us as professional as possible is put to its first test as I bite back my scathing comment on the dress.

She stops beside the back door but makes no attempt to get inside the idling vehicle, blinking up at me expectantly.

My temples throb as, knowing what she's waiting for, I grit my teeth and reach down to open it for her.

Blair beams, tossing her curtain of glossy hair over her shoulder as she folds herself elegantly into the darkened back seat of the car. I feel her eyes on me as I push it closed, a touch harder than I ordinarily would, and round the front of the car to the driver's seat.

"It's a perfect day for a drive, don't you think, *Diable*?" Blair asks cheerfully, almost as soon as I've buckled my seat-belt. "That's devil in French, in the likely event you aren't cultured enough to be aware."

Every ounce of self-preservation I possess is bellowing at me to *flee*. Willingly locking myself in an enclosed space with this woman for the better part of the morning seems like a recipe for disaster, and yet I have no choice but to put the car in drive and pull away from Thornhurst's front steps. "Yes," I agree at last, and a nerve in my jaw twitches as the smell of her perfume invades my lungs. "A great day for a drive."

Only twenty-four hours ago, I was covered in mud and pinning her to the forest floor, trying to decide whether I wanted to scream in her face or fuck the brat out of her right then and there. There was no disguising what it did to me, no pretending I wasn't hard as stone from having her under me like that, and the worst part—the part I couldn't help but relive over and over again in the day since—was that I wasn't the only one turned on by it.

I'd seen the pretty pink flush spreading over the parts of skin not covered in dirt.

I'd heard the way her breath caught when she realized what she'd done to my cock.

I'd felt the way she squirmed and pressed herself against me.

For the briefest of moments, the defiant, stubborn little brat had submitted to me in a way she's resolutely refused to otherwise, and even the memory of it has me hard all over again before we've made it past Thornhurst's front gates.

Fucking hell. *I need to get it together.*

"I want to make some extra shopping stops while we're in Wyngate," Blair informs me from the back seat. "Schedule permitting."

"No."

Even without looking, I know exactly the way she's pursed her lips at my denial. "It was my mother's idea, actually. Alba and James' engagement party is coming up, and I suspect there will be even more events like these as the election approaches. She agrees it's absolutely *vital* that I look presentable."

"It's more *vital* for you to behave yourself. How are those studies going, by the way?" I retort, my mouth twisting as I throw out the tried-and-true pressure point that I know will get under her skin.

Slowing the car to a stop, I roll down my window and reach out into the cold October morning to input the six-digit gate code into the box. The black iron gates open smoothly, and I drive through, trying to ignore my mounting sense of dread as I do.

Blair sighs, as if I'm the most wearisome man on the planet. "Fabulous, actually. I'm top of my class."

I don't have the mental capacity to call her on the lie, so I keep my mouth shut and my eyes on the road as we pull out onto the country lane.

A quick Google search confirmed that, since Blair was recalled to Stelland, there have been numerous "charitable appearances" just like the one we're headed to. From what I could see, they're typically attended by Lord and Lady Porter, sometimes accompanied by either or both of their two older children.

Blair being added on to this one so last-minute seemed significant. It suggested that the reporter who turned up at Thornhurst had been sniffing around elsewhere, too, and as I suspected, an article was published only yesterday which noted the absence of their youngest daughter from the campaign trail.

When I'd discussed the particulars of the job with Lord Porter the day we met at his club, he'd seemed convinced the time away from the spotlight would do his daughter good.

It's infuriating that this determination to keep Blair out of sight for her own safety evaporated with a single gossipy article. The foul, threatening letters have only just stopped arriving. Now, barely a month into her "period of improvement," the Porters have decided that trotting her out in public to quell rumors would be worth any renewed risk to their daughter's safety.

The facade of parental concern the Porters put on to justify locking their youngest daughter away from the world is looking flimsier by the day. They don't call her, or me, to check in, for that matter, and I'm convinced that if she hadn't ended up in the news, they would have turned a blind eye to the partying until the end of time.

None of it's surprising to me, but I'm still disgusted.

"Should we play a game?" asks Blair from the back seat, apparently unable to stand being left alone with her thoughts for longer than five minutes.

"No."

I'm not the least bit surprised when she ignores this completely. "I spy with my little eye something oversized and brown-haired, that missed a spot while shaving this morning."

This is going to be the longest drive of my life.

Unable to help but vent some of my mounting tension,

my knuckles go white on the steering wheel. "You are aware that I'm the one operating this motor vehicle, aren't you? Doesn't it seem unwise to antagonize me when we're driving past a cliff?" To the left of the car, there is nothing between us and the rocky cliffs, apart from a rusty guardrail.

Blair considers this for all of six seconds. "Nah, not really," she decides. "You'd be splattered right along with me. Mutually assured destruction."

"We've been over this. I think you're overestimating my will to live when you're speaking."

Uncharacteristically, she doesn't have a scathing retort to this, but before I can do more than wonder whether I've actually hurt her feelings this time, movement registers in the corner of my vision. I glance over to find her leaning over the center console, eyes narrowed and frowning.

"Who's Leo?"

My stomach plummets as I follow her gaze. My phone is resting in the cupholder beside me, and I can see the name displayed on the screen, announcing an incoming call. It takes an inordinate effort not to snatch it up and shove it away in a rush, but reacting strongly to that question would only invite more notice.

Moving slowly and attempting to exude annoyance rather than panic, I reach over to shove the device into the glove box without a second look. "An old friend," I inform her crisply.

Blair gasps. "You? A friend? How much do you pay them?"

Ha. "More than you'll be able to afford if Daddy takes away your golden key, princess."

I glance up at her reflection in the rearview mirror when I bring the car to a stop at an intersection. Blair tilts her head, gazing back at me with the mischievous glint in her eye, the one I've learned to associate with trouble approaching. "You refer to my father as '*Daddy*' a lot," she muses. "Is this your way of telling me something?"

Despite myself, I feel my lips twist. "Yes, Blair. Well spotted. I am your father's secret lover, and he gave me this job so I could make myself more available to him. He likes to be the little spoon, in case you were wondering."

A delighted, wispy laugh bursts from between Blair's lips. "Oh my god, that was *so specific*! Satan! Have I stumbled upon your deepest, darkest secret? Wait, though... No. It can't be." She recoils theatrically, clutching her hands to her chest. "A gay man would *never* wear those shoes."

———

The rest of the drive passes in more or less the same manner.

Despite my best efforts, I'm on edge, waiting for her to bring up what happened in the forest yesterday. Last night, whilst dreading this drive, I managed to come up with about a dozen excuses and justifications for my hard dick being pressed against her.

None of them is even remotely believable.

However, in the first bit of mercy I've had in months, Blair never brings it up.

She talks, of course. A lot. The woman keeps up a constant stream of commentary over the three-hour drive, touching on topics which range from my haircut—dubbed "deeply unfortunate"—to the several thousand-euro handbag she's *literally praying* the luxury department store will have in stock. I notice the chatter develops an increasingly wild edge as the arrival time on the car's GPS ticks closer.

"Oooo, I hope we see the queen," she giggles as the car slows to join the line of traffic below a large, blue sign, announcing we're entering Stelland's capital.

A weight seems to drop right into my chest at her words, and I have to clear my throat before responding. "I doubt it."

"I guess you'd know, huh? Since you worked for the Ashwells."

It shouldn't surprise me that she knows this, but it does. "Who told you that?" I demand before I can stop myself, and though I keep my eyes on the car in front of us, I can feel the weight of Blair's questioning gaze on the back of my head.

The subject of my relationship with the most famous family in the country is, quite literally, the last topic on Earth I'd like to discuss with her. Even engaging in a conversation about our foray into mud wrestling—and its effect on my dick —sounds preferable. I have no idea what Blair was or wasn't told about my background, but it seems likely she was given an incomplete picture if she's aware I was an employee, but not that I'm a "distant cousin" of Araminta's.

The last weeks have taught me better than to underestimate her, however, and for all I know, she's on a fact-gathering mission, hoping to lead me into disclosing more than I should, or catch me in a lie.

"Was it a secret?"

I'm biting my tongue so hard that I taste blood. "No," I admit. "I'm just surprised your father shared that kind of information with you."

It's an underhanded, mean little comment, exactly the kind I've thrown her way since the day we met. Except, for whatever reason, this time my stomach twists with regret.

"Well, I suppose there are some things you don't know, Satan," Blair offers after a pause, an airy quality to her voice. "It's pretty cool you worked for them, though. My parents were obsessed with getting Alba to marry the king. They kept trying to get her invited to all these palace events."

Trivial gossip, blurted out by a woman who has nothing better to contribute to a conversation, yet it makes some of the tension bleed from my stiff shoulders. I hit the blinker, turning the car out of the worst of the traffic. "Did they?"

Blair hums. "Obviously, it didn't go their way. You must have met the queen, then? If you only left a few months ago?"

Eager to keep her talking and distracted, I reply, "Yes."

"Well, I'm obsessed with everything she wears. Doesn't she have the best taste?"

The question almost makes me smile, but instead sends a deep pang of grief and longing through me.

If things were different, and that question had been asked in the presence of my brothers, I would have said, *"Maybe, but not in men."* It would have made Leo laugh and Ben roll his eyes, even as he fought a smile because the grumpy prick knows damn well his wife is miles out of his league.

Even kings have to face facts.

Fifteen

Blair

The salon my mother selected for me is bustling with activity when we arrive, exactly ten minutes before my scheduled appointment. It's exactly the sort of place I expected she'd send me; chic, upscale, and apparently inhabited exclusively by rich, middle-aged women.

All of whom give my frowning companion their full attention when we step inside.

Heads turn. Conversations falter. One woman actually swivels in her chair for a better view, her eyes lingering openly, while another smiles at him like she's just been handed a piece of fat-free cheesecake.

My stomach twists.

"You must be Blair!" exclaims my stylist, who appears from a back room. She plasters on the fakest smile I've ever seen as she leans in to air-kiss me twice, missing my cheeks entirely.

"I'm Stephanie," she announces, beckoning us to follow

her farther into the gleaming salon. "Lady Porter was kind enough to send over *extensive* notes."

Of course she did.

I catch my reflection in the mirror as Stephanie steers me into a chair—eyes wide, shoulders hunched forward. Over my shoulder, Mallory is lingering a step behind my stylist, hands in his pockets, looking like he'd rather be anywhere else.

The feeling is mutual.

"And you." Stephanie rounds on him, landing a light, flirty swat on his bicep. "You are welcome to have a seat over there." She points to a small waiting area in the center of the ring of salon chairs, where a few ladies are already stationed with their hair in foil, pretending to flip through magazines in between sneaking peeks at him.

He meets my eyes in the mirror, but looks away just as quickly, retreating to the area Stephanie indicated. The moment he sits, one woman leans toward him, saying something I can't hear. He doesn't move closer, but he smiles politely at her, and it makes him look like a stranger.

Probably because he has never looked at me with anything other than frustration or dislike.

When I got the call from Candice about the trip today, I was excited. Obviously. Getting out of Thornhurst for the day, buying new clothes, and getting made up sounded like paradise. It didn't take long before the initial buoyancy began to fade, however, and every minute I spent in the car with Mallory, my stomach dropped a little further.

I just... I don't want to mess it up.

God knows my family has never exactly seen me as an asset, and after those pictures, my status dropped from *least favorite child*, right down to *ugly family heirloom we keep in the attic out of obligation*. Being invited along today is good, a sign that the ice may be thawing a little, and I'm determined not to waste the opportunity to show them I'm not as useless as they think.

I don't complain as Stephanie trots me around the salon like a prize pony, determined to transform me into a more palatable version of myself.

I don't complain as my hair is washed, attacked with a pair of shears, and layered in highlights, supposedly intended to *"soften the natural color."*

Or when my eyebrows are plucked until my eyes run.

Or as the makeup I got up early to do myself is wiped away, replaced instead with a look that's more *"elegant"* and reminds me of my mother.

And, all the while, Damien Mallory lingers in the corner of my vision, barely visible in Stephanie's mirror. Every time I open my eyes after another round of transformation, they seem to be dragged right back to him.

Since getting the news, I've been too preoccupied by the prospect of *"family time"* in Wyngate to spend much time thinking about what happened in the forest yesterday. As I watch Mallory being charmed by an endless rotation of rich, glossy, perfect, age-appropriate women, however... I can't *not* think about it.

The man has made it really clear he hates everything about me, and that he thinks I'm immature, idiotic, and spoiled. But, even with all that, I made him hard.

I wonder if he hates being attracted to me as much as I hate being attracted to him.

When Stephanie is finally finished with me, and I'm allowed back on my feet, he's at my side in an instant.

"Finished?"

"Yup."

My stylist, who seems to have misconstrued the nature of our relationship, glares at him playfully. "Isn't she *gorgeous?*"

Before he's even opened his mouth, my belly goes hard,

instinctively bracing for impact. I'm not disappointed. Mallory offers me the most perfunctory, brief glance before his lips twist, as if he's tasted something foul. "That's not the word I would use, no."

And with that, he sweeps me from the salon and out onto the street.

"You could have at least been polite," I tell him bitterly, as we march along the sidewalk toward the public garage where we parked. It's a glorious autumn day, and the city is bustling, its inhabitants eager to take advantage of the last pleasant weather before winter sinks its claws into Stelland.

It's hard to enjoy any of it, however, as the man at my side lets out a hard, humorless laugh. "You want me to lie?"

On an ordinary day, I would have a retort for that. I'd think of something clever and insulting to throw right back at him. He wouldn't know he hurt me, or made me feel small, and I'd be able to walk away from this interaction with my head held high. Today, though... I don't know what's wrong with me.

So, I stay quiet.

My appointment at the salon ran slightly longer than expected, so we needed to hustle to make it across the city to the luxury department store, Century, where my mother set up an appointment with her personal stylist.

This place, thankfully, doesn't seem to operate entirely at the whim of Lydia Porter.

The private showroom we're led to is pleasantly cozy and warm, with a couch, beverage station, and a door leading off into the dressing area. Rack after rack of pre-pulled garments are arranged along the far wall, and I must not be too downtrodden, because I take one look at the pantsuits my mother had them pull and flat out laugh.

"Can you find me some things that would be appropriate for someone under the age of sixty?" I ask the shopper as I step up onto a small platform before a fan of mirrors, allowing her to verify my measurements. She agrees without hesitation, offering me a commiserating look that assures me I'm in good hands, and heads off to pull some things.

Left alone, I look to Mallory, who wasted no time taking up residence on the couch, and is typing away on his phone. "So, if you worked at the palace, you must have lived here in Wyngate, huh?" I ask, attempting to distract myself from the unsettled restlessness gnawing away inside me.

He doesn't so much as glance at me. "Yes."

"I bet you know the best food places. Do we have time to get something to eat after this? I'm starving." The only thing I've eaten today is a bag of chips from the convenience store we stopped at on the drive, and my stomach is objecting accordingly.

"You didn't bring a three-course meal in that giant bag of yours?" He nods to the tote leaning against the side of the dressing platform.

"What? No. I brought clothes."

That has his attention, and he finally looks up at me, eyes wide with disbelief. "Why are we *here*, then?"

"For something to wear to dinner, and any other events they may need me at." I look away, wandering over to the beverage station in the hopes of finding a snack. My heart lifts at the little packs of biscuits I find there. Taking one, I lean back against the counter, fidgeting with the wrapper. "It felt shitty to walk into a building full of people who are struggling, wearing expensive clothes. So I brought some other things. Simpler, you know?"

Satan looks back to his phone, a tension in his shoulders that wasn't present a moment ago.

Bitterly, I shove a biscuit into my mouth, chewing it as I glare at the back of his head.

"Alright, I think we have a good start here," my stylist

announces as she backs into the room, her arms laden with a fresh selection of clothes. She winks at me as she takes them into the dressing room and reemerges a moment later. "I'm going to go grab some things from the new winter collection, it hasn't even hit the floor yet. I'll be back soon to check on you."

I let out a heavy sigh when she's gone and toss the biscuit wrapper into the bin as I traipse into the smaller dressing room, my shoulders heavy. Closing the door behind me, I turn to the rack of clothes and blink, staring in surprise at what she pulled.

The wink is making a lot more sense, because it's clear my hair stylist wasn't the only one who thought the scowling giant on the couch outside was my boyfriend.

Along with a few perfectly respectable but still trendy dresses, there is a dazzling selection of lingerie and sleepwear—absolutely none of which is designed to remain on one's body for very long. In a daze, I reach out, running my fingers over the many hangers of satin and lace as a flame leaps in my belly.

The man just outside the door might hate me, but his hard cock pressed against me yesterday meant more than his being attracted to me.

It means I have a weapon, and with it, I can make Damien Mallory hate himself. Just like he makes me hate myself.

My lips curve as I reach for the first one that caught my eye, a pink lace babydoll which comes with a matching pair of cheeky panties. The demi-cups aren't transparent, and the panties are the same, but the garment reveals plenty, and I'm almost dizzy with the rush of adrenaline that comes as I put them on. There is no mirror in here, but I feel hot, and that will have to do.

I reach out but pause with my fingers on the handle to the dressing room, blood rushing in my ears.

Despite some pretty bold behavior in the past, I've never

in my life flaunted my body purely to prove something. And, on top of a flood of insecurities, the longer I stand here, the more doubt manages to worm itself into my certainty.

Mallory getting hard might have more to do with the situation than with me. Maybe it was adrenaline, or he has a bit of a primal play kink, or just didn't have time to jerk off with his conveniently stored bottle of lotion and tissues that morning.

Or—my chin lifts determinately—the asshole wants me.

Before I can talk myself out of it, I open the door and stare out at the profile of the man on the couch, who still hasn't realized what I'm about to throw his way.

"What do you think?"

The look on Mallory's face when he turns is all the validation I'll need for the next decade or so.

He *stares*, jaw slack and eyes bugging out of his head, for at least fifteen seconds. Until his brain catches up with his cock, and he remembers he isn't supposed to be looking at me when I'm not wearing clothes.

God, who needs drugs when you can force Damien Mallory to confront his attraction to you? *The rush.*

"That bad, huh?" I muse, strolling past him to stand on the little round platform, surveying my body in the three-way mirror. Granted, I've only been at it for a month or so, but running hasn't changed my body in the way I thought it would. I haven't lost my curves or anything, but there's a hint of quiet strength beneath the softness now.

I think I like it.

And so, apparently, does Mallory.

"Put your clothes on, Blair," he hisses, and in the reflection, I see he's resolutely fixed his gaze on the wall, his fingers digging into the arm of the couch.

"Come on, you have to admit I look *a little* hot. Even demonic entities can experience sexual attraction. I think they can, anyway." Shaking off this unknowable question, I sigh, twisting this way and that to examine the effect of the pink lace on my body.

It really is gorgeous. I think I need it.

A choking noise comes from the chair behind me. "Blair. *Fucking Christ*, put your clothes on. Now." He's begging, literally begging, and there's no way in hell I'm going to let him off the hook that easily. If he really wanted to leave, he could go stand outside the door of the private room, and yet *here he is.*

Is it tacky to wonder if he's hard?

Whatever. Tacky or not, I'm wondering.

I got him with the shock of it all, but I don't for a minute think that Mallory will sit there and let me get away with trying everything the stylist brought me. If I had to guess, I'd say I have one more chance to make an impression before he flees or gouges his eyeballs out or something.

"Fine. Your loss." With a pretend sigh of resignation, I head back into the tiny dressing room and close the door behind me. Alone, I shift my weight onto my hip, frowning appraisingly at the remaining selection of lingerie. Frankly, I don't think I could possibly go wrong here. All of it is wicked, and yet when my eyes finally find the very last garment on the rack, it's like a warm weight has dropped into my pelvis.

Yup. *That one.*

My pulse is racing as I step out of the first set and carefully remove the second from its hanger. It's a bralette and panty set, made of the most delicate, white cotton imaginable, the material unadorned apart from the thin blue ribbon which weaves through the rouching.

If I were to get wet wearing the panties, they would be practically transparent, the material clinging to my folds like it doesn't exist at all. If someone were to suck on my nipples through the bra, you'd be able to see what color they are.

The quiet thud of the dressing room door hitting the jamb

has Mallory's head whipping around, and even from three yards away, I can see his pupils dilate.

This time, there are no demands for me to put my clothes on.

I draw forward and stop just in front of him, intoxicated by the rush of what I'm about to do. "This one's probably no good either, huh?" Biting my bottom lip, I allow my hands to drift down my sides.

Mallory lets out a sharp, winded noise. "Enough," he hisses, jaw locked tight, even as he can't seem to stop himself from looking. An interesting reaction from a man who said it would be a lie to tell me I look nice after a haircut.

I step closer, until my knees brush his, and even the material of his trousers against my bare skin makes heat leap in my core. "Tell me how terrible I look."

"You—" He blinks, his eyes flitting from my tits to my eyes, then down again. Lower. "You—"

Leaning forward, I brace my hands on the back of the couch, boxing him in. This close, I can smell the ocean on his skin and see the tiny lines at the corners of his eyes, a reminder that I am currently seducing a man almost twenty years my senior.

Why is that so hot?

I let out a soft, thoughtful hum. Not pausing to allow him the opportunity to find his voice, I crawl up onto the couch, my thighs bracketing his hips as I settle my full weight in his lap. My hands find the warm, solid breadth of his shoulders, and it occurs to me that this is the first time I've ever touched him, if you don't count a hand gooped in mud.

"Tell me how you hate seeing me like this." My voice is a soft, breathy plea, as I feel the unmistakable, hard length of him pressing right against my core through the paper-thin panties.

Mallory groans, his chest rising and falling heavily as both hands curl into fists on the upholstered surface below us, as though he's forcing himself not to grab me. The battle is lost, though, when I allow my hips to rock over his stiff cock. His hands fly to my waist, so large that they make me feel dainty and delicate by comparison, and it's all I can do to hold back my moan as his touch sends heat rushing through my entire body.

For the first time, I feel a pinch of sympathy for what I'm putting him through.

Just not enough to stop.

"Tell me you don't like how this feels." I lower my lips to his neck, and without thinking about it, my tongue darts out to taste the patch of skin below his ear. In response, his hands tighten on my waist as he lets out a near-silent groan that goes straight to my clit.

This is more than I bargained for. When I stepped out of that dressing room, all I was thinking about was how to affect *him*, without a thought of what it would do to *me*.

Now, I'm aching with how badly I want him, how much I want this to be real, but I know it isn't. We're in the middle of a public place, and any minute now, my stylist is going to come back with a fresh selection of clothes.

I wish she wouldn't.

I wish we were back at Thornhurst.

I wish he would guide me onto my back and cover my body with his.

I wish he would kiss me until I forget how much I hate him.

Letting out a shaky breath, I rock against him. My lungs are burning, and the room spins around us as I issue the last, most important challenge. "*Tell me you don't want me.*"

Silence.

Pulling away is almost physically painful, and as I lean back to meet his inky stare, I know it is for him, too. I smile, even if there is nothing in the world less amusing. "Not such a lie after all, huh?"

The warm, tight grasp of his hands vanishes from my waist, and Mallory's expression shudders, apparently lost for words as I get back to my feet. The air of the showroom is somehow much colder than it was before, but I ignore the goosebumps, sweeping my newly done hair over my shoulder.

It seems to take an age for the man before me to come back to himself. He stares up at me, the line of his erection visible through his trousers, and I think maybe—just maybe— he feels as flayed open as I do right now. Finally, his gaze falters, and he looks at the floor rather than me, his broad shoulders heaving.

Yes, I think. I'm more dangerous than you thought.

Muffled female voices sound from outside the room, and I turn, striding back into the dressing room. Closing the door behind me, I lean back against it, pressing my hand to the place over my heart, which is beating harder than after one of our runs.

A quiet knock sounds from behind me. "How's it going in there?" comes the bright, cheerful voice of my stylist.

I swallow, letting my hand fall back to my side. "Great!" I call back, loud enough to ensure Satan can hear me, too. "I'll wear the white set to go."

Sixteen

DAMIEN

It's been hours since I delivered Blair into the hands of her father's campaign people.

My original intention was to spend the afternoon running errands, checking on my house, and taking advantage of a few free hours in Wyngate. Those plans were forgotten, however, in the wake of recent events.

Instead, I found myself parked and waiting in a line of dark SUVs behind the shelter where the Porters are making their appearance. For hours now, I've been sitting in silence, struggling to make sense of what the fuck is happening, and getting no closer to the answers.

Blowing out a rocky breath, I rake my hand through my hair, staring at the rain-soaked windshield before me, without truly seeing it.

I could handle Blair insulting me.

I could handle her lack of discipline.

Fuck me, I could even take her defying and undermining me at every possible opportunity.

What I can't stand, the development that has me questioning every choice I've made thus far, is wanting her.

The relationship I have with Blair is unlike any other I've had in my life. I've never dreaded seeing someone, while yearning for it too. No one has driven me out of my mind the way she has.

My only defense was denial, and I clung to it for so long. Even as the tides rose higher and higher, I held my ground, clinging to the utter, deluded certainty that *I couldn't possibly want her.*

It was a mistake. A massive, earth-shattering mistake that I didn't realize I'd made, until the woman I *couldn't possibly want* was on my lap in a public dressing room, wearing little more than scraps of paper-thin cotton.

This entire situation has gotten so wildly out of hand. I need to correct course, to get us back into professional, neutral territory, but after what happened this afternoon... *How?*

Space would be ideal, but as desperately as I need to escape her presence, there is no way of doing that. Not today, at least. A quick glance at the dashboard confirms today's event will wrap up soon, but afterward, there's her family's scheduled dinner at their Wyngate residence. Only once that's over will we be permitted to leave the city and spend nearly four hours in a darkened car together for the drive back to Thornhurst.

It feels as if I'm being conspired against, as though the universe has been quietly putting things in motion, setting me up to fail. *Again.*

With a rough growl of frustration, my fist comes down on the dashboard, rattling the panel violently, and I slump back in the seat, my chest heaving.

There is no more time to grapple with this, however, because out in the alleyway, I hear the sound of muffled voices. Beyond the rain streaming over the windshield, indistinct, shadowy figures appear, moving around.

Closing my eyes, I brace myself and reach forward to turn the key in the ignition. The engine has barely come to life before the passenger side door is ripped open without warning, and Blair throws herself into the seat beside mine. She pulls it closed behind herself, not looking at me.

I stare at her profile through the semi-darkness, and at the way tension radiates from every line of her body, like she's waiting to be attacked.

For a moment, the only sound is the quiet rumble of the engine and the rhythmic fall of raindrops atop the vehicle.

"I'd like to go back to Thornhurst now," Blair tells me, her voice calm and determinately steady.

Something is wrong.

Steeling myself, I tear my gaze away from her, reaching out to turn on the windshield wipers. "You have dinner at your parents' house."

Even not looking at her directly, I see the way she shrinks in on herself, and when she finds her voice again, it's only for a single word. "*Please.*"

A deep, violent ache spreads outward from the center of my chest.

I want to give her what she needs, to bundle her up and get her as far away from these people as possible, but—even discounting the shit I'd get for allowing her to skip the dinner —that isn't something I can do. Now, more than ever, I need to maintain my professionalism and authority over this woman. Allowing her to believe that pulling what she did earlier might get her what she wants is a dangerous precedent to set, and I can't allow it.

"You don't make the rules," I hiss, hating myself, and my muscles are stiff as I put the car in drive.

I half hope she'll argue, but she doesn't.

Lights gleam on the rain-soaked hood of the car, casting brief patches of light on the silent woman beside me as we make our way across Wyngate to her parents' house. It's located barely five miles from the shelter where they spent the afternoon, but might as well be another world entirely. The farther we drive, the more the city transforms, giving way from overflowing trash bins to sleek, marble facades and luxury storefronts.

And as we go, Blair Porter transforms, too.

I watch it happen out of the corner of my vision. I see her lift her chin and steel her expression, see as she pushes her shoulders back and sweeps her rain-dampened hair off her face.

The wound in my chest pulses painfully as I realize she is donning the same armor she so often wears for *me*, gathering all her strength to pretend, and I know—I know too fucking well—how much it costs her to keep it up.

We turn onto her parents' street, and I see the towering stone townhouse up ahead, all lit up, yet still so cold.

Fuck.

My hands tighten on the steering wheel as I try to remember the reasons I need to stop the car and let her out. If I'm going to make it through another seven months at the end of the earth, locked up with this woman I can no longer pretend I don't want, I need to stop.

It's a tiny movement, barely anything at all, to move my foot from the gas to the brakes.

I can't do it, though.

We drive by the house, and Blair turns in her seat to look at me. "It was back there," she whispers, and there is no hope in her words, as if she knows better than to expect kindness from me.

Swallowing my guilt, I keep my attention focused on the road, taking us farther and farther from our intended destination. "Are you sure you want to go? You look sick to me."

As quiet as it is in the car, I can hear her breath catch. "I—
yes. Yes, I'm sick."

"Okay, then."

There is no more discussion.

———

We stop at a gas station about halfway back to Thornhurst.

Blair goes inside, while I stand at the pump, staring off into the stretch of unlit field across the road. We've long since left the city behind, and after driving through the darkness, everything feels surreal under the shop's bright, fluorescent exterior lights.

It's nothing, however, compared to the muddling effect of the woman who steps out of the shop's glass door, holding a brown paper bag in one arm.

Blair's gaze meets mine over the roof of the car, and my heart stalls as I watch her step off the curb, crossing the empty parking area in calm, measured steps. She isn't wearing any of the day's luxury clothing purchases—which I barely remember loading into the trunk—but a very ordinary sweater and skirt that she'd changed into before we went to the shelter.

Nothing has changed.

I need to keep my distance.

Even acknowledging the sliver of humanity I've seen in her, Blair still represents everything I turned my back on. She is making me do things, say things, become a person I don't recognize, and—my god—*it infuriates me.* The things she makes me feel, jumbled together and all at once, are *infuriating*.

I hate that she has that power over me.

I hate the overwhelming, all-consuming urgency of it, which demands I *do something* before it swallows me whole.

I hate her. It's the only possible word, the only possible

emotion strong enough for what she does to me, and yet, somehow, it still isn't enough.

Something reckless and fierce is rising inside me as she draws nearer, growing more powerful with each beat of my pulse. The fuel pump clicks off under my palm, but I don't move, watching as Blair moves around the back of the car, coming to a stop just before me.

Neither of us looks away, and her lips curve in a silent challenge as she reaches into the paper bag.

As focused as I am on her, it takes me a moment to register what she's holding out. It's a miniature travel container of pretzels, in the brand and flavor I like, but rarely bother buying. In fact, since we met, I've had them only once. They'd been sitting on my desk the time she'd come by the security office, complaining about the noise from the electrician.

The oxygen vanishes from my lungs.

With a noise like a snarl, I close the distance between us, sending her purchases clattering to the ground. My hands find her face, and suddenly, I'm guiding her pointed chin up, angling those perfect fucking lips for me to kiss them.

If anyone could call it a kiss.

It's harsh and demanding and fast. Within a second, I've turned us, pressing her into the car with my body. In the next, my tongue is teasing the seam of her lips, and I swallow her noise of shock as the taste of her—honey and apples and *Blair* —floods my senses.

There's no stopping this.

All the want I tried for so long to ignore has been released, surging over us both in an overwhelming, inescapable wave.

She's touching my arms, my chest, my neck, her fingers twisting in my hair.

I'm crushing our bodies together, devouring her without a thought of teasing or finesse, driven by the same reckless, fierce need that rose inside me when she stepped outside.

Her teeth graze my lip, and I hear myself groan, pressing my cock into her belly.

There's heat, so much heat, and in this moment, I would do anything to be inside her. Would, quite literally, commit a crime if it meant I could tear away the barriers between us and fuck her, raw, hard, and dirty.

She likes it that way. I *know* she likes it that way.

The longer this goes on, I'm pulled farther from my reservations, my common sense, my own goddamn mind. I am—quite literally—lost. The only thing I know is her, and the illogical certainty that Blair needs this as deeply as I do.

Every noise of pleasure, every throb of pain, the pressure against my aching cock...

And then, before I can even brace myself for the end, it's over.

The crunch of tires filters back to me through my lust-muddled mind, and I tear myself off her, throwing myself back into the corner of the fuel pump.

Chest heaving, I stare at Blair. She's still leaning against the side of the SUV and gazes back at me through wide pupils, her kiss-swollen lips parted in shock. Headlights beam over us both as another vehicle pulls into one of the neighboring spots, and still neither of us moves.

Nearby, a chorus of doors slams shut, and a gaggle of teenage boys walks past us into the shop, casting sly, approving looks in our direction.

Fuck. *Fuck.*

"Get in the car," I tell her, and my voice is so rough I hardly recognize it.

Blair blinks, her fingers drifting to touch her lips, as though checking she can still feel me there and that it was real. "What—"

I shake my head mutely and tear my eyes away, staring at the scattered snacks at our feet as I scramble to get myself together. "The car," I say again, the words just as rough as they were seconds ago. Clearing my throat, I try again, "Please, just get in the car, Blair."

She doesn't respond this time, and I turn away, busying myself with the fuel pump while Blair stoops to scoop up the fallen food. Neither of us says a word as we get back in our respective seats. The mundane sounds of bags crinkling and seatbelts being clicked back in fill the silence, but none of it is louder than my own racing thoughts.

I did this. *Me.* Nobody else is responsible for such an epic lapse in control, and my chest burns with an unsettling emotion that should be regret but isn't.

Blair sets the container of pretzels in the cupholder between us, and I start the engine, still not daring to look at her. I'm reaching for the gear change when the noise of a phone vibrating fills the darkened space.

Grateful for something else to focus on, I seize the device from the center console, but my heart drops when I read the notifications.

"What is it?" demands Blair, who has obviously seen my shock register.

The rush of adrenaline that came from kissing her had only just receded and is now flooding my system once again. Jaw tight, I put the car in drive, pulling out onto the road at a much faster speed than I would ordinarily.

"Damien," Blair prompts again, a note of panic in her voice now.

I let out a long, determinately steady breath, staring at the dark road ahead. "Somebody broke into Thornhurst."

Seventeen

Blair

’m not sure what I expected when Mallory said "break-in," but this is pretty anticlimactic.

The high metal gates are securely closed as always when we finally arrive back, the headlights from the Land Rover beaming over the darkened driveway. My companion is on high alert, though, every line of his body tight with tension, like he's waiting for someone to run out of the woods and attack us in the time it takes to enter the gate code.

"I'm going to lock you in the car when we get to the house," he tells me as he rolls up the window and the car moves again. Ahead, Thornhurst's exterior lights are on, illuminating the closed front door and windows on the first floor.

Everything looks normal.

I swallow, glancing at him. "Are you *positive* someone was in there?"

"No," he admits, his lips pressed into a grim, flat line. "But I'm also not sure someone *wasn't*."

He'd said more or less the same thing to the local police when he'd phoned them on the way back. The man he got didn't sound concerned and said we should call back if we had more reason to be suspicious. "Sensors malfunction all the time," the officer had grunted. "We're not driving all the way out there for a maybe."

Mallory hadn't been a fan of that reasoning. He'd hung up, muttering venomously about lazy law enforcement and substandard something-or-other, while I sat beside him, trying not to touch my lips. I can still feel him there, even now, and it's the only evidence I have that the kiss we shared in the gas station parking lot wasn't a figment of my imagination.

That and the fact that he hasn't looked in my direction since it occurred.

I start as Mallory reaches past me to open the glove box, but as he loops two fingers under the handle to pull it open, I reach out, snatching his wrist before I can think better of it.

My heart is in my throat as he freezes, his eyes finally meeting mine through the pale glow cast by the dashboard.

"I'm scared," I blurt out, my pulse fluttering. "Don't leave me in here by myself."

Mallory's expression tightens. "These windows are bullet-proof, and I'm going to leave the keys with you," he explains, totally calm in the face of my mounting anxiety. "Don't open the doors for anyone but me. If you see anyone else, I want you to lay on the horn. You're good at making some noise; it should come naturally." His attempt at humor does nothing to lighten the situation.

"What about *you*, though?" I whisper, too frightened to pretend I don't care.

He's mean and rude, and I hate him, but if the panic I'm feeling is any indication, I *really* care.

"I'll be fine," Mallory assures me wryly and looks away. Under my hand, his forearm flexes gently, and the glove box falls open. There's a light, and I squeak in surprise when I see what's nestled in a holder inside.

"Oh my god! You have a gun?"

He glances at me, clearly bemused. "Of course I have a gun." Reaching inside, he takes it. I sink back into my seat, watching as Mallory opens and closes little latches, checking to see if the device is loaded. When he's done and apparently satisfied, he presses the keys into my hands. "I mean it, Blair. Stay put. If I don't come out in fifteen minutes, drive to the village and call the police. Do you understand?"

I nod, numb with disbelief that this is actually happening. "Yes. I—I understand."

"Promise me." He utters the two words so seriously, so gravely, staring right into my eyes as he says them.

My vision blurs, my throat tightening to the point of pain, as I manage a nod. "I promise."

I want to say something else, maybe a plea for him to be safe or not do anything heroic, but before I can find the words, he's gone. The door closes with a quiet thud behind him, and I lean forward, watching as Mallory prowls along the side of the house, until he's swallowed by the darkness.

Seconds later, before I've even had time to process that he's gone and that I'm truly alone, the lights in the car fade, and I'm swallowed up too.

I look at the clock on my phone, the numbers even more difficult to differentiate than usual, thanks to the tears blurring my vision. Wiping them away impatiently, I look up, staring out at the house, searching for signs of movement.

Surely if there had been a break-in, the person or persons responsible would be long gone by now. We got the notification at the gas station almost forty-five minutes ago, and what kind of burglar would hang around for that long? They'd take what they came for and go.

Right?

Five minutes pass, then ten, and with each one, my panic mounts higher.

Despite what I promised him, I'm not at all sure I could just leave Mallory here by himself. What if he's hurt, and I drive away, leaving him wounded and alone? What if—I squeak, lurching forward and straining my vision to see the figure moving toward me through the darkness.

I can't see his face, but I'd know those shoulders anywhere, and by the time he is close enough to see properly, I've already unlocked the car.

"Did you find anything?" I demand, turning sideways in my seat to watch as Mallory gets inside the car, his expression grim and set.

"There was definitely someone inside who shouldn't have been," he confirms, putting the safety back on the gun and sliding it back into its holster. "Whoever it was is long gone, but it isn't safe for you to stay here tonight. The house is too big for me to do a thorough search on my own." He holds out a hand, and I return the keys to the Land Rover without hesitation.

"Are we going to a hotel?" I ask, sinking back in my seat as some of my panic recedes.

Mallory shakes his head, already turning on the car. "I'm taking you back to my cottage tonight, you'll be safe there while I deal with the police. I called them when I confirmed someone had gained entry, and they're already on their way."

I'm not sure what to say to that, so I stay quiet, still a little numb with the shock of it all as he puts the car in drive and pulls away from the main house, moving down the access road toward his cottage.

"How could you tell someone had broken in? Was there damage?" I ask when we stop outside the cozy, stone structure.

"A bit," he replies vaguely, all business as he reaches for the gun again and opens the door, stepping out onto the dark drive.

I feel more vulnerable out here in the middle of the forest than I did parked amidst Thornhurst's sprawling lawn. Anyone could watch us from the dark trees as we make our way up to the porch. Mallory unlocks the cottage, moving out of the way so I can enter first.

It's the same as I remember it, sparse, clean, and impersonal. I wrap my arms around my middle, watching as he goes around, closing all the curtains and lighting lamps.

"Are you sure this is a good idea?" I ask with a shaky little laugh. "Leaving me here by myself?"

"Whoever broke in got what they came for," he assures me. "They're gone. And, even if they're not, this place is secure."

That makes me laugh. "Are we forgetting that *I* gained entry? With practically no effort?"

Mallory shoots me a dark look and pauses beside one window, pointing to a tiny white box mounted at the very top of the frame, the same color as the paint and barely noticeable. "This is a motion detector," he explains. "I installed them on all the access points after moving in."

My mouth falls open as I look around, spotting one on every door and window. "*That's* how you knew I was in here?"

Shaking his head, Mallory sighs, striding over to the kitchen area and reaching up to take something from on top of the cabinets. Lowering his arm, he sets a small red canister down on the kitchen table. "This is pepper spray. You won't need it, but keep it with you, just in case. The police should be here soon. I'm going to the gate to meet them and walk them through the house. After that, I'll need to call your father's team, brief them, and get them down here for a more comprehensive sweep of the property in the morning. Go to sleep, it may take a while."

I watch silently as he shoulders off the nice wool jacket he'd worn for the trip to Wyngate and takes his favored pullover from off the hook beside the door. The chances of me actually being able to sleep seem pretty slim, but I sink down in the lone armchair beside the dark fireplace as the adrenaline pumping through my veins finally thins.

When he's ready to go—gun hanging in a holster on his hip—Mallory glances at me, his expression set in his familiar, disapproving frown. "You can sleep on the couch."

I smile weakly. "I was wondering when I'd be seeing you again, Satan."

All business, Mallory scoffs, heading outside without a goodbye. A second passes, and then I hear the deadbolt clicking into place, locking me in alone.

The muscles in my body seem to give up the fight all at once, and I sag back into the chair, tucking my knees up under my chin as the finer points of the day I just had sink in.

Six hours in the car with Mallory, grinding all over him in a department store dressing room, and being put down by my father's horrible campaign staff—who made it clear I was only there to smile, wave, look pretty, and *definitely* not talk—on top of making out with Mallory in a gas station parking lot and now, a break-in at Thornhurst... yeah, maybe I'll be able to sleep after all.

I'm too weary to do much snooping, but I steal a T-shirt from Mallory's drawer, and when I go into the bathroom, the first thing I do is open the medicine cabinet. The watch is where I last saw it, wound and ticking gently on the top shelf.

As I turn on the shower and wait for the water to get warm, I take it down and stare at it, watching the tiny hands move in circles until the bathroom fills with steam. Setting it back with a sigh, I close the cabinet door and strip down, laughing softly to myself when I see the thin white panties and bra I'd worn out of the store.

There hadn't been much of a choice, considering the state of them.

While my mother's influence over the Century employees didn't seem too firm, I can't imagine word wouldn't get back to her if I'd left a pair of drenched panties in the dressing room.

The hot water is heaven on my back, and I take my time, washing every inch of my skin with Mallory's body wash. Doing so, it's hard not to let my mind wander to what happened at the gas station, and heat floods my lower belly as I remember the way he crushed my body against his.

He'd kissed me like he hated he had to, but he *did* have to.

I've had plenty of sex before. I've explored my body and my kinks, and had lovers who made me feel alive. None of them had needed me, though. Not like Damien Mallory did when he devoured me against the back of the car, furious with himself and me, but doing it anyway.

When I'm finished in the bathroom, I leave the panties and bra hanging over the rack beside his towel—which I used, ignoring the clean ones on the shelf—and smirk to myself as I pull the borrowed T-shirt over my damp hair.

The cottage is still empty when I poke my head out of the bathroom, and I cross to start a fire and turn off a few lights before trotting back over to Mallory's bed. He can sleep on the couch if he's so unhappy about it. For all I know, the business with the police will take all night, and there's no use in waking up with a sore back when there's a perfectly good bed right here.

I might also like the idea of him coming back late and finding me here.

Fighting a smile, I pull back the blankets—which are tucked neatly under the mattress, because Mallory is an insane person—and get in, my lungs filling with the heady combination of ocean air and Satan's distinct, masculine scent. The bed is comfortable enough, but I'm still a bit wired from all the excitement.

Are the police here by now?

Rolling over, I reach for the curtains on the nearest window, pulling them back just a few inches so I can peek out into the darkness. Through the trees, barely discernible, red and blue lights are flashing beside what I know is the house, and I sink back into the mattress with a heavy sigh, feeling a bit more at ease.

I have a lot of questions about all this, and I think I deserve an answer as the estate's only full-time resident, apart from the man whose bed I'm currently resting in. Something tells me Mallory isn't going to want to hand over any specifics, but I'm not going to take no for an answer. Even if it means calling my parents to get them.

They won't be upset I skipped dinner.

Candice, who can always be trusted to remind me of my place, was kind enough to inform me I was only included to quell speculation on what they'd "done with me" after the pictures ended up in the papers.

The ice was never thawing.

They weren't trying to include me because I'm part of the family.

God, I know I'm a mess, I know I fucked up, but I am still their daughter, aren't I? Were my mistakes so ruinous they've written me off forever? It seems that way. The only time they looked at me at campaign headquarters, and then again at the shelter, was when the cameras were pointed in our direction.

At first, I'd been angry, devastated, even, but somewhere in the midst of it all, it occurred to me that even for perfect Alba, or Saint Cedric, who fell in line and do everything they possibly can to uphold the esteemed Porter name... we're chess pieces, being pushed this way and that on the board. All to serve a larger purpose.

A sad, cold finality settles over me as I lie back in Mallory's bed, staring at the ceiling and listening to the soft popping and snapping of the fire in the hearth.

I might not know who I am, or what I want, or where I want to go. But when this is all over, and I can leave Thornhurst behind for good, I never want to see those people ever again.

I doubt they'll even miss me.

Nobody is ever bothered when a pawn is taken off the board until another sacrifice is needed.

Rolling over, I bury my face in Mallory's pillow and squeeze my eyes shut, breathing in the scent of him lingering on the sheets. It seems impossible that I could actually sleep, with my mind wide awake and turning over the events of the day, but my body must be tired enough to drag me under.

I don't remember when I succumbed, but the next thing I know, my body is pleasantly warm and relaxed, and for a moment, I can't understand what woke me up.

As I open my eyes, however, I see him.

From the bed, I have a clear view of Mallory standing just inside the cottage, his weary profile visible through the blueish morning light. I watch as he drags his sweater over his head and rakes a hand through his hair as he braces one hand on the wall, toeing off his shoes, before leaning down to set them in a row with the others.

Heat blooms low in my belly, and I shift restlessly, rustling the bedding as I do.

He straightens up, and his eyes meet mine.

I expect a frown, or maybe a cutting word for finding me in his bed despite his express orders, but Mallory does neither. His footsteps are slow and heavy as he makes his way across the cottage, coming to stand at the foot of the bed.

Rolling onto my back, I prop myself up on my elbows, gazing up at him through my eyes that are still itchy with sleep.

"You can't ever do as you're told, can you?" God, I don't remember ever appreciating his voice quite as much as I do right now. Low, rumbling, and warm, it makes the muscles in my abdomen tighten.

I let out an unsteady breath, smiling weakly. "Where's the fun in that?"

Mallory lifts a hand to his face, rubbing the stubble that's grown in since we left yesterday morning. He looks exhausted, and yet there's something in his gaze that is sharp enough to slice right through me. "It's been a long night, Blair."

I'm not sure if it's my imagination or not, but I could swear there's a warning in his voice. Not like the kind I've heard before—cross me or else—but something different.

Something way better.

Trying to ignore the heat spreading outward from my core is becoming more difficult the longer I lie here, looking up at him and being looked at right back. I swallow, trying and failing to steady my racing heart. "You should come to bed, then."

The murmured invitation hangs in the air between us, and still, he doesn't look away.

After an age, Mallory's eyes fall, running over the shape of my body, still covered by his bedding, before coming to meet mine once again. He seems to choose his words carefully, speaking in that same slow, deep, warning tone. "If I share a bed with a woman, we aren't sleeping."

The words raise a surprising pinch of jealousy, but the feeling is nearly drowned entirely by the overwhelming, inescapable surge of desire which rushes through me. I hadn't allowed myself to entertain the possibility of this ever happening when our relationship has been such an unending battle of wills.

Something seems to have shifted in the deep blue light of early morning, and I get the sense we're both just so, *so* tired.

"Okay," I whisper, and the breath leaves my lungs in a short, shallow rush as, slowly, I reach over and pull back the covers. "Let's not sleep."

Eighteen

Damien

As I drove back to the cottage, bone-tired from one of the longest twenty-four-hour periods of my life, part of me had already known what I would find when I stepped inside. For Blair, whose least favorite thing is being told what to do, followed shortly by discomfort of any kind, the temptation to defy an overt order would be too much to resist.

I told myself I was prepared for the sight of it, that I wouldn't let it—or her—affect me.

Except, as I stepped inside the cottage and saw her there in my bed, shrouded by deep, dreamlike shadows and my own exhaustion... the reasons I shouldn't do this fell to the floor with every step I took toward the bed. So as I stood over her, staring down at this beautiful, bold creature, all I knew was that I wanted her.

Just as woefully unprepared as I was to accept my desire for her, I'm equally disarmed in the face of denying her. When she pulls back the blankets and offers her soft, sleepy invitation, there is nothing to hold me back. I simply can't do it.

The T-shirt she must have taken from my drawer is twisted around her body, its hem casting a torturous shadow over the space between her bare thighs.

Thighs that part, making room for me as I drop to my knees at the edge of the mattress, crawling forward to get between them, as ravenous as a starving man being welcomed to a feast.

I don't waste time, gripping the backs of her knees and lifting them over my shoulders, opening her up for my mouth to descend on the slick slit waiting for me there. She's already so fucking wet, and as I drag my tongue through her seam, I hear my groan of approval before I realize I've issued it.

Maybe I really was starving, because as her taste flows over my tongue, a dark, possessive beast roars into existence. I'm a man obsessed, lapping greedily at every drop her body has to give me, and when it's thinned, fucking her opening with my tongue to get more.

Fingers tighten in my hair, and the edge of pain makes my cock pulse, precum leaking from the tip to join the spot already soaking my boxer briefs. I should have taken them off, should have removed every fucking barrier between us, but the foresight was lost to my urgency as I saw her lying here.

"Holy shit," Blair sobs, grinding her greedy cunt against my mouth. "Don't stop, please don't stop!"

She doesn't have to worry about that.

We've barely begun, and already I know neither of us will be getting any sleep, not for a long time.

I'm going to make her come on my face. Then, I'm going to do it over and over again, until she's puffy and slick and so sensitive that she's trying to pull me off. Only when I'm satisfied she's at her limit am I going to take my dick out and unleash weeks of frustration on the swollen hole between her legs.

The thought has me pressing my hips into the mattress, aching and aroused beyond belief. Already, I'm perilously close to finishing, but I don't attempt to stop it, grinding myself against the bed as Blair's thighs begin to shake under my hands.

I pull her clit between my lips, suckling on the firm little nub as the woman beneath me breaks apart with a cry.

Feeling her come for me, because of me, is the equivalent of adding gasoline to a raging fire. Her honey-sweet cum is dripping over my chin as I push her legs open wider, holding her open for me to feast as the tension building in my groin finally gives way.

My groan is muffled in her sex as I spill in my trousers, and even if it isn't what I need, I'm grateful for it. I can focus now, and after I've come down, the way I eat her cunt is fucking exacting. I pay attention to every moan, every whine, every little tilt of her hips. I learn she likes my fingers inside her as I suck her clit, and she likes it more when I spread them, stretching her. The pain of it makes her whine and squirm, but she comes harder when I do it, and after three more orgasms, I know she's finally getting close to where I want her.

I'm hard again, my erection slick with my own cum, and throbbing angrily. The mattress won't be enough to get me off this time.

"Oh, fuck. I can't. Please, *I can't*," Blair whines, trying to squirm away from me as her most recent orgasm fades, and I redouble my efforts on her poor, abused cunt.

She's swollen as hell, and there's a wet spot under her ass from her cum and my saliva. As I push two fingers inside her hole, my dick leaps at how much tighter she's become. *Almost there.*

Whimpering, Blair pulls my hair, trying to drag me off.

I allow her to pull my mouth a few inches back from her pussy and glare up at her. "It's going to hurt, but you're still going to give me one more."

Breasts that I still haven't laid eyes on are heaving beneath the crumpled T-shirt as Blair thrashes her head back and forth, eyes wide and pleading. "I can't."

My two fingers are still inside her swollen channel, and she pants unsteadily as I ease them in and out, stroking her G-spot. "You're going to do it anyway." My voice is so rough that I barely recognize it. "You're going to come again. Then—" My fingers part, stretching her until she cries out, bucking against it. "And then you're going to get on your hands and knees, and I'm going to fuck you. *Hard*."

The words make Blair moan, and the slick arousal that greets this plan leaves me little doubt how she feels about it. "Please," she gasps, "you can fuck me now. Please fuck me now?"

My lips, coated in her cum, curve in a dangerous smile. "You want to get fucked?"

Gasping and trembling beneath me, Blair nods. "Yes. Please. I want it."

My cock likes this proposal, but I scoff. "You know what you need to do, then. *Beg for it*."

Blair's breathing stutters, but she barely hesitates. "Please, please make me come one more time? *Please, Damien—*"

I don't think I've ever felt more powerful, more wholly in control, than I do in this moment. The sight of her like this, so outside her own head, so fucking desperate for me to fuck her she'll abandon her bratty attitude for one goddamn minute… Christ. My cock throbs painfully as I go to work again, sealing my mouth over her flushed, slick cunt.

She's so sensitive, so far gone from what I've already done, that it won't take long. I drag the flat of my tongue over her clit, lapping at the bud as I fuck her with my fingers. The overstimulation has to be uncomfortable, painful, even, but she takes it.

Blair's fingers are still knotted in my hair, twisting and pulling painfully whenever I get overzealous, sucking too hard, or grazing my teeth against her overworked clit. The way she's rough with me is almost as arousing as the way her inner walls clutch and tremble around my fingers, a promise for what my cock will be in for, as soon as my good little brat does as she's told and gives me one more.

It's a special kind of intoxication to feel her responsiveness, to feel every little tremor and hear her cries grow louder, knowing I've done this to her. None of it compares, though, when Blair's back snaps off the bed, her entire body convulsing from the earth-shattering orgasm I draw out, and out, and out.

When she's finally gone boneless and limp beneath me, and I sit back to look at her, I find tears streaming down the sides of her face, and plump tits heaving beneath the dark cotton T-shirt. My stomach hardens, raw, animalistic lust blanketing my mind, meeting her glazed eyes.

She's still dazed and trembling, but one look is enough to remind her what's expected of her. In seconds, she's scrambling unsteadily onto her hands and knees in the middle of the mattress, presenting herself for me.

Fuck yes.

I want to see her tits, but the promise of relief for my aching cock is too goddamn much. I have no concept of how much time has passed since I arrived back to find her in my bed, but the light in the cottage has grown warm and soft since we started this. Even if I haven't slept in twenty-four hours, my exhaustion is nowhere to be found as I rip my T-shirt off and shove away the pants and boxer briefs that are drenched with cum from my earlier release.

"Are you on the pill?" I demand as I follow her onto the

mattress, gripping my base in one hand, and reaching between her legs to give her pussy a sharp little spank with the other.

Blair moans, but her back arches, silently begging for more. "W-what?" she asks, sounding dazed.

"Birth control," I snap impatiently, half out of my mind with the sight of my cock hanging, heavy and swollen with need, so close to her bare cunt.

"Yes," she finally responds raggedly, arching her back to push her plump ass higher, "I have an implant, and I was tested, please put it in—" Her words break off, turning to a scream of mingled relief and shock which splits the quiet stillness of the cottage.

Her cunt, even after everything I did to it, isn't prepared for me. Her inner walls stretch snugly around my shaft as I bottom out, impossibly tight and wet and hot—*fuck*.

Even after finishing in my trousers, I need a moment to steady myself. Closing my eyes, I allow my head to drop back, gripping her hips to keep myself fully seated inside her.

"Ow," whines Blair, squirming against my ironclad hold. "You're too big."

Arousal twists in my gut as I look down, seeing the way her entrance strains around my base. "From where I'm standing, it looks like I fit just fine, princess," I grunt and lift one hand, bringing it down on the side of her perfect, round ass in a loud smack, hard enough to leave a red mark after I return my grip to her hip. "You'll take it because I told you to, and because I know what this bratty cunt needs. Do you understand?"

She exhales, hanging her head and, at last, makes a tiny noise of agreement. "*Yes*."

"That's what I thought." My eyes stay locked on the place where we're connected as I pull halfway out, my shaft already shining with her arousal, and push back in. She's so fucking tight that one pump has pleasure settling at the base of my spine, making me grateful I allowed myself to finish once already.

A part of me—the one I've shoved to the back of my consciousness, determined to ignore it—knows this won't happen again, *can't* happen again, but I'll be remembering it with my hand around my dick for a long, long time.

"I'm going to fuck you now," I rasp after a few more thrusts, each one harder than the last.

Blair pants in response, her fingers digging into the white sheets beneath us. "*Please*," her voice breaks, "I can take it."

Yeah, I know she can.

Dragging my dick out until only the crown remains inside her, I use my hold on her hips to pull her back onto me, and the sensation of it tears a snarl from my lips. Abandoning my control, I allow my body to take over, setting a fast, harsh pace that makes the headboard bang loudly against the wall and Blair's wails to fill the quiet cottage.

I fuck her like I'm punishing us both.

I fuck her like I'm ruining us both.

I fuck her like my life depends on it.

Blair's orgasm comes out of nowhere, and her inner walls clamp down on me so hard that I have to pull out to prevent her from milking my orgasm right out of me.

I'm not done yet.

And even then, even with pleasure spreading through my groin and her swollen, used cunt milking me with every thrust, it isn't enough. *Doing this only once isn't enough.* We haven't even finished yet, and I'm already battling with the urge to take more.

My hand comes down on her ass again. "I want to see your tits. Ride my cock."

Blair complies at once, swinging a leg over my hips eagerly as I take the place where I found her sleeping not long ago. She bites her lip, gazing down at me through heavily lidded eyes, as her fingers find the hem of my T-shirt, lifting it over her head at last.

Even if I could hold back my groan, there's no way she could miss the way my cock leaps against her ass at the sight of them; full, plump, perky tits, tipped in palest pink, and providing an uncomfortable reminder I've taken a twenty-six-year-old to bed.

Not that it's enough to stop me now.

"Fucking Christ," I snarl, reaching up to tease her nipples and rolling the pebbled buds between my fingers as she rises onto her knees. "Sit on it. *Now*."

Reaching between her legs, her fingers wrap around my shaft, still sticky with her arousal. "You're so bossy," she complains with a breathy giggle, even as she guides the head of my cock to her opening and lowers herself slowly onto my length.

A deep, approving groan rumbles low in my chest as her ass settles in my lap, my bare dick buried inside her once again.

The sight of this woman, totally naked and sitting astride me, may be the most erotic moment of my entire life.

"What now?" Blair teases, eyes sparkling down at me, as she circles her hips slowly. "Should I just sit here?"

Not a bad idea.

A loud smack splits the air as my hand comes down on her ass once again. "You know what I want, now give it to me," I snap, and her inner walls clutch my length as I give her another spank for good measure. "Or, if you'd rather not have my cum dripping out of you for hours, I'll go finish myself off in the shower."

The way her breath catches at this is telling.

"*Hmmm*," Blair sighs, pretending she's really considering this. "I suppose that sounds okay." She nearly earns herself another spank for the attitude, but my hand falls to clutch her hip as she rises off me, sending pleasure tearing through my abdomen and up my spine.

If the sight of this woman sitting on my dick was life-altering, it's quickly eclipsed by watching her ride me. I find myself panting, totally lost in the sight of her tits bouncing and the wet noises of her pussy leaking over me. She's unbelievably responsive, and when I tilt her back, angling our bodies so my tip hits her G-spot, Blair's moans turn to gasping sobs.

"Oh my god, oh my god," she chants, her fingers digging into my chest. She's trying to maintain her pace, to keep getting me off, too, even as her body is wracked with tremors which signal her most intense orgasm yet is approaching.

I take over, letting out rough grunts as I hold her hips in place and pound into her from below. In seconds, she's coming, and there's no way for me to escape doing the same. I'm not ready for this to be over yet, but I don't have a choice.

My own release surges through me, and I drag Blair down with a guttural groan, sealing our bodies together. She collapses over my chest, her inner walls still convulsing around me, drawing out my orgasm as I pump her full of my cum.

It's an effort to open my eyes again when it's all over.

Both of us are damp with sweat and panting, tangled together atop the trashed bedding. The air is cold on my skin as Blair slowly pushes herself off me, falling onto the mattress at my side.

Neither of us speaks, lost in our respective shock at what just transpired.

Fuck.

"You should get some sleep," she whispers at last.

I nod, still staring at the ceiling. "Your father sent a few security guards, and they're stationed at the entrances of the house. You're safe there."

Silence.

"Okay." Blair's voice reveals nothing, and I listen to the sound of bedding rustling as she leaves my bed.

I wait until I'm confident she's dressed again before pushing myself onto my elbows to watch as she slips from the bathroom, pulling her hair from beneath her sweater. Her eyes are on the floor.

"Blair." She stills, listening. I swallow. "That isn't going to happen again."

For once, she doesn't have a retort.

THE PORTER CAMPAIGN FACES A RELATABILITY PROBLEM

PERFORMATIVE POLITICS WON'T HELP THE FALTERING PORTER CAMPAIGN

When Lord Albert Porter's campaign announced a visit to the Wyngate Women's Shelter "to listen," even his fiercest supporters winced.

Facing an increasingly close race, Porter—who owns several estates, properties all over the country, and a majority share of the venture capital firm his father built—has lately been criticized for his lack of relatability, particularly with so many voters living paycheck to paycheck.

Unfortunately, Porter's visit on Friday did little to help combat this. Nothing screams *"out of touch"* quite like a choreographed display of empathy, and with poll numbers sliding, the visit felt less like outreach and more like desperation.

The Porter family arrived as they always do—on time, well-lit, and impeccably packaged.

Wyngate Women's Shelter, for those unfamiliar, is not a backdrop. It's a working shelter with scuffed floors, hardworking volunteers, poorly paid staffers, and residents who have heard these kinds of promises before.

Stationed before a cafeteria full of weary onlookers, Lord

Porter launched into his remarks, offering polished commentary on how Stelland must *come together*," and *"leave no one behind."* The phrases landed with the familiar thud of words that have been correct but had little in the way of actual substance.

At his side, Lady Lydia nodded at appropriate intervals, offering sympathetic smiles to staffers and residents, which weren't returned.

Cedric, the Porter's eldest son and current CEO of Porter Capital—currently one of the highest-grossing investment firms in Stelland—stood stoically beside his sisters, polite if uninvested in the proceedings.

Alba attempted charm, which might have worked elsewhere. Here, it read as distance: practiced smiles, polished small talk, and a gentle recoil when a resident's toddler reached for her bracelet.

And then there was Blair.

Lord and Lady Porter's youngest is best known lately for the topless photo scandal in early September, which landed her father's campaign in hot water, and notably hasn't been included in any press since.

Has she been forgiven for her behavior? Or simply useful when optics require it?

Regardless of why she was there, however, Blair's demeanor contrasted with the Porters' controlled presentation. While the rest of the family hovered, Blair sat. She asked names and remembered them. When a woman spoke about the difficulty of finding childcare after leaving an abusive partner, Blair didn't respond with policy or platitudes; she embraced the woman and commended her for her courage.

When a volunteer apologized for the coffee, Blair laughed, joking that she would take caffeine however she could get it, then went back for a second cup.

Blair's clothes—understated, unbranded, and forgettable—

became a quiet counterargument to the Porters' reputation for "taste."

Observers picked up on the contrast immediately, and while there were no cameras on her at first, that may be exactly the point.

By the time reporters did pick up on Blair, the story had already shifted. Photos from the visit captured Blair as the unlikely hero of the visit, fully engaged and listening in a real, meaningful way as, in the background, her parents watched on with a polite smile that looked a little thin.

If Lord Porter is serious about bridging the gap with his voters, he might consider a radical shift in strategy: less spectacle, more listening.

Nineteen

"Are you being more sadistic than usual to make me forget about the sex?"

The question is pretty unnecessary. Mallory's attitude toward me—which wasn't exactly warm and fuzzy to begin with—has gotten about ten times worse since I spent the night at his cottage, and it doesn't take a detective to work out what he's trying to accomplish with it.

The King of Evil and Darkness accidentally showed weakness. He forgot he hates me, gave in to the sexual tension, and now he's doubling down on being a crap nugget in an effort to make both of us forget it ever happened.

If only understanding the sado-masochistic phenomenon would make it more pleasant to be on the receiving end.

I peek over at him, jogging at my side, and see Mallory's jaw tighten, though his eyes stay glued to the horizon. "Speak when you're spoken to, Porter. The sound of your voice this early in the day makes me nauseous."

Porter. That's new too. Before the sex, I was *Blair,* or

princess if he was feeling particularly condescending. Neither name was ever uttered with any semblance of warmth or familiarity, but it's pretty depressing for my identity to be reduced to my family name.

Especially given my current feelings toward them.

"The sight of your face makes me nauseous, so I guess we're even," I retort, trying not to let my pace slow, even as the burning in my leg muscles increases with every stride. We've been at it for over a month now, running every other day, rain or shine, but it's hardly less torturous than it was at the start. I keep expecting it to get easier, to fall into a rhythm with it—that's what the nice fitness coach lady on YouTube was assuring all 2.4 million of her viewers—but it just hasn't happened.

I'll have to add running to the long list of things I'm terrible at. Or I can save myself the trouble and let Mallory do it for me. He's even better at pointing out my shortcomings than I am and often manages to draw my attention to ones I hadn't even considered before.

My self-esteem probably looks like Swiss cheese with all the holes he's punched in it.

It's miraculous, really. Every time I think I can't possibly feel more unimportant, or lonely, or lost, Damien Mallory finds a way to push me down.

"You know, maybe it would be good if we talked about the sex," I puff as we turn the last corner of the path, crossing over the forest's edge and onto the frosty back lawn. Even if I know it will end in him lashing out, I can't seem to resist poking the bear a little. "It would be good to clear the air, don't you think? Healthy?"

Healthy communication clearly isn't a priority for Mallory. He lengthens his stride, effectively leaving me in the dust and, instead of depositing me at the back kitchen door as he usually does, veers off toward the cottage and security building. When it becomes clear he isn't going to look back, I slow to a walk, clutching the stitch in my side.

It's pretty pathetic that even missing out on a few minutes of snarling, snapping, hateful company feels like a loss. Lately, it's felt as though days at Thornhurst have slowed to a crawl, inching through an endless cycle of monotonous, isolated drudgery.

I wake up to Mallory banging on my door.

I run with intermittent reminders of what an entitled, lazy, spoiled brat I am.

I shower and dress.

I spend several hours forcing my uncooperative, malfunctioning brain through coursework.

I eat lunch.

I receive bad marks on my coursework from the previous day.

I stare out a window.

I die a little more.

Maybe it's a little melodramatic to think that way—that I'm dying—but I'm really starting to wonder. Every time I look in a mirror, it's like there's a little less of me than there was when I last looked.

All at once, I'm being forced to confront all the ugly truths about myself and my life that I've spent years running from, and even if I do make it through this, I have no idea what I'm going to do. Could I go back to traveling? Partying? Probably not, when the memories of pulsing music and flashing lights now seem almost as empty as the void of time and space that is my ancestral home.

Miserable, I trudge over the back lawn, staring across its expanse at Thornhurst's many dark windows. Today is November first, but the wind off the sea is already so cold that it burns my cheeks and the exposed skin of my hands. True winter will be here before we know it, and while Satan hasn't indicated whether we'll be running through the snow or not, the insulated black jacket he wore today seems like an ominous sign.

Really, I should have known better than to think things couldn't get worse.

As I approach the back kitchen door, I halt, staring at the unfamiliar car parked in the little area set aside for staff. It's Saturday, which usually means the housekeeper will be in. We have a whole routine going now; I wish her a good morning, and she frowns at me disapprovingly, saying something in Polish that I can't understand but sounds judgmental. Following this, we continue to coexist with the help of nods and awkward smiles until she leaves for the day.

That isn't Yolanda's car, however, and when I enter the kitchen, it certainly isn't an old Polish woman I find polishing the refrigerator.

I have never seen her before, but the stranger is closer to my age, possibly a few years younger. She's dressed in the same blue uniform of trousers and a polo shirt as Yolanda, with the logo for the housekeeping service embroidered on the breast pocket. Her dark blonde hair is long and wavy, but tied back in a high, neat ponytail.

She starts when she catches sight of me hovering in the doorway, and drops the paper towel she was holding, a flush rising on the apples of her cheeks. "Oh! Good morning, Miss Porter."

If the accent is anything to go by, I'd guess she's American. *Interesting.*

"I'm sorry to disturb you." I move further into the room, shouldering off my fleece, and offer her a tentative smile as she bends to pick up the fallen rag. "You're not our usual house-keeper, are you?" I ask unnecessarily, hovering at the end of the long marble worktable as the unknown woman straightens up, wiping her hands on the pants of her uniform.

"Ah, no," she admits, not quite meeting my eye. "To be honest, I can't remember the name of your usual lady, but she's moved to be closer to her daughter, and the agency sent me."

After having no company for weeks apart from Satan, it's embarrassing how eager I am to have someone new to talk to. "And you're American, if I'm not very mistaken?" I surmise, leaning against the table. "What brought you to Stelland?"

She seems a little disoriented by my interest, but nods. "Yes, I'm from Pennsylvania. Here for university."

Port Briar, which is home to Stelland's oldest and best-known university, Orwick, is actually the closest city to the estate. My parents undoubtedly pay better than the restaurants or bars closer to her school, but even so. It's a forty-five-minute drive between here and there, and with the terrible weather approaching, I wonder if this poor girl has any clue what she's in for.

"Will you be here every day?"

"Two afternoons a week, then for the day on Saturday." She steps back to retrieve her cleaning bucket, apparently deciding I don't mean any harm. "I have a night job at a bar, too, and I teach some community art classes during term breaks."

I'm not sure how to respond to that. My exposure to people my age who weren't born with a whole mouthful of silver spoons is pretty limited. None of my friends ever had jobs, or if they did, they were more of the "*Daddy made me a vice president of his company*" variety and came with a corporate car, travel card, and unlimited vacation time. Certainly, no one I ever knew had to work two jobs while going to school.

My stomach sinks as I wonder what she must think of me, so clearly bored out of my mind and so desperate for company that I'm keeping her from her work.

My eyes fall on a spray bottle and rag sitting on the kitchen countertop. "Do you need any help?" I ask impulsively, gesturing to the bottle.

The girl—whose name I still haven't learned—looks at me like I've grown two heads. She doesn't respond, simply stares at me, apparently trying to decide if she's being led into some kind of trap. Deciding to save her the stress, I march forward to seize the bottle. "Just show me what needs to be done." I smile, trying my best to seem friendly and not like the psychotic rich girl Mallory loves to assure me I am.

It must work a little, because, shyly, the girl smiles back. "I was about to start on the downstairs bathrooms."

Encouraged, I step back to allow her to pass. "Lead the way!"

So, she does. I trail after her down the hall and into one of Thornhurst's many bathrooms. The space is furnished in lots of glowing white marble and glass, with the faint scent of eucalyptus hanging in the air. It's the sort of room that's generally used by guests, and I've never really taken notice of it.

Summer Johnson—because she finally tells me her name when I ask—sets her bucket down beside the toilet with a thud.

When I start poking at the front dial on the bottle, however, Summer winces.

"Okay." She bites her lip, obviously apprehensive. "Please don't be offended, but... Have you ever cleaned a bathroom before?"

I open my mouth, then close it again. Lying seems a fool's errand in this instance. "I have... been *in* a bathroom before. Many bathrooms, in fact."

She snorts before she can stop herself. Clapping a hand over her mouth, Summer's eyes go round, clearly horrified she laughed at me, but I just grin, strangely pleased. "I'll take that as a no, then." She giggles, shaking her head in amusement when it becomes clear I can take a joke. "It's really not that hard. I'll show you what to do."

Stooping down, Summer retrieves a toilet brush from beneath the sink and straightens up, offering it to me.

My expression must reflect some of my sudden panic, because Summer's expression softens. "You don't have to do this, you know. It's my job, not yours."

"I know." With a renewed sense of determination, I steel myself and step forward to take the toilet brush. "But I'm committed now."

As it turns out, *"not that hard"* is a bit of an overestimation for someone who has never cleaned anything in her life. In the split second Summer turns her back, I squirt half a bottle of toilet cleaner directly into the water. Then, after she shows me the correct way to distribute a smaller amount around the edge—which does seem more logical when I stop to think about it—I sort of jab at the blue liquid with the brush held as far away from my body as it can go.

I am one hundred percent certain I look like an idiot, but Summer is patient with me. After my clumsy attempts to help in the first bathroom, we move on to another. By the fourth, I seem to be getting the hang of it.

It takes hours, but we talk as we work—about Port Briar, Summer's terrible roommate, and how she hates night shifts at the bar because drunk people think tipping is optional. I don't exactly have a lot going on, but tell her about the estate, and this guy who tried to pick me up at a club in Denmark wearing only a banana-printed G-string, and the friends whose calls have faded away as my time away stretched from days to weeks.

I don't mention Mallory, or my parents, or why I'm here all alone.

Summer doesn't ask.

"What are you going to school for?" I ask as we finish up

the final bathroom on the ground floor and start back toward the kitchens, walking side by side.

Summer hesitates. "Art," she tells me at last, tucking a wayward lock of hair back behind her ear. "My focus is mainly on classical form."

My eyebrows lift in surprise. "You must be really good to have gotten into Orwick for that. Can I see some of your stuff?" We've reached the kitchen, and Summer sets her bucket down on the tile floor, her cheeks pink.

"I'm still learning," she cautions me, reaching into her back pocket to retrieve her phone. I step closer and watch as she pulls up her camera roll, scrolling until she finds what she's looking for.

All the air goes out of me as I stare at the tiny screen. "You did that?" I demand, leaning in closer to see.

In the picture, an unfinished canvas is sitting on the floor, its moody palette of grays and blues standing out vividly against the plain white wall behind it. The man in the painting isn't distinct, but isn't quite a silhouette, either, more shifting color than actual form. He has his collar pulled up to his ears, and it looks like he's walking, his eyes on the ground. If I lift my focus to one corner, the others seem to change, as though my eyes are dragging the light with them.

I think I could look at it for an hour and still be discovering different ways to see it.

"Summer, it's remarkable. You're so talented."

"Thank you," she replies softly, slipping the phone away, and casts me a quick, sideways look. "I'm here on a scholarship, so I always feel like I need to..." She trails off, waving away the statement with a dismissive little laugh. "Never mind. Let me get all this put away."

Summer heads off to the supply closet, but I stay where I am, probing the sharp ache which appeared in my chest when I first laid eyes on the painting. The feeling is strange—like admiration threaded with shame—and after the past few months, it isn't difficult to deduce why I'm having this reaction to such an innocuous piece of information.

I've never *earned* anything like that. My education was probably decided before I could spell my own name. I went to the very best schools, had the finest tutors, and was handed opportunities someone like Summer probably had to fight tooth and nail for.

And, worst of all, I didn't deserve a single one of them.

"Thank you for letting me tag along," I tell Summer when she reemerges, shoving aside my feelings of inadequacy. "I know I wasn't exactly helpful."

She casts a quick, reassuring smile over her shoulder as she crosses to retrieve her purse from the hook beside the door. "Don't be silly. You got the hang of it in no time."

I linger awkwardly as I watch her prepare to leave, wondering if she was just being polite or really meant it. When Summer finally turns to say goodbye, though, I think her smile is genuine. "This was fun," she tells me with an embarrassed little laugh. "To be honest, I thought this job was going to suck. No offense. Will you still be here when I come back on Tuesday?" Her cheeks go pink yet again. "Not that I'm expecting you to clean with me or anything. Which I'm definitely not."

The ache which appeared so suddenly in my chest eases a little.

"I'll be here."

Summer leaves with a wave, and I watch through the kitchen window as she crosses toward the staff parking lot and out of sight.

I think I just made a friend, and as the looming prospect of coursework threatens to puncture the full, happy feeling that's risen inside me at this realization, I decide the classes can wait.

Twenty

Damien

For weeks, it's felt as though something terrible and inevitable is closing in on me.

I didn't notice at first, too preoccupied with my many attempts to put Blair Porter back in the box she belongs —the one which labels her as the bratty, self-important, lazy, and entitled daughter of my employer—and failing over and over again.

I've tried to put my finger on when it happened, exactly, running through the past weeks in my mind and examining every interaction I had with her. Nothing has come to mind, however, no moment when I realized the lid didn't quite fit correctly, or when the box began to pull apart at the seams.

She is too young and too impulsive, and her fucking attitude might drive me into an early grave.

I don't like her.

I shouldn't want her.

I definitely *shouldn't have fucked her, or be desperate to do it again.*

The less sense I can make of it, the more infuriating the situation becomes.

So, when I received an email from Porter's PA late last night, blaming *me* for not properly ensuring Blair completes her coursework—*the coursework she told me she was on top of*—I seized upon the situation with relish. While I'm not particularly concerned with Lord Porter's opinion on my competency, there's an element of pride involved now, too.

Being here alone with her, having her in my face constantly, getting under my skin in the worst fucking way... Things got out of hand. Now, it's a relief to have something to point at as incontrovertible proof she is exactly what I need her to be: *impossible*.

"If you're going to behave like a child, I'll treat you like one."

Blair, whom I just directed into the chair behind the unused desk in the security office, merely smirks, crossing her legs. "Okay. I have a follow-up question, though. What is your stance on spanking?"

I grit my teeth, trying to remain authoritative and stern, while simultaneously dismissing the memory of my hand coming down on her bare ass, or the sounds she made when I did it.

The worst part of this is that Blair knows exactly what she's doing. The typical, snarky repartee that's existed between us since day one has taken on a decidedly sexual, bordering on flirty, edge, and no matter how cold I am with her, I haven't managed to get us back to less *charged* territory.

The only way I've managed to get this woman to drop the attitude was by making her come on my face five times in a row, a remediation strategy which is now firmly off the table. No matter how much I wish it weren't.

"Show me the modules you've completed," I demand, not acknowledging her attempt to steer us off course.

Blair hums thoughtfully, tapping one manicured nail on the edge of her laptop. "So, just to be clear, that's a no on the spanking? What a pity."

If I bite at that, we'll be bickering for an hour, and I have shit to do today. "*Now*, Blair. Christ."

Letting out a loud, weary sigh, she opens her computer and inputs the password—changed since I guessed it in one try—and clicks around for a moment, before leaning back in her chair, expression guarded.

Holding my breath so I don't catch the scent of her hair—because even the smell of her fucking shampoo sends blood directly to my dick these days—I round the desk and lean down to examine the home page of her study program.

I go from irritated to incensed in seconds.

Of the fifteen modules she ought to have completed by now, Blair has gotten through three.

"What the fuck?" I snarl, straightening up and looking down at the woman sitting before me, who is busy picking dirt from beneath one of her nails with the head of a mechanical pencil. "It's been weeks since you started this. What have you been doing all day? Are you so lazy that you can't manage an hour or two of actual cognitive activity?"

She doesn't look at me, but there's a stiffness in her shoulders which suggests my words have found their mark.

Shaking my head in disgust, I cross back to my own desk, gathering up my keys, wallet, and phone. "I have to meet the electrician at the main house shortly. Stay here until I get back, and work on your courses. If you haven't made any progress by the time I return, I'll send your father an email to inform him you are no longer cooperating. I'm done with this crap."

Pausing only when my hand is resting on the doorknob, I look back—another set of warnings on the tip of my tongue—and see Blair seems to have curled in on herself. She's staring at the computer before her like it's the stuff of nightmares, arms wrapped around her middle, and eyes glassy.

If we'd never met, I might even feel sorry for her.

I *do* know her, all too well now, and I certainly know better than to think she deserves sympathy.

This woman has had every advantage in life, every opportunity, and more money than most people—including me—will ever see in their lives, and what has she done with it?

Why she is so committed to doing absolutely nothing with her life defies all logic.

Frustrated, bitter, and tired of the fucking games, I let out a noise of disgust. "I don't know what is wrong with you, but you should be fucking embarrassed, Blair. A grown woman, with all the privilege in the world, and you can't even be bothered to do your homework."

For fuck's sake.

I don't want to look at her anymore. I don't want to be anywhere near her. So, with one last furious, disbelieving shake of my head, I open the door and stride outside.

Even as frustrated with her as I am, I can't help but experience a prickle of guilt as I cross the grounds on foot, my mind on the exchange we just had. I was harsh with her, cruel even, but even telling myself it was for her own good doesn't absolve me, and I know why.

It isn't just my attraction to her. The more time we've spent together, the harder it's become to see Blair Porter as a two-dimensional character. She might be everything I expected—spoiled, entitled, and bratty—but I've also seen traces of humanity in her that aren't so easy to dislike.

Could I have been so cruel to the beautiful young woman who was singing to herself in the kitchen that day? Or the quiet, withdrawn one who threw herself into the car following the event in Wyngate?

Probably not. Because I'm not a fucking monster.

Though I haven't been employed by them long, it's been enough to deduce that the Porters are very like the family my brothers were born into; one that comes with obscene levels of wealth and privilege, yet is emotionally bankrupt.

Plenty of people come from shitty, loveless families, however, and plenty of people rise above it. Blair isn't unintelligent. She has the ability to go out into the world and make a life that will make her happy, but she *won't fucking do it*. I refuse to feel sorry for her. There are actual victims of circumstance, but Blair Porter isn't one of them.

I'm still seething when I reach the main house.

The electrician wrapped up in the basement yesterday, and I need to check his work is completed as the contract specifies before I write a check for the next phase of the project. My boots have barely hit the gleaming wood floor in the downstairs hall, when I have to step back against the wall to avoid running headlong into a woman.

"Sorry!" gasps the new maid, Summer, clutching her chest. She's an American college student, brought in part-time by the household staffing agency, and I only completed her background check a few weeks ago.

"No problem, it was my fault." I shake my head and offer her a reassuring smile, already moving past her.

Before I can get far, however, Summer calls after me. "Can I ask—" She winces as I turn to face her, frowning. "Sorry, it's none of my business, I was just wondering if Blair is alright?"

"Blair?" I echo, bemused.

"Porter? She lives here?" Summer clarifies hesitantly. "We've become friendly since I started, and usually she's around when I get in. She said she'd be here today, so I just wanted to make sure she wasn't sick or anything."

This is news to me. I've wondered what Blair does with

the time she isn't driving me mad, but paling around with the maid certainly never made the list.

I cross my arms. "She's fine, doing some schoolwork in the security office. Less distractions out there. I hope she hasn't been bothering you."

Summer's eyes widen. "Oh! Not at all, she's been really kind. My first day here, she offered to help me with the bathrooms, and it's become our thing. Work and chat, you know—not that I expect her to!" she hastens to assure me, obviously worried she's said too much, and that allowing the lady of the house to scrub floors might be forbidden.

It seems to take more effort than usual to swallow. "She's fine. Just busy today."

Bobbing her head, Summer retreats, scurrying off in the direction of the kitchens.

I don't move, though, still reeling at the news that Blair has been helping the maid clean Thornhurst.

Why?

In the few short interactions I've had with Summer, she seemed like the soft-spoken, mild-mannered type, quite the opposite of Blair. For the life of me, I can't imagine what interest the new maid would hold for Blair, unless... My stomach sinks.

I haven't kept up on monitoring Blair's communications. As days turned to weeks and she still hadn't attempted to do anything illegal or forbidden by her parents, to do so began to feel less like precautionary surveillance and more like spying. There is a difference, ethically anyway, so I reduced my check-ins to weekly scans of her call and text logs, ensuring there weren't any numbers popping up that might raise red flags.

There haven't been.

In fact, there have been very few calls at all.

When I finally manage to thaw my stiff limbs, I resume my

path to the back door, moving at a brisker pace than before. I'm possessed by the need to set eyes on her, as if to verify my memory of her is correct, and she hasn't changed form since I left the office an hour ago. It's undoubtedly wrong, but a not-small part of me is praying to find she hasn't done a single part of her homework.

Nevertheless, it's impossible to shake the gnawing suspicion I'm forgetting something.

Before I've even made it back to the truck, my phone vibrating in my pocket has me coming to a halt yet again. Gritting my teeth, I pull it out, staring down at the name of the groundskeeper whom I've met only a few times, and has certainly never called me about anything.

Fucking hell.

"What?" I snap, taking the call even as I resume my stride to the truck.

"Sorry to bother you, Mr. Mallory," he tells me, clearing his throat loudly as I throw myself into the driver's seat. "Ah, I just wanted to let you know I've let someone through the main gate to see you."

My mind goes instantly to the tabloid reporter I sent off a few weeks ago. "What?" I snarl, not quite able to believe anyone would be so stupid. Why the fuck does he think we have the gate there? "Why would you do that?"

"Jeez, man, no need to get up in arms about it. I was leaving just as he was pulling up, and didn't think he should wait—"

"So what if he has to wait? Let him! You are aware we had a break-in recently? Jesus. Did you get his name, at least?" If this man has let someone dangerous onto the property, I'll have his job for it.

"Ah." The groundskeeper lets out a quiet, uncomfortable chuckle. "That's the thing. I didn't need to get his name."

I stare at the steering wheel of the truck, blood rushing in my ears. "You know him?"

"*Everyone* knows him, sir. It's Prince Leopold. *The* Prince Leopold. He said he has urgent business with you. Don't worry, I was real civilized and sent him right to the security office—"

I hang up before he can get another word in, and turn the keys in the ignition with a shaking hand, my heart thundering in my chest. The engine roars as I pull out of the little parking lot behind Thornhurst without pause, driving far faster than I should.

Fucking hell, Leo.

How he found out I'm here is anyone's guess, but even as panicked and irritated as I am, I can't exactly blame him for turning up. Not when I've been dodging his calls for months, and there is very little my youngest brother cares about more than his family, broken and dysfunctional as we may be.

My chest burns as I speed across the narrow service road which leads away from the main house and toward most of the estate's secondary buildings, kicking up a cloud of dust in my wake. I need to reach the security office—and Blair—before Leo does. She's already asked questions about my relationship with the Ashwells, and there isn't an excuse in the world to justify the king's brother turning up at my office for a chat.

For what feels like the first time in months, I get lucky.

The taillights of a gleaming, black luxury sedan are just rounding the corner to the office's parking area as I approach, and my palms are damp as I skid the truck to a stop between it and the building, blocking us from view of the window.

I'm on my feet and striding around the hood before Leo has even opened his car door.

My brother's familiar features, so like my own, are tense behind his wire-rimmed glasses as he steps out of his vehicle, searching my face.

"You're alive, then," Leo declares dryly, pushing his door closed behind himself. "I wasn't entirely sure. Considering."

All the air goes out of me. "What are you doing here?"

Leo's nostrils flare. "*Why am I here?* That's really all you have to say? Why do you *think* I'm here, Dam?"

I swallow with difficulty and glance past the truck toward the office. If Blair is where I left her—an admittedly unprecedented event—she won't be able to see us, but I think I see movement beyond the rippling glass.

Dread is heavy in my gut as I look back to my brother. "Let's go to my cottage to talk."

With an absolutely disgusted look, Leo scoffs. "Last I checked, we don't talk, so I don't see how it should matter."

"I don't—" I scrub my hand over my face, gut twisting with panic and guilt. Even the thought of lying to him is like ash on my tongue. Regathering myself, I swallow. "I'm sorry. Things have been... busy."

"Busy," Leo echoes, and I can't recall ever seeing my brother this angry before. "It's been *m-months*."

Of Fabian Ashwell's four sons, Leo was always the quiet, reasonable one.

When Arthur, Ben, and I fought, it was Leo who called for peace, and even if it was never discussed, the three of us seemed to live by the unspoken agreement to shield him whenever possible. Not just because of his speech impediment, or his diagnosis, or even his being the baby of the family.

No, we protected him because he was the best of us.

My youngest brother isn't a boy anymore and hasn't been for a long time. Old habits die hard, though, and I would sooner hurt myself than hurt Leo. Which is, of course, what has made the last months so difficult.

I stare out at the familiar patch of trees which disguises the running path I take with Blair every morning. "I know. I'm sorry."

"You damn well should be," Leo snaps. "You leave the palace with no notice, there one day and gone the next. You've been ignoring my calls, *and Zelda's*." His voice drops in furious disbelief at the mention of my sister-in-law, who is perhaps the kindest person either of us has ever encountered, and deserves far better. "Then to find out you're working for *P-P-Porter* of all *p-people*? What the fuck happened?"

His impediment worsening has always been a tell that Leo's lost his hold on his emotions, and more than anything he's said, the obvious effect my absence has had on him makes me feel worse than ever.

Hollow with regret, and staring into my brother's furious, hurt expression, I have to force myself to respond. "Nothing."

"Nothing?" He lets out a harsh, impatient noise, staring at me in disbelief. "Just *f-f-felt* like a change? Decided to *q-quit* your job and shut out your only living family for the fun of it?"

"It wasn't—" I break off, shaking my head. Christ, I wasn't prepared for this conversation. For the past month, I've allowed myself to get lost in the storm that is Blair Porter, and a part of me welcomed it. Easier to be angry at someone other than myself. Easier to focus on hating Blair than trying to come to terms with why I'd done what I did.

Now, I've been backed into a corner, scrambling to think of some reasonable explanation for my behavior, something to tell my brother that isn't the truth, and isn't a lie.

A cold wind sweeps through the clearing, sending a flurry of brilliant foliage down around us and rustling the leaves already on the ground.

"I... did something," I admit at last. "Something bad. It was a long time ago, but recently..." Again, my words falter, and I shake my head, helpless to say the words my brother deserves to hear; that it was only recently that the full impact of my terrible choice has come to light, and that I was too much of a coward to be reminded of it every day when I saw her face.

"Dam." Leo stares at me, and his expression is impossibly grave. "*What did you do?*"

Again, I glance back at the security office, straining my vision for signs of Blair watching from the window. If she is, I can't see any sign of it, and my chest has grown impossibly tight in the time it takes me to look back at my brother.

Finally, I can't put off responding any longer. "I can't tell you that, Leo. I'm sorry." The admittance is hollow, and the apology even worse, but it's the best I can do.

Leo doesn't respond right away, and another gust of wind sweeps through the clearing, rustling the branches above our heads. "So, this is how it will be, then?" he finally asks, a weariness to his voice I haven't heard often. "You hiding away from all of us for some crime we didn't know you committed?"

"*No.*" The denial sounds like a plea. "I just need..." Again, my words fail, the incomplete sentence hanging in the air before me.

More time? Some space? If only it were that simple. No, what I need is a way to put the burden of my actions on myself, rather than the people I love.

That isn't possible, though. So, now, I need to find a way to live with myself.

"How's Ben?" I ask, a little desperately.

Again, Leo pauses, considering. "Happy," he assures me at last, his voice gentler than it was before. "More so than I've ever seen him. He *m-m-misses* you, though." I feel those words like a physical blow, and something in my silence must suggest there is more to the inquiry than brotherly concern, because Leo's next question hits me squarely in the chest. "Dam, this bad thing you say you did... was it to Ben?"

I close my eyes, focusing on the breath leaving and entering my lungs, a reminder that this hasn't all killed me.

When I open them, I meet my youngest brother's familiar, dark eyes. Leo smiles weakly, seeming to sense I have exhausted my ability to explain. He was always good about that, able to read between the lines. A rare quality in a family of rich, powerful men who crashed forward without concern for who or what was upset in their wake.

I'd always thought I was different from them, that the nature of my parentage automatically excluded me from the less favorable characteristics often seen on my father's side of the family. It's only now, as a grown man, that I'm starting to realize how very not unlike them I have always been.

Bastard or not, at my core, I am Fabian Ashwell's son.

"I'll go," offers Leo sadly, taking a step back.

Even after avoiding this moment for months and hating every second of our interaction, I'm gripped by the almost overwhelming impulse to ask him to stay. I push my hair off my face, watching helplessly as my youngest brother turns toward his car.

"Leo," I call, and my throat aches as he pauses, turning cautiously to face me once again. Swallowing, I attempt a smile. "How's the baby?"

My heart aches as I think of my niece, the tiny girl whom I ought to have protected with my life, but who will instead bear the full burden of my mistakes.

Leo smiles gently. "Getting big. She's crawling now and pulling herself up on things. I swear she looks more like her mother every day."

I let out a weak laugh. "Thank god."

Reaching out, Leo rests a hand atop his car, and I know he's trying to decide whether or not to tell me something. "Ben's birthday is coming up," he tells me, apparently making up his mind. "Z is putting together a party at Fernmoor that night. It will only be friends and family. You should come."

"He's angry at me." I smile sadly. "It's better if I stay away."

A weary, exasperated look comes at this. "Surely you don't really believe that."

He's right. I don't. This would all be so much easier if I could.

"I don't know what you think you've done, Dam, but this"—he gestures toward the main house with a pained grimace—"isn't the answer. Sort it out."

I stand back, watching as he gets into his car and pulls out onto the access road. He offers me one brief, pained smile before he's gone, and I'm left staring at the space between two trees where I last glimpsed his taillights.

For all my panic about Leo being here, now that he's gone...

Unable to stand being left alone with my own company, I turn toward the office. I'll feel what I have to feel later, find a way to block off the chasm of grief and guilt yawning open inside me, but not now.

My chest is hollow as I step inside. Blair is where I left her, shoulders bunched up and staring miserably at her computer. If she got up at any point to peek out the window, she doesn't give any indication of it.

"Let me see what you've done," I grunt, careful to keep my eyes from her face as I cross the room and take her laptop in my hands, turning it so I can read from this side of the old metal desk, rather than get too close.

As I lean down to read through the question and answer portion of the lesson she's working on, for a moment, I can't understand what I'm seeing. It's been over an hour since I left her here, and in that time, Blair has only managed a single, clumsy attempt at one of the twelve questions on the reading assignment.

Even for someone who's been away from school for years, it's bad.

Much of her response is totally unreadable, words misspelled and mashed together with others, only to be repeated correctly later on. There are sentences which look as though they've been copied and pasted from the internet, right beside others that might have been composed by someone who didn't read the material at all.

Lifting my eyes from the screen to look at Blair, I find her staring at her lap. "What is this?" I hiss. For once, however, she has no witty retort.

The thing that rises inside me at her silence is ugly.

Disgusted, I shake my head, straightening to my full height. "Jesus, Porter. Are you too good to do the damn reading? What the hell is wrong—" But the sentence dies as, for the very first time since we've met, I watch my horrible, cruel words hit their mark.

A single tear falls from Blair's downturned face to her lap, and in the quiet of the office, I swear I can hear it.

I can't breathe. I'm not sure I can even think. Certainly not of anything other than the realization which has poured in, with the sudden, inescapable rush of a dam breaking.

It fits.

The voice notes, the lack of texting, the avoiding school-work... *It fucking fits.*

God help me, if everything I thought was wrong with her was really a symptom of something she could never help—*Fuck.*

I want to be wrong.

Please, let me be wrong.

"You're not too good for it," I croak, and the pressure on my chest is so intense it may break as another tear falls to her lap. "You can't."

She hisses, recoiling as if I've slapped her. And, before I

can fully process what this means, or even begin considering the depths of my terrible behavior, she's on her feet, rushing past me. The door slams behind her, and I'm left staring at the disjointed, misspelled words on her computer.

Words that were written that way because the woman I've called an idiot, and lazy, and an embarrassment, isn't any of those things.

Blair is dyslexic.

TWENTY-ONE

I've had a lot of lows recently.

Being plucked from my life and shut away from the world—with only an inconveniently gorgeous asshole for company—was abrupt and brutal. I've had to face that the people I thought were my friends really weren't, and that in twenty-four years of life, the only thing I'd succeeded at was humiliating my family.

God, I can't even count the number of times I've curled up under the blankets in my bed, sobbing my eyes out because I was so embarrassed, or lonely, or just plain sad.

Even with all that, no matter how embarrassed, or lonely, or sad I got, I never thought of leaving Thornhurst. Not one single time did I consider fleeing right through the front gate, consequences be damned.

Until now.

It seems the look of pity on Damien Mallory's face is the straw that broke the proverbial camel's back, the final indignity I couldn't weather, and now... *I have to get out.*

In the back of my mind, I know I'm not behaving logically, that I'll live to regret this, but *I don't care*. Nothing my father or the world can throw at me would possibly feel worse than having to look that man in the eye again. That intelligent, handsome, perfect *asshole* who really, truly *hates* me, but not as much as I hate myself.

The thought of it alone is enough to puncture a hole right through me as I storm down the long drive, my breath burning in my lungs and tears blurring at the edges of my vision. It's so cold that the wind burns the skin of my exposed hands and cheeks. I make no effort to pull down the sleeves of my coat or wrap my scarf higher on my neck, too intent on my newly formed resolution, and keeping my gaze glued to the high black gates in the distance.

He won't come looking for me. I'm sure of it. Undoubtedly, whenever Mallory realizes I've gone—probably tomorrow morning when I'm nowhere to be found for our run—he'll sound the alarm to my father and issue final confirmation that I really am as stupid as everyone thinks I am.

The thought fills me with a sick swoop of vindictive pleasure.

It's easier to sink into it, to confirm what they all believe, rather than work my ass off to prove them wrong. Why bother with being a well-adjusted human being? Who gives a shit? I'll be a dumb, irresponsible liability for the rest of my life, and what better time to accept it than *right now*?

Whether from the cold or the rush of adrenaline, my hand is shaking as I reach the security panel beside the gate and stare into the camera thing that Mallory put in. Part of me is expecting it not to work, to find I really have been locked in, but the mechanism grinds to life at once, opening onto the country lane which I've only ever seen from the back of a car.

I don't hesitate, marching out onto the road, and turn left, heading in the direction of the nearby village. Brisk, ocean air nips at my face as I finally relent and shove my cold-reddened hands into my pockets, my boots crunching on the gravel and loose debris resting along the bank of the asphalt.

Now is about the time I should be trying to think of a plan.

Some of the rush that propelled me from Thornhurst is fading, leaving behind a deep, sorrowful ache that seeps further into my nervous system with each step, taking me farther and farther from the security of my prison. Already part of me regrets leaving, but I don't stop or turn back. I won't. Not knowing who I'd have to face if I did.

God, the way he looked at me...

Impatiently, I swipe at the hot tear that manages to escape down the side of my cheek and feel my bottom lip tremble.

There's no way I have cell phone service out here, but when I get to the village, I'll get in contact with Summer. She's the only friend I have, and I refuse to be a burden to her, but maybe she'll let me crash on the couch in her apartment for a few days, at least until I can figure out what my father's next move is going to be.

Yet another man who holds my entire life in his hands. It must be so gratifying for them to have that kind of power, to toss it this way or that, sending it up in the air and catching it when they see fit, while letting it crash into pieces on the floor at others.

I know it's my own fault.

I know I'm a disappointing mess.

I know I deserve whatever is coming to me, leaving like this, but at least it will be my choice. Not theirs.

The weight of my conflicting emotions is so heavy, I think it might make my knees buckle, but I carry on anyway.

I have no idea how much time has passed since I left Thornhurst, but my entire body aches, and my toes are going numb with cold as the trees begin to thin along the side of the road. Finally, they give way entirely, and I pause at the edge of a rocky outcrop. The ocean wind nips at my exposed skin as I stand there, allowing my breathing to even, and watching as the sea crashes onto the rocks below.

Maybe some self-sabotaging madness runs in the Porter blood. Who else but a prideful fool would see such a place and decide to make it their home?

"Blair!"

The sound of my name is almost drowned out by the wind, the crashing waves, and my own thundering heartbeat, but I know I'm not imagining it and whip around automatically. I hadn't heard a thing, but the estate's green work truck has pulled off onto the curb a little way down the road. Through the windshield, my eyes lock with those of the unmistakable figure sitting in the driver's seat.

The very last person I wanted to see right now.

As we stare at each other, a thing I can't name seems to pass over the distance between us, and, too late, I realize how red my eyes must be. I turn away anyway, my throat tight.

Listening for it now, I hear the sound of Mallory's boots crunching over rocky soil, moving toward me, and then stop. "Get in the truck, Blair."

His tone surprises me. It isn't angry, or frustrated, or any of the other negative emotions I've managed to bring out in him thus far.

I let out a hard, miserable laugh, my chest aching so badly the poor thing could split open, and it would be a relief. "I left," I point out unnecessarily, still watching the waves. "That means you don't have to deal with me anymore. Congratulations."

Another hesitant step, and when he speaks again, Mallory's voice is a low, raspy plea. "I'm not telling, Blair. I'm asking. Please come home."

I allow my head to fall to the side, as my spiraling mind

catches on the last word, the word that fills me with a deep yearning. Home. "It's not," I tell him weakly. "My home, I mean. Thornhurst isn't my home."

My heart leaps in surprise as a jacketed elbow brushes mine, and I look up, meeting Satan's dark eyes. We both look away and stand in silence for a long time, staring out at the gray, churning waves.

"Where is?" he asks at last.

That is a surprisingly loaded question, but for once, I don't think he means to wound me. Lifting a shoulder, I smile grimly. "Here and there. Wyngate, if we're going by where I spent the most time."

The man at my side considers this solemnly. "I don't think time spent is what makes a place home."

"What does, then?"

He doesn't seem to have an answer for that, and when I chance a peek over at him, I see a tired sorrow in his familiar features, as if this conversation has reminded him of a very old wound.

For a long time, neither of us speaks. We stand side by side, silently watching the waves crash over the rocks far below, lost in our respective thoughts. Until Mallory voices the conclusion I really hoped he would never make.

"You're dyslexic," he says. It isn't a question, and he isn't asking.

The word alone makes me want to start crying all over again.

Until now, I've been strong. I kept it together when I was in his presence and refused to allow him the satisfaction of knowing he had an effect on me. Even if he hurt me with his harsh accusations and assumptions, I held my head high and threw them right back at him.

Apparently, providing this man with final confirmation of

just how right he was about me has eliminated whatever remained of my pride.

"Yes," I spit, glaring at him. "And before you ask, *no, I can't help it.*"

Mallory rubs the stubble on his jaw, lowering his inky eyes to meet mine. "I know you can't help it. Why didn't you tell me?" He winces almost as he's finished asking the question, as though he's answered it himself.

I let out a hard laugh. "What a lovely idea. Here, Mr. Shark, let me cut my foot open and stick it in open water for you."

"I'm not..." He trails off, his lips curving unhappily.

Unable to stand the silence long enough to let him find his words, I steel myself. "Look, you've made it really clear what you think of me, and my—my *thing* doesn't change the fact I'm a stupid, useless brat, does it? I don't want your pity."

"I don't pity you. I'm just..." Again, words seem to fail him.

My hands ball into fists at my sides, a flicker of irritation momentarily dispelling my self-pity. "You're just *what*?" I demand incredulously, and even raised, my voice is almost carried off by the wind. "Say what you have to say, so we can get this over with."

Mallory doesn't seem capable of responding right away. For a long time, he just looks at me, his entire body stiff with tension. When he manages it, though, nothing could have prepared me for what he says.

"I'm *sorry*." He really sounds it, too, and all the air goes out of me as we look at one another, apparently both rocked by those two simple words.

It takes an inordinate effort to swallow past the mass lodged in my throat, and I turn away again. "You're sorry," I echo, because I'm still half expecting him to mean something else, something that isn't expressing actual regret for the way he treated me.

"Yes," he confirms, "I'm sorry. I didn't know. Nobody told me, and if they had, I wouldn't have handled things the way I did. I wouldn't have said those things to you."

A selection of *those things* comes immediately to mind.

His not knowing isn't a surprise to me. I'd guessed as much, considering my parents have done everything they possibly could to forget or dismiss my diagnosis. In a way, I don't blame them. They did all they were taught to; they threw money at the problem and expected it to be taken care of. No amount of special tutoring or school aids could help me, though. Not when my problems went so much deeper than the inability to read.

"Come home. Back to Thornhurst, I mean." Mallory's voice is unbearably gentle, like he's coaxing a wild animal into taking food from his hand. It's not a tone he's ever employed with me before, and I don't know how to respond to it. Fighting fire with fire is the only dynamic I know with this man, and if it's extinguished... What should I say? How do I act?

I think of him smiling at that woman in the salon.

I think of him laughing with the electrician and clapping him on the shoulder.

I think of the fact that he has never once smiled or laughed with me.

"Nothing has changed," I retort bitterly, pulling my coat closer, as I lower my gaze from the sea to my boots. "You were right about me. Everything you said was right. Being dyslexic doesn't absolve me from being a spoiled, entitled little brat, does it?"

"No," he concedes gruffly. "But it adds context, and as the saying goes, you reap what you sow. I have to assume that the way I treated you from the start set the standard for the way you would behave in response. If I had been kinder, if I had listened, and treated you as the person you are rather than what I assumed you'd be, maybe we wouldn't be here now."

My eyes burn, and even though he's the one being vulnerable, somehow it opens me up, too. "Maybe," I admit quietly, still not looking at him.

Mallory sighs. "I can see now that my judgement was clouded. My own experience with generational wealth isn't positive. My father's family has money—*old* money—and the things it does to people..."

I look over and see he's shaking his head, expression creased in resentment and disgust. He hasn't ever spoken about his personal life to me, and this fragment of information sends a dull jolt of surprise through me, a distraction from the miserable self-loathing. I want to ask more, but I'm afraid to shatter whatever fragile understanding has settled over us, so instead, I wait.

At last, Mallory shifts his gaze from the sea to my face, and something warm spreads through my chest at what I see there. "It wasn't fair for me to treat you according to my own assumptions and prejudices, and I'm sorry for it, Blair. Truly sorry. If you come back with me, you have my word that we'll find a new way to do things. *A better way.*"

Twenty-Two

DAMIEN

I don't sleep that night.

I can't.

For hours, I toss and turn, trying and failing to clear my mind, but it's no use.

All I can think about, all I can see, is the endless list of cruel, hateful words I've spat at Blair Porter. Even as I try to tell myself that *I didn't know*, that I couldn't have possibly guessed at any of this, in my heart I know the truth.

If I hadn't been so quick to shove Blair in the box I believed she belonged, cramming the lid on to protect myself, regardless of whether it truly fit... well, maybe she would have told me, maybe she wouldn't, but now, we'll never know.

Regardless. One apology doesn't seem like enough.

At around one in the morning, I give up on getting any sleep.

Instead, I take out my computer and sit on the couch to research dyslexia.

Having only the most surface-level knowledge of the condition—that it mixes up letters and makes reading difficult —I feel woefully unprepared on how to properly support Blair now that I know the truth. Learning more seems like a pragmatic, appropriate first step, but as I dig in, reading through everything from firsthand accounts from adult dyslexics, to medical journals, and descriptions of what can happen when it goes unsupported.

Educating myself doesn't lessen my guilt.

If anything, each of the cold, clinical facts I learn, sheds a new, terrible light on the way I treated Blair.

It isn't limited to making reading difficult, as I'd thought. Dyslexia can affect everything from the ability to process verbal instructions, memory retrieval... the list goes on and on, and my chest feels as though it may cave in when I finally reach an article about the long-term effects of untreated or improperly treated dyslexia. Words like *poor self-esteem*, and *higher rates of anxiety and depression* jump out at me, as does the paragraph describing how many adults with the dyslexia will avoid situations which might force them to confront their limitations.

All of it fits perfectly.

By no fault of her own, the way Blair's brain operates is different than mine, and most of the population's. She has a disability, and one that was so clearly never addressed as it should have been.

If I were to guess, the fucking Porters threw money at the situation and expected that would be enough to solve it. Then, when it wasn't, they made it Blair's fault. Easier to write her off, to call her lazy, or stupid, or impulsive, rather than face that they had failed her.

The same way I failed her.

It's easy to point fingers at her parents and to blame them

for not supporting her in the first place, but much more difficult to hold a mirror to my own behavior, seeing it for what it truly is for the first time.

How many times did I get exasperated with her when I told her something and had to repeat myself?

How many times did I call her lazy or an idiot?

How many times did I allow my own prejudices to color the facts, warping them into a picture which best fit the narrative I'd been telling myself about Blair Porter from day one?

Exactly like the Porters, I clung to what was easy and familiar to *me*, without a care for what it was doing to *her*.

By dawn, my vision is blurry with exhaustion, and I'm sorely tempted to go back to bed, if only to allow myself a temporary respite from the debilitating guilt. Instead, I push my weary limbs into a standing position and begin to dress for our run, possessed by the need to lay eyes on Blair, and to see her clearly for what is perhaps the very first time.

As usual, she isn't in the entrance hall when I arrive at the main house, but when I pause in the dimly lit hall outside her bedroom door, there is a line of light spilling from beneath it, and the indistinct sounds of someone moving around inside.

I raise my fist, knocking softly. Only a few seconds later, it's thrown open, and I find myself looking at Blair. She's dressed for the run, but looks about as tired as I feel, and the knife buried in the center of my chest twists when I see the hint of red lining her eyes.

"Sorry," she murmurs, not quite looking at me as she works her hair back into a ponytail. "I meant to be downstairs on time."

I think I would prefer it if she cursed or threw something at me again.

"It's not a problem." I step out of the way, allowing her out into the hall, and watch in silence as she finishes her preparations.

Side by side, we start toward the stairs. "Did you, uh, sleep alright?" The attempt at normalcy, at civility, feels forced and awkward.

Blair must think so too, because in the corner of my vision, I see the corners of her lips pull into a tiny, wry smile. "Not really," she admits calmly. "You?"

"Not really."

Her jacketed arm brushes mine as we turn onto the sweeping main staircase, descending toward the entrance hall. There are large crates and boxes set along the wall to the side, decorations for her sister's upcoming engagement party which arrived a few days ago. By next weekend, the house will be filled to the brim with Blair's family members and their closest, wealthiest, most important friends. Already, my inbox is filled with about a dozen information requests from various security teams, and I anticipate some debilitating headaches to come.

None of that is a concern for me at the moment, though.

Right now, all I can think about is the quiet, pale-faced woman at my side, who seems to have lost that bright, impossible fire which has burned so fiercely inside her from the day we met. A fire I tried to extinguish over and over again, but now that I've succeeded, I can think of little else but bringing it back to life.

Fuck. *Fuck*.

We stop in the center of the checkered, marble floor, but as Blair raises her arms over her head, preparing to stretch for the run, I find myself proposing something I never have before.

"Why don't we do something else today?"

She pauses, staring at me. "Something else?"

"Something you'd like to do. Instead of running," I clarify, and my pulse thuds in my throat as, slowly, the woman at my side lowers her arms.

"Something I'd like to do," she echoes, disbelief evident in her tone. "That *isn't* running."

"Yes."

Blair blinks. "But you *always* run."

"Not *always*." I fractured my metatarsal two years ago, and then there was the flu I had last winter; apart from the odd one-off incident, however, she's right. Maintaining a strict, regimented routine is a holdover from my days in the Royal Navy, but *I like it*. The predictability is steadying, especially when so many significant, altering parts of my life have been totally outside my control. In fact, I can't remember the last time I willingly relinquished a single part of it for someone else.

Shifting her weight onto one leg, Blair folds her arms over her chest, studying me. "I'm not sure what you're trying to prove here, but—"

"I'm not trying to prove anything, Blair."

Her expression hardens. "Well, I don't want your pity. You hate me, remember? You've always hated me. Don't stop now."

Reaching up, I drag my hand through my hair, looking back at her with a twisted mix of fondness and exasperation.

Why did I imagine she would stop driving me mad after all this?

And how the fuck could I ever convince myself I don't like it?

Though I hadn't realized it until now, this new insight into Blair didn't just turn my beliefs about her on their head, it did the same to my beliefs about our relationship. The way I see her—*us*—is fundamentally different than it was even yesterday, and I'm struggling to orient myself to this new reality.

"I never hated you."

The words hang heavily in the air between us. I can see it

in her face that she doesn't believe me. Why would she, when all I've done is prove the opposite?

"What would you do today? If you could do anything?" I try again. "Anything at all."

Blair heaves a sigh. "I don't know." She hesitates, apparently wracking her mind for something far-fetched and ridiculous enough to prove me wrong, and I know she must have found it when she brightens. "I would leave this house." There's a challenge in her green eyes.

"Okay," I agree without the slightest hesitation. "What else?"

"I've always wanted to go to one of those places where you drink beer and throw axes at a target."

"Alcohol and axes, sounds like good, safe fun. What else?"

She seems to scramble for another item to add to the list. "I would learn how to make real pasta from scratch."

"And?"

"I would invite Summer."

"Summer, the maid?"

Blair's nostrils flare. "Summer, my new friend, who is very kind, very talented, and who *happens* to work part-time as a maid."

I nod, trying not to grin. "Okay, fine. Go get dressed in something appropriate for ax throwing, beer drinking and pasta making with Summer."

She looks over her shoulder at me at least three times as she ascends the staircase back toward her room, as if expecting me to change my mind at any moment.

I won't, though.

Tomorrow, I'll find a way to navigate our increasingly complicated relationship and attempt to build some trust between us so I can help her through this, while maintaining some semblance of professionalism. If such a lofty concept is even possible for us.

Today, I'm going to give Blair Porter whatever she wants.

When she's finally vanished from sight at the top of the stairs, I turn toward the kitchen, already pulling my phone out of the fitness holder on my arm.

I don't have a game plan. This decision wasn't made with any kind of foresight, and perhaps if I had thought I would give Blair carte blanche to call the shots today, I would have thought to offer her some feasible options.

Options that are private and come with little risk of Blair being seen or photographed.

As I sink down at the kitchen table, I decide that the not-so-small hazard of bringing her out in public will simply need to be overcome, because I won't take back the offer now. I'm resolved to make each and every one of her ridiculous offers happen, even if I need to go out to buy beer and erect an ax-throwing target myself.

To my pleasant surprise, however, having a college town within an hour's driving distance—one which happens to be the home of her *"friend who happens to be a maid"*—makes fulfilling Blair's wishes less complicated than expected.

Port Briar, which is situated further south of Thornhurst on Stelland's western coast, isn't unfamiliar to me. The city boasts both the Royal Naval Academy and its oldest university, Orwick. The two entities are situated almost side by side, making for a bizarre collision of military life and academia. I lived there for years while I was in the academy, renting an apartment around the corner from the posh townhouse where Ben and Leo lived while attending university

Looking back, it was one of the happiest periods of my life, and I find my heart lifting at the prospect of a day there.

It only takes a few minutes to find a bar—located at an address I recognize as part of Port Briar's bustling downtown district—which has a full back room dedicated to ax throwing and arcade games, and make a reservation for two.

The pasta making is a bit more difficult to wrangle, but I find an Italian restaurant that occasionally hosts cooking classes, and send them an email, offering to pay a premium for a last-minute private pasta-making demonstration before they open for dinner.

By the time Blair comes back downstairs—dressed in a cozy knit dress which emphasizes her hourglass shape and makes my mouth go dry—I have a reasonably concrete plan.

"Alright," I tell her, standing up. "Let's go."

She still doesn't believe me. I can see it in her face, even after I've pulled around the estate's Land Rover and have gotten back into the driver's seat after a brief detour to my cottage to change out of my running things.

"You should know that if this is an extremely elaborate plan to murder me, I will be quite annoyed," she informs me as we approach the gates, folding her hands neatly in her lap.

I roll down the window and lean out, allowing the newly installed biometric access to scan my facial features. When the tech is satisfied, the gates open, and I pull through, humming thoughtfully. "No plans at the moment, princess, but I'll keep you updated as the day progresses."

Blair purses her lips. "Is that a reminder to behave myself?"

No, all my homicidal inclinations are self-directed as of yesterday, but I don't tell her that, keeping my eyes trained on the road.

The storm is already dying away, but there's a mix of ice and slush covering everything, which makes for a treacherous drive. Apart from a call to Summer—who is more than happy to abandon a day of cleaning to join her—Blair is mainly quiet, her eyes on the landscape as we pass.

I can tell she's disoriented by my abrupt change in attitude toward her, likely unable to accept it could have been prompted by something other than pity.

While I fully intend to do everything I can to show her

that isn't the case, since I took the job at Thornhurst, I find myself troubled by the *lack* of time left on my contract. Is seven months enough to undo the damage I inflicted in the first one? It should be, and I can't understand why I'm suddenly so bothered by this end date.

The drive isn't a long one, and when we pull up outside the coffee shop where we're supposed to be meeting Summer, Blair looks confused when I don't turn off the car.

"Put your hair up. You'll be less recognizable," I tell her calmly, handing over my own black, knitted winter hat. "The reservation at the ax-throwing place is at six, and all paid for, but I was waiting on the Italian restaurant to confirm the cooking lesson. I'll send you a voice memo when I hear back from them."

Her lips pull down at the corners. "You aren't coming with me?"

I'd intended to, had thought that hovering discreetly in the background would be the safest course of action. "No. Are you saying you'd like me to?"

This question is met with a scoff. "Of course not. I just thought..." She trails off, glancing toward the glass-fronted shop, then back to me.

"I'll pick you up in front of the bar, and I won't be far. If you need me, call." My voice is steady, calm, but inside, something is twisting painfully.

"You're not worried I'll cause trouble? End up in the paper?"

I shake my head. "Go have fun with your friend. I trust you."

Despite this reassurance, Blair still looks as though she expects me to stop her as she pulls her pale red hair up into a bun and covers it with my hat. I say nothing when she opens the door and gets out onto the sidewalk, and lean back in my seat, letting out a heavy lungful of air as I watch her cross to the door, and pause, looking off down the sidewalk.

The slim blonde I recognize as Summer bounds into view, and I watch as she throws her arms around Blair. The pair of them smiling widely as they separate and carry on into the shop, elbows looped together.

And, for the first time since we met, I'm positive I've done the right thing for her.

Twenty-Three

There hasn't been a single day since he arrived that I didn't dread seeing Damien Mallory's face. Starting your morning with a person who hates you and thinks you're the biggest idiot to ever live is pretty shitty. Throw in a run through the icy grounds, the looming promise of literally nothing to look forward to, and getting back on my seasonal depression meds was starting to seem like a no-brainer.

Then the other day happened, and for a minute there, I was sure my life was going to get a whole lot worse.

Except it didn't. And, when I open my eyes the morning after my day of freedom, I find myself not dreading the sight of Damien Mallory's face quite as much as I did yesterday.

There is still *some* dread, though, as the wind howls loudly outside my bedroom window, promising an even more miserable running experience than usual. It's only the thought of muddying the slate he seems to be trying to wipe clean that has me forcing my stiff, reluctant limbs into a standing position and shuffling over the cold floor into the bathroom.

As in, *on my own* with time to spare. No banging on the door or ice water required.

Yesterday was probably the best day I've had in years. Summer and I walked all over Port Briar. She showed me all her favorite haunts, and it was nice to know that the easy, familiar friendship we'd fallen into on the days I helped her clean the house translated to the real world, too.

Though I caught a glimpse of the black Land Rover parked down the street from us a few times, Mallory kept his word, allowing us to enjoy the day without him shadowing me. The only time I heard from him was when he sent a voice memo with the specifics on our confirmed pasta-making demonstration. The simple thoughtfulness of that—sending the information in a way that wouldn't force me to stop what I'm doing to squint at my phone screen for five minutes, or use the text-to-speech app in front of Summer—took me off guard.

I didn't call him to pick me up until nearly nine, when my feet were aching from all the walking we'd done, and both Summer and I were yawning. She hugged me goodbye in front of the bar, promising to see me at work on Tuesday, and I was still smiling when I dropped into the passenger seat beside Mallory.

When I'd thanked him for organizing it all, he'd merely hummed, pulling out into traffic.

I'm still not quite clear what his motivations are here—a personality transplant also seems possible—but as I move through my typical morning routine, washing my face and brushing my teeth, I allow my mind to wander to the sexually charged element of my relationship with Mallory. Before all this, I'd been committed to using his attraction to me as a weapon against him, but now that he's actually being *nice* to me...

Am I supposed to just ignore it? Pretend I *didn't* flounce out of a Century dressing room in nothing but sheer cotton and grind all over his dick? Forget about the kiss we shared on the way back to Thornhurst, and the life-altering, impossibly hot sex we had the morning after?

A weight drops into my pelvis at the memory, spreading heat through my core, but I focus on brushing my hair into a ponytail, resolutely ignoring it.

For the first time ever, it's exactly six o'clock when I leave my bedroom and make my way through the quiet, darkened house to the foyer. Mallory is already there, dressed for the weather in a sporty jacket and sweatpants. He glances up at me as I descend the staircase, a hint of pleasant surprise in his expression.

"Good morning," he offers when I stop beside him, already shaking out my stiff, achy limbs.

A perfectly civil greeting, for the second morning in a row.

"Good morning," I reply, wishing I could banish the lingering heat in my core, which flared noticeably at the sight of him.

Lacing my fingers together, I stretch my arms up and over my head, eyes on the door. "You should know that I've decided to stop calling you Satan. As a gesture of commitment to our peace treaty."

"Very generous." My heart flutters as a quick glance to the man on my right shows his lips have quirked into a wry smile —*Those freaking dimples.* "I'll have to think of a comparable offering."

Promptly, my imagination provides a selection of offerings he could give me which would be more than sufficient.

We go quiet. Our sneakers squeak against the floor as we move through the familiar stretches to warm up, and though I keep catching sight of his movements at the edge of my vision, I keep my attention focused away.

Ordinarily, we'd be on the move by now. However, as wind buffets the house, rattling the large, paned glass window to our right, I get the sense that we're both dawdling.

I hazard a glance over at him. "I *really* don't want to run in this," I confess with a feeble, watery laugh, as another wave of freezing rain lashes harder against the windows.

Even with our new peace treaty in effect, I don't actually expect him to call it off, though. Satan—*Mallory* is nothing if not committed to his morning routine, and even if I don't particularly enjoy running, I've settled into it, too. Just not today. Today is going to suck.

He surprises me, though.

"Neither do I," Mallory admits, and I see him grimace as he looks out at the stormy sky beyond the window. "Unfortunately, the closest gym is a forty-five-minute drive from here. With the weather turning, maybe we'll have to look into getting some treadmills."

I have another idea.

Hesitantly, I let my arms drop back to my sides. "Do you swim?"

"Swim?" He glances at me, frowning. "I know how to, if that's what you're asking."

Good enough for me.

Without offering further explanation, I nod toward the back of the house. "Come on. I have a less terrible alternative to running through freezing rain."

I can tell he wants to ask more but seems to be endeavoring to play nicely because he allows me to take the lead. We don't speak as I lead the way through the house, only stopping when we've reached one of the unmarked doors at the back of the kitchen.

"When I was a child, I called this the grotto," I tell him,

casting a sly smile over my shoulder as I open it, and we're hit by a wall of warm humidity. It's an effort not to laugh at the wary expression on his face.

A flight of stone steps descends into the foundation of the house, curved, so you can't see what lies at the bottom. Without offering further explanation, and relishing his confusion a little, I move forward.

Located in what was once a root cellar, the pool lights cast an unearthly, greenish light onto the arched stone ceiling. The room is quiet and still, apart from the gently swirling water, and I hear Mallory's surprised intake of breath as he comes into view and realizes where I've brought him.

The air is warm, much warmer than the rest of Thornhurst, and I used to spend hours in here when we visited, pretending it was a secret mermaid cave, and I was the only human they trusted.

"You didn't know this was here?" I ask, and the question echoes through the whole room as I stop when I reach the bottom of the stairs, breathing in the salt and stone that hangs in the air as I toe off my sneakers.

He doesn't answer right away. Moments pass before I hear the soft thud of his shoes on the stone behind me, like he had to convince himself to follow. In the weeks that I've known him, I haven't seen this man hesitate over much of anything, and the fact that I've taken him off guard is beyond satisfying.

"No," he finally says from behind me, and his voice sounds different, confined in this small, darkened space. "Freddy didn't include this in his tour. On the blueprints, it's marked as a cellar." There is an air of suspicion in his voice, like he knows why our old head of security neglected to mention it, but he doesn't elaborate.

I'm in the process of stripping off my socks when he moves past me.

Straightening up, I watch cautiously as he walks a slow

circle around the pool, taking everything in. He's trying not to show it, but I can tell he likes it here. As he concludes his inspection, his shoulders lose a fraction of their tension, and his inky eyes have softened just a bit.

We stand side by side, staring at the glowing pool.

My fingers find the hem of my thermal running shirt. "So, you're telling me you *don't* know everything, then?"

Mallory glances at me just in time to see me lift the garment over my head. In the time it takes me to toss it onto a nearby bench, however, he's already looked away. His throat bobs. "I never claimed to know everything."

That makes me laugh, the noise echoing off the walls like a strange, fading song. "You certainly had me fooled."

A weight drops into my core as I hook my thumbs beneath the waistband of my leggings and peel them down my legs. Under my clothes, I'm not wearing anything special at all, just a black sports bra and cheeky pink panties. It's more coverage than the average bikini, and he's already seen every inch of me. Still, there's something about undressing in front of this man when we're wholly and completely alone that has a prickling, uneasy desire spreading beneath my skin.

It takes more courage for me to look at him than it did to undress, but when I do, I find Mallory's eyes already on me. His mouth pulls into something between a scowl and a smirk.

That's all it takes for my pulse to stutter, and the muscles below my bellybutton go taut.

"I didn't bring swimwear," Mallory retorts, crossing his arms as if that objection settles the matter.

I arch a brow and shoot him a look that says, *please, I've seen your dick.*

"You're wearing running clothes," I point out, drawing away from him and toward the water as, from behind me, there comes the sound of a low groan.

"Blair—"

"It's either this," I interrupt, speaking over my shoulder, "or running in the freezing rain, but didn't you say you'd be more *flexible*?"

Again, he goes quiet. It's not the kind of silence I've come to associate with him, which is heavy with annoyance or judgement. This is something quieter. Something that feels like he's actually thinking about me instead of defaulting to his preconceived notions.

I'd wondered whether yesterday was his attempt to "make it up to me" and once his conscience was clear, he'd go back to being an asshole, maybe without the insults regarding my intelligence. That doesn't seem to be the case, though.

Interesting. He really is trying.

I shouldn't get my hopes up. It hasn't even been a full forty-eight hours since he apologized for his attitude, and who knows if this newfound peace will hold. We do seem unusually good at getting under one another's skin, and maybe this time next week, we'll be back to Dictator Damien and Bratty Blair.

"I did say that," Mallory admits at last with a hint of regret, as if keeping such a promise is much more difficult than he expected in the present situation.

Even so, the tiny admittance feels like a victory as I dip my toes into the pool, letting out a breath of pleasure at the feeling of the warm water on my clammy skin. I've been avoiding this place. In the month since I arrived at Thornhurst, I haven't come down here even once, too lost in my spiral of depression and hatred of Mallory to indulge in anything that I actually enjoy.

I'm hyperaware of his eyes on me as I lower myself onto the topmost step. The warm water laps at my calves, soothing muscles that have ached for weeks, and by the time the heat reaches my hips, I feel my shoulders releasing tension I hadn't realized they were holding.

How had I forgotten how good, *how safe*, this room used to feel?

I sink lower with a happy sigh, letting the water rise to my collarbones, as I finally lift my gaze to where Mallory is standing.

Staring.

Not at the pool, or the stone ceiling, or the lights. *At me.*

He blinks, tearing his eyes away when he realizes I've caught him, jaw tightening as he runs a hand through his already messy hair.

"Are you getting in?" I call, my voice carrying through the chamber in the same melodic, echoing song. "Or is swimming laps instead of running them a little too flexible for you?"

His eyes cut to mine. "It might be."

"You need therapy."

This retort prompts a bark of laughter. "Probably." He admits it so dryly that I find myself smiling, holding back a laugh of my own as—finally—he bends to remove his shoes.

I sink lower in the water, letting it cover my lips as I watch Mallory undress.

This is different, *heavier* than it felt to see his body before. During those unforgettable moments we shared in his cottage, I can barely remember him taking his clothes off. I'd been too far gone, too unbelievably desperate for him to fuck me, after the heaven and hell he'd just unleashed on my pussy.

At the thought of our one and only sexual encounter, I press my thighs together beneath the surface of the water, watching as Mallory strips off his shoes, socks, and zip-up coat. He's methodical about it, putting each sock in its appropriate shoe, and folding his jacket before putting it on the bench beside my things. When the compression shirt goes next, though, I find my mouth suddenly bone dry.

Good Lord. This was such a bad idea. I didn't need to see... all that again.

My recollections of Mallory's body were, unfortunately, very accurate. His chest is broad and well defined, without being obnoxiously muscular. Dark hair is dusted over the center and trails down to beneath the waistband of his sweatpants, an honest-to-god happy trail that I instantly imagine tracing with my fingers.

He has tattoos, too. Above his heart, there are several lines of slanting, cursive script–impossible to read from here—and on his bicep, I see the corner of what I remember is an anchor. There's another one too, a curving ocean wave on his upper right flank, but I'm too distracted to appreciate how beautiful the aging ink looks on his skin, because the pants go next.

The temperature of the water seems to rise by degrees as Mallory folds his sweats and lays them carefully with our other things. He doesn't look at me as he moves to the edge of the pool, following me into the water in nothing but black boxer briefs, which cling to his strong thighs.

Thighs that strained when he was fucking me, and... *oh, fuck.*

I am not okay.

In the interest of self-preservation, I turn away, my cheeks burning as I push off toward the far end of the pool, eager to put as much distance between us as possible. Mallory seems to be thinking along the same lines, because he diverts to the opposite end, meeting my eyes across twenty yards of shimmering, greenish water.

"Twenty laps, then break," he calls, apparently recovering his sense of superiority and authoritarianism.

Finally, I thought there might be something seriously wrong for him to go two whole days without barking an order at me.

I don't argue, though.

Where running is new, and my muscles seem to pull back

against it, swimming seems almost effortless. I haven't been in a pool for anything other than a party in years, yet within two laps, I've found my stroke again. Here, I'm fast and strong and capable. Instead of being dragged down, my heart lifts as I push against the burning in my muscles and kick off the wall, only to realize Mallory is just ahead of me.

I'm faster than him.

The realization sends a thrill of triumph through me, and I kick harder, pull faster.

He isn't letting me win, either. His clean front stroke falters when he catches sight of me in his periphery and does a double take beneath the surface, arms pulling through the water faster as he tries to pick up the pace. I feel my lips pull into a wide, unseen smile when I push away from the side and pass him as he goes to do the same.

I lap him once.

Then, after another few well-executed kicks off the pool's rocky wall, I lap him again.

I have no sense of how long we've been at this, and my attempt to keep track of my progress fell off somewhere along the way. We might have swum ten laps or a hundred, but I don't want to stop. I'm soaring, addicted to the feeling that comes every time I catch sight of Mallory's legs beating the water ahead of me, signaling another victory is fast approaching.

He must not be getting the thrill out of this. I am, though, because after about my fourth cycle of outpacing him, the next time I see him, he's standing in the shallows.

I stop ten feet away and stand, too, wiping the water from my eyes. My heart is beating hard, but my breathing is under control. Unlike Mallory, who is gasping and clutching one of his sides.

The sight of this man truly winded is a victory unto itself.

"Weren't you in the Navy?" I call, breathless but unable to disguise the delight in my voice.

"In the Navy, they preferred us to stay *on* the boat," Mallory pants, pushing his dripping hair off his forehead with a disgruntled grimace.

My laugh reverberates off the stone walls and ceiling as I sink back into the water with a happy sigh. God, I never would have expected myself to need this, but I really, really did. How long has it been since I had a win? A real, hard-earned victory?

"Where did you learn to swim like that?" Mallory asks unexpectedly, his brow furrowed.

I was wondering if he would be sour about losing, after weeks spent setting the precedent of him being my superior at all things. His ego appears to be intact, however, because he doesn't sound put out, only curious.

"Swim team until I was—*gosh*—fifteen, I want to say? Something like that." I allow my legs to float up, enjoying the buoyancy of the water. "It's been a while."

"Why did you stop?"

At this angle, I can't see him, and I'm grateful for it as my smile slips. Just a little, though, and not for long. I don't allow the pinch of an old scar to detract from my happiness at the present. God knows I'll probably feel sorry for myself about all sorts of things tomorrow, but after the lowest weeks of my life, I want to feel good a little while longer. "My grades got too bad," I reply simply, and I'm pretty proud about how blasé I sound, like I'm not ashamed at all.

My toes skim just above the surface of the water, and I pull them back under with a little splash, gazing up at the arched, stone ceiling.

"There are accommodations, aren't there? For people with your..." He trails off awkwardly, the words muffled a bit by the water lapping against the sides of my face.

"You can say it," I reply, amused despite myself. "Dyslexia

isn't a bad word. Hard to spell, though. Whoever invented it had a sick sense of humor."

Mallory makes a low, impatient noise, and I turn my face to look at him. He's still standing where I left him, his hands resting on his hips. Up close like this, I wish I could make out the script tattooed over his heart, but the letters blur together, and discerning it would take a lot more staring than is good for me.

Catching my eye, he frowns.

I turn away, allowing my eyes to close.

"Yes, of course there are accommodations," I admit. "Maybe they would have helped, but it's hard to accept you're different at that age. The most important thing in the whole world is fitting in, and nobody can fit in with a fifty-year-old woman named Suzanne following them from class to class or sitting in a classroom for an extra hour to finish a test while everyone else is on a field trip," I scoff, annoyed at myself for the edge of bitterness which colors the words. "It was easier to pretend I didn't care, and that I didn't need to, when I'd get control of my trust fund when I turned eighteen."

Mallory doesn't respond for a long time. I don't even realize I've been pushed closer to him by the gently lapping water until my foot brushes the bare skin of his abdomen. I suck in a gasp, and my eyes snap open, instantly meeting the darkened gaze of the man standing over me.

I drag my arms through the water, pulling myself away, my stomach in knots. "Can we do this again sometime? Instead of running?"

I'm fully prepared for him to say no. Even after all his talk about doing things differently, I don't really expect the dynamic of our relationship to change much. Why would he compromise the way he does things when he has been handed all the power in this relationship?

In my experience, people don't change unless they have to.

Mallory surprises me. "Okay," he agrees, his voice barely discernible over the water lapping against my head, and though I don't look, I can feel the weight of his eyes on me. "We'll do it your way, princess."

Twenty-Four

Apparently, I swim now.

In the days since Blair showed me the secret pool in the cellar of Thornhurst, our mornings have fallen into a new routine. One day we run, the next, we swim.

Compromising the way I live to accommodate someone else's needs isn't something I'm familiar with. Apart from a few short-lived relationships, interspersed with the occasional, impersonal hookup, I've been on my own for a long time. My brothers have been the only consistent presence in my life, and they're the only people I would ever have considered adjusting my behavior for.

Until Blair.

We seem to have found a fragile state of détente. I wouldn't call us friends, but we're not enemies either, and the newly established peace feels more dangerous than the weeks of psychological warfare that preceded it. At the time, I hadn't realized it, but now I can see the constant bickering and hurling insults were a way to vent *the other things* I feel for her.

Unfortunately, there is limited time in which to find another way to vent *the other things*, because come tomorrow, Thornhurst will be busier than I've ever seen it. Over two hundred prestigious guests will be flooding into the estate from around the world to attend the "intimate" engagement party for Alba Porter and His Grace, James, the Duke of Fairborne.

Even if they're secretly disappointed the title doesn't come with a crown, Lord and Lady Porter appear to be sparing no expense to celebrate their middle child's marriage. Caterers, florists, decorators, and an army of cleaners have been coming and going from the estate all week, which means that my job—keeping track of every-one, and ensuring they don't wander into an area of the house they aren't meant to be—has been unusually hectic.

As an added complication, Lady Porter fired the party planner who'd originally been hired to manage the whole affair —I wasn't aware seating charts could be considered a "*disaster*" until all this—and Blair was drafted into overseeing the setup.

The Porters themselves will be arriving tomorrow, along with the future bride and groom, and their accompanying flurry of high-ranking staff members, for an additional layer of tension to the preparation proceedings.

Which means that, for the past few days, I've seen very little of Blair.

It shouldn't bother me. Yet every time I enter the house, I find myself... paying attention.

Having an intense awareness of one's surroundings is something of an occupational hazard in my line of work, but this is different from what I'm accustomed to. When I strain my hearing, or scan the room I enter, I'm not looking for something wrong—I'm looking for her.

It. Won't. Fucking. Stop.

It's unrelenting, and infuriating, and it's no use trying to convince myself that I'm not doing precisely that. Not when I do encounter her, and her presence rushes through me like a stiff drink, making me warm, a little woozy, and—worst of all—thirsty for more.

This isn't just attraction. I've been attracted to women before, had feelings for women before, and those instances seem flimsy and insubstantial when I put them against what Blair Porter inspires in me. Obsession might be more accurate.

When we're not together, I wonder what she's doing.

I've caught myself searching for reasons to go to the main house, in the hopes of seeing her.

When I do see her, I can't seem to stop filing away inconsequential details about her, as though my ability to do my job hinges on knowing how she takes her coffee or the types of jewelry she favors.

It's driving me mad.

Yes, we're getting along for the most part, but *nothing has changed*. I'm still employed by her family and hold the keys to her freedom at the end of this. The power imbalance, the age difference, the mountain of emotional baggage I've been dragging around... Nothing should have happened. Letting it go so far was an inexcusable lapse in judgement, and one that I'm determined not to repeat, for both of our sakes.

Right or wrong, however, I'm not capable of forgetting it ever happened.

I remember, in painful clarity, every minuscule detail of the morning after the break-in. The morning I found her in my bed and was too fucking exhausted to stop myself from giving in and taking what I'd wanted from the moment we met—try as I might to deny it.

It was a mistake.

I know it was a mistake.

So, naturally, I find myself pushing open Thornhurst's kitchen door during my lunch hour on Thursday, holding an enormous bouquet of flowers under my arm.

The kitchen, which I'm used to seeing empty, is now crowded with boxes of party rentals, large stainless steel tray racks, and several members of staff preparing for tomorrow's event.

"Looking for Blair?" asks Summer as I enter, pausing in the act of removing several hundred crystal goblets from their packing cases.

The innocent question is surprisingly loaded, and I wince, adjusting my hold on the vase as one of the catering assistants hurries past, bearing a large crate of smoked salmon.

"Yes," I admit, nodding to the blooms, as if delivering three dozen long-stem roses to a woman is going to make this look casual. "Need to see if there's someplace she wants these."

I must be projecting, because Summer doesn't appear to think anything of this, and merely smiles cheerfully as she turns back to her work. "She was in the ballroom a minute ago."

Not waiting around for further questions, I thank Summer and head through the house to the entrance hall, which has been bedecked in garlands, holly, and a twelve-foot Christmas tree for the occasion.

The ballroom doors stand open to the right, and I pause in the doorway, taking it all in. Large, round tables, draped in deep red, have been arranged along the right side of the room. On the left, a line of glittering Christmas trees stands evenly between the high windows. Everywhere you look, there are ribbons, ornaments, and all the trappings of an elaborate holiday-season party.

Even I, who am not the largest fan of this house or the people throwing this event, have to admit it's beautiful.

And none of it compares to the young woman standing at the center of it all, alone in the vastness of the room.

Blair hasn't noticed me yet. She's frowning, listening intently to whoever is speaking through the phone held to her ear, free arm wrapped around her middle. Sighing, her head drops back, allowing herself an unseen moment of exasperation as she speaks, her voice carrying clearly over to me. "Don't worry, Alba. I triple-checked, it's all here. *Yes*—even that."

The corners of my mouth tug, and I find myself fighting a smile as I watch her lift her fist into the air in front of her, shaking an invisible person.

"*Yes*, Alba." There's no mistaking her irritation now, and her sister must think so, too, because Blair's next words come with an air of forced calm. "No, I'm not making fun of you. It's very reasonable to be concerned about the well-being of the centerpieces; however, I assure you, they're all present and accounted for. Just like they were present and accounted for when you called me about them this morning. We're just waiting to put them on the tables until tomorrow, in case they drop any petals. What? What's that? You're breaking—*shhhh* —up! *Alba?*"

And she ends the call.

"Nicely handled."

Blair whips around and, seeing me in the doorway, smiles sheepishly. "She and my mother are driving me crazy," she admits, shoving her phone into the pocket of her dress. "They don't trust me to do any of this but refuse to disrupt their schedules to come take care of it themselves."

"Must be nice."

"Right?" She rolls her eyes. "Are those for the infuriating bride?"

For a moment, I'd forgotten why I came in here, but recover quickly. "From the Swedish Ambassador and her husband," I tell her, moving farther into the room. "Apparently, they're not able to make it, but send their most sincere apologies and best wishes." I stop before her, holding out the bouquet.

Blair's fingers brush mine as she takes it, setting the arrangement atop the nearest table with a sigh. "How nice for the Swedish Ambassador and her husband. I wish I couldn't make it."

I clear my throat, turning my gaze to the nearest, non-Blair attraction in the room—the nearest Christmas tree. "It looks great in here."

"Does it? I've spent the past forty-eight hours being told everything that's wrong with it, so my judgement might be a little screwed." She says it wryly, but as my eyes dart automatically back to her, I see a hint of bitterness in her familiar features. "I was going to ask whether all siblings are this infuriating, but I actually don't know if you have any."

My stomach drops, and it's difficult to keep my expression impassive and not react. "I have—*had*—three brothers." I feel Blair's eyes on me as I stroll over to the nearest Christmas tree, examining the ornaments without any real interest as I wait for the inevitable follow-up to that.

"Had?" There's a hint of something—sorrow, maybe—in her voice.

"My eldest brother died several years ago now. We weren't particularly close."

As I glance back, I see her face has fallen. "Still," she says softly, "I'm so sorry, Damien. That's... I mean, Alba and Cedric and I aren't particularly close, but I would still be devastated."

I've always felt a little funny claiming any sympathy for Arthur's death. What I told Blair is the truth; we *weren't* close, not like Ben, Leo, and I. The late king avoided acknowledging our shared paternity whenever possible but still asked for my help managing our two younger brothers when necessary. I believe he viewed me as a bridge of sorts, useful on occasion, but otherwise ignored.

That bridge burned about six months before his death, however, when I refused to stop Ben from divorcing his nasty first wife. I have many regrets surrounding my family, but that, at least, isn't one of them.

Eager to escape this conversation, I offer Blair a slight smile. "Never mind all that. Do you need help with anything?"

To my relief, she moves on, letting out a weary sigh. "You'll have to be more specific. Is this assistance limited to party planning, or could I get you to rub my back? I pulled something while lifting a bag of linen napkins." She's teasing, trying to lighten the mood, but even the suggestion of putting my hands on her has blood rushing south.

Fucking hell, I am a grown man getting hard at the thought of giving this woman a back rub?

What is wrong with me?

My answering chuckle is strained. "Dangerous business, party planning."

"It is when Alba is the bride." Shifting her weight, Blair stares at me. "I was joking, by the way. About the back rub. I'm trying not to bring up... what we aren't bringing up. I know it makes you uncomfortable."

There's a hint of color high on her cheeks now, as memories of what we aren't bringing up echo between us. *Her hands planted on my bare chest, tits pressed together, as she rolls her hips over my*—no. Uncomfortable isn't the word I would use.

With difficulty, I swallow, shoving my hands into the pockets of my coat. "What makes you say that?"

Her lips twitch. "Oh, just the look on your face when you're reminded of it. Like a deer in headlights."

Yes, I would imagine that's an accurate assessment. I glance toward the door, ensuring that none of the staff have wandered into earshot. Part of me is hoping to find someone there, to have some reason to cut this conversation off at the knees and not have to tell her it can happen again.

We're quite alone.

Stepping closer to her, I lower my voice. "It isn't something that can happen again."

"Oh?" Blair hums, and there's a mischievous, playful glint in her eyes which experience has taught me to be wary of.

I stop five feet away from her. "Yes."

"Why?"

"A lot of reasons."

Blair takes a single step closer, eyes sparkling. "Such as?"

"I'm too old for you." My cock—regrettably—hasn't gotten the memo on that.

The maddening creature before me actually laughs. "I'm twenty-six, not eighteen, and"—her eyes drop to my body for a fraction of a second before returning to my face—"you look good for your age."

Her praise could make me throw out my chest and strut. Instead, I frown. "Blair. That isn't the only reason, and you know it. I'm in a position of authority over you."

"If I don't want to sleep with you, are you going to tell my father I'm not following his rules and get my trust fund taken away?"

My jaw goes slack. "*Of course not.*"

Grinning, Blair steps closer, reducing the distance between us to less than a foot. Too close to be considered casual if anyone walked in. I should step back, but—of course—I don't move. "Well then, one could argue this authority you have over me isn't relevant to the situation at hand," she muses, reaching out to pick a bit of lint off the breast of my coat. My heart stalls as her eyes lift to mine. "Do you ever think about it? What happened between us that morning?"

I don't need to ask what *it* is, and ball my hands into fists in my pockets, resisting the urge to reach out and grab her. "Blair."

"I think about it. A lot. I've never had sex that good before. Have you?"

"*Blair*," I snarl, trying to maintain my resolution as the scent of her invades my lungs. I could drag her against me in seconds, could be kissing her, touching her... This house is full of empty rooms. If we were fast, I could be inside her again in minutes.

Before I can act on the impulse, however, the woman before me sighs deeply.

"Don't worry, your virtue is safe with me, Mr. Mallory." She smiles softly. "I'm pretty tired of forcing you to admit you're attracted to me. It gets old, you know? A girl has to have some pride. I pinky promise, I'll let you live in denial from now on."

My lungs are burning and—*fucking hell*—how does she do this to me? "I'm trying to do the right thing, Blair."

"I know." She draws back, putting space between us again, but doesn't look away. "And I respect that. Which is why I'm going to make it much easier for both of us. My mother was kind enough to forward a very specific section of tomorrow's guest list to me, and I told her I will put my absolute best foot forward. After all, how often does a girl get the opportunity to meet so many single, *age-appropriate* men without even leaving the house?"

Blood is rushing in my ears. I should be relieved at what she's telling me, happy she's moving on from whatever it was that happened between us, and that I won't need to worry about it happening again because she's taking it off the table.

Relief is *not* what I feel.

"I think this will be good for me, actually. Healthy." Blair nods to herself, apparently satisfied by the number she's done on me, and doesn't wait for me to formulate a response. Drawing over to the flowers, she scoops them up, beaming at me. "You know, I'm betting my parents' *no guests, no leaving the house* rule would be relaxed if I were dating someone they approve of. Something to look forward to, right?"

Twenty-Five

BLAIR

This dress is a knock-out.

Ordinarily, I reserve my best wardrobe selections for parties that I actually *want* to attend. However, with my social calendar currently void of any such occasion, and a newly established resolution to make Damien Mallory crawl and/or beg to fuck me again, I think tonight's event warrants an exception.

It's actually well worth the—admittedly exorbitant—amount of money I spent on it, because this dress isn't just pretty, sparkly, and ridiculously hot on me, it's armor.

I'll need it to successfully navigate my role as the only piece in a four-way game of chess, being played by people who all want to move me in the direction that suits them best.

Damien, who'd like me to remain single and available to him, without ever treating me as such.

My mother, who is clearly hoping to have me married off and safely someone else's problem.

The single, socially appropriate fuckboys who absolutely

do not want to get married, but would very much like to have sex with me.

My sister, who would prefer me to be as quiet, unassuming, and boring as possible.

That's a lot of conflicting responsibilities for anyone to juggle in one night, but fortunately, this dress makes it possible. Or, at least, it makes it possible for me to fake it, while pursuing my own ulterior motives.

As I turn this way and that, admiring my reflection in my bathroom's floor-length mirror, however, I experience a brief moment of concern that I might be being a little mean. Damien is trying to do the right thing.

On paper, us getting further involved is a terrible idea. I should definitely respect his wishes, take our newly established peace, and be grateful I don't have to spend the next six months coming up with fresh nickname variations for Satan.

Should, but won't.

The problem is that the light, breezy attraction I felt for that man when we met, has become a fully-fledged hurricane. I've seen a hint of what could exist between us if that big, bossy buttface would just let it happen, and *I want it.*

I want it so, so bad, and unfortunately for Damien Mallory, I refuse to let the stick up his ass get in the way.

He'll thank me later.

Reservations dismissed, I smirk at my reflection, watching myself smooth my palms over the front of the dress. It has an art deco vibe, with its gold beading and velvet material, and is cut in such a way that emphasizes my curves when I'm standing still, but catches the light whenever I move, toeing the line between sexy and sophisticated.

The garment is a little more daring than I would ordinarily attempt with my mother present. However, my efforts to get things in order for the party this week must have bought me some goodwill, because she merely purses her lips when I finally join her in the sitting room. I'm a little late, too, after taking my time on the journey across the house, making sure I was in full view of all Damien's temporary security cameras the entire time and throwing in a strategically angled shoe adjustment for good measure.

"People will begin arriving any moment," she informs me, as if I could have missed the flurry of last-minute activity in the entrance hall.

Despite myself, I glance toward the camera I know is hidden in the shadows of a nearby bookshelf, wondering if he's already seen my outfit choice for the evening.

I'm saved from making conversation with my mother by the sound of footsteps in the hall and the arrival of Ced. I'm not sure if it's my imagination or not, but I think he looks a little ill. Certainly, he's paler and more distant than he was when I last saw him in September.

He barely acknowledges either of us, offering only a curt nod before stalking over to stand beside the fire and pulling out his phone.

"Cedric, you can't possibly be thinking of wearing that," Mom squawks, her eyes round in alarm at the sight of my brother's dark pressed trousers and plain white button-up.

"Would you like me to be in attendance?" he replies cooly, not lifting his gaze from the device in his hands.

Mom splutters, "Of course. You—"

"Then this is what I'll be wearing."

His response leaves no room for argument, and I stare at him as our mother heads to the bar cart, obviously intent on pretending the exchange didn't happen. Even for Ced, who is stiff and unfamiliar with nearly everyone, he's historically been at least *polite* to our parents.

God, whatever.

My brief flicker of interest in this new development in the family dynamic dies nearly as soon as it sparks. Despite seeing them more than I have in years, I've never felt so detached from my parents, brother, or sister. More than anything, I finally understand what that cold, echoing emptiness inside me is, and that I will never be whole if I wait for them to fill it.

Muffled voices interrupt my brooding, and seconds later, Dad and Alba enter the room.

I haven't actually seen Dad since everyone arrived this morning. He went straight to his study and didn't emerge, but now, it's clear he looks nearly as weary as Ced, though seems to be taking the trouble to pretend otherwise.

At his side, my sister is wearing six-inch heels, a white cocktail dress, and makeup that is so flawless, you'd never know she has a pore.

"Guests will be arriving shortly," Mom echoes the news she just relayed to me, clutching her newly poured glass of wine. "Alba, make sure to call dear Princess Araminta in the morning, apparently she wasn't feeling up to the journey."

"Of course."

"Oh, and—"

Alba, who has stopped just beside the door, shoots her a venomous look. "Why don't you email your requests to my secretary, so I can enjoy my engagement party without your to-do list on my mind?"

In response, Mom downs half her remaining glass of wine in a single gulp.

Okay. What is going on? *Something* has obviously happened, and I can't decide whether I'm thrilled that nobody thought to tell me or annoyed they're including me in the fallout anyway.

"Be right back, I'm going to sneak upstairs to change my shoes really quickly, I think I'm getting a blister," I hedge, inching toward the door. Nobody stops me, and I make my escape from the bubble of simmering tension, filled with unbridled relief as I stride back across the house toward the stairs in my unusually comfortable heels.

I don't make it far.

One second, I'm passing the very first bathroom I helped Summer clean, barely noticing that the door is ajar.

The next, a hand has wrapped tightly around my wrist, and I find myself being pulled sideways into the familiar, marble-tiled space. Disoriented, I blink, watching as Damien closes the door behind us, locking it with an audible click. "What are you—"

The question is silenced as he reaches out to grip my waist, dragging me into his warm, firm body. I get a glimpse of a tight jaw and darkened, hungry eyes, before he's bowing to kiss me with all his might.

Oh my god.

My pulse is humming, flooding my body with a violent, reckless need as he crowds me backward into the vanity. I moan into our kiss as my butt hits the cabinet, and I feel the unmistakable, stiff ridge of his cock. My hands fly to his hair, clutching the silken strands as our lips work frantically, devouring each other. Barely fifteen seconds could have passed since he pulled me in here, and already, heat is blooming low in my core, my pussy aching to be filled.

Damien hisses as my teeth graze his bottom lip, but doesn't pause or say a word as his hands tighten on my waist. Seconds later, I gasp as, without warning, he lifts me right off my feet and onto the edge of the cool, marble countertop.

I whimper as he shoves my thighs apart, filling the space between them with his hips.

"Is this what you wanted?" Damien mutters against my lips as between us, he rocks his erection against the narrow strip of fabric covering my pussy. "Are you happy now?"

He must not really want a response, because the question has barely been asked before he's kissing me again, devouring my noises of pleasure as the friction of the arousal-coated material drags over my clit.

Yes, I wanted this.

Yes, I'm happy now.

Yes, I will take literally anything he wants to give me.

Yes, yes, yes.

Damien doesn't stop me as my hands move to his belt, fumbling helplessly with the loops and metal pieces as I tilt back, trying to maintain the connection with his lips and cock as I work them apart.

Dimly, I hear a strand of my dress's detailing break, sending a wave of tiny gold beads onto the bathroom floor. It's not important, though. I don't care. Especially not as I finally manage to get the belt open. The room spins, and flames flare higher in my belly at the promise of what comes next.

Gathering my dress in his hands, Damien shoves the garment up to bunch around my waist, letting out a low grunt of approval as I manage to free the button of his trousers from their loop. Both of our hands are clumsy with urgency, clawing at the garments between us in our desperation to remove them.

He pulls my panties over my hips and down my legs, shoving them to the floor along with one of my heels.

I shove his briefs down, and my lungs burn from the lack of oxygen as I wrap my fingers around the hot, heavy base of his shaft, stroking him.

And, through it all, he never stops kissing me.

"Fuck me," I whisper against his lips, my heart leaping into my throat as a set of footsteps passes by the bathroom, and the distant murmur of voices reminds me that we aren't alone.

In my hand, Damien's bare cock pulses. "We don't have a lot of time. Show me you're ready," he mutters, his voice a low, rumbling order.

For once, I don't hesitate to obey.

Releasing him at once, I brace one palm on the counter behind me and lean back, ensuring he can see what I'm doing. He can. Damien watches, his pupils going wide as I press my free hand down to the juncture of my thighs and slip two fingers between the slick, naked lips of my cunt.

His breath stutters as I part them, showing him every inch of myself, and how wet he's made me.

How impossibly turned on I am by what we're doing.

How much I need him.

I have to bite my lip to mask my cry as he reaches out, circling the bud of my clit with the pad of his thumb. "Stay like that," Damien mutters, as he takes himself in hand, fisting his base and guiding our bodies into alignment.

We're both still dressed, me in my crudely pushed-up dress and him in a fitted black pullover, pants still hanging loosely on his hips.

If anyone paused outside the bathroom door, they would hear our ragged breaths and my poorly stifled cry as Damien circles my opening with the bulbous crown of his cock. It's impossibly hot, and I'm so turned on that even his tiny, controlled ministrations sound wet in the small room. Unable to help myself, I arch closer, needing to feel him split me open once again.

Damien's fingers dig into the flesh of my hip, stopping me. "Don't fucking move," he hisses, not lifting his eyes from my pussy.

The coppery, iron taste of blood floods over my tongue, and I realize how hard I've been biting my lip. "We don't have time." I remind him, squirming. "*Please—*"

My begging turns to a soft, choked moan as, finally, I feel the pressure of his cock against my entrance.

He pulses his hips ever so slightly, and we both stare as my body stretches, permitting the tip of him inside me. I expect him to go further, to give me more, but as the seconds pass, Damien still doesn't move.

"How's that, princess?" he muses, pulling out and pressing back in again. Still, he doesn't give me more than the tip.

A desperate, broken whine escapes from between my clenched teeth. "I need more. Please—*fuck*—please, Damien."

He ignores me, continuing to fuck me in slow, agonizingly shallow thrusts. The teasing is getting me wetter and wetter. It would be effortless for him to sink deeper, but he doesn't, maintaining his ironclad control.

Meanwhile, I'm shaking. "Oh my god, you suck so bad," I half-laugh, half-cry, tightening my legs around his waist in an unsuccessful attempt to pull him closer.

Gripping my waist with both of his massive hands, Damien finally tears his eyes from my unfilled pussy to look at my face. He smirks. "You want more?"

I dig my nails into his forearms, panting. "*Yes*, you asshole."

Still not letting me move, he leans forward to brush his lips over my jaw, still maintaining the teasing, shallow thrusts. I'm literally dripping now, tits heaving against him, and growing more frustrated by the second. "If you want more," Damien murmurs, his deep voice rumbling through me too, "You'll come find me after the party."

Is he joking right now?

I can barely stifle my cry of protest and have to grit out my hushed, furious retort from between clenched teeth. "Oh my god, what is wrong with you?"

Goosebumps erupt up my spine as Damien presses his lips chastely to my pulse point, stubble rasping against the sensitive skin there. "You will be good and *not* attempt to drive me out of my mind with jealousy. Do I make myself clear?"

My head drops back against the wall with a dull thud, and

it's an effort to stop myself from collapsing as a rush of understanding washes over me. *Holy shit.* The attempt to provoke him into action may have worked a little too well.

Apparently, denial is not on the table.

"I—" Words fail me, and the muscles in my legs ache with how tightly I'm clinging to him.

His lips brush the line of my jaw, and I feel the rumble of his silent laugh as I let out a little whine to vent my discontent. "Now you know how I feel, princess. How does it feel to need someone so badly it drives you out of your mind?"

My heart somersaults in my chest and I clutch his forearms harder than ever, because the truth is, *I already knew.*

Damien leans back, his eyes on my dripping pussy as he permits himself a few slow, controlled thrusts, his jaw tightening as he watches himself fuck me. "You're so goddamn wet for me," he mutters. "I should send you to the party with this cunt painted in my cum."

If I wasn't already soaked, the idea of this would definitely do it.

"You can," I plead, my voice soft and ragged. "You can do whatever you want. Please, just, just..." My words fall away, turning to a muffled sob as he pulls out entirely, settling his hard cock against my pussy. The distance between our bodies is only a few inches, but it's enough that I can't do more than grind helplessly against his length, unable to get enough pressure on my clit to do more than tease myself.

"Later," Damien assures me, his lips curving in an infuriating little smirk as he watches me try to relieve the ache he left me with. "If you're good, tonight."

Disentangling himself from my legs, he steps back, and I sit up, snapping my thighs back together. "I hate you so much," I hiss, watching him tuck his cock away, apparently satisfied he's accomplished his mission.

Damien doesn't respond right away, stooping to retrieve

my fallen panties and shoes from the bathroom floor. He only meets my eyes as he sets them on the countertop beside me and, despite the furious indignation I'm feeling toward him at the moment, I find myself melting as he tilts my chin up and lowers his lips to mine one more time.

This kiss isn't like the last. It's soft, controlled... *sweet*.

When he draws away, moving toward the door, the smirk has turned to a grin. "You know, princess?" he muses, resting his hand on the doorknob. "I don't think you do."

Twenty-Six

Damien

"I've gotta admit, man. It was a surprise to hear you'd taken this job."

The personal protection industry in a tiny island nation with a low crime rate, admittedly, isn't large. There are only a handful of people who do, or have done, the same job as me, and Stelland's heavily intermingled elite class means we run into one another a lot.

Kingsley MacLeod—more commonly known as "Mac"—who has handled both personal and professional security for the Duke of Fairborne for years, is someone I've come across a lot. If I'd stopped to think about anything other than Blair Porter for the past month, I would have assumed he'd be here tonight, ensuring I'm adequately covering his boss's engagement party.

Unfortunately, foresight is apparently a bit beyond me presently, and my office, which I'd once thought an excessively large space for just myself, is starting to feel crowded. Along with Mac, there are a handful of Porter's NPS—National Protective Service—officers, and a few other miscellaneous bodyguards and personnel milling around.

Leaning past Mac to turn on the last in a row of monitors, I offer my colleague a noncommittal grunt. "Needed a change."

To accommodate the great number of guests who will soon be arriving at Thornhurst, I've spent the better part of the past week setting up a temporary system of security cameras throughout the downstairs of the house. The familiar rooms are now displayed on the ten monitors set up before me, each of them alternating between differently angled views of the room to which it's been assigned.

Humming in acknowledgement of my lie, Mac's lips curve in a thoughtful frown as he leans in, studying a view of the downstairs back hallway, where a server is hurrying over the plush runner, laden with a tray of champagne flutes.

"Heard you had some trouble here a few weeks back. A break-in?"

I bristle, instantly annoyed that word of the incident had made it so far. "Their system was about two decades out of date. It's been a process, getting things properly shored up."

Mac holds up both hands. "Hey, I'm not saying it was your fault, Mallory. Porter is a piece of work; you've probably had shit coming at you daily."

"It's harder when you aren't kept informed," I admit quietly, casting him a dark, significant look. While I ordinarily wouldn't divulge issues with an employer to a colleague, my tolerance for Lord Porter—which was already rapidly waning —took a sharp dive toward pure loathing after learning about Blair's learning disability.

Having his NPS officers go over my head to coordinate with the police about the break-in, while leaving the man on the ground in the dark, raises serious red flags. *Something* is going on, and it's becoming increasingly difficult to tolerate being treated like a fucking security guard.

Mac's unsurprised expression only serves to intensify my suspicions.

The office is busy, with members of Porter's NPS team coming and going, but nobody is paying attention as Mac edges closer to me, lowering his voice. "As a friend, I'd advise you to *unmake* this little career change, if at all possible."

"Yeah?" I question. "Why's that?"

Mac goes quiet, and I get the sense he's trying to decide whether I can still be trusted, given my new employment status. I glance over, offering him a weary smile. "It's a job, Mac. Just a job. My contract is up the day after the election."

It's mostly the truth, but lately, I've felt myself becoming increasingly invested in the situation. While it's obvious I'll never get the transparency necessary to adequately do my job, it's not the possibility of my professional reputation being tarnished by association that has me worried.

It's Blair.

How is it possible that in under two months, she's gone from my own personal nightmare to my primary concern?

Mac's lips flatten into a grim line, and he glances over his shoulder to ensure we won't be overheard. Apparently satisfied, he turns back, letting out a heavy sigh. "Between you and me, the duke isn't happy. He was getting pressure from his mother and grandmother to settle down, have a couple heirs, you know the deal with these people. Alba Porter is hot, knows how to handle herself in society, is young enough to have a few kids, and comes with a trust fund that will make the Fairbornes one of the richest families in the country. Then, her brother offered his firm a massive contract... well, needless to say, it was a no-brainer."

"But?" I raise my eyebrows expectantly.

Mac scoffs, shaking his head. *"But* you know as well as I do that skeletons don't stay in the closet when someone steps into the national spotlight. Men like Porter"—he inclines his head toward the main house, expression twisting—"think that having enough money, or enough power, makes them untouchable. Now, the skeletons are starting to come calling, and the duke isn't pleased to find himself stuck on a ship full of 'em."

I swallow, falling silent as I let this information sink in, reconciling it with what I already know. "Porter is being blackmailed."

Mac taps the side of his nose with his index finger. "Not confirming or denying anything. Just tread carefully, that's all I'm saying. The man's a crooked piece of shit with a whole lot of money." He can't say more, though, because three more members of the NPS are filing into the office, looking around for the man in charge.

I'm not at all happy that this dubious distinction belongs to me.

Edgy and restless, I answer their question, fighting the impulse to look back at the cameras all the while. Guests are flowing into the estate, and I'm itching to ensure Blair doesn't spend the evening flirting with the *single, wealthy, age-appropriate* men her mother undoubtedly invited specifically to meet her.

Going over there earlier today wasn't the plan, nor was the round of teasing that my balls still haven't recovered from. Even this morning, I was resolved to let her do what she wanted. It was for the best, after all. In no universe can I be the man who gives Blair everything she wants, and after all I've done, it would be selfish to stand in the way of her finding happiness.

As the party grew nearer, however, I felt my conviction weakening.

She might have been tired of forcing me to admit my attraction to her, but I... I was fucking exhausted, and it all came crumbling down when I glimpsed her heading downstairs in one of the security monitors.

There isn't a doubt in my mind that she knew exactly what she was doing with that fucking dress, but in that moment, I didn't care.

I still don't.

After I've helped—what feels like—every member of support staff do their jobs, the party is well underway, and I'm itching to return to the monitors.

"Give me a moment," I tell the latest swarm of NPS officers to enter the office, all of whom seem more keen on talking shop and sniffing out any useful connections I may have in the palace than doing their jobs.

Rubbing a twinged nerve in my neck, I edge through the crowded room, making my way back to the wall of screens. There are discreetly dressed guards on hand in the house, ready to step in if anyone wanders off somewhere they shouldn't, and three men already on surveillance duty.

I'm not here because I'm concerned about a drunk head of state wandering into Lady Porter's dressing room, however.

My eyes roam over the crowd, searching for a familiar head of light red hair, and feeling increasingly unsettled as my first scan comes up empty. Then, just as I'm beginning a second scan of the room, I see her.

Chest burning, I lean in, discreetly watching as she enters the ballroom behind Alba and James.

I hadn't noticed earlier, but she's done something with her hair that I haven't seen before. The strawberry strands have been twisted into two braids and knotted at the base of her neck, with only a few strands falling loose to frame her features. The dress she's wearing—the ignition point for this entire situation—looks as incredible as I remember. Diamond studs glitter on each of her ears, and as she reaches up to tuck a wayward curl behind one, the camera quality is good enough for me to notice she's had her nails painted gold to match.

A man in a dark suit moves past her, temporarily obscuring my view, and I don't think I breathe until she is in sight again.

The temporary cameras I set up may be discreet, but they're thorough. There is hardly a single inch of the house left uncovered, and my eyes jump from screen to screen, inhaling and exhaling in slow, shallow breaths that burn my lungs. There are other guests, ones I really should be more focused on, and yet their existence seems like a foggy, insubstantial reality compared to the one, wholly real thing in the center of the party's ecosystem.

Blair.

Amidst a room of well-dressed, important people, she seems to radiate a magnetic sort of energy.

As the night goes on, it doesn't matter how many times I attempt to look away, returning my focus to my job, I find my eyes drawn back to her again and again. Even as my chest feels like it might cave in on itself when I do.

It *hurts*. Looking at her actually physically *hurts*.

So why the fuck can't I stop?

Blood rushes in my ears as one of the trussed-up, blond-haired dipshits—obviously one of the men her mother thought to invite—approaches her, a glass of wine held loosely in one hand, grinning like he's already confident in the outcome of this exchange. I watch, barely breathing, as he leans in to speak in her ear.

He's young, maybe early thirties, and annoyingly not hideous.

Blair listens, but when the blond dipshit leans away, I see her step back. Her mouth moves, speaking words I wish I could hear. Then, she's turning, slipping back into the crowd.

Blond dipshit frowns, disappointed, and moves on.

My chest feels as though it might burst open as, for the first time tonight, I feel myself start to relax.

Twenty-Seven

Blair

I wait until everyone is asleep before sneaking out.

It isn't exactly the first time I've sought the refuge of *literally anywhere* that isn't occupied by my family, and I consider myself something of an expert at slipping away undetected.

Even before he'd set his sights on politics, my father was a wealthy, ambitious man. We always had some degree of security presence hovering in the periphery of my childhood, which tends to be a fairly significant obstacle for any underachieving teenage rebel to get past. I was creative, though, and learned the key to not arousing suspicion was to not appear suspicious.

"Good evening," I murmur, smiling wearily at the pair of NPS officers standing in the kitchen when I move through the room, already pushing my arms into my coat.

"Good evening, Miss Porter," the older of the two replies, nodding respectfully to me as I pass, and I hear them continuing with their conversation as I close the kitchen door behind myself.

Even if my gut tells me nobody is watching, my evasive maneuver isn't complete.

I walk off across the grounds, moving in the opposite direction of Damien's cottage, or any of the estate's outbuildings. My pace is leisurely, and I make a point to stare up at the full moon, which is clearly visible through the scattered clouds, amidst an impossible number of stars.

If anyone happened to be watching me, they'd suspect I'm headed for the path which winds along the cliff's edge, perhaps hoping to clear my head with a walk before bed. As far as most would know, there is nothing in this direction but wilderness. It's only from nearly two months of running through these woods that I know of a tiny trail which loops back around the edge of the grounds, ending only a hundred yards from Damien's cottage.

The night is so still that the waves crashing into the cliffs sound like a roar, and for once, I enjoy the reassuring predictability of it. Even the smell of this place steadies me now, and a part of me wishes I could hold onto it, wherever I go.

My memories will have to do, however, because something tells me when I leave Thornhurst, I will never, ever come back.

Damien's cottage is dark, with only a few lines of firelight escaping through the gaps in a few curtains. I'm careful to be quiet as I step up onto the porch and reach for the handle, not wanting to wake him if he's gone to sleep, unburdened by the same urgency which possessed me to walk through the cold to come here.

He must be expecting me, however, because the door is unlocked.

I inhale deeply as I step into the cozy, warm space, which is lit only by the fire burning away in the hearth and a single lamp beside the bed. Damien is nowhere in sight, but the bathroom door is closed, and the muscles in my belly tighten as I hear the sound of water running from beyond.

Suddenly unsteady, I drift toward the table, unbuttoning my coat. Even the material brushing my arms as I slip it off my shoulders makes my skin tingle, and no sooner have I laid it over the back of a chair than I'm drawing toward the closed door, acutely aware of the slow, deep rhythm of my own heartbeat.

I don't pause to consider whether I should be here or wonder whether he'll regret what happened earlier. Not when instinct—overwhelming, undeniable instinct—bellows it will be the opposite. The hinges on the old door groan softly as I open it and am hit at once by a wall of steam and the scent of Damien's soap. The shower curtain wrenches back.

He's naked.

Obviously, I knew he would be, but the air seems to vanish from my lungs as we stare at one another through the hazy, yellowish light. Water drips from the ends of his hair and runs down his body, caressing parts of him I've never had the chance to touch myself, and something inside me burns as I watch it.

Jealousy. Over *water*.

Damien doesn't speak or make any attempt to cover up, as, slowly, I close the door behind myself.

I don't say anything, either.

It's only been seconds, but already, steam is clinging to my skin, and my core body temperature is rising. I can barely breathe as, holding the wordless gaze of the naked man in front of me, I begin to remove my clothes.

Damien has gone unnaturally still since I entered the bathroom, but as my top hits the bathroom floor, I see his pulse leap and, lower, his cock begin to grow hard. It's a heady feeling to watch the effect I have on him grow stronger with each article of discarded clothing and every new piece of skin exposed.

Knowing very well what my intention was for tonight, I'd dressed carefully, and the quiet groan which punctuates the rhythmic rush of water makes my efforts more than worth it.

"Leave it," Damien hisses suddenly, as my thumbs loop beneath the waistband of the same thin white lingerie I'd worn for him in the department store, preparing to push the panties over my hips.

I nod slowly, not lowering my gaze from his. "The bra, too?" My fingers brush over the blue ribbon which lines the material.

Jaw tight, he inclines his head in the tiniest, jerkiest of nods.

It's not surprising to find my pussy is already wet with arousal when I step out of the jumble of fallen clothes, drawing toward him. Damien only moves when my foot finds the shower floor, shifting to the side so I can fit inside the tiny, enclosed space with him.

The sound of my breath catching is lost in the metallic rasp of him pulling the shower curtain shut behind me.

"You came," he mutters, his eyes on my body as the hot water washes over me, turning my flimsy undergarments transparent in a matter of seconds,

It's difficult to swallow my moan as he crowds me into the shower wall, his massive hands coming to hold the curve of my waist. "I was careful," I promise, running my hands from his chest to cradle his face. "Nobody saw."

A low grunt meets my words, and I get the sense that he wouldn't care, even if *everyone* saw.

"What about what I can see?" he asks as he drags his palms over my wet skin to my breasts, cupping them through the sodden material. A peek down confirms that what he can see is everything, and desire twists low in my core at the sight of his large, rough hands squeezing me greedily.

My tongue darts out to wet my lips. "I can leave, if you'd rather not." The offer is like ash on my tongue, and though I'm teasing him, a tiny part of me braces for him to agree. I would go, of course I would go, but he doesn't let me worry for long.

A low, disbelieving laugh rumbles in his chest, and I whimper as he backs me more securely against the wall, his rigid cock pressing—hot and urgent—against the softness of my belly. "I can't think of anything I'd rather be looking at, princess."

And before I can respond to that or do more than recognize the way my heart expands at his words, Damien is lowering his lips to mine, and it isn't possible to think of anything else. Nobody has ever kissed me the way he does now, slow and savoring, as though he wants to make it last.

He's patient, controlled, but there's something else simmering beneath the surface, something that's mirrored inside me, but I still can't name. It surges through my veins as large, callused hands press flat to my back, one over the other, and drag me closer as our kisses become more urgent.

My bra falls away, and I'm so turned on that even the friction of his chest hair against my heavy, tender breasts makes me gasp. The sound seems unnaturally loud over the ringing in my ears and the heavy drum of water over us both, but it's nothing compared to Damien's throaty noise of approval.

My hands fall to his shoulders as he stoops, dragging my panties down until they fall with a wet slap to the shower floor. I look down, watching as he presses his lips to my mound, the curve of my thigh, the place below my belly button, leaving worshipful kisses every place he encounters.

His nose brushes the sensitive skin along the jutting curve of my pelvic bone, and my knees might have collapsed if he hadn't wrapped his hands around the back of them at that exact moment. My belly swoops as he stands, taking me with him.

I'm lifted right off my feet, and my back hits the cool shower wall, my body pinned open like a butterfly by this giant, confusing, perfect man between my legs.

The water, the tile, his skin against mine, and the way my body responds to it... It's sensation overload, bordering on too much, but as Damien reclaims my lips with a deep, satisfied groan, all I want is more.

I groan, too, my arms looping back around his neck to hold him so close that even the water can't find a way between our bodies. His shaft is pressed into my slick seam, and as we kiss, he rocks against me, coating himself in my arousal, which is slicker and more lasting than the shower pouring over us.

It's intoxicating to get so lost in someone that you forget the outside world even exists. Years and years of running from myself, my family, and the expectations that I could never quite meet... None of it ever made it fade quite as much as it does now.

Oh god, I'm falling for him.

I'm *really* falling for him.

That's bad. *So, so bad.*

The realization sends a rush of hot panic through me, but it still isn't enough to end this. Especially not as Damien shifts my weight, angling my body back just a little, and allowing himself room to press the crown of his cock to my slick core.

Our kisses falter, but we stay close, lips brushing as he breaches my entrance, and the sound of our ragged breathing fills the tiny space. Unlike the first time we did this, he goes slowly, easing his way deeper with each pump of his hips. He doesn't stop until his hips are pressed to mine, and I'm fully impaled on him, my inner muscles struggling to adjust.

Fuck, he's *everywhere.*

I whimper, squirming, and Damien's hands move from the backs of my thighs to my ass, his fingers digging into my flesh, hard and unapologetic. It isn't punishing, though. It's desperate.

"That's it," he hisses against my lips when at last I manage to convince my body to relax. "You like being stuffed full, don't you?"

His words send molten heat to pool in my core, and I let out a short, breathless laugh, my legs tightening around his waist. "Fuck you."

Damien nips at my bottom lip. "Are you trying to provoke me, princess? Need I remind you of your current position?" My response never comes, the words turning to a pained cry as he pulls out and drives back into my unguarded sex, giving me a sharp, warning thrust.

Maybe I was trying to provoke him. A little.

As my head swims, almost drunk on lust, I decide that provoking him a little more might be a good use for my *current position*.

"Is that supposed to scare me?" I ask breathlessly, kissing the corner of his mouth, as I run my hands over his broad shoulders, savoring the way my touch make the muscles bunch and tighten. "Consider your mission unsuccessful. Better luck next time."

I bite my lip to stop myself from crying out. "Was that adequate?" Damien murmurs, feigning concern as his fingers dig into my ass. "Or should I try again?"

This time, I can't hold back my moan as he bottoms out, the plush head of his cock pressing snugly against the very deepest part of me. "Yes," I plead, forgetting the games. "Again, *again*."

He doesn't give it to me, though. Instead, smirking, Damien leans back, reaching out to shut off the water, which I now realize has gotten cooler since I got in here with him.

Dignity forgotten, I whine in protest as he pulls out, lowering me back onto the weight of my own shaky legs.

My heart lurches when he lowers his head to kiss the damp skin of my cheek. "Don't pout, you little brat. You'll get what you want."

I'd better.

Regardless of this reassurance, I find myself pouting anyway, as he pulls back the shower curtain and leans out into the steamy bathroom, reaching for the stack of clean towels resting on a shelf. His fathomless gaze meets mine as he returns to hand me one.

"Bold of you to assume you know what I want," I tell him petulantly as I wrap the terrycloth material around my middle, hiding my body from view.

Unconcerned, Damien scoffs, lifting the towel to his hair. I lean back against the shower wall, trying not to let my eyes linger on the curve of his biceps, or drop to his cock, hanging heavily in the space between us, still streaked with milky lines of my arousal.

When he lowers his hands, his hair is tousled but still darker than usual. He holds my gaze as he steps over the lip of the shower and lifts his chin toward the door. "Get in my bed, princess."

The words seem to have a direct line to my pussy, making my clit throb and my inner walls contract, mourning the fullness which had stretched them only moments ago. Letting out a lungful of air, I do as he says, feeling the weight of his eyes on my back as I open the door, stepping out into the dimly lit cottage.

Even with the fire blazing in the hearth, the air is cooler out here, making me shiver as I draw toward Damien's neatly made bed. Pretending I don't notice him watching, I keep my movements unhurried and casual, drying myself with a lot of unnecessary bending over.

If he's determined to torture me, I'm happy to torture him right back.

Finally, when my pussy is so wet I'm nearly dripping down my thighs, and I think I might burst from how badly I need him, Damien seems to reach his breaking point, too.

Large, strong male hands appear on my waist, dragging me back into his warm chest with a grumbled, "*Fucking tease.*"

There's nothing even a little bit funny about the situation, but I find myself giggling, my cheeks aching from the size of my smile as he marches us forward. Pushing me playfully, I sprawl on the mattress, rolling over in time to see he is smiling, too, his dimples so big that they make my heart lurch, before he comes down on top of me.

My hands find his face, pulling his lips down to meet mine.

He comes without resistance, and a low groan rumbles in his chest as I wiggle beneath him, spreading my legs to give him enough space to settle between them. Our skin, still a little damp from the shower, sticks together when I reach down to wrap my fingers around his cock. The angle is awkward and complicated by Damien's apparent reluctance to allow any space between our bodies. I manage to stroke him, though, and his shaft twitches under my hand, a bead of precum smearing on my inner wrist.

I like the feeling of it so much that I think of tracing the shape and having it tattooed there.

He doesn't let me play for long.

Though I don't remember closing them, my eyelids flutter open as Damien pushes up onto one forearm, allowing himself enough space to reach down and replace the hand I have on his cock with his own. Firelight glints off our skin, and I stare in rapt fascination as he lines himself up with my entrance.

I watch as he pushes in, my body yielding to his.

See how my legs leap higher on his hips and my back curves off the mattress beneath me, as though his thick cock entering me is seismic activity which carries through my whole body.

See the way his abdominal muscles tighten, and his chest heaves, overcome by how good I'm making him feel.

See my arousal coating his shaft as he pulls out and hear him groan as he sees it, too.

And, as he rolls his hips, entering me in a second deep pulse, that is the last thing I see.

My eyes squeeze shut as, disoriented, I realize I'm coming. It makes no sense. Even as I gasp and moan, heels digging into his ass and thighs trembling against his hips, my mind can't quite comprehend this is happening.

How could I... we've barely even begun?

"Fuck, *fuck*—" Damien curses, and even through my muddled, pleasure-drunk mind, I feel him moving between my legs, making it last for me as long as he can.

My eyelids flutter open, and I tilt my chin up, desperate for his lips on mine. He doesn't hesitate to give me what I want, ducking down to kiss me with a rough noise of pleasure.

"That was the hottest thing I've ever seen," he growls against my lips, "Were you that worked up?"

"Yes," I whisper, so far past pretense as my nails dig into the planes of his broad, muscular back. "I've been wet for you all night."

Damien groans, setting a deep, rolling pace between my thighs, still not allowing even an inch of space between us. "You're driving me out of my mind."

Yeah, I know the feeling.

We kiss again, and I feel the tremor run through his body as I clench my inner walls over his length, making myself tighter for him. There is nothing especially kinky or hot about what we're doing, missionary in the semi-darkness hardly qualifies as exciting—*but it is*. I'm not sure I've ever felt so present, so close to another person during sex, that even his lips brushing my neck is downright erotic.

I come again, my body convulsing and my cries splitting the air in the quiet cottage, as Damien's thrusts grow more frantic.

"Yes," he snarls his approval, one hand tightening in my hair to keep me close. "Christ, I love the way you come."

Lifting my hips higher on his abdomen, his tip hits a deeper place inside me, and I feel myself getting wetter at the possibility of him finishing inside me again. I think of begging for it.

Instead, my tongue darts out, teasing the seam of his lips, and Damien doesn't hesitate to give me what I want. He kisses me so deeply it makes my heart twist, as between my legs, his thrusts finally falter.

Heat blooms low in my belly as he shoves himself as deep as he can, and comes, panting against my lips. I hold him through it, my heels digging into his ass and my hands spread on his back, kissing him until he can kiss me in return.

At last, when Damien finally regains the ability to lift his head to look at me properly, his eyes meet mine and something expands in my chest.

This time, there is no going back.

LORD PORTER'S IMAGE PROBLEM ISN'T GOING AWAY

PORTER FAMILY'S TONE-DEAF CELEBRATION RAISES CONCERNS.

With poll numbers continuing to slide and critics questioning whether his "for the people" message still connects, the Porter campaign needed a win. Last night's engagement party for his daughter, Alba, and James, the Duke of Fairborne, could have helped to steady the ship.

Instead, it further underlined the problem.

The timing alone raised eyebrows. The celebration was held on the three-year anniversary of the tragic plane crash, which claimed the lives of King Arthur and Queen Lillian, who perished alongside their two teenage sons. For many, the date remains one of quiet remembrance—and a somber marker in the national calendar.

To host a glittering engagement party on that anniversary struck some observers as, at best, tone-deaf, and at worst, deeply insensitive. Flags around Stelland flew at half-staff, while online tributes to the late royal family trended throughout the day. By nightfall, images of champagne towers and chandelier-lit ballrooms were competing with memorial posts.

Hosted at the Porter family's ancestral home, Thornhurst

Estate, the event was polished, exclusive, and unmistakably blue-blooded. Senior MPs, donors, aristocrats, and media figures filed inside the glittering mansion, greeted by Lord and Lady Porter themselves.

Power, prestige, and glamour were in high supply. Relatability… less so.

This event, landing only a month after the Porter family's joint appearance at Wyngate Women's Shelter—a visit widely described by many voters as *an obvious PR stunt*—and set on the anniversary of a national tragedy, only served to widen the gap with voters.

At a moment when many citizens of Stelland are skeptical of elites playing dress-up as populists, a formal engagement party at an ancestral estate—following a shelter visit which felt more performative than sincere—raises uncomfortable questions about the Porter campaign:

Is Lord Albert truly a prime minister "for the people"?

Twenty-Eight

Damien

When I step into Lord Porter's study the afternoon following Alba and James' engagement party, I find the man reading a news article on his tablet. He's frowning, and when he glances up to find me in the doorway, the deep, worried lines in his forehead don't ease.

If what Mac told me is accurate, the stress of the man's choices seems to be taking its toll.

"Ah, Mallory. You requested a meeting?" The Lord's words of welcome are edged with exasperation, as if he can't quite believe I—the man he hired to ensure the security of his family's ancestral home and supervise his adult daughter—might have something to discuss with him.

"Yes," I confirm, and sit down in one of the high-backed armchairs stationed in front of his desk, not waiting for his invitation. "This won't take long. I wanted to touch base about some of the police reports I requested from your team. Regarding the break-in."

Lord Porter sets down his tablet, flipping the case closed. "What about them?"

It's an effort to conceal my irritation. "I have reached out to your office multiple times to get them and the files on the threats directed toward Blair, but have been met with a lot of... resistance." I pause, studying him. "It's vital I have access to all the information regarding any ongoing security concerns, in order for me to do my job correctly."

Before he can respond, there's a quiet knock on the door behind me, and Lord Porter looks up.

"Oh, I'm so sorry to interrupt, sir," comes a woman's bright, professional voice. "You have a conference call with Cunningham and Howard in five minutes."

The man across from me inclines his head in acknowledgement. "I'll be on, this won't take long." The door closes again, and he lowers his gaze to me. "Regarding the break-in reports, my team evaluated and determined there was nothing of significance to be found in them. Likely a local, looking to make some quick cash."

Christ, I hate this man. The scenario he's just presented doesn't strike me as even remotely plausible, and it's an insult to my intelligence that he thinks I'd believe it. Criminals hoping for some quick cash would have taken the silver candlestick holders off the dining table or the jewelry that was sitting out in Blair's bedroom—*not old account records from His Lordship's office.*

After the break-in, I'd double and triple-checked the valuables in the house, and to this day, I can't find evidence of the intruders taking anything other than some paperwork.

Swallowing the sour taste which has flooded my tongue as this conversation progresses, I push forward. "And the threats against Blair?"

Porter heaves a heavy sigh. "They've faded away, just as we expected. While I appreciate your *thoroughness*, unless you have reason to believe my daughter is in any imminent danger, I don't see how it would do any good to go poking around and stir it all back up. Now, if there isn't anything else." He gestures to the phone on his desk. "You'll have to excuse me."

I don't move.

"It's difficult to determine whether or not your daughter is in any imminent danger when I haven't been given the luxury of seeing the entire picture."

There's a steely glint in Porter's eyes as he leans forward in his seat, tapping his pen against the posh leather desk mat. "I'll say it again, Mallory. *My team has investigated*. While I appreciate there may be an element of professional pride at play here, I think it is a good time to remind you of why you were hired. It was not to conduct investigations, but to secure the estate, and make sure my daughter doesn't irreparably damage her reputation for a second time."

Chest burning, I force myself to nod.

Whatever suspicions I had about this man's priorities before this conversation took place have only been confirmed, and the blackmail Mac alluded to the other night is looking more like fact than fiction.

Someone has *something* on this asshole, and he isn't going to risk telling me a damn thing. Even if the price is compromised security.

As I get to my feet, preparing to leave, however, Porter speaks again.

"You know, after we had our meeting at the club, it occurred to me that we'd met before. Years ago."

I swallow, trying to banish the sudden sound of ringing in my ears, which deafens all but the voice of the man before me. "Did we?"

Porter's answering smile is dangerous. "Yes. You probably wouldn't remember it, you couldn't have been older than twelve or thirteen at the time."

It takes everything I have not to react, as his words raise a cold sweat over my palms and up the back of my neck. "Maybe a picture of you back then would help jog my memory."

The lord lets out a cold laugh. "Perhaps. Lydia and I had only just gotten engaged, and we were visiting with her godmother, Princess Araminta. I took a wrong turn on the way to the restroom and happened to spot three boys sitting together in the garden." His head tilts slightly to the side, studying me. "At first glance, I thought it was Prince Arthur. I remember thinking to myself how nice it was to see three brothers so close. It certainly wasn't the sort of relationship I shared with my own siblings."

Fuck. *Fuck*.

My resemblance to Ben and Leo is, and has always been, problematic. For years, I'd managed to hide behind the anonymity brought by my uniform. Now that I've taken it off, however, my shared likeness with two members of the most famous family in the country is much more dangerous than ever before.

Porter seems to sense my discomfort. The man is a shark, and even the hint of blood in the water has him zeroing in on my largest vulnerability. He leans forward, lacing his fingers together atop the leather desk mat. "It *wasn't* Prince Arthur, though, was it?"

I let out a determinately steady breath, trying and failing to calm my racing pulse. "I wouldn't know."

"Wouldn't you?" he hums. "King Fabian did quite a good job of covering up his *indiscretions*, but even so. There were rumors back then."

Of course, I would be intimately acquainted with the *rumors* which must have been circulated *back then*. Pieces of my life's story, whispered back and forth amongst gleeful aristocrats, fodder for their social standing. They ring in my ears as I stare at Porter, hardly able to believe I've found myself in this situation, trapped by my identity, yet again.

"Have you heard? People are saying the king has been very occupied with a cocktail waitress who works in his club."

"I was told from the most reliable of sources that the king's little mistress had a child. I do hope the man insisted on a test before getting her situated."

"My brother's butler started off as a footman at the palace. Did you know the king keeps his proper family for the cameras, but hides another in the North Country?"

"Rumor has it that the king's mistress died. No clue how it happened. Apparently, he's sent the boy to live with Araminta."

My hands tighten reflexively on the back of the chair, my fingers aching with how hard they're digging into the upholstery. "You don't know anything about me."

Porter, apparently satisfied he's arranged things to his benefit, lifts a shoulder arrogantly. "I know more about you than you believe you know about me, Mallory. Remember that the next time you think of questioning my judgement." Atop his desk, his phone lights up. He reaches for it, still looking at me. "Now, run along and do what I pay you for."

Chest burning and reeling with furious disbelief, I have no choice but to comply.

There are people, staffers, and the Porter's house staff—brought with them from Wyngate—milling around the downstairs as I move through the familiar halls, replaying the conversation I just had on a loop, feeling worse with each successive recollection.

After being cautious about my identity for years, all I've done to protect myself, and the most separate from my family that I have ever been, *still*, I've found myself backed into a corner.

Will I ever be free of this? *Ever*? Or am I doomed to have

the choices of two people, now long dead, tear through my life like a slow-moving bullet?

It seems likely.

My very existence is a weapon to be used against me, to rob me of my privacy and keep me beholden to the same fucking people I wanted to escape from.

Porter knew who I was the first day we met.

Hell, I wouldn't be surprised if he wanted me for this job because of who I am. The man is a spider, spinning a web of blackmail, secrets, and lies around himself, and I've somehow become another fucking insect trapped and at his mercy.

My lungs burn from the shallow, insubstantial breaths I've been taking, and the edges of my vision swim as I burst through the kitchen door. The biting ocean wind hits me like a physical blow, and I double over, bracing my hands on my knees and sucking in big, greedy gulps of oxygen.

I want to leave.

I want to pack my shit, get in the car, and drive somewhere. Anywhere. The middle of the fucking Sahara sounds preferable to this godforsaken place. When I think of the reasons I can't, though, it isn't Araminta, or Lord Porter, or my paycheck that comes to mind.

"Damien?" I start, whipping around to face the woman stepping out of the kitchen door behind me, wrapped in a thick knit sweater, her features rapt with concern. "Is everything okay? You walked right past me..."

Christ, I hadn't even noticed.

Raking my hand through my hair, I glance toward the kitchen window, which we're in full view of. Anyone could see us talking out here, and at this point, I don't trust myself to appear unaffected by her presence.

"I'm fine." My tone is short, clipped, and the tiny flicker of hurt in Blair's face has me shaking myself. "I'm sorry. You didn't do anything. I—" I cast around, searching for a way to describe what I'm feeling, as if there is a word in existence which might come close to describing *this*.

Blair edges closer, but remains a respectable distance from me, her lips turned down. "Do you want to talk about it?"

I don't respond right away, looking at her standing out here in the cold, her beautiful face pinched with worry *for me*. Care I'm not sure I deserve but still crave. Care that softens the storm of turmoil churning inside me, the paranoia, the anger... all of it.

I've battled with Blair Porter nearly every day of our relationship. From the very start, she has possessed the unique ability to make me do, say, and think things I didn't believe myself capable of. She frustrates me, and exhausts me, and may send me to an early grave out of sheer exasperation.

Yet, before I'd even realized it was happening, she found her way under my skin, into my blood, and through my fucking heart.

Somehow, this woman I was so sure I hated has become the most immovable, grounding part of my life.

Warmth spreads through me as, lost for words, I step toward her. "Come here," I mumble as I approach, reaching out to pull her into my chest the moment I'm close enough.

Blair comes willingly, wrapping her arms around my waist and hugging me back, right here in the back parking lot. Anyone could see, and a single word of it to the Porters could cost me my job.

I don't care.

Closing my eyes, I kiss her temple, breathing in the familiar scent of apples, honey, and the wind which lingers in her hair. Blair's arms tighten around me, and we stand there for a very long time, holding each other.

"They're all leaving tomorrow," she reminds me when we

finally part, gazing up at me through those wide, moss-colored eyes. "We'll be alone again."

I brush my thumb over the apple of her cheek, unable to bring myself to let her go quite yet. "Good."

Twenty-Nine

Being fucked by Damien Mallory is the closest I've ever come to a religious experience.

Not because of how much he makes me come, or the number of—admittedly creative—ways he positions my body, or how good it all feels.

It's the way his hands dig into my flesh, holding me so tightly it's like he isn't entirely in control of himself.

It's the way he looks at me, as though the sight of me, naked and squirming beneath him with my thighs spread wide and his name on my lips, is the most erotic thing he's seen in his life.

It's the way he could happily spend hours with his head between my thighs, ignoring his own needs in favor of fulfilling mine.

Following the night I snuck out of the house and into the shower with him, part of me was still bracing for a regression to *the before times*, with lots of icy silences and spiteful commentary. Even if it *felt* different, I couldn't quite trust that

Damien wouldn't get angry at himself for giving in, and that we'd be back to suffering through another few weeks of sexual tension before he worked on pulling his head out of his ass again.

That wasn't the case. Like, *at all*. If anything, it seems like the lingering frustration needs to be worked out, and once would never be enough.

So, to commemorate the end of the bang-blockade, the departure of my insufferable family members, and no more psychological warfare in Thornhurst, we have been having sex. *A lot* of sex.

"Fuck, princess. You're so goddamn wet for me."

In response to Damien's praise, a broken cry falls from between my parted lips, and my pussy—which was dripping to begin with—gets wetter.

I'm kneeling on the bench in the poolroom, holding on to the back for dear life as Damien fucks me in rapid, punishing thrusts from behind. One hand is gripping my hip, aiding him in dragging me back and forth, as the other paws roughly at my bouncing tits.

The slap of skin-on-skin echoes off the stone ceiling, and his deep groan of approval is louder than I've ever heard it. The sound of it turns me on so much and is almost certainly responsible for yet another wave of fresh arousal over his shaft.

Finding my voice, I let out a breathy laugh and allow my head to drop back, arching my ass higher for him. "Are you sure it isn't from the pool?" We'd been swimming before he finally lost patience with me "accidentally" pressing my ass against his crotch at every possible opportunity and hauled me out of the water to "teach me a lesson."

Oh no.

Not a lesson.

Darn.

Damien growls and pinches my nipple, tugging on it

hard enough to make me squeal. "Such a fucking brat." Abandoning my nipples, his hand drops to the space between my thighs and presses two fingers to my clit immediately, circling the slick bud with just the right amount of pressure.

"Shit," I half-laugh, half-moan, "that's perfect. Oh god, please don't stop."

His free arm loops around my torso, and I gasp as I find myself being hauled up until my back is pressed flush to his chest. I can't hold on to the bench like this or anchor myself to anything other than him. Twin moans echo off the stone ceiling as I clutch his arm with one hand, while the other finds its way to his neck

"You don't want me to stop?" Damien hisses directly in my ear, his fingers slowing threateningly. "Tell me who made this bratty cunt so fucking wet."

Zero hesitation is required.

"You," I cry, grinding into his touch now, "you make me wet."

"Yes, princess, I do." He rewards me with more pressure on my clit, still driving his cock into my body in brief, punishing thrusts. "Christ, you drive me crazy. I can't even do my goddamn job. All I can think about is getting you under me again, getting inside you, getting my cum as deep as I can —" He breaks off with a groan, and if he wasn't holding me up, I would have collapsed.

"Yes, yes, yes," I hear myself chanting, hiccupping in pleasure as heat spreads outward from my tender, hard-used pussy.

The man behind me groans as my inner walls clamp down on his length, instinctively trying to keep him inside me as my body convulses, falling over the edge into an orgasm that makes lights burst behind my eyelids.

My head has fallen back, and Damien's hand tangles in my damp hair, dragging me around so he can meet my parted lips in a hungry, searching kiss. I'm still trembling and panting as he devours me, and the rhythm of his thrusts begins to falter.

He isn't ready for this to be over, though.

I cry out as he pulls out without warning, leaving me empty. Before I can think to look around at him, though, his hands are on my waist, turning me. I find myself on my butt, blinking up at the tight-jawed man towering over me. His cock is long and veiny, the ruddy skin gleaming with my cum, and I moan at the sight of it.

As I reach for him, though, Damien shakes his head curtly, and I realize he's guiding me to lean further back. "Push your tits together," he snarls, using the same furious tone he did when we threw mud at each other that day in the woods.

God, how much of our behavior back then was sexual frustration without us even realizing?

"Like this?" I breathe, gathering my tits together as Damien follows me onto the bench, bracketing my torso with his knees, and he grips the base of his dick, guiding it through the tight space between my breasts. *Fucking them.*

Oh my god. Why is this so hot?

I can't do more than watch, dizzy with lust as he rolls his hips into me, using the wetness he forced me to admit I made for him as lube.

"You have no idea how many times I've thought about doing this," Damien mutters, and when I finally manage to look at his face, I see the whole of his focus is on the glide of his shaft through the tight space. "Every time I looked over at you running and saw these goddamn tits—" He breaks off, and the tendons in his neck strain as he lifts his hands to cover mine, pushing them in harder than ever. "Fuck—fuck!"

The curse echoes through the room around as, with a few more shallow, desperate thrusts, he stills.

A whimper escapes from between my lips as I feel the first hot lash of his release against my skin, and I'm panting when he finally relaxes the pressure of his hands on mine, getting back to his feet.

My breath catches as I let my hands fall too and get my first view of his cum smeared over the globes of my breasts and dripping through the space between them. Dazed, I drag my index finger through the thickest section, and my heart is beating wildly as I lift my gaze to meet his. Slowly, I dip the finger between my lips, sucking his cum off the tip.

Damien's pupils dilate.

Something heady settles over us as he leans over me, bracing one hand on the back of the bench and lifting the other to the hollow between my breasts. Neither of us says a word, and our labored breathing slows as Damien gathers a thick bead of release on the pad of his thumb, dragging it over each of my pebbled nipples in turn.

This isn't the result of dumb lust; it's darker, more proprietary, and the muscles in my belly tighten as he pauses to take more. This time, he stares directly into my eyes, cataloguing my reaction as he brings the digit to my oversensitive clit and gives it the same treatment.

"That's it," he mutters approvingly. "Do you want some inside you, too?"

Damien chuckles quietly as, instantly, my thighs spring wider apart. I must look a little embarrassed, because he leans in, kissing the corner of my mouth and murmuring the words, "*Good girl.*"

My breath hitches, and I'm incapable of looking anywhere other than at his face as Damien carefully gathers up the last creamy drops of cum, his attention focused on the task at hand. Heat floods my lower abdomen as he eases two fingers inside me, carefully curving them to stroke my G-spot.

Hoooly shit.

Another soft kiss on my cheek, and he eases his fingers free, straightening up at last.

"Well, aren't you a sight for sore eyes," he rumbles approvingly, and the accompanying dimple/smirk combination does *not* help my state of mind. Then—because he's still kind of a turd—Damien reaches out, offering me his hand. "Come on. We didn't finish our laps."

"That wasn't enough exercise for you?" I ask, rolling my eyes, as I allow him to pull me to my feet.

Grinning now, he draws backward toward the pool, not releasing his hold on my hand. We are both naked and ignore the pile of abandoned, sodden swimsuits resting on the floor beside the bench. Damien jumps off the edge into the water, and I have little choice but to stumble after him, colliding with his body beneath the surface.

It's just deep enough for my toes to brush the bottom, but my attempt to push off toward the shallows is thwarted. Tall enough that he can stand, Damien pulls me into his chest, and I bite back a smile, allowing my legs to wind around his waist.

The words tattooed on his pectoral draw my attention, and thoughtfully, I run my fingers over the slanting script. It's faded with age, and the edges are a little blurred, which makes it even more difficult for me to read. Now, half covered by water in the shadowy pool, it's next to impossible.

"What does this mean?" I ask quietly, because I've seen it enough to be pretty sure the words aren't even in English.

"It's Latin," he tells me. "It means *duty before all else.*"

I trace the ink, silently mouthing the words. *Duty before all else.* The phrase is vaguely familiar, but I can't quite place it. "Is it from your Navy days?" I ask but receive only a lazy hum in confirmation.

Water laps quietly against the wall of the pool as he gathers me closer. We kiss, and in my heart, I know the water is only partially responsible for my feeling of buoyancy.

"That was incredibly hot, by the way," Damien murmurs when we part, his voice gravelly and warm.

I know what he's referring to, and I have to agree. "Can I ask you something?" I pose, voicing another of the many questions that's been on my mind the past few weeks. "Have you ever had sex like this before? It's okay if you have. I'm just... curious."

Damien's smile turns to a thoughtful frown, but he doesn't seem to need clarification on what sex I'm referring to.

To me, it's different, but it's hard not to be a little embarrassed by the question. I'm younger than him and less experienced. Maybe I've been having sex with the wrong people, or he is just particularly good at it. Either way, I don't want to read into things any more than I already have if, to him, this uncontrollable need is totally normal.

Under the water, Damien's fingers ghost up and down my spine, leaving goosebumps in their wake. "No," he admits at last. "I haven't had sex like this with anyone but you." My heart flips, then flips again, as the dimples make a sudden reappearance. "Try not to look too pleased with yourself, princess."

I hum, enjoying the way his skin feels against mine beneath the water. "Would it help to know this is new for me, too?"

"It would help a lot, actually," Damien admits quietly, and my breath hitches as his hand finds its way to the back of my neck, guiding my lips to his.

My eyes fall closed, and it's like my entire awareness is centered on our slow, sensual kiss. It goes on and on, without ever growing more heated.

There is a moment when we part, and as my eyes flutter open to meet his, it's in time to see Damien's lips stretch into a slow smile. Then, he draws us back together all over again, brushing his fingers over the column of my neck, and I swear I feel it all the way in my toes.

This isn't lust—It's *so, so* much better.

When it ends, neither of us acknowledges the undercurrent of something deeper which just passed between us, but Damien still doesn't let me float away. "Just think," he muses, "only a month ago, you were dropping mud down my pants."

Laughter bursts out of me, ringing off the walls and ceiling, as he allows us to drift apart at last.

His eyes glint as, still grinning, Damien lifts his chin toward the far end of the pool. "Now, finish your laps, princess."

THIRTY

DAMIEN

Though my employment contract stipulates I'm off duty on the weekends, I have never actually taken advantage of that time.

After all, what would I do?

Make the three-hour drive to Wyngate? Visit the friends I haven't kept up with? Spend time with the brothers whom I've pushed away? Free time was dangerous; it left too much time for thinking, and being left alone with my thoughts was the last thing I wanted.

With the break-in, the upgrades being completed, and those disgusting letters sent to Blair after the pictures were published, I told myself I should stay close. Then, as our relationship drifted from obsession to something else entirely, I've felt disinclined to leave for very different reasons.

This morning, however, when Blair cheerfully informed me Summer would arrive soon—all but sprinting out the cottage door to go meet her—I found myself unexpectedly confronted with an entire Saturday to myself.

The worst of Thornhurst's security concerns have been addressed. I don't *need* to stay on the property every minute of every day.

Without a real plan, I paused only to send Blair a voice memo with a heads-up that I was leaving, and double—then triple—checking all the sensors and alarms were online, before I got into my seldom-used personal car, and left.

It wasn't until I was halfway to Port Briar that I realized what my intention was. Then, when I did, I was tempted to turn around and return safely to my pattern of avoidance. I didn't, though. Something kept me moving forward, even as the knot of guilt and regret inside me pulled tighter and tighter with every mile I drove.

My brother's aging, neo-Gothic townhouse is situated on the corner of a quiet, tree-lined street, only a few blocks from Orwick University and insulated from Port Briar's hectic, downtown district. I pause when I get out of my car, staring across the quiet lane at the familiar structure, struck by a rush of memories.

The stone facade, crawling ivy, and iron handrails leading up to the glossy black door look exactly as they did when Ben and Leo lived here together during university.

My younger brothers coexisted very comfortably, united in their complete disinterest in socializing or leaving the house for anything other than class. They'd been annoyingly reluctant to get into much trouble, but I was determined they leave with *a few* memories and succeeded in necessitating the Palace Press Corp's involvement on at least two occasions.

Those few years we'd all lived in Port Briar were brief, but happy.

I'd been the first to leave, heading north to my first officer assignment, and eager to truly step out from the shadow of the Ashwell family for the first time in my life. Ben followed me the year after, recalled to Wyngate and to his duties as a working royal.

Leo stayed.

Port Briar might have been a stopover for Ben and me, but our youngest brother had found his home. He collected degrees in art history, chemistry, and conservation before accepting a full-time faculty position at the university and settling down for a quiet life in academia.

He never left the townhouse.

He never married or had a significant romantic relationship, as far as I'm aware.

He walks the same path, takes the same lunch, and exists mainly within the same four-block radius as he has for decades.

It might seem grim to some, but Leo disentangled himself from the Ashwell family in a way Ben or I never have. He found a place where he can excel, and, of us three, I believe he's the most free.

The distance between us, I could almost stand, but since Leo's unannounced visit to Thornhurst... I hate how we left things. In the back of my mind, I've begun to accept the only true way out of this, but coming clean and telling my brothers everything—even if it means they hate me for it—isn't something I'm ready to do.

So, why am I here?

Shaking myself, I shove my keys into my back pocket and cross the road, jogging up the stone steps to ring the bell before I can convince myself not to.

There's a good chance he isn't even at home. Leo's obsession with his work certainly isn't limited to business hours, and after a moment passes, with no signs of life within the house, I've accepted this is the case. I'm just on the point of turning back toward my car—feeling foolish for even attempting this—when the door is yanked open abruptly, and I find myself looking at my youngest brother.

Leo's eyes widen. "Dam," he greets me, his tone lifted in surprise. "What are you doing here?"

If only I knew.

I smile weakly. "If you're busy—"

"Come in," Leo interrupts, sounding surprised but pleased, and steps hurriedly out of the way to let me inside.

My shoulders are stiff as I move over the threshold, casting a look around at the familiar space.

The decor, at least, has changed a lot.

Originally decorated at the behest of Leo's late mother, the family-owned property was once filled with many posh, ugly wallpapers and uncomfortable pieces of antique furniture. Now, all that is gone, and instead, the house boasts evidence of my brother's one true love: *really old art.*

An eclectic assortment of paintings occupies nearly every inch of wall space in the narrow entryway. There are even more leaning against the baseboards, with sheets of foam and vellum paper carefully situated between each of the antique frames, protecting them from damage.

The front door closes, and Leo casts me a slight smile when I catch his eye. "Come through," he says, already passing me by, and leads the way into the dimly lit hall—lined with even more art—which takes us into the sitting area.

Admittedly, his mother wouldn't have approved of any of Leo's modifications, but this room... This room alone would've made the dearly departed queen depart even earlier from sheer shock.

Even I, who is well used to Leo's eccentricities, am brought up short, *staring.*

Apparently seeing no need for ordinary household comforts—like a television or couch—Leo has now dispensed with such frivolities.

Instead, the room is now cut in half by what appears to be a giant, white tent. Though I can't see through the tarp-like walls, the space is lit, and classical music plays quietly from a speaker somewhere inside. The quiet drone of an air filtration system is the only other noise in the room as Leo moves over to a table that's crammed against the far wall, hitting the "on" switch of an electric kettle.

Fucking hell.

"Leo," I begin, hovering in the doorway as I take in the scene before me. "What's going on?"

My brother blinks, following my gaze to the tent, as if only now realizing it's there. "Oh, this? I set it up a few months ago. I thought it would be prudent to have a controlled environment to get work done at home."

Prudent isn't a word I would use to describe this development.

Scrubbing a hand over my stubble, I watch as Leo hurries over to take a stack of papers off a worn leather armchair, dropping them onto the floor beside it with a smile.

"Sit down," he offers cheerfully, as if this is all very normal. "I'm glad you came." I don't move, however, torn between guilt and trepidation as I try to decide how best to handle this.

My youngest brother's ups and downs were always severe. Even before college, Leo swung between periods of wild efficiency and hyper-focus to deep depression and isolation, with no apparent trigger.

No one in the family was particularly surprised by his diagnosis of bipolar two, and I suspect it was my father and his wife's primary motivation for permitting Leo to escape the royal institution for a life in academics.

He's been medicated and stable—or, mostly stable, anyway—for a long time, and I'd clearly taken it for granted.

"Leo," I begin carefully, edging further into the room, as

my brother drags a folding chair out from behind the bookshelf, "have you been good about your meds?"

"Of course." A flicker of irritation passes over his face, but he doesn't look at me directly as he unfolds the plastic chair and drops it onto a vacant section of floor across from the armchair. Then he's off again, heading back to silence the whistling kettle. "Earl Grey?" he casts over his shoulder, busying himself with the mugs and packets of herbs.

My mouth is dry as, with difficulty, I swallow. "Yes. Thanks."

Even if Leo *is* off his medications—which I have no actual proof of—there isn't much I can do here. He's an independent adult, and my absence over the past months hasn't exactly left us in a place where my interventions would be welcome. Then, there's my recent experience with Blair, and what happened when I appeared in her life and tried to change it to my liking.

I bite back my questions as Leo gingerly hands over one of the mugs and sinks down in the folding chair, letting me have the nicer of the room's two seats.

"How have you been?" he asks, with rather a forced air of normalcy.

Sitting down too, I set the mug on the ground beside it and lean back, gazing at him helplessly. "Okay. I'm sorry to just come by like this. It wasn't planned."

Leo regards me appraisingly, his head tilted to the side. "In the area?"

"No, not at all, actually."

Silence falls, but before I can drum up a neutral topic of conversation, Leo's next question brings me up short. "Are you seeing someone?"

Totally taken off guard, I stare at him. "Why would you think that?"

Chuckling, my brother drops his gaze significantly to a point below my chin. "You have a rather noticeable *bruise*, just there."

Immediately, I pull my phone from my pocket and turn the camera on, angling it so I can see the place he described. Sure enough, with the first two buttons of my knit shirt undone, the material has gaped away just enough for a mouth-shaped bruise to be visible in the hollow above my collarbone.

Christ, princess.

Shaking my head, I shove the device away again and offer my brother a guilty smile. This was not a topic I wanted to address today, but in the absence of any alternatives... "Yeah," I admit, chuckling wryly, "I've been seeing someone."

Leo's plastic chair groans as he leans back, obviously pleased at his detective work. "Is it serious?"

Yet another fairly unprecedented line of questioning. I've dated in the past, of course, but I can't recall either of my brothers asking me that. "What? Do I have a receipt for an engagement ring stuck to my shoe?" I joke and make a show of lifting each foot to check.

"No," Leo counters calmly when I'm finished with the theatrics, "you just have a particular look about you. It's the same one Ben had at the beginning, when he was pretending he wasn't entirely gone for Z. Like a stray dog that's been taken in and given treats for the first time."

"I've been given plenty of *treats* before now, thank you very much," I retort, even as the sentiment stirs something in my chest, because I also remember *that look* our brother had.

Leo merely stares at me expectantly and helps himself to another sip of tea.

Recognizing defeat, I groan. "It's complicated."

"Yes, it always is," Leo agrees sagely.

"Don't be patronizing, you little twerp. It's *very* complicated. She's..." I trail off, searching for the correct combination of adjectives to describe Blair Porter.

Funny?

Beautiful?

Clever?

Impossible?

Infuriating?

Adorable?

All are correct, and yet they fall short. I have no idea how to explain this woman who has consumed my entire life. It seems almost inconceivable that only a little over two months have passed since we met, when so much has changed in that time.

It took convincing, but last week, she finally agreed to email the director of the educational program she's enrolled in, requesting accommodations for her dyslexia.

If they hadn't come through, I was fully prepared to go to war on her behalf, but, thankfully, it wasn't necessary. The school responded well, going so far as to offer individualized remote tutoring sessions to help Blair improve her literacy foundation.

She doesn't enjoy it, of course, but I've seen the genuine effort she's putting in—no nagging, threats, or coercion necessary—and I'm *so fucking proud of her.*

Admitting to myself that I want this woman was the equivalent of a dam breaking. What happened next was out of my control. I was swept up by the current, carried from fucking her, to wanting her, and now, falling too.

"She's great," I finally manage, somewhat lamely, after what must have been a full minute of silently simpering, given my current state of mind.

Fuck, *what is she doing to me?* I made fun of Ben for this shit.

Leo appears to be having quite a bit of difficulty holding back his shit-eating grin as he asks, "What's her name?"

"Blair."

"Blair?"

I gnash my teeth, bracing myself for the inevitable commentary. "*Porter.*"

"*Porter?*" my brother echoes with an incredulous laugh, his eyes bright. "Oh, shit."

Yeah, "*oh, shit*" about sums it up.

"I told you it was complicated," I retort, scowling at him.

"You were not understating it," Leo admits, though he still appears to be finding the entire matter very amusing. "Did I see a picture of her—"

"No." I lean forward, narrowing my eyes. "You didn't see any pictures."

"Of course I didn't. My mistake." He takes a long sip of tea, but when he lowers the mug, Leo's smile has faded somewhat. "Does she know? About you?"

I don't need to ask what he's referring to. "No," I admit, leaning forward to pluck my mug from the floor, just for something to do with myself. When I straighten back up, I find Leo eyeing me speculatively. "We had a bumpy start," I tell him, a little defensive now. "That isn't something you just... tell people."

It also isn't something you *don't* tell people, at least not people you care about. Unfortunately, I have limited experience in disclosing my personal history.

There may be people, like Blair's father, who have their suspicions about my identity. The only ones who know for sure, though—Leo, Ben, and Araminta—always have. The sole exception, my now-sister-in-law, Zelda, is the only person who has been let in on the secret. In her case, though, I'd been protected by the NDA she'd signed when dating my brother.

"Well, I'm eager to see how this all plays out," Leo informs me with a mild smile, finishing his tea and rising from the folding chair.

I blink, watching him cross back to the table in the corner. "What, no words of wisdom?"

"Is that what you came here for? A brotherly pep talk?" he asks over his shoulder, setting down the mug.

It seems I need one, but as my eyes find the plastic sheet cutting across most of the room, worries about my relationship with Blair are momentarily eclipsed. An unpleasant weight settles in the pit of my stomach.

I clear my throat, schooling my features into something resembling a smile, rising from my chair as well. "No, I didn't come here for a pep talk. Do you need to go?"

"Yes, actually." He checks his watch but doesn't elaborate.

My chest is hollow as I follow Leo through the house to the front door, waiting silently as he dons his coat and changes out his house shoes for loafers. It's only when we're outside on the front stoop and Leo has locked up that my brother glances at me. "Is this unexpected visit a sign?" he asks. "That you'll be ready to talk soon?"

With some difficulty, I nod. "I'm working on it."

Apparently satisfied, Leo grips my shoulder briefly, and we walk side by side down the old stone steps. "I'll see you soon, Dam," he calls meaningfully over his shoulder, strolling around the corner and off in the direction of the Orwick campus.

I watch him go.

Instinctively, I know that something isn't right. But, after months lost in my depression and guilt, all but entirely removed from my brother's life, I know I have no business interfering. Not yet. The inevitability of *someday* needing to tell Ben and Leo the truth has now become much more pressing.

Ben is newly married; he and Z have a baby to raise and an entire country to run. After everything I've done, the least I can do is monitor Leo and make sure he isn't spiraling.

As I get back in my car, the reality of the situation settles upon me; I no longer have the luxury of being checked out.

Thirty-One

"Okay, what was the exact time of your birth?"

Summer is perched on the kitchen counter, her bare feet dangling over the freshly washed floor, and the whole of her focus on the phone in her hand. She technically got off work an hour ago, but a flurry of snow had appeared out of nowhere just before the end of her shift, and I persuaded her to spend the night instead of braving the drive back to Port Briar.

I haven't seen Damien since this morning. Shortly after I left his cottage, I received a very long voice message from him with the news that he was leaving Thornhurst to run errands for the day. This was followed by instructions he'd already given me on how to activate the security system and the locations of all the house's fire extinguishers.

Now, we're hanging out in the kitchen, having a marvelous time surrounded by every snack we could find, and have big plans to spend the night binging the newly released season of a reality dating show where the contestants all seem to be the most horrible people the producers could find. I bet my parents would like it a lot.

"Can I ask your opinion on something?"

Summer's eyes lift from the phone in her hands to meet mine. "Non-star chart related? I'm hyper-fixating pretty hard right now."

She's teasing me, and I offer her a playfully exasperated look in response before voicing a question I've been turning over in my mind for weeks. The one that's suddenly begun to feel much more pressing as my relationship with Damien has grown—impressively—even more complicated.

It's pretty difficult to convince myself I'm *not* falling for him, but even as we've gotten closer, fucking more than fighting, and even edging closer to something more intimate... he's lying to me. Or, if not outright lying, at least omitting the truth.

Damien has secrets, and every time I feel my heart flutter at the sight of him or find myself fantasizing about what it would be like to be with him—*actually* be with him—those questions never fail to bring me up short.

I didn't dare voice any of this or ask about him to my family while they were here, terrified of drawing attention to my interest in Thornhurst's head of security. After weeks of wondering, I can't hold it in anymore.

Fiddling with the can of flavored water clutched in my hands, I try to decide how best to say it. "You know Damien, right? The estate's head of security?"

"*Damien*, huh?" Summer asks, raising her eyebrows. "I've noticed he isn't Satan or Evil Incarnate anymore? What—or perhaps *who*—could Mr. Mallory have done to bring about such a dramatic change of attitude toward him?"

Even as preoccupied as I am, I can't hold back my laugh. "God, you're the worst."

"I definitely am," she beams, unrepentant. "Come on, I'm

aggressively single. It's pathetic, really, and you're a bad friend if you don't lessen my patheticness by letting me live vicariously through you."

Shaking my head, I groan, relenting to the blatant manipulation. "We've been hooking up," I admit, prompting a gasp of glee from my friend. "It's not... nothing, you know?"

"Nope. I don't know."

"I don't either," I laugh helplessly, looking around as if a definition of mine and Damien's relationship is going to be painted on the wall. When that fails, I look back to Summer with a sigh. "I like him, but it's just hooking up. We're here all alone and—"

"Decided that fucking is a more enjoyable way to pass the time than murdering one another?"

Pretty much. "I'll keep you posted," I promise her. "Seriously, there's not much to tell."

Summer pops a piece of popcorn into her mouth. "You can tell me about the sex. I've only been in a room with both of you that one time, and *the tension*." She fans herself. "Oh my god, I could die. Is it hot? I bet it's hot."

It is indeed very hot. Unfortunately for Summer, that isn't what I'm interested in discussing at the moment. I glare at her. "It's always the quiet ones, isn't it? What happened to the shy art student I met last month?"

"You feed her, routinely help her do her terrible job, and now look." She gestures to herself, swathed in a borrowed pair of my sweatpants, her hair pulled up with one of my favorite scrunchies. "She's imprinted on you like a baby duck. You'll never be free again."

My heart tugs with fondness for my new friend, who already might be the best one I've ever had. "A duck who needs to get herself laid, so she can stop perving over my sex life," I retort, fixing her with a playful glare.

Summer throws a handful of popcorn at me in response.

Laughing, we hop down to clean it together, and when we straighten up, I finally voice the actual thing I wanted to discuss.

"Does Damien kind of look like Prince Leopold to you?" I ask Summer hesitantly, cataloguing her reaction. "The king's brother, I mean. In case you aren't up on Stelland's royal family."

It's been on my mind since I saw them arguing the day outside the security office.

I'd even gone so far as to look up a picture of the prince to make sure I was remembering correctly, and covertly compared the two when Damien wasn't paying attention.

There are differences, of course. Damien is older and a little more rugged than Leopold. His hair has the same wavy texture, but a shade lighter, though even that could possibly be attributed to his being outside so much. There's a resemblance, and I'm not really sure what to make of that, but coupled with the other mysterious facts I've stumbled (or snooped) upon, I can't convince myself to ignore it, either.

A thoughtful line appears between my friend's brows. "I know who Prince Leopold is; he's a bit of a local celebrity at Orwick. And now that you mention it... Yeah. Mallory does look like him a little." It's more than a bit, in my opinion, but this resemblance doesn't seem as interesting to Summer as it does to me. "What's your time of birth?" she asks again, returning to fixation on star charts.

"How should I know?" I demand with a laugh, temporarily distracted from my preoccupation with Damien's links to the royal family.

"Text your mom!"

Of course that would be Summer's solution. I learned recently that she has a group chat going with her entire family, and is always recounting news from their life back in Pennsylvania, like it's totally normal to know when your little sister fails her driver's test for the fourth time, or that the "*darn baler*"—I had to look up what that one was—is acting up again.

My mother, on the other hand, would probably think I'm on drugs if I texted her out of the blue to ask what time I was born.

I reach for the grapes in the bowl resting beside me and pop one into my mouth. "February third. Take it or leave it."

Summer heaves an exaggerated sigh as she resumes tapping away at her screen. "Your chart changes *hourly*, Blair. This won't be nearly as accurate."

"So, you agree they look alike? Mallory and Prince Leopold?" I ask carefully, fingering another grape.

"I guess so."

I fall silent, considering. It might be a coincidence, sure, but in combination with everything else I know about him... There are a lot of connections, too many to be easily written off.

According to Alba, Mallory came to be here because my mother's godmother, Araminta—sister-in-law of the late King Fabian—recommended him personally. By his own admission, he worked for the royal guard for years, and in that time he... what? Just so happened to strike up a friendship with King Benedict's notoriously private younger brother? Was Leopold the "Leo" who was calling him in the car the day we went to Wyngate?

Then there's the watch, the royal heirloom piece that I discovered in his medicine cabinet the day I broke into his cottage. Damien isn't sentimental. He wouldn't have kept something like that if it didn't mean a lot to him.

My stomach sinks.

I keep reminding myself that he's older than me and has a past that goes back much longer than I've been alive. The problem is that I'm afraid asking about that past would lead to his telling me no. That I'm too young, or silly, or foolish, and that this thing we've been doing always had an expiration date.

I have feelings for him. More feelings than I should, given the circumstances, and I'm not sure I've ever felt quite so in danger of having my heart broken before.

The sound of a door closing has both Summer and me looking around, staring at the far side of the kitchen as Damien steps into view, brushing snow from his winter jacket. He stops short at the sight of Summer and turns his gaze to me.

"We're having a sleepover," I inform him cheerfully. "That's not an issue, is it? Unless you want Summer to drive into a snowbank and freeze to death, helpless and alone. Is that what you want, Damien? For Summer to *die*?"

He crosses his arms, scoffing at my dramatics. "No, I do not want Summer to die. However, I'll point out that we've only gotten flurries, and it's due to stop within the hour."

Summer, who has been watching this exchange take place, and looking as though Christmas has come early, suddenly scowls. "Are you trying to get rid of me so you can bang my friend? If you are, and I really do freeze to death, please be advised I intend to turn into a ghostly entity whose sole purpose for existence is seeking revenge on you."

Damien stops ten yards away from us, frowning at Summer. "I thought you were shy."

"She fooled us both," I commiserate.

Summer brightens suddenly, pointing at Damien. "Hey, I bet *he* knows his time of birth. What's your time of birth, security man? I need the exact hour and minute, otherwise there's no point."

"Unfortunately, February third is the best I can do."

His words have made me lean back, though, reeling. "No, February third is *my* birthday."

Damien arches his eyebrows, and my belly flutters as he turns his gaze to meet mine. "Well, it's mine, too."

"Wait, seriously? We share a birthday?"

"Apparently."

I'm not sure why this learning piece of information—which is totally just a strange, random coincidence—makes me feel so *off balance*. We're still looking at each other, and I let out a nervous little laugh, finally forcing my eyeballs off him and onto Summer, whose entire face is split in an expression of sheer delight.

Recovering herself, my friend blinks rapidly, rearranging her expression into something more composed. "That's... um. Definitely a super normal thing to happen, and I will not be researching it for any higher astrological significance when he leaves."

Experiencing the bizarre combination of exasperation and fondness, I glare at her. "Why are you like this?"

She shrugs, unrepentant. "I have no idea. But heads up, it tends to get worse the longer you know me."

"Okay, just to be clear, the whole *ghostly entity whose sole purpose for existence is seeking revenge* thing? Does that apply to homicide, or is it exclusive to Damien sending you to a snowy grave because he wanted to bang me?"

"Oh, I trust you, girl. I'm sure if you kill me, I'll deserve it. No hauntings necessary, it's totally my bad."

I press my hands over my heart. "That is so sweet, Summer! Thank you!"

"*Goodnight!*" a loud call comes from the doorway, and we both look around, frowning at the place Damien was standing a second ago. He's gone, and seconds later, we hear the heavy thud of the back door closing.

Grinning, I lean past my friend to peer out at the snowy grounds, where I can just make out Damien's form striding toward the truck, shaking his head. When I look back to

Summer, though, I see her smile has faded. "Wow." She turns away from the window, frowning distractedly. "He really does look like Prince Leopold. I wasn't looking for it before, but now that you've said something... Yeah."

"Yeah," I agree, and I want to say more, to tell Summer about the watch, and his work history, and what Alba told me about Araminta recommending him personally. We might not have known each other for long, but I trust Summer more than any of my supposed friends in the glittering, fake life I used to have. Still, something about all this feels heavier than an ordinary relationship problem you'd discuss with your friend, and out of respect for Damien, I keep my theories to myself.

It stings to realize you trust someone more than they trust you.

Thirty-Two

Damien

"You're a menace to society."

Blair, who is running at my side, dodges neatly to the right to avoid the spank I try to land on her ass. "You're so sweet. Thank you for saying that. It means a lot," she pants, beaming at me as we round another corner of the trail, our shoes crunching over the thin layer of packed-down snow. "But you should consider it, because there are *at least* three major benefits."

I find myself grinning, too. "Do tell, princess. What benefits are there to me fucking you over your father's desk, specifically?"

Her pace is slowing, likely because she is using her breath for talking rather than exercise, but I don't call her on it. I'm in too good a mood.

She holds up one finger. "One, I'm a huge fan of you fucking me over things. Super hot."

"A great time for all parties involved," I acknowledge with a chuckle. "And the second?"

Another finger rises, and her smile turns vicious. "He would hate it. Obviously."

"Obviously."

We round another bend in the trail, and Blair scowls when she sees I've had the groundskeeper clear the long trail back to the house, but not the shorter, more direct route. This way takes us through the woods bordering the property and past the gates, where we can finish our run on Thornhurst's main drive.

The minor storm that swept through last week was just the beginning, and only six days into December, the grounds are already covered in a few inches of snow. I made sure Blair was properly equipped with winter gear, and we've so far been able to keep to our routine of running one day and swimming the next, but it's only a matter of time before the trails become inaccessible.

I haven't told her about the treadmills scheduled to be delivered on Friday.

"And the third?" I prompt, as apparently exhausting her ability to run *and* talk, Blair slows to a walk. Following her lead, I shoot her a halfhearted, warning look. "Your muscles are going to cool down."

As if to illustrate the point, a light wind moves through the trees, sending a flurry of snowflakes down around us.

"The third is that it's an excellent way to keep me warm," Blair teases breathlessly, even as she picks up the pace again. "Practical."

Before she can get far, I lurch forward, catching her gloved hand in mine, and pull her into my chest, meeting her lips in a brief kiss. We've already fucked once today, hence the late start time for our run this morning, but the taste of her alone has my mind wandering to when I'll have her in my bed again.

Thankfully, that time will be tonight.

"Come on." I smack her ass playfully and draw back so we can set off again, grinning. "Only a mile to go."

Blair groans. "Curse you, *Demonan—Demonician?*" She screws up her face, trying again. "*Demonian?* Damn, I'm getting rusty. What's a good conjugation of *Damien* and *Demon?*"

"Surely you can't expect me to do the heavy lifting on this one."

"*Dameon?* No. What is wrong with me today? I'm better than this!"

"You'll get there, princess. I have full confidence in you."

"Do you know what would make me feel better?"

I have a feeling I know where this is going but play along anyway. "What's that?"

Puffing, Blair glances over at me, wearing a breathless, mischievous smile. "If you fuck me over my father's desk."

This time, the spank makes her squeal, picking up the pace to get away from me as we cross the forest's edge, running through the narrow, makeshift trail that will intersect with the front drive. My attention is on her, and I'm not paying attention to our surroundings. Not the way I should be.

We're nearly directly in front of the gate, when I realize—too fucking late—that we aren't alone.

"Good morning!" calls a man's voice, and Blair and I both stop dead, staring at the familiar white sedan which is idling outside the gates.

It's the same reporter who came by, asking about Blair, shortly after I started work here. He's dressed in a thick coat and woolen hat, leaning against the hood of his car, with an eager glint in his eye as he looks at the woman beside me.

My heart drops, and automatically, I step in front of her, blocking her from view. "You're trespassing. Leave immediately."

He pushes off the car, drawing closer to the gates. "Good

to see you, Miss Porter! Funny, when I was here before, your friend here told me you weren't home. Glad to see you've made it back, safe and sound!"

"I am not fucking around here," I snarl, reaching behind me to grasp Blair's arm, ensuring she doesn't move. "This is private property, and if you're not gone in the next—"

"Not to worry, I'll be out of your hair in no time," he assures me easily, apparently not the least bit bothered by my threats. "Before I go, though, I was wondering if Miss Porter would like to comment on the search warrant which was executed this morning."

Before I can stop her, Blair pulls her arm free, stepping out from behind me. "Search warrant?" she demands, staring at the man.

His smirk widens to a triumphant grin. "At Porter Capital. I would have thought you'd have been informed, as a shareholder and sister of the current CEO."

"Blair," I hiss, reaching out to touch her shoulder. "Let's go inside and figure out what's going on. Don't say anything to him."

Too intent on what he's just told her, she ignores this, brushing me away as she draws closer to the gate. "What were they looking for?" she calls, a tremor in her voice.

"Your guess is as good as mine, Miss Porter. There seems to be a lot you aren't being informed of, though." He sighs, pretending to be sympathetic. "I have a source in your father's inner circle who told me you weren't even told about *the threats*? That can't be true, though, can it?"

Blair opens her mouth, eyes wide, but again, I step between her and the man, this time facing her. "We need to go inside," I tell her urgently, my adrenaline flooding my system, as my greatest priority in this situation—removing her from this man's vicinity—rises to critical status.

Blinking, she pulls her gaze from the place beyond my shoulder, looking at me directly at last. "What threats?"

It's difficult to breathe.

She shouldn't have found out like this.

"Please, Blair. He's a slimy tabloid reporter, trying to get you to say something he can spin. Let's go inside, and I'll tell you what he's talking about."

Vapor from her breath curls through the space between us, uneven and shaky. "Okay," she agrees at last, but the look on her face...

My relief is minimal.

Pressing my hand to the center of Blair's back, I turn her toward the house, throwing a filthy look over my shoulder at the man. "I have your plate numbers, and I'm calling the police."

He gives me a thumbs up, grinning.

My heart is pounding as we walk up the drive, not exchanging a word. Even if it doesn't bode well, I'm relieved to have a moment to think this through, to disseminate my reasoning for not telling her into something resembling a defense.

It wasn't reasonable, though.

At first, I'd been doing my job and listening to the orders of the man who signs my paychecks.

Later, the threats were gone, and—because my feelings for her obviously hold more sway than my logic in this situation—I didn't want to scare her. Maybe I would have told her eventually, but it isn't the sort of thing one just drops into a conversation.

When we've gotten farther from the gates, and a glance backward confirms the reporter has gone, Blair stops dead, rounding on me. "What was he talking about?"

I swallow, staring back at her. "It's important to me that

you first know you are safe and always were. Even before we were together."

Exhaling sharply, Blair's expression tightens. "Damien. I swear to god, if you don't tell me what is going on—"

"When I met with your father about the job, he informed me that after those photographs of you were published, the campaign office started receiving some extremely unsettling communications. There were also some sent here, to Thornhurst, as well as your parents' Wyngate residence."

She blinks, panic shining in her eyes now. "What kind of communications?"

My stomach churns as I remember the few I had read before turning them over to the police. "The kind you would expect, given the fact that tens of thousands of strangers saw your half-naked body." Blair doesn't respond, but hugs herself, swaying slightly on the spot. "Your father didn't feel you were in a place to handle that kind of information."

Her lower lip trembles. "You mean he couldn't trust me not to react emotionally and possibly embarrass him. And you agreed."

"*No*," I plead, frantic now. "No, Blair. I wanted you to be informed, but it wasn't my call. They stopped quickly, though, and I didn't want—"

"To trust me?" she suggests with a wild laugh, tears shining in her eyes. "Of course not. I'm an idiot, right? An irresponsible, spoiled brat?"

My own words hit me squarely in the chest, knocking the oxygen from my lungs. It feels like a very long time since I said those things to her. So much has changed, and neither of us is the person we were before, but it hasn't been that long.

A month isn't long enough to erase the damaging things I said to her. I should have known that.

"You are not an idiot, or irresponsible, or a spoiled brat," I tell her, my voice choked. "Please, Blair. You have to know…"

My words falter, though, as she shakes her head, and I wish the ground would open to swallow me up with her next words.

"That's not the only thing you haven't told me, though, is it?"

It isn't really a question. The way she's looking at me is like this is confirming something for her, and I can't stand it. Blair is more intelligent than anyone, including me, gives her credit for. Of course she would have picked up on me hiding something and would take that personally, given how our relationship began.

Snow crunches under my feet as I take an unsteady step forward, reaching for her, and my heart plummets when she steps out of the way, misery shining from every part of her beautiful face.

"That's what I thought," she whispers, her voice wavering.

"Blair," I plead, "I didn't keep these things from you because I don't think you're capable of handling them, or don't trust you. There are things about me, about my past, that no one outside my family is aware of. Even they don't know the full story."

"Forgive me, but doesn't it seem a little convenient to you, Damien?" She lets out a hard, miserable laugh. "For months we've been—" But her words falter, and the second half of the sentence falls away, leaving a chasm of regret inside me.

For months, we've been falling in love.

That is what's been happening: each of us learning how to love the other, and I refuse to let *this* be the mistake that ends that. I won't fucking allow it.

Except, in my silence, Blair seems to have reached the end of her patience. She steps back, her expression shuttered. "It's freezing out here. I'm going back to the house." Her voice is hollow.

"Let me come with you. We can talk." But she's shaking her head before I've even finished speaking.

"No. I need some space," she tells me, sounding so tired, so fucking defeated.

I exhale sharply, trying and failing to center myself. "You have become the most important person in my life, princess. I know I fucked up here, but I swear, I'll find a way to tell you everything. Take your space, if that's what you need, but please don't write me off yet."

Blair's eyes drop to the snowy ground beneath us, and after an age, she finally gives a tiny nod.

I stay where I am—smothering my natural inclination to fix this immediately—and watch as she walks alone back toward Thornhurst, never once pausing to look back at me.

The door might not be closed, but I know I'm one fuckup shy of having it slammed in my face for good.

ASHWELL PALACE ANNOUNCES DEATH OF PRINCESS ARAMINTA

ANOTHER DEATH IN THE ROYAL FAMILY SENDS STELLAND INTO MOURNING

Princess Araminta Ashwell, sister-in-law of the late King Fabian and wife of his younger brother, Prince Clement, died Friday morning at age seventy-three. Her passing was announced in a brief statement by Ashwell Palace Press Corps, noting that the princess died peacefully in her home after a brief illness, and that flags across government buildings will be flown at half-staff this week in remembrance.

Born Lady Araminta Loxley, eldest daughter of the Duke of Halifax, she married into the Ashwell family at a defining moment in Stelland's modern history. Throughout the decades that followed, she became a notable figure within the royal household, known for her formality, discipline, and observance of protocol and tradition. Her marriage to Prince Clement was characterized by a shared devotion to public service and philanthropy, together supporting a number of charitable, cultural, and civic organizations.

Later, Princess Araminta's role within the monarchy would take on greater significance following a series of deep and profound losses. Within the span of a few decades, the Ashwell royal family endured the deaths of her husband, her brother-in-law King Fabian, and, most recently, the tragic passing of her nephew, King Arthur, along with his family.

In the aftermath of these events, Princess Araminta was widely regarded as a stabilizing presence, one whose unwavering commitment to duty helped maintain a sense of order during periods of uncertainty and transition.

A formal funeral service will be held next week at Saint Clement Cathedral, the cathedral named in honor of her late husband's namesake, followed by a private memorial wake at her longtime home, Willow Bend House. Members of Parliament, senior officials, and representatives from allied nations are expected to be in attendance, alongside the royal family.

Thirty-Three

A ripple seems to pass through the room as they enter it. While the wake of Princess Araminta could hardly be called a joyful affair, whatever ease existed a moment ago vanishes as Stelland's king and queen join the mourners.

Conversations falter mid-word.

Drinks are lowered without being sipped.

Shoulders are dropped, chins lifted, and dresses smoothed flat.

I'm stationed against the far wall beside the refreshment table, as far from my family as possible, and watch at a distance as the royals enter, joining the crowd of black-clad guests filling Araminta's sitting room.

Today is not the first time I've seen King Benedict. My parents dragged me to more than a few parties and charity functions where he was in attendance, but it's been ages since I laid eyes on him in person. In that time, a great change seems to have settled over the man. He's still not the cheerful sort, but today, he seems more at ease than I can ever recall, and there is a softness in his expression when he glances at his wife.

"*Your Royal Highnesses.*" I wince as my father's voice cuts through the low rumble of voices, and bring my wine to my lips, grateful to be hidden from his view by the hangers-on who drift toward the royals.

I'm ready to go back to Thornhurst.

When I woke up the morning after my fight with Damien, it was to about a dozen missed calls from Candice, my parents, sister, and even one from Ced. I hadn't even had an opportunity to say goodbye to him before I was being swept off to Wyngate to "comfort" my mother during her time of "grief."

In reality, my comfort was limited to when the cameras were pointing in our direction, and I had to endure several excruciatingly long press conferences with my arm looped through hers. All the while, trying to appear appropriately sorrowful while my father droned on about how much Araminta had meant to our family.

As if the last time I saw the woman, she hadn't called me *Bella*.

While not exactly grieving, the whole affair must have drained my limited supply of self-control, because days later, when Dad informed us over dinner that the circus had gained him two whole polling points, I'd been sent to my room for "making a face."

I can tell my presence has been wearing on them, because nobody protested when I requested a car to return me to Thornhurst immediately following the funeral.

One more hour.

I can do this.

Taking another sip of wine, I survey the crowd as my mind returns—for about the tenth time in the past hour—to Damien.

He'd called me, the first evening I was in Wyngate. We

hadn't spoken long, but he'd promised we could talk when I got back and made sure to tell me—twice—that he didn't like leaving things "unsettled" like this.

After hanging up, I stared at the wall of my bedroom for a full fifteen minutes, replaying the brief conversation in my head, and struggling to make sense of it all. Not so long ago, Thornhurst was a battlefield. There have been so many games, so many ups and downs, and it seems a little insane to hope for something good to come out of it. I had to practically force the man to admit he wants me, but there's no denying, now that he has, there has been another seismic shift in our relationship.

I've been clinging to the negatives, keeping my focus on the secrets he so clearly has, and our less-than-conventional history. But when I set all that aside and ask myself how he makes me feel, I can't deny the truth.

Damien cares, and what's worse, *I care, too.*

And caring is dangerous.

God, I've actually avoided it. For so long, people, places, and possessions have slipped in and out of my life. Everything was so fleeting, a moment to be enjoyed, but not held. I hadn't realized it at the time, but I was temporary, too.

Then, suddenly, I had no choice but to stand still, and now... Now, I've found myself wanting to be more than a moment to Damien Mallory.

"I'm leaving." At the words, I blink, looking around. Lost in my thoughts, I hadn't noticed my brother coming to stand beside me.

He hasn't been around much in the past week, popping up here and there for press stuff, and we haven't spoken more than a few words to each other. Up close, I can see he looks even more weary than he did at James and Alba's engagement party, and there's a nearly empty tumbler of Scotch clutched in one of his hands.

Nothing has been published about the search warrant executed on Porter Capital, and none of my family members has mentioned anything. I'm not sure what to make of that. Was the reporter at the gate lying to try to get a reaction out of me, or—more likely—is my father exercising his influence to stop anything from getting out and distracting from the election?

I frown, momentarily distracted from thoughts of my confusing relationship status. "Is everything okay, Ced?"

My brother casts a brief, weary glance at me before returning his gaze to the swarm of funeral-goers hovering around the King and Queen. "It's fine, I just have things to do at the office. I can't waste a full day on this."

I tap my nail on the side of my wine glass, biting the inside of my lip. "No, I meant... You look tired, that's all." Showing concern for one another's well-being isn't in the Porter offspring rulebook, and I can tell the question has surprised him.

Ced clears his throat, still not looking at me. "Our father's political aspirations have put the family under very heavy scrutiny."

He hasn't told me anything, not really, but the vague statement still makes my heart drop. "What do you mean?" I ask carefully, trying not to sound too interested.

Lifting his drink to his lips, Cedric downs the remaining Scotch in a single gulp and, wincing, sets the tumbler down on the nearest table. "It's none of your concern, Blair."

Without another word, he retreats, moving briskly through the crowd toward the exit, his pace not faltering, even when he inclines his head toward James and Alba.

God, these people suck.

My temples throb, promising a headache is approaching, and I seize upon the excuse to slip out for a moment. Craning my neck to ensure neither of my parents is paying attention, I abandon my wine and drift toward a door I seem to remember leading to the powder room.

Nobody even glances at me as I drift through it and emerge into a carpeted hall. There is a line of glossy white doors lining the wall to my left, and sunlight spills into the narrow space from the large windows opposite them. At the very end of the space, an exit leads into the snow-covered garden.

The noise of the wake is muffled back here, and my shoulders sag with relief as I edge forward, trying to remember which of the doors is Araminta's powder room. Before I can get far, however, the sound of a familiar male voice makes me still, my heart shooting into my throat.

"—I've been better."

My first instinct is to deny it. Even if I would know that voice anywhere, the possibility of Damien being here, of all places... The most logical conclusion is that my mind is playing tricks on me. I want to hear him, I miss him and wish he were here, but that doesn't mean he is.

Except, as I linger by the wall, straining my hearing, it quickly becomes clear that I am not hearing things.

"Still. It's good of you to come, Dam," says another male voice, smoother and more polished than Damien's familiar rasp.

"Yeah," Damien agrees, sounding weary and noticeably more subdued than usual.

Pulse thudding heavily, I edge forward, my eyes glued to the corner at the end of the hall, around which I suspect Damien and the unknown person are standing. My confusion only deepens when a cheerful, high-pitched squeal sounds, undoubtedly issued by a baby.

"Oh, damn, will you take her for a moment?"

"I'm not sure—" Damien's words falter.

I can't decide whether I should turn around and go back

to the wake or continue on. Surely he knew I would come here today, but didn't say a word about being here himself. That, and the fact he's lurking in a back hall instead of attending the event, makes it quite clear Damien probably never intended for me to know.

More lies. More secrets.

I'm hurt, of course, and more than a little confused, but more than any of that, I'm absolutely furious with him. God, he makes it as difficult as possible for anyone close to him, doesn't he?

Heat burns in my chest as, abandoning my sneaking, I push away from the wall, striding forward with a fierce sense of purpose. I don't know what I'm expecting to find when I turn that corner, but my genuine shock when I do suggests I truly didn't think I'd find *this*.

Damien is there, dressed in a suit, and holding a dark-haired baby in his arms. At his side, Prince Leopold is bent over and shuffling through the contents of a pink diaper bag, presumably searching for something to clean the white spit-up on his lapel.

I stop short, staring, as both men turn to look at me.

Damien's face falls.

"Hello," offers Prince Leopold politely, not quite meeting my eye as he straightens up, a wet wipe clutched in one hand.

My throat is so tight I can barely respond. "Hi," I whisper, watching as the baby tries to grab Damien's nose with her chubby hand.

"Blair—" begins Damien hoarsely, searching my face.

But before he can think of an excuse for this, I'm stepping back, shaking my head. "I'm sorry. I was just looking for the powder room."

"Blair," Damien says again, more insistently now, and there's a hint of panic in his voice as he adjusts his hold of the baby in his arms.

It's only then that I notice that the little girl is not just any baby. I've seen her face before, plenty of times, often accompanied by her very well-known parents in the news or online.

Damien is holding the future Queen of Stelland.

A quiet, disbelieving cry escapes from between my lips, and I take another step away.

"Sorry!" comes a bright woman's voice from behind me. An *American* woman's voice. "We were surrounded the moment we walked in there." The speaker brushes past me, and my mouth falls open, staring in disbelief at the addition to our little group.

Queen Zelda, who is dressed in a neat black collared dress and pearls, stops short at the sight of Damien holding her daughter and beams. "Oh my gosh, this is the cutest. Keep her for a bit, Dam, you two need some time together." Then, glancing over at me, her smile slips. "Sorry, I don't think we've met."

The only noise I seem to be capable of producing is a high-pitched squeak.

"Zelda, Leo, this is Blair Porter," offers Damien, and though I don't look at him, I can hear the tightness in his voice. "She's—I've been working for her family for the past few months."

Working for my family.

His words make my chest ache and my eyes burn, but finally, I have enough sense to step away. "I'm very sorry to bother you, Your Royal Highness," I whisper, addressing the queen, and sink into a brief little curtsey.

"No bother at all," she replies kindly. "It's very nice to meet you, Blair."

I can barely breathe through my shock as I draw back. "Pardon, I mean excuse me—*Oh, god*. I'm sorry. I should go." And, ignoring my mortification, I make a break for it.

Before I've even made it halfway back up the hall, Damien calls after me. "*Blair.*"

My pace doesn't slow.

"Blair," Damien tries again, sounding more panicked now.

I don't look back as I reach the last door and tear it open, reemerging in the crowded sitting room I'd wandered away from only a few moments ago. It closes behind me with a quiet click, and I pause beside it, my heart hammering.

Damien doesn't follow.

It's saying a lot that the room full of high-profile mourners for Princess Araminta now feels like a sanctuary.

I stand beside the door for a long time, breathing shallow breaths in and out through my nose, struggling to process what just happened. My suspicions about who Damien is and his connections to the royal family have only grown more confusing and disjointed as time went on. Now, though...

While I may not have much firsthand experience in loving, close families, I've seen enough from the outside to know that's what Damien has. The queen and Prince Leopold care about him—*love him*—and suddenly, all the scattered clues I've gathered about Damien Mallory's identity over the past months have turned into a theory.

A far-fetched, impossible theory *that fits.*

"Blair?" From her place amongst a circle of well-dressed middle-aged women, my mother has spotted me. She raises her eyebrows expectantly, and I force myself away from the wall to join her, smiling robotically as I'm introduced to each in turn.

"What is wrong with you?" she hisses under her breath when the other ladies have turned away, temporarily distracted by a platter of miniature puff pastries.

I swallow with difficulty, not looking at her. "I'm not feeling well."

Mom sniffs. "Too much wine? You should return to Thornhurst."

I don't care enough to defend myself.

"Fine." As I begin to move away, however, Mom's hand snatches my wrist, stopping me in my tracks. Automatically, I turn, meeting her eyes. They're the same shade of dark green as my own, but even on my worst day, I'm not sure I've ever looked into a mirror and seen so little warmth.

Her mouth pinches, but after a moment of silent indecision, she drops her hold on me without offering an explanation.

I blink, still not moving. "Is everything okay, Mom?"

In an instant, her expression transforms, turning from icy to fond in the blink of an eye. "You're so sweet to check on me, darling, but please go home; you look exhausted."

My mother hasn't called me darling since I was very small, and despite myself, the crumb of affection has my heart lifting. "Are you sure?" I ask, genuinely hesitant about leaving her for the first time.

At least until a voice comes from behind me. "I wish my daughter were so devoted. You are so fortunate, Lydia." I glance over my shoulder, and the moment of connection I'd felt with my mother turns to smoke, as I see her friends have all returned their attention to us.

Of course her love would only be for show.

"I am," Mom tells them. "Blair has been such a comfort to me during this terrible time."

A round of affirming commentary follows this, before I'm finally allowed to escape with a last kiss on my mother's cheek. I feel like a ghost as I move through the crowd, passing my father, sister, and future brother-in-law without saying goodbye.

It's not until I've folded myself into the back of the waiting car and we're pulling off down the drive, that I breathe freely. Resting my forehead against the cool glass, I stare outside at the long line of vehicles, just like mine, parked and waiting for their very important owners to finish pretending to mourn Princess Araminta Ashwell.

I squeeze my eyes shut as—for the first time in twenty-six years—I begin to wonder whether the money is really worth it.

If I were given a choice, I think I would prefer people love me while I'm alive and miss me when I die.

THIRTY-FOUR

I beat Blair back to Thornhurst by only fifteen minutes.

The fire in the cottage's hearth is still coming to life, the coffee machine still spitting noisily atop the kitchen counter, when I get the notification someone has accessed the front gate.

Abandoning the email I was responding to, I pull up the security cameras on my laptop to watch as one of Porter's chauffeurs delivers Blair and her bags onto the front steps. Leaning forward, I stare at the video feed, not relaxing until she's made it inside and the man has left the way he came.

I wait, selfishly hoping she will reemerge and come find me, but the doors stay firmly closed.

Finally, when I can't stand it any longer, I close my computer and rise to pour myself a cup of coffee, feeling older and wearier than I can ever remember.

Even with the current distance between Blair and me, I should be relieved. After over an hour spent with my family members and our aunt's attorney, it finally became clear that Araminta's last will and testament—which was ridiculously long and accounted for every last teaspoon—did not include me. My anonymity and the secret I've carried for my entire life are secure.

At what cost, though?

For so long, protecting my privacy was the most important thing in the world to me. I'd seen firsthand what my brothers went through, what it was like to grow up in view of the entire country, and the expectations which come with the Ashwell name.

I didn't want that—I still don't—and yet my relationship with every single person I care about has been damaged as a result.

Christ, I've allowed it to damage my relationship with *Blair*.

Blair, who has gone from being the worst part of my day to the best.

Blair, who I showed the ugliest parts of myself, yet still looks at me like I'm worth something.

Blair, whom I was so convinced I couldn't possibly want, but now will for the rest of my life.

I've never told anyone the full story. Right to my core, I believed I would take my secrets to the grave, and there was nobody I could ever trust with all of it.

For whatever reason, I'm filled with the bizarre urge to laugh as I set down my mug in the sink and take my coat off the hook beside the door. The sun is setting behind the clouds as I leave the cottage behind and make my solitary way across the snowy grounds, my eyes on the lights shining in the windows of the grand old house.

I let myself in, but bypass the sitting room and stairs, heading straight for the pool. It's a hunch, but my instincts prove correct when I open the cellar door, and the soft lapping of water carries up to me from the chamber below.

Ignoring the painful knot which has formed in the center of my chest, I lower my foot to the first step and begin my descent into the familiar space, only stopping when the room comes into full view.

Blair is sitting on the side of the pool, her hair dripping and water spreading over the stone floor below her, as if she's only just pulled herself out. Her eyes are downcast, but even from a distance, I see her features tighten as I enter the room.

As I look at her, it registers that losing this woman terrifies me in a way that having my identity revealed never has.

"Hi." The single syllable echoes through the room, and Blair's shoulders stiffen.

She doesn't respond, doesn't look at me, but doesn't stop me or send me away, either. Given the circumstances, it's the best I can hope for, and I'm encouraged as I take the last few steps down to the cellar floor.

Blair kicks aimlessly through the water, her fingers gripping the edge, as I strip off my boots, socks, and coat. Not waiting for her invitation, I roll my pants up to the knees and cross to sit beside her, putting my feet in the water alongside hers. I have no idea where to begin, and stare at the arched, stone ceiling above us, lost in the familiar cavern of grief and guilt, as the woman beside me waits for me to find my words.

Finally, lowering my gaze to the water, I decide on the beginning.

"My mother's name was Nora Mallory."

Blair stills, listening.

It's been years since I said her name aloud, and even longer since I actually talked about her. *I didn't expect it to hurt.* My relationship to my mother feels tenuous at best, and I have never quite worked out how much of that can be attributed to my being so young when she died, or whether the significance of my father overshadowed her.

"She was working as a cocktail waitress at a private club in Wyngate when she met my father. He was older, and wealthy, and," I scoff, "married. I believe he loved her, in his way, and they were having an affair for a year before she became pregnant. He put her up in an old property belonging to his family, one that hadn't been used for many years, and that was where I was raised for the first part of my life. My father continued to visit, sometimes staying for days at a time, but never longer."

It had confused me when I was young, why the other boys in school had fathers who they saw every day, and mine only came when he could. At least until my teacher at the village school put on a live broadcast of the King of Stelland giving a speech.

Even now, decades later, it's all too easy to remember the rejection, betrayal, and confusion that rose inside me at that moment.

Sitting in the classroom, I'd watched my father stand behind a podium in full ceremonial garb, speaking into a microphone about duty and honor and loyalty to one's country. To his side stood a thin-faced woman I'd never met, and three boys who were very like me, and just about my age—the brothers I didn't know existed.

I couldn't reconcile that man was the same as the one who'd helped me repair my bicycle, or who brought my mother flowers and danced her around the kitchen. The man who always left and seemed to take a piece of her with him when he did.

Everything I thought I knew about my very existence was thrown to the wind on that day, and I'm not sure I ever fully recovered the pieces.

My heart lifts as, impossibly, I feel Blair lean over, resting her cheek on my shoulder. The warmth of her skin, the weight of her... It steadies me. This woman, whom I was once so determined to hate, has now become the center of my universe.

"My mother died. When I was eleven."

A tremor wracks Blair's body. "Oh god." Her voice breaks, devastation evident in every syllable. "I'm so sorry. So, so sorry, Damien."

My hand finds hers in the space between us, and I squeeze it in silent reassurance. "It was a long time ago. I've made my peace with it. As much as anyone can, anyway."

A part of me is steeled, bracing for the inevitable question of how *it* happened. I would tell her, if there is a soul alive who deserves the truth, it's her, but the weight of this moment is already impossibly heavy. The next part of my story is difficult to recount for very different reasons, and gratitude expands inside me when Blair seems to sense the topic isn't something I'm ready to discuss, and stays quiet, waiting patiently for whatever I'll tell her.

I stretch out my leg beneath the water, hooking her foot with mine as I continue. "After that, I was sent to live with my father's widowed sister-in-law. Araminta."

Blair lets out a heavy, disbelieving breath. "Damien. What —" I look over, and watch as she shakes her head slightly, as though needing to dismiss her impulse to write the question off as foolish. "What was your father's name?"

My lips twist as I stare back at her, my heart beating like a drum inside the hollow cavern of my chest. "Fabian," I reply at last. "Fabian Ashwell."

At last, Blair lifts her gaze from the water to look at me, her features stricken. "Fabian Ashwell. *King Fabian Ashwell*?"

I manage a weak smile. "Yes."

She sits back, pushing her damp hair back from her face. "You're... Is this real? You're serious?"

"No one knows," I tell her carefully. "No one outside the family, anyway."

And now her.

A hysterical giggle bubbles from Blair's lips. "I'm sorry. This is... this is a lot to take in."

"I know it is." Squeezing her hand again, I drag my thumb over the back of it. "I understand."

"God, I thought I was losing it," she half-laughs, wiping the corners of her eyes. "That day I saw you and Prince Leopold outside the security office. I thought..."

Of course, she was spying.

Chuckling weakly, I gaze at her, my chest full to bursting with affection. "We look alike." I acknowledge grimly. "Less so, believe it or not, than me and Ben."

Blair's mouth falls open, and she gapes at me in muted disbelief. "*Ben?*" she splutters. "Oh my god, your brother is the king. You call King Benedict, *Ben.*"

"I also call him a shithead occasionally."

"Damien!"

"He deserves far worse, trust me."

Blair covers her face with her hands, shaking her head. "I can't believe this. Even with the watch and everything, and then seeing you with them this morning, I couldn't really believe... *Holy shit.*"

My pulse leaps. "The watch?"

Looking a little bashful now, she lifts one shoulder in a halfhearted shrug. "I found it and saw the engraving the day I broke into your cottage. At first, I'd wondered if you stole it, but that didn't seem right. You wouldn't keep it there, or wind it every day, if it wasn't precious to you."

By now, I would have thought I'd learned my lesson in underestimating this woman, but she has managed to shatter my expectations yet again. Dragging my thumb over the side of her hand, I stare at her profile and realize I'm smiling. "What else did you work out?"

Blair casts a wary look at me, but the unguarded devotion I'm currently experiencing must reflect in my face, because her apprehension softens. "Alba told me that Araminta had recommended you for the job to my parents, but it seemed weird she would even know the name of a palace staffer, never mind be aware you'd resigned. Then, after I saw you talking to Prince Leopold, I remembered the call from *Leo* you'd gotten when we were driving to Wyngate." She wrinkles her nose. "There were a lot of little things, to be honest. It hadn't occurred to me that you were King Fabian's son, specifically, but I wondered whether you were related to the Ashwells."

"Why didn't you say anything?"

At the question, her face falls, and something strains inside me as she looks away, staring back into the depths of the pool. "I guess I was afraid," she admits softly. "That you'd tell me it doesn't concern me."

Doesn't concern her?

I turn the words over in my mind and wonder how many times this woman's genuine care has been cast aside, dismissed, or rejected? *Fuck.* Never again. Not from me.

"Blair?" At the sound of her name, mossy-green eyes lift to meet mine once again, apprehension shining in them. My hold on her hand tightens. "I'm your concern. If you want me to be."

Her bottom lip trembles. "Are you—I mean," she lets out a watery laugh, "Are you sure?"

In response, I pull her into my lap, right there on the side of the pool.

Blair is still wet from her swim, but I couldn't care less. I hold her against me, pressing my lips to her temple as water seeps through my clothing. "There is more to the story, things I haven't told you yet. Some parts of my history…" The familiar, bitter, corrosive guilt spreads through my center, and I shake my head helplessly. "I'm not merely a victim of circumstance, love."

Love.

Christ, all this time, I've been such an idiot. What the fuck else could it have been?

She doesn't acknowledge my slip, but Blair's fingers lift to play with the hair hanging over the back of my neck, resting her cheek on my shoulder. "Just to be clear, you're telling me you're not perfect? Damien, *I used to call you Satan.*"

My laugh booms unexpectedly from my chest, echoing over the water and off the vaulted ceiling. "I believe there were a few other iterations of the sentiment, too, if memory serves."

Blair lifts five fingers and begins ticking off names. "Bringer of Darkness, Evil Incarnate—" I catch her hand in mine and drag it to my lips, kissing the translucent skin on the inside of her wrist as the insults turn to giggles.

"Yes, yes," I scoff, not quite able to believe this conversation I never thought I could have has resulted in laughter. Allowing her hand to fall back to her lap, I turn, pressing my lips to her forehead. "My point is that I've done things I'm not proud of. There are pieces of this that *no one* knows, including my brothers, and I'm not sure you would see me the same way if I told you."

Blair's hand settles on the side of my neck, and it sends warmth spreading through my entire body. "Do you want to tell me?"

My response comes instantly. "*No,*" I croak, "I don't. But there's one thing I want even less, and that's to keep secrets from you. Especially if it means you're hurt by it."

If there was any way around telling her this, any way at all, I would take it. Even as the unspoken offer hangs in the silence between us, I pray she won't accept it. She isn't the only one who is afraid, but I've done too much damage to the people I love, and I can't shoulder the guilt of more mistakes.

Is that why I fought this so hard?

At last, Blair lifts her head from my shoulder. She gazes at me, a soft, sad smile playing on her full lips, as she smooths her thumb over the line of my jaw.

"Tell me everything."

Thirty-Five

Maybe I should be more wary of what Damien is going to tell me.

It's not every day that someone offers to divulge all their deepest, darkest, most closely held secrets, after all. I could see the torment in his face, feel the tremors that wracked his body as he tried to warn me off, but somehow, I'm not afraid.

On the contrary, the knowledge that he trusts and cares about me enough to offer the whole truth seems to have healed something I hadn't realized was broken.

Damien sits on the end of my bed, waiting as I strip off my swimsuit and change into a fleece-lined sweatsuit. Then, we bundle up in our outerwear and leave Thornhurst, crossing the dark grounds to his cottage. He offers me a sad, resigned sort of smile when we get inside, as though preparing himself for the worst.

"Why don't you put some logs on the fire?" I suggest as we

strip back out of our winter things, offering him a soft, reassuring smile. "I'll make tea."

Damien agrees quietly, and we separate to opposite ends of the cottage, moving through the ordinary, domestic routine of our respective chores. A shadow hovers over us both as we do, growing more and more oppressive and difficult to ignore.

Finally, I set two steaming mugs on the kitchen table, just as Damien steps out of the bathroom in his own sweatpants. He doesn't smile as he meets my gaze, moving across the cottage to sink down in one of the old wooden chairs.

I've never had someone care enough to make themselves vulnerable to me.

"When did you meet your brothers?" I ask because I can see in the sad, helpless way he's looking at me that Damien doesn't have the first clue how to begin. "Did you always know them, or…"

Leaning back, he rests his hands on the tabletop between us, offering me a slight, grateful smile. "I was eleven and had just moved in with Araminta. It wasn't an easy transition, as you can imagine. My father must have seen I needed company and sent Ben and Leo to stay with us for the summer."

"That must have been…" I let out a ghost of a laugh as words fail me. "A lot?"

"In some ways," he agrees. "I was so sure they would despise me—living, breathing proof of our father's infidelity. They didn't, though. Like me, they were curious, and the three of us bonded quickly, united against a common enemy: Aunt Araminta."

Something deep in my chest tugs as I see the fondness in his expression as he talks about them. "You love them very much," I deduce.

"Yes." His voice breaks on the word. "If any good at all came from my mother's death, it was getting to know my brothers. They accepted me without question, and were there for me during the loneliest, hardest part of my life."

I sense there is more to the story and stay quiet, ignoring the burning behind my eyes at the thought of the boy Damien going through so much.

He seems to be forcing himself to continue, and when he speaks again, his voice has grown tighter. "Ben always had a very strong sense of justice. It bothered him when things weren't fair, especially things that could be helped. From the time we were young teenagers, he felt strongly that our father should acknowledge me as his son, regardless of the inevitable scandal. For a time, I believed I wanted that, too, but as we grew, I began to truly understand what it meant to be part of the royal family. You"—his lips slant unhappily—"unfortunately, may have had a similar experience."

My heart aches as the meaning of his words sinks in.

Yes. I think I did.

Reaching across the corner of the table, I cover his hand with mine, gazing at him. "I don't blame you for not wanting this, Damien." God, I was born into this, and at twenty-six years old, I'm only beginning to realize I don't want it.

He doesn't meet my eyes, though, staring at our hands.

Silence stretches on, and my entire chest aches at the self-loathing in his expression when Damien finally lifts his gaze to meet mine once again. "The thing is, my brothers didn't want it either. They've struggled under the burden of it every day, but they didn't have a choice, Blair. They never had a choice."

"Neither did you!" I protest. "You didn't ask—"

"I did," he interrupts, his voice sharp for the first time since we started this conversation. "I did have a choice. When my father learned he was dying, he told me it was time and that he wanted to acknowledge me as his son publicly." He lets out a rocky breath and pulls his hand from beneath mine to scrub over his face, obviously tormented.

I stare, horror clogging my throat, as Damien drops his hands to his lap and continues on bitterly.

"I told him no. It was... I didn't want it. None of us did, of course, but my joining the line of succession wouldn't have changed anything. Arthur was going to be king. Arthur was always going to be king. I didn't see a reason to push the family into scandal during that time and upend my life, when it wouldn't make a difference." Cursing, he shakes his head. "It *would have* changed something, though. I'm ten months older than Ben."

My stomach sinks as the meaning of what he's told me truly sinks in.

King Arthur died, and if Damien had accepted his father's offer, those ten months would have made the difference between the crown landing on his head instead of his brother's.

Finally losing the battle to stop myself from crying, a tear escapes from the corner of my eye, flowing over the side of my cheek as I gaze at him. "Damien," I whisper, my voice shaking. "You couldn't have known. It wasn't your fault."

He shakes his head as a tremor wracks his body. "I was there, sitting beside him, when we got the news that the plane had been found, and Ben realized he was king. All I could think was that I'd made my choice nearly a decade before and took the easy way out. Watching him struggle through those first months..." Damien's voice breaks. "I've regretted it every day since, but there was nothing I could do. Nothing."

"Damien," I whisper. "Look at me. Please."

It seems to take an inordinate amount of willpower for him to raise those endlessly dark eyes to meet mine. I reach out, resting my hand on the table, palm up, and to my relief, he takes it.

"*You didn't know.* Nobody could have known. You didn't

ask for any of this, and if your brother holds you responsible for protecting yourself when—"

"Ben doesn't know."

My lips part. "What? *Why?*"

"Because it was my burden, not his."

"Or," I counter, staring imploringly at him. "Your brother loves you just as much as you love him, and you know he will forgive you."

Damien exhales sharply. "It isn't that simple. His isn't the only forgiveness I need. Not anymore."

Oh. Swallowing past the lump lodged in my throat, I tighten my hold on his hand. "The baby?"

He nods curtly, and for the first time, I see his eyes shining. "I could almost stand it when it was only Ben whose life I ruined. I could support him, be there for him... The baby, though..." A choked noise breaks from between his lips. "I couldn't stay and see her every day, playing the devoted uncle, when I'd taken her future before she was even born. Knowing she would shoulder the weight of the duty I shirked."

Slowly, I rise from my chair, reaching out as I step to his side of the table.

Part of me is expecting him to push me away, to reject any sort of comfort, but he doesn't. Folding his thick arms around my middle, Damien drags me to stand between his legs and presses his face into my stomach. I feel him break. "You didn't know," I whisper over and over again, pressing my lips to his hair and struggling to be strong for him, to keep myself from breaking down, too, as silent sobs wrack Damien's body.

God, he's carried the weight of this for so long, all by himself.

I can't imagine the courage it took to tell me this, but despite his fears, I don't think any less of him. Not even a little.

On the contrary, as I hold him, tears spilling silently down the sides of my face, a surreal sense of clarity seems to settle over me.

Of course I would have fallen for him.

Of course I would.

How could I—who has only known the coldest, most conditional kinds of love—not have been drawn to this brave, loyal man, who loves his family so fiercely that even inadvertently hurting them has all but destroyed him?

My eyelashes are still damp when, after his body has stopped shaking and his breathing has evened, Damien finally loosens his hold on me and sits back. I don't move, lifting my hands to his face and wiping away the lingering wetness. "You are the best man I've ever known," I whisper, unperturbed by the tremor which wracks his body at my words. "This doesn't change anything for me, but I'm not the only person who needs to hear it."

His hands tighten on my waist, but I'm encouraged when he doesn't look away. "I know," Damien admits at last, his voice hollow. "They deserve the truth."

"We'll talk about it tomorrow," I assure him, because if *I'm* exhausted from the day's events, I can only imagine how he's feeling.

Damien allows me to pull him to his feet, his eyes never leaving my face as I tug him backward toward the bed, leaving our cold, untouched tea abandoned on the table. The corners of his lips pull into a wry smile as I pull his shoulders down, guiding him to sit on the edge of the mattress. I stand back, watching as he pulls his sweatshirt off and drops it to the floor beside the bed.

"You didn't even fold it?" I tease gently but swat his hand as he reaches automatically for the fallen garment. "*Oh my god, I was joking, Damien. Leave it. You can be a lazy slob, just this once.*"

Chuckling quietly, he allows me to push him back into the

pillows. "Habits are important. If you let things slide, you might find yourself being managed by a woman half your age who once called you Satan."

I purse my lips as I begin removing my own clothes, making a point to drop my sweatshirt on the floor beside his. "I'm not *half* your age. And, besides, if I were fifty and you were sixty-six, nobody would care."

"*Hmmm*," Damien hums, his eyes already closed as he shifts to the side, holding out his arm in invitation. I join him, pulling the blankets over us both as I settle against him, loving the steady, reassuring beat of his heart beneath my ear. "You seem to have put some thought into this, but I suppose only time will tell," he murmurs. "We'll have to take a general survey when you're fifty, and I'm sixty-six."

For some reason, the words make me want to weep all over again, and I turn my head, pressing my lips to his chest. "Or," I suggest, tilting my chin to stare at his shadowy profile, "you could just admit I'm right."

Damien doesn't open his eyes, but I see his dimples deepen, as if he's holding back a smile. "Where's the fun in that, princess?"

Thirty-Six

Apparently, the days of quiet family gatherings, attended by only myself and my brothers, have come and gone.

Blair and I left Thornhurst early this morning, a week and a half after Araminta's funeral, driving straight up the coast and through the mountains to attend the celebration I'm not at all confident I will be welcome at.

Fernmoor House, the once-abandoned country house that my sister-in-law took upon herself to restore, has become the default venue for all informal family gatherings over the past year or two. Far from the posh formality of Ashwell Palace, this place is a home, beautiful but lived in, and I can see why they like it so much.

As we step inside, the foyer is empty, but it's clear where everyone is when a chorus of laughter erupts from deeper inside the house.

My stomach sinks.

It seems poor timing to divulge all this only a week before

Christmas, and on Ben's birthday to boot. After five months of minimal contact, however, I have no idea how I could attend without offering some kind of explanation for my absence. That, coupled with my lingering worries about Leo's mental health, and the thought of hurting Zelda's feelings by skipping another family event, left me with little choice in the matter.

Telling Blair everything was one of the most difficult things I've ever had to do. Even if having the same conversation with my brothers will be worse, I know it's time.

"I promise, they're going to like you better than me by the end of this," I assure the woman at my side, who has been uncharacteristically quiet for the past hour, and is currently clutching my hand for dear life.

Blair blanches, "You're not the one who made the world's worst first impression *to the queen*."

Even with the weight of the upcoming conversation hanging over me, it's difficult not to laugh. "When you're friends, ask her to tell you the story of how she met my brother. Trust me, Zelda has quite a high tolerance for clumsy starts."

"*Hmm*. Are you telling me that it's a family trait to behave like a royal turd when interested in a woman?"

Despite myself, I snort and reach down to nudge her chin up, lowering my lips to hers in a brief kiss. "Come on," I say when we've parted, glancing over my shoulder as the volume of the party surges unexpectedly, with many voices trying to talk excitedly over one another. "Let's go."

Keeping her hand in mine, I lead the way deeper into the house, following the noise to the formal dining room. We stop, lingering in the doorway, to take in the scene laid out before us.

The long table is laden with dirty plates and empty dishes, scattered amongst half-burned tapers.

Ben is sitting at the head of the long table, leaning back in his chair and holding his small daughter to his chest. My heart twists as I watch him laugh, though the noise is lost in the many sets of voices filling the room. His attention is on the man sitting to his right—his brother-in-law, Calvin Flowers—who is so covered in tattoos that un-inked skin seems to be the exception rather than the rule, and is talking animatedly, his smile wide.

Cal isn't the only member of the California contingent in attendance, either. Zelda's other siblings, Sterling and Sybil, are also seated at the table, and the three Americans seem to be responsible for most of the cacophony. Leo is there, too, and Zelda's friend, Davina, along with a pair of men I recognize as Leo's professor friends, Kian and Eric.

Amidst the chaos, nobody notices us. However, moments later, as Zelda enters the room through the door to the kitchen, her arms laden with a platter holding a handmade cake, Ben looks up. His gaze catches on Blair and me, hovering in the doorway, and regret wells in my throat as he looks away, smile fading.

Everyone launches into a boisterous rendition of "Happy Birthday" at different times and at different pitches. Calvin tries to conduct with a fork and knife, to no avail, and there's quite a bit of laughter amidst the applause as my brother's wife sets the cake on the table before him, pausing to kiss his cheek.

A cheer goes up as he blows out the candles obligingly, maintaining a careful hold on Alice to prevent her from grabbing the cake. "Thank you, darling," he tells his wife when the noise has died away, and, at last, he looks to me again.

The room quiets as several people follow his gaze and finally notice Blair and me. Her hand squeezes mine in silent encouragement.

"I hope we aren't too late," I manage.

Zelda breaks the silence. "Oh my god, of course not." She

hurries across the room, her face shining, and I release my hold on Blair to accept a hug. "He's missed you so much," she whispers when she pulls back, gazing up at me with a pleading look.

I wish I could tell her it could all be set aside so easily.

"Zelda, this is Blair Porter. You met briefly at the funeral," I tell her, and Blair looks downright petrified when Zelda turns her attention onto her.

"Of course. Welcome, Blair. Do we have you to thank for Dam's presence tonight?" she asks warmly.

Blair's cheeks go pink. "*Your Royal Highness*. Thank you for having me in your home, I'm so sorry to come without an invitation and—"

Zelda silences her with an airy wave. "There's actually a rule in Fernmoor House that we take quite seriously, and it's that titles are left at the door. Call me Zelda. Now, come sit, we'll introduce you to everyone."

There's an underlying tension in the room, the party much more subdued, as Zelda produces two more chairs, and everyone shuffles over to make room. Blair and I end up between Leo and Sybil as cake is distributed, and finally, Ben meets my eyes over his daughter's head.

I smile weakly. "Happy birthday."

"Thank you," he tells me quietly, and though the words are stiff, they seem to take some of the lingering awkwardness from the room.

I'd like to ask him if we can talk later, but the hubbub around the table has escalated in volume again. My brother seems to sense it, however, because he inclines his head toward the door, a question in his eyes.

Throat tight, I nod and lean forward to look at Leo. He also understands the unspoken request, and after Ben has handed off Alice to Cal, the three of us stand.

Fuck.

"We'll be back shortly," I tell Blair, leaning down to speak quietly in her ear, and she offers me a soft, encouraging smile, her hand coming out to squeeze mine.

If anyone at the table thinks anything of us leaving halfway through dessert, they don't comment, and before I'm quite ready for it, I find myself filing out of the room after Leo and Ben.

"You look familiar," I hear Davina tell Blair as we cross the threshold into the hall, an air of playful delight evident in her voice. "Did I see a rather spectacular picture of your breasts on the cover of a magazine?"

Christ.

Confident Blair can handle herself, I follow my brothers down the hall and into a warmly lit study. Leo closes the door behind me, and even the quiet click of the handle has my stomach twisting.

"Why have you come, Damien?" asks Ben without preamble, leaning back against his desk, his expression hard.

My gaze catches on a framed portrait on the wall above the desk, which depicts Ben and Zelda sitting together before a nondescript blue wall. In Zelda's arms is a swaddled infant, and even in the formal, painted image, both of them look so happy.

I force myself to meet his eyes, swallowing the shame and guilt which have grown even further inside me since we stepped inside Fernmoor. "To tell you I'm sorry. For leaving the palace the way I did." Exhaling heavily, I sit down in the other vacant chair, struggling to keep track of the words I swore to myself I would tell him tonight. Though I'd rehearsed them many times in my own head over the past week, and talked it over with Blair, now that I'm here...

"This isn't me asking for your forgiveness," I finally manage, addressing Ben as I shove down the clawing fear. "But you deserve an explanation for my absence the past few months."

So, I tell them.

It takes far less time than it did when I had this conversation with Blair. After all, Ben and Leo were there with me for most of this. They don't need to be given any backstory when they lived it.

Neither of them speaks or reacts in any way as I make my confession, and though it is the most difficult thing I've ever done, something seems to have loosened inside me as I near the end.

"I left the palace because I couldn't look at her. Alice," I confess at last, staring up at Ben. "When I came to meet her," my voice cracks, "she was perfect, you know? Nobody had ever hurt her, or tried to make her anything she isn't, or—fuck." I shake my head, desperately trying to dispel the burning behind my eyes. "It should have been my responsibility to protect her, but instead, I'd pushed her into the line of fire before she was even born."

The silence that follows this is painful, but shorter than I would have believed possible given the information I just disclosed.

I look up as, slowly, Ben pushes off his desk, turning to look at the portrait hanging before him. "It's changed my perspective so much," he muses, "being a parent."

His expression becomes thoughtful. "After she was born, there were nights I would stay awake for hours, holding her while she slept. I remember thinking that I would do anything for her, anything at all." At last, my brother turns to meet my eyes. "I was so angry at our father for so long, but now that I've experienced that kind of love... I can't imagine how broken he must have been not to have felt it too."

His words have an immediate, powerful effect, as though a knife has been driven into my chest. I understand, though, that the pain is there because what he said is true. Even for me, who saw a better side of Fabian Ashwell than my brothers, I know he never offered the unconditional love that Ben just described.

I, at least, had a mother who loved me that way, even if it was only for a brief time. Ben and Leo had none of it at all.

I'm in awe of him; my little brother, who had every reason to be broken, angry, and cold, now wholly committed to loving his wife and daughter in a way he never experienced himself.

Raking my hand through my hair, I let out a thin breath. "I'm sorry—*so goddamn sorry*. None of this was my intention, and I know the way I handled it was…"

"Poor?" Leo supplies dryly, speaking for the first time since we entered the room.

"I was going to go with *fucking shit*, actually," Ben counters, casting a dark look toward me. "Christ, Dam. Did you actually believe we would hold it against you? As if either of us wouldn't have opted out of this madness if we had the chance?"

Reeling, I sit back. "But Alice—"

Ben scoffs, waving this away. "Alice will be fine. She has the significant advantage of being raised by parents who love her and prioritize her mental health. If Zelda or I have concerns about her ability to handle it, then perhaps her younger brother or sister will be up to the task. If not, then…" He trails off with a shrug, as if to say, *let it burn*.

It takes a moment for the meaning of his words to fully sink in, and a quick glance at Leo confirms he is just as stunned by this development as I am. "Z is pregnant?" I demand, my heart expanding.

Smiling slightly, Ben nods. "We only found out a few days ago, so it's still a secret for now, but yes. She's due in August."

The emotional whiplash I've experienced since entering this room is fairly insane.

Letting out a weak laugh, I get to my feet, and Leo and I take turns hugging Ben, congratulating him on the addition to their family.

"I understand why you've struggled with this," Ben tells me at last, speaking slowly, as if he's choosing his words with care. "And I understand why you needed space to work through it. We never know the full impact of our choices, though, Dam. All we can do is our best with the information we have. And, with any luck, learn from our mistakes."

"Christ, Dam, look what you've done," Leo tells me, chuckling warmly, and breaking the sudden seriousness of the moment. "You've forced him to be wise."

Ben, in turn, flips him off. "It's called growth, you little twerp."

To my intense embarrassment, I realize my eyes are burning once again. *I fucking missed them.*

"Will you be coming back to the palace, then?" Leo asks me, frowning. "Since you've finally learned to communicate?"

I hesitate. "To be honest, I'm not sure it's the best idea. I've learned it's very difficult for me to be impartial or logical when it comes to the lives of people I love. We can discuss it when things are a bit more stable. Blair's family situation is... complicated. More complicated than ours, if you'll believe it."

"I know enough about Porter to believe you," Ben supplies grimly. "Is there anything I can do?"

"She's important to me," I explain, as somewhere out in the house, there is a muffled chorus of laughter. "This isn't something I can leave her to grapple with on her own, and I wouldn't feel right, influencing her decision one way or another. Especially when it may mean walking away from an insane amount of money. Listen, I've cast a shadow on your birthday celebration enough. Let's forget it for now."

Leo claps my shoulder, his smile wide and unconcerned. "Leave it to you, Dam. Going into self-imposed exile and returning with a *t-topless* socialite. Quite the remarkable journey of self-discovery you've been on."

I glare at him. "She's fully clothed now, thank you. And it wasn't entirely self-imposed." I explain briefly about Araminta's part in all this, and both my brothers look furious by the end.

"*P-perhaps* we shouldn't speak ill of the dead, but in this instance—" Leo begins but is swiftly cut off by Ben.

"She's a terrible human being and always has been. Did you know, she has had every pet dog she's ever owned stuffed after they passed, and kept them in storage to be buried with her? Can you imagine the level of narcissism required for something like that?" He shudders. "Well, at least we're rid of her. Back to the party, then?"

While we've been away, everyone appears to have abandoned the table, and we find the group gathered in the sitting room. Most of them are clustered around a board game in the corner, but as my eyes search the space, they find Blair removed from the revelry.

My heart stalls, and for a long moment, I'm capable of nothing but staring.

She's reclining on the couch, and Alice has fallen asleep on her chest, her tiny lips parted and back rising and falling steadily under Blair's hand.

When Blair meets my eyes, she lifts her free hand to point at the baby, mouthing *"look,"* her entire face shining with delight.

Before I can cross to them, however, Zelda appears at my side. "So, is she going to end up *Aunt* Blair?" she asks quietly, eyes sparkling.

She will if I have anything to say about it.

"I hope everyone was on their best behavior," I remark, glossing over the question. "Congratulations, by the way."

"Oh, he told?" She grins. "Thank you. And yes, they were perfect, but I do think she can hold her own." As if to illustrate this point, Sterling leans over the arm of the couch to touch Alice's tiny fist, and Blair slaps his hand away with a pointed glare. Z squeezes my arm. "By the way, no pressure, but I'll kill you if you mess this up for me. I've always wanted a cool sister-in-law."

She doesn't need to worry about that.

Heart full to bursting, I leave Zelda's side, crossing the room to take the empty place on the couch beside Blair.

"Isn't she the prettiest baby you've ever seen?" Blair murmurs, her expression full of wonder as she gazes down at my niece. "Look at her tiny little ears. They're just like regular ears, but in miniature."

"Yes, I think you'll find tiny human features quite common in eight-month-olds." My words are dry, but I lean in nevertheless, kissing her shoulder.

Tearing her attention from Alice, Blair peeks over at me, a hint of worry in her expression. "How did it go?"

I consider this. "If I tell you it went well, are you going to be insufferably smug about it?"

"Oh, I definitely will. I like you and all, but a girl has to have some standards," she replies promptly, and, not quite able to contain my affection for her, I drape my arm over her shoulders and shift closer to her and the baby.

"I suppose I'll have to bear it, then," I say, keeping my voice as quiet as possible. "It isn't settled, not entirely, but I think it will take longer for me to forgive myself than it will for them."

Blair's look of ease slips, just a little. "Will you go back to Wyngate? Araminta is dead. You've cleared things up with your brother."

"No," I reply simply, running my fingers over the column of her neck. "No, I'm not going anywhere without you." People are moving around the room, talking, laughing, living, but I'm wholly unable to look at anything or anyone but her.

Blair is looking back. "Even if I'm insufferably smug?" she teases, her eyes glassy with unshed tears.

"Yes," I assure her, "even then."

Movement registers in the corner of my eye, and reluctantly, I turn to find Ben standing over us. "I'm here for my child," he informs Blair wryly. "If we don't get her into her bed now, she'll be there all night."

"I don't mind," she assures him, a little pointedly. "Look at her, she's so comfortable! Also, have you seen the tiny little ears? How cute are they?"

This argument holds little sway with my brother, but his smile is amused as he eases Alice into his arms, kissing the crown of her head when the whimpering begins.

Blair groans, leaning forward to watch them leave the room with Zelda. "Just a heads-up," she informs me, once they've gone and she has slumped back, dejected. "If you're serious about me, I've just now decided that I would like about ten of those."

"Ten?" I scoff. "That seems excessive, love."

"*The ears*, Damien. *The ears.*"

"Of course, I hadn't taken *the ears* into account. My mistake." Gathering her into my side, I sigh, recognizing that some of the heightened emotions of the past day have settled. Not just the recent stress about our upcoming visit, either. I haven't been this relaxed in—fucking hell—months.

I feel Blair's smile as she kisses the side of my neck, cuddling closer. "Hey," she drops her voice to a whisper, "you're not running and screaming."

"*Hmm*, no. I suppose I'm not."

"Aren't guys supposed to run and scream when you tell them you want to have their babies?"

Superbly unconcerned by this sentiment, I turn to look at her. "I'm not a *guy*, love. I'm a grown man with a house, and money, and enough experience to know what I want in life. Which is to make you happy, in case I haven't been clear enough on that already."

A slow, radiant smile has spread across Blair's face as I speak, until she is all but glowing. "I'm not going to lie, that was the hottest thing you've ever said to me."

I let out a bark of laughter and lean in to steal a brief, searing kiss from her, feeling my heart expanding as I do.

For the first time since I recognized my feelings for this woman, I'm not concerned about anything.

This is going to work.

I'll make sure of it.

Thirty-Seven

Blair

"We don't have time."

Damien's scheduling concerns must not be too dire, because seconds later, his hands tighten in my hair, a groan issuing from deep in his chest as he guides my mouth over his cock.

I gaze up at him, and molten heat pools between my thighs as I take in the straining tendons in his neck and the tightness of his jaw. It's like he's doing everything in his power to stop himself from fucking my mouth, and honestly, how disrespectful.

I'm doing my best work here; the least he could do is make me gag.

Deciding to take matters into my own hands, I lower my head past the point of comfort until his tip hits the back of my throat and I'm forced to pull back, panting. Undeterred, I dive back in for more, licking and sucking eagerly, determined to see an end to his self-control.

He's unbelievably hard, the veins raised in thin ridges up

and down his shaft. They throb under my hand as I stroke what I can't fit in my mouth, holding tight enough to make him curse. I gag again, and his hips lift slightly off his chair, a tremor wracking his body.

"Fuck," comes the strangled snarl from above me. "That's it. Just like that, princess."

I would smile if my mouth wasn't a little full at the moment. Recent experience has taught me I'm *princess* when we're fucking, *love* when we're living our lives, and *Blair* when he's genuinely annoyed.

My clit throbs, begging for attention, as he drags me up and down, and I move from wet to *fucking soaked*.

I'd fantasized about this very scenario—before we learned more enjoyable methods to release our frustration with one another—and when I entered the security office to see him before my meeting, inspiration struck. Without a single word, I'd rounded the desk and dropped to my knees, working his belt open as he rapidly tried to conclude the phone call with Thornhurst's internet provider.

He's right, we don't have a lot of time, but I'm confident that won't be an issue.

Redoubling my efforts, I moan, and a ribbon of heat ripples in my belly as his cock grows—somehow—even harder.

Above me, Damien curses, fisting my hair tighter than ever. "I'm close," he rasps. "Swallow, do you hear me? *Take it —Fuck—*"

His words break off as he pulls me down, letting out a deep, masculine groan of satisfaction as his cock swells in my mouth, flooding the back of my tongue with his cum. It drips down my throat, and I do my best to breathe through my nose and not choke.

When Damien's grip on my hair finally relaxes, I lift my head, grinning at his dazed expression. "That good, huh?" I ask brightly, rolling back to my feet and snatching a tissue from the corner of his desk to dab the saliva from the bottom half of my face.

Slumped in his chair with his half-hard cock out, Damien merely blinks at me, apparently still coming back to himself. "Sorry, what?"

"You're adorable," I beam, bracing my hands on the arms of his chair and leaning in for a quick kiss. "What time is it?"

Shaking himself, he leans over to check the computer. "You've got five minutes," he tells me gruffly, as his hands move to tuck his cock away. "Definitely not complaining, but can I ask what prompted that?"

I shrug, already refocused on checking my makeup on my phone screen. "I was nervous, and figured it would be distracting, *and* give me something to look forward to when it's all over." Because, if there's one thing I've learned about this man's sexual preferences, it's that unreciprocated orgasms are off the table. There is no way in hell I won't be generously paid back for this little stunt.

"Brilliant," supplies Damien, sounding very amused. "Does this mean I get to eat your cunt when I need to take my mind off things?"

"Anything for you." Satisfied my face and hair bear no evidence of what we just did, I shove my phone away, feeling the first prickle of returning anxiety.

He must see it, because Damien stands, taking his coat from the back of his chair. "I'll drive you over there," he offers casually, and wraps an arm around my shoulders, leading me out to the truck.

My knee starts bouncing in the time it takes him to close my door and round the front of the vehicle to his own. As the engine rumbles to life, his hand finds mine in my lap, giving it a little squeeze. "Hey, it's going to be okay."

"I know." I don't actually know anything of the sort, but I'm hoping that's the case.

Upon realizing I wanted out of the Porter's toxic generational trauma party, the next big thing to consider was *how*. Learning who I am and growing up a little was the first step, but I have no idea what I want to do with myself when all this is over. Even if I've been working on my literacy and learning better ways to support my dyslexia, the prospect of actually going through with my father's college plan was daunting.

When I told Damien I was thinking of finding an attorney to learn more about the actual legal specifics for my trust fund, he'd promised to help. This help translated into him shamelessly exploiting his relationship with the King of Stelland to get me not just any lawyer, but a *really* good one.

After sending Mr. Allister every intimidating legal document I have, he called, asking if he could "*stop by*" for a "*quick chat*."

As we pull up to Thornhurst's kitchen door, Damien takes out his phone, frowning at the screen. "He's here."

My stomach churns. "Will you come in with me?" I ask, a little hysterically, as I watch him remotely open the gates, allowing my new attorney into the grounds.

With a gentle smile, Damien shakes his head. "No, love. Whatever he has to say, whatever options he gives you on how to proceed, it needs to be your decision. I don't want to influence this choice, one way or the other."

A panicked little giggle bubbles from between my lips, and I gaze back at him, pleading. "I appreciate the vote of confidence in my decision-making abilities, but my track record isn't exactly stellar. Come on, you love bossing me around."

"Not this time." He leans over the center console to kiss me and uses my temporary distraction to open the door.

Resigned to my fate, I screw up my face in a halfhearted glare. "Well done, sir."

"On your way, love. I'll be waiting."

Stomach in knots, I get out of the truck and go inside. As is often the case when I'm dreading something, time seems to be moving much faster than usual, and in what feels like about ten seconds, I'm opening Thornhurst's massive front doors.

Mr. Allister, who is a tall, reedy man with very little hair, greets me with a handshake and a nod. He follows me into the dining room, and upon setting down his bag, immediately begins pulling out paperwork.

Nauseous now, I slip into the chair across from him. "Thank you for coming all this way," I offer, simply to break the silence.

Glancing up at me, he offers me a tight, professional smile, shuffling the papers before him. "Of course. This is rather a complicated case, and if you decide to hire me as your counsel, I'll need your signature on some things."

"I'm dyslexic," I confess, ignoring the familiar prickle of embarrassment that comes with voicing that aloud. "There's an app I use to read through things like this for me, but when it's really complicated..." Trailing off, I wince, despite myself. "I haven't been as informed about the actual legal technicalities as I should have been."

Beneath the table, I twist my hands together in my lap, but to my relief, Mr. Allister doesn't look surprised.

"Even for someone without a learning disability, this is not a simple matter. It took me several days to get my arms around the way your parents and late grandparents have structured things." Clearing his throat, he sits up a little straighter. "Well, I suppose we'll get into it, then."

Just as he said, it's complicated. *Really* complicated.

Even giving me the simplified version, there are so many legal loopholes and protections in place that nearly every explanation Mr. Allister gives me comes with a "but if" attached. By the end of an hour, however, I think I'm getting the gist of it.

"So, basically," I clarify, rubbing my temples and gazing blearily across the table at my new attorney. "When I was young, and my grandparents died, my parents used my inheritance to buy a portion of Porter Capital, and the profits from that portion go into my trust fund, from which they are *reinvested* into Porter Capital."

"Basically," Mr. Allister agrees, looking extremely relieved we're finally getting somewhere. "The majority of your financial holdings are directly tied to the family company."

My shoulders weigh about ten times more than they did an hour ago, and I slump back in my chair, gazing at him helplessly. "So, I'm stuck, then. I don't have access to my trust fund, so I can't sell my shares or whatever."

"You are not stuck," Mr. Allister counters, and there's an enthusiastic gleam in his eye, which is pretty unfathomable to me, considering we're talking about the most boring stuff ever. "When your father initially ran for Parliament, he was required by law to divest himself of his controlling interest in the firm. To do this, he used—pardon me—some very questionable legal work."

While not surprised—given what Damien told me about his blackmail suspicions, and my experience being raised by the man—this definitely has my attention. "What do you mean?" I ask, as, picking up on whatever thrill Mr. Allister seems to be getting from this, my heart lifts.

"It means, at first glance, Lord Porter handed over his shares of Porter Capital to you and your siblings, just as was required of him by law. It wasn't a gift, though; it was a loan. Every month, your trust fund pays your father for the shares he divested to you, *with interest*. This would be legally questionable on its own, but there are stipulations hidden in the contracts, which essentially means he can collect interest proportional to your returns on Porter Capital shares. For example, if *you* make a ten percent return, *he* will make a ten percent return. There is no material gain for you in those shares, which makes your trust fund a funnel for his own financial gains without him technically needing to own anything."

Holy... I stare at the man across from me, stunned by what he's telling me, and totally unable to comprehend how he still looks happy. "I'm sorry, but none of that seems like good news for me."

Mr. Allister's smile widens. "It means you have a tremendous amount of leverage, Blair. Trust me, your father does not want this contract put before a judge. For one thing, the dispute would become public record, and for another, the judge may choose to honor the spirit of the contract. Which was to facilitate your father's divestment of his financial interests, in order to hold public office." He leans forward, staring into my face. "You may walk away with his shares of Porter Capital, free and clear. A gift, as it should have been."

Swallowing, I gaze back at him, as the full implications of this settle over me at last. "What if I don't *want* his shares in Porter Capital?" I ask. "Or my own, for that matter. What if I want nothing to do with it?"

I don't mention Damien's suspicions about the break-in, or the search warrant, which was supposedly executed at my brother's office, that still hasn't been publicly reported.

While his smile fades, Mr. Allister seems to have suspected this would be the case, because he doesn't need time to think about it. "There are two ways we can make that happen," he informs me promptly. "The first is to take your father to court and challenge the validity of the contract. At the end of which, you would be able to sell your shares at full market value. It would be a very long, very public process, but in the end, it would result in a significant amount of money."

Oh, is that all?

"And the second?" I ask, a little pleadingly, because I'm really hoping it's better than option one.

Like he knows what I'm thinking, Mr. Allister chuckles. "I could approach your family members and their legal counsel, privately, and notify them of your intention to challenge the contract in court. They would be given the option to head this off early, and to buy you out of your ownership shares, at a below-market rate. The proceeds of which would be put into a new trust, which is controlled by you, and you alone." He winks. "It would be quieter, faster, but may result in a slightly smaller yet still significant amount of money."

A hysterical little laugh bubbles from between my lips because a slightly smaller yet tremendous amount of money sounds just fine to me, and I don't need long to think about it. "I would like option number two, please."

"Yes, I thought you might," agrees Mr. Allister, the corners of his lips still turned up as he shuffles through his paperwork, searching for a contract. "I should mention something else, though. Having litigated cases like this in the past, family matters which involve a great deal of money, I can tell you they very often end in estrangement."

I'd figured as much, but if even the tiniest part of me still craved the love of Albert and Lydia Porter, I wouldn't be feeling the way I am now, as though a tremendous pressure I've been bearing all my life was suddenly lifted away.

"Thank you. I understand." I get to my feet, offering Mr. Allister my hand over the table. He stands, too, and takes it before handing over the form—which he explains gives him my consent to act on my behalf in this matter—and tells me to take my time looking it over.

Once I've seen him out, I go in search of Damien.

Thornhurst is silent as always as I stroll through the familiar rooms, my eyes roaming over the paintings, draperies, and furniture, seeing it all with fresh eyes. Even given the association this place has with my family, my memories here aren't all bad.

This is the house with the pool that reminded me I'm an excellent swimmer.

This is the house where I lost my independence and took it all back.

This is the house where I fell in love.

Thornhurst gave me a lot, but I don't owe this place anything. When I leave, I'm never coming back.

I find Damien in the kitchen, arms folded and face solemn, staring out the window at the snowy grounds. Hearing me enter, he turns, his expression softening. "How did it go?"

"Good, I think." Crossing to where he's standing, I pull myself up onto the counter across from him, sitting with my feet dangling against the cabinets, and stare into his face. "My parents seem to have structured the whole thing as incomprehensibly as humanly possible."

His warm brown eyes wrinkle at the corners. "Sounds about right."

"I think I've got the gist of it, though." I hesitate, gripping the edge of the countertop. "Dad has been doing some really shady stuff with Porter Capital and my trust fund, stuff that would look bad for him if it went before a judge. Mr. Allister thinks I'm in a position to settle this quietly, sell my shares of the company, and walk away. I would make more money if we went the court route, but who knows how long that would take, and if they're under investigation of some sort..." I trail off, lifting my shoulder with a grimace. "What do you think?"

Smiling gently, Damien shakes his head. "It doesn't matter what I think. This is your decision, Blair."

Trusting myself and my instincts isn't something I have a lot of experience in, but I give it a shot, listening to the new but growing voice that comes directly from my heart. The corners of my vision swim as I stare into the face of the bossy, noble, perfect man I've fallen in love with and tell him, "I don't really want to be a Porter anymore."

Damien moves forward immediately, closing the distance between us in a single stride and hugging me.

He holds me while I cry. *And cry. And cry.*

Every time I think I've processed this and grieved the family I wanted but never had, something will remind me I haven't. Now, though, the pain is different because knowing what I do now, I understand my parents in a way I didn't before.

Albert and Lydia were frightened of me.

They treated me like my siblings by default and assumed that providing me the same lifestyle, privileges, and education would produce the same result. Only, it was too late that they realized what they had done; handed the power to undo them, directly into the hands of the child they could not control.

They wanted me to stay frivolous and ill-informed.

They wanted me too occupied with partying to ever turn my mind toward more important matters.

They wanted me to be controllable, so I could never control him.

When I've finally run out of tears to cry, and the bonds around my chest have loosened, I lift my head to look at Damien. He meets my eyes and slowly lifts his hands to cradle my face, carefully wiping away the tears still wet on my cheeks.

"I'm not sure if anyone has ever told you this," he tells me calmly, "but you are a force of nature, love. Nothing and no one can control you without your consent. If you've decided you don't want to be a Porter anymore, you won't be."

The love I feel for this man might have grown to be a force of nature unto itself.

Sniffing, I reach out, settling my palms on his chest. "I want you to know I am being one hundred percent serious when I say that if anyone is rude to you ever again, I'm going to ruin their whole life."

A bark of laughter greets my words, and he leans in to kiss my forehead. "I know you will," he assures me placatingly.

Bristling, I lean back to glare at him. "Damien! I'm not kidding!"

"Of course you aren't."

We fall silent, and I look around at the cavernous kitchen we're currently occupying, as another issue occurs to me. "We can't stay here," I tell him weakly. "When they find out what I've done... I don't want to be around for it."

Turning my attention back to the man before me, I meet Damien's steady gaze, and whatever strain I felt at this eases. "Thankfully, I have a solution to that."

"Oh?"

My heart flutters as I watch his handsome face stretch into that adorable, dimpled smile. "Run away with me, princess?"

PORTER RESIGNS AMIDST INSIDER TRADING SCANDAL

FROM RICHES TO RAGS: WILL LORD PORTER'S FALL FROM GRACE EVER REACH ROCK BOTTOM?

Only months after the election for Prime Minister that he was once favored to win, Lord Albert Porter (61) has now bowed to calls for his resignation from his seat in Parliament.

This announcement comes days after Stelland's National Police formally announced charges would be filed against his family-owned venture capital firm, Porter Capital, as well as its Chief Executive Officer, and Porter's son, Cedric Porter (35). Prosecutors have confirmed these charges include securities fraud, insider trading, and other minor related financial offenses, which stretch back at least six years.

Investigators accuse Porter Capital of leveraging confidential government information to execute highly profitable stock trades before major announcements, allowing the company to benefit from impending investments and subsidies before those contracts were made public. Legal analysts suggest that, if proven, the charges could result in prison sentences and steep financial penalties.

Cedric Porter has denied wrongdoing, calling the charges

"trumped up and politically motivated," and although Lord Porter himself has not yet been charged with a crime, his proximity to both political decision-making and the firm's activities certainly raises eyebrows.

Legal proceedings for Cedric Porter are scheduled to begin next summer, but Lord Porter's future remains uncertain. Once the frontrunner for Prime Minister, he now faces the prospect of permanent political exile, and in the court of public opinion, the verdict may already be forming: Even if he avoids criminal charges, the damage to his reputation may prove to be irreparable.

EPILOGUE

Two Years Later

Damien

I've never considered myself to be a particularly vengeful man.

Yes, there are people in my past who have wronged me, and yes, in an ideal world, I would like for them to see some consequences for their actions. Yet, with one notable, misguided exception, I've never gone out of my way to personally facilitate justice being served. I've always been of the opinion that assholes will typically continue to behave like assholes until they inevitably piss off someone who is bigger, meaner, and more vengeful than they are.

I hadn't realized that *anyone* can become that bigger, meaner, more vengeful asshole under the right circumstances. Unfortunately for Lord Albert Porter, for me, it seems those circumstances are met by anyone who hurts my wife.

It's been well over two years since we left Thornhurst, and in that time, neither of us has had any contact with the

Porters, except through Blair's attorneys. The matter of her trust fund and shares in Porter Capital was settled very quickly. Presumably concerned about this turning into a court battle, her father agreed to all her terms, on the condition that Blair had to sign an NDA. Even on his way out of her life, it seemed Albert couldn't help but provide one last reminder that he valued his reputation over his daughter.

She'd signed anyway, eager to begin living her new life—*our* new life—and never looked back.

After Thornhurst, we moved into my house in Wyngate, where Ben lured me back to the palace with a position as his domestic security advisor. Meanwhile, Blair committed herself to a skill she'd mastered a long time ago—*spending a lot of money*.

Now, fortunately, it's on things more substantial than designer clothes or handbags.

Her very first stop, once the legal formalities with her trust had been settled, was the shelter she'd visited with her family months ago as one of her father's campaign stops. Except my wife didn't just talk about how important it was to help them, she actually did it.

The place is unrecognizable now, clean, safe, and well-staffed. Still not satisfied, however, Blair then roped Zelda into it. In no time, the two of them had dozens of businesses signed up to provide paid internships and on-the-job training for the shelter's single mothers.

As if I needed further reason to be madly in love with her.

While the wounds left by her family are painful from time to time, Blair has moved on with her life. She's found her place in the world, surrounded by people who adore her, becoming a devoted wife, friend, sister-in-law, aunt, and soon, mother.

Our first child, a boy, is due in six weeks, and this fact is undoubtedly responsible for my newly discovered *bigger, meaner, more vengeful* side.

Thankfully, my wife is still unaware, and I'm determined to keep it that way. After all she's gone through to bring our son into the world, she deserves a surprise.

"Have you settled on a name yet?" asks Zelda from her place across the table from us, offering Blair a sympathetic smile. In her arms, my nephew, Rowan, is sleeping peacefully.

Beside me, Blair shifts uncomfortably in her seat, pressing her hand to the side of her very swollen belly. She wrinkles her nose at the question. "No, but he's going to be called something embarrassing if he doesn't stop kicking me like this."

It's Friday afternoon, and we're seated beneath an awning in the rose garden behind Ashwell Palace, taking advantage of the first day warm enough to eat outdoors, and watching Ben chase his squealing daughter through the shrubbery. Ordinarily, I would be taking the heat off for him a bit, but lately I've been reluctant to let my wife out of my sight unless absolutely necessary.

Zelda considers. "You could call him Mallory? Mallory Mallory? That's awful, he would almost certainly get teased."

"Pringlefritz?" suggests Blair, as, with another wince, she rubs her side in the place our son has obviously decided to use for target practice.

"Snoorlock?"

"Fiddlebum?"

"Turnip?"

I zone out as the two continue to go back and forth, proposing increasingly ridiculous baby names, and lift my wrist to check my watch for about the fifth time in the past half hour. It's nearly time, and after looking forward to this for weeks, I feel like a kid on Christmas morning. Except, instead of the remote-controlled car I asked for when I was nine, I'm getting the satisfaction of finally besting my father-in-law.

I doubt Lord Porter failed to make the connection when I abruptly resigned my position as Thornhurst's head of security, and his daughter vanished from the premises. Whether he knows I married her, or that my son will be his first grandchild, is unclear.

At the sound of giggles, I look around, grinning at the sight of Ben approaching the table—flushed and clearly winded—with Alice thrown over his shoulder like a sack of potatoes.

"Ready?" he asks casually as he meets my gaze, and I get the sense he's avoiding looking at Zelda or Blair directly, as if they'll pick up on our subterfuge if he makes eye contact.

While not quite as invested as I am, Ben has heard plenty about Lord Porter and must be similarly looking forward to what is about to occur. He seems to have grown very fond of his sister-in-law over the past several years, presumably warmed by her unconditional love of his children, and the creative nicknames she conjures up when annoyed with me.

"Where are you going?" asks Blair, frowning as I stand up.

I'm saved from having to respond. Upon hearing the voice of her very favorite person, Alice squeals, squirming until her father sets her on her own two feet, and rushes over to squeeze onto her aunt's lap.

"We'll be back," Ben assures our wives, "just a quick meeting." And, before either of them can question this further, we're striding back through the gardens and toward the palace, side by side. "I have to say, Dam," he tells me as a footman opens the garden door, and we enter the palace's east corridor. "Exacting revenge against her father is a strange gift to commemorate the birth of your first child."

"She's going to love it."

A quick glance confirms my brother is unconvinced. "I got Zelda a very expensive handbag after she had Rowan. Are you quite sure Blair wouldn't like one of those?"

I can't help but laugh, clapping Ben on the shoulder. "Your wife is into sunshine and rainbows and—Christ, I don't know—fluffy kittens? You know I love Zelda, but the woman is completely devoid of bloodlust. I bet she has never once dropped mud down your pants."

"Wait, Blair dropped—"

We make the turn toward Ben's study and the palace's official meeting rooms, and I wave this question away impatiently. "*The point being*, Blair can buy her own very expensive handbags. Do you know what she can't buy?"

My brother pauses. "Revenge against her father?"

"Correct."

As we pass one of the palace's smaller, secondary lobbies, a familiar voice calls after us. "Good afternoon, gentlemen."

Slowing my pace, I grin at Leo, who is strolling toward us in a tweed vest, hands shoved deep in his pockets. "Thanks for making the trip."

"You're in on it, too?" Ben demands incredulously, obviously still wrapping his head around this.

Leo hums in confirmation, falling into step beside us. "I'm an advisor, too. Technically."

With an impatient scoff, Ben shakes his head. "Yeah? How many King's Council meetings have you attended this year—no, actually—in the past *decade*?"

"I thought my participation would be a nice gesture," Leo tells him, sidestepping the question. "Dam's gone to all this trouble to arrange a very considerate gift for his wife—"

"I got Zelda a handbag, and she loved it."

"Yes, I'm sure she did," Leo agrees patiently, "but Blair is rather more—ah—*spirited* than Zelda, isn't she? It's good that Dam is giving her a present that is appropriate to her taste. Besides, the asshole deserves what's coming to him, doesn't he?"

Ben, who has obviously seen he won't convince anyone that Blair would like a handbag instead of retribution, leans past me to frown at Leo. "You've had a wife for about five minutes, and already you have all the answers?"

I'm saved from enduring more bickering by our arrival at the conference room where the appointment is taking place. Both my brothers fall silent, gazing at the closed wood door. Technically, this began fifteen minutes ago, but our tardiness isn't an accident.

The old fuck can damn well wait.

"Ready?" asks Ben, casting me a long, sideways glance.

My lips curve. "Ready." And, without further delay, I step forward to grasp the polished brass handle, leading the way inside.

This room was yet another very deliberate choice to set the stage for today's proceedings. Earlier this week, I spent the better part of an hour going into every single meeting space in Ashwell Palace, searching for the least desirable one I could find. With its unusually uncomfortable wood chairs, proximity to the air conditioner, and a window looking out on the kitchen dumpsters, I thought this particular room sent a clear message: *you are not important.*

"Good afternoon, Lord Porter," Ben offers cooly as we file inside, moving to sit in the three chairs across the table from Blair's father.

He stands hurriedly, inclining his head respectfully as we take our seats. "Your Royal Highness. Thank you for your invitation." As he lifts his face to look at us directly, however, I see his features harden as he realizes who Ben has brought with him.

It's with no small amount of satisfaction that I see the past two years have taken their toll on Lord Porter. After his resignation from Parliament, he only narrowly escaped criminal charges for his role in the insider trading scheme for which his son is currently doing time. Porter Capital, the diamond of his empire, is no more, dissolved and sold off in parts to the same firms he was once in competition with.

Ben clears his throat and rests both hands atop the table, waiting for Porter to retake his seat before continuing. "I have two members of the King's Council here with me today. Allow me to introduce my brother, Prince Leopold, and one of my most trusted advisers, Mr. Damien Mallory."

A muscle leaps in Porter's jaw as he stares at me. "Actually, I've encountered Mr. Mallory before. I employed him. *Briefly.*" The words ring with feeble bravado, and I have to bite back a laugh. He hasn't changed. This is exactly the sort of posturing he utilized during our first meeting at The Lord's Club.

"A few years back, yes," I confirm calmly, reclining in my chair.

"Quite the ascension, from managing security to advising the king," Porter sneers. "I would love to hear how this came about. These things don't often happen without considerable connections."

Before I can respond to this, however, Ben lets out a low, impatient noise. "We aren't here to discuss Mr. Mallory's employment history, Lord Porter. I summoned you here in regard to your peerage."

The mention of his title has Porter's attention immediately. Abandoning his pursuit of me, he rounds on my brother, his jaw tight. "Of course, Your Highness, my apologies."

To my right, Ben tilts his head, considering the man before us. Despite his reservations about the advisability of this gift for Blair, it's clear my brother has decided Leo was quite right when he said *the asshole deserves it*, and is now a wholehearted participant. "I believe the Porter title was originally bestowed by my great, great-grandfather on yours. A gift given for his dedication and loyalty to the crown."

What a dignified way of saying he's the descendant of an ass kisser.

"It has been one of the greatest honors of my life, Your Highness," Porter boasts, but I can sense wariness in his tone for the first time.

Ben does nothing to settle his sudden apprehension. "As you are undoubtedly aware, in Stelland, peerages such as yours are settled at the discretion of the monarch. It is my right to give them, and to take them away... when the occasion calls for it."

There is no possible way Porter has missed the proverbial writing on the wall, but he seems determined to remain calm and not react. Stiffly, he inclines his head, never once taking his eyes off his king. "I am aware of that, yes."

"It is a considerable responsibility, and not one I take lightly. However, considering your recent conduct—"

Abandoning the pretense of civility, Porter cuts across him, nostrils flaring. "I have not been charged with a crime."

"Your heir has," Ben counters. "And I'm afraid to say, your conduct is not up to the standard I would like to see in an individual who represents the crown. This meeting is merely a formality. I have already submitted a formal order to Parliament, which strips you of your title, peerage, and all associated honors."

With a snarl, Porter is on his feet, his chair grinding noisily over the wood floor. "This isn't about Cedric or my conduct," he seethes, jabbing a finger in my direction. "This is about *him,* and my traitorous daughter. They want the title, is that it? You'd like to strip me of my birthright and give it to King Fabian's bastard?"

At this, Ben hesitates. "Actually, I hadn't thought of that." He glances at me, a glint in his eye. "Do you want it?"

I require exactly no time to think it over. "Nah."

"Alright, then." He turns back to Porter, smiling blandly,

and wholly unbothered by the fury radiating off the man before us. "It appears Mr. Mallory isn't interested. However, I'm afraid it changes nothing, as your conduct and your heir's conviction are the deciding factor here, not my personal loyalties."

Porter sneers. "If you think I won't go to the press about him—"

"You could," I concede with a polite, unaffected smile. "Unfortunately, when Blair dispensed with her interest in the Porter family holdings, you insisted she sign a non-disclosure agreement. She did so, but only after her attorney requested a slight modification"—I lean forward, adrenaline rushing through my system as I stare into his icy eyes—"that you needed to sign one, too."

Incensed, Porter glares at me, his chest heaving. "I have no intention of bringing my daughter into this."

"Your daughter is *my wife*. There is no possible way to bring the hammer down on me without doing the same to her. By all means, you're welcome to attempt it, but if the NDAs are invalidated... well," I chuckle, rising as well, "you have a lot more to hide than I do, and it won't change the outcome."

We stare at one another until Porter's expression contorts into a twisted sneer. "Funny. I truly believed my daughter could not possibly disappoint me more."

He's trying to provoke me, and for the briefest moment, it almost works. Instead, I think of my wife, and I smile. "Your disappointing daughter has done more to help her community in two years than you have in your entire life. *She* is currently enjoying lunch with the queen, while *you* are about to be thrown out of the palace. There's only one disappointment here, *Mr. Porter*."

Ignoring the furious hiss at the reminder of his new status, I step out from behind the table, following my brothers out of the room without a backward glance. The entire encounter can't have taken longer than ten minutes, but I feel like a new man as we start back toward the gardens, pausing only to direct the guards to see the former Lord Porter out.

"I have to admit, that was immensely satisfying," Ben concedes cheerfully, after we've left the conference room well behind.

Leo nods, grinning from ear to ear. "It really was. Do you have any more revenge to enact on your wife's behalf, Dam? If so, count me in."

Pushing open the door to the garden, my attention is drawn immediately to Blair. She's standing amidst the roses, her chin tilted up, and her lashes lowered to her cheeks, enjoying the warmth of the sun on her face. As though sensing eyes on her, she turns, meeting my gaze from across the garden, and my heart swells as her face splits in a mischievous smile.

"I have no idea," I admit, and honestly, I couldn't be less bothered.

My wife has been a surprise from the start, and I can't wait to see what she has in store for us next.

Bonus Epilogue

Want more of Blair and Damien's story? Download this FREE bonus epilogue, set over a year after the end of Revelation!

THANK YOU

Thank you for reading Revelation!

If you have a moment, **please consider leaving a rating or review for the book**. Feedback from readers is so important to me and vital to help new readers find my work!

Want to stay updated on my releases, events, free book promos and what I'm working on?

- **Subscribe** to my newsletter @ www.authorcle owhite.com
- **Join my Patreon** for exclusive character art, bonus chapters, and updates on my work
- Buy **signed books** directly from me through Beventi
- **Follow me** *@authorcleowhite* on Instagram, Tiktok, Goodreads, Pinterest or Facebook
- Join my Facebook **reading group** to connect with me and make like-minded reader friends – Cleo's Cliterature Collective

Thank you again!
xo,
Cleo

Cleo White's affinity for all things dramatic, and hopelessly romantic began the day she was born, which happened to be in the middle of a record-breaking snowstorm on Valentine's Day. Her love of literature came soon after, and she spent the better part of her childhood with both a book and a notebook full of unfinished stories in hand. Later in life, she found a love of writing spicy books with complicated characters and dysfunctional family drama. Cleo currently lives in Vermont with her husband and two daughters. When not writing, she can be found hiking, gardening, painting, and consuming excessive quantities of caffeine.

Also by Cleo White

Standalone Titles

Out of Sight

In Pieces

Age of Shade

You're It

Second Edition

Triple Tidings

Royally Forbidden Series

Coronation

Revelation

Creation

Daddy Issues Series

Chilled and Thrilled

Kissed and Missed

Charmed and Alarmed

Acknowledgements

Writing a book is way more of a team sport than most people realize, and I am certainly not the only person responsible for Revelation becoming the story it is.

In the interest of not writing the words about fifteen times, I'm going to express one big fat ***THANK YOU*** (See, I put in in bold and everything!) to all the people below;

My husband, Ethan, for his unfailing support and certainty that I am excellent, even when my imposter syndrome thinks differently. Every single love story I write has pieces of ours in it.

To my daughters, M & R, who I sincerely hope never read this or realize they've been acknowledged.

To my assistant, Danie, who deals with more nonsense, listens to more discombobulated voice memos than anyone ought to, and deserves the whole world. (Danie, you are greater than you think you are. Stop being mean to my PA.)

To my Alpha readers; Jen (June), Dani, Rose and Nika.

To my Beta readers; Ashley, Megan, Kelsey, Rae and Megan.

One more, special thank you to the members of my Patreon, The Smut With Soul Society, for their consistent support, encouragement, and enthusiasm for my work.

These members include, but are not limited to; Kesia Joy, Evelyn Hudson, Caitlin, SpicySeoulReads, CamillaDamsted, NaShara Goodwin, Samantha Sullivan, Roxy C., Katie Thayer, Lina, Cindy Velazquez, Megan Smith, Sarah Buckley,

Ashley Jo, Louise Baaz, Jessica H. Galloway, Betsy, Stephanie Kelley, Molly Smith, Luna D, Samantha S Sullivan, Amy Alarcon.

Content Warnings

Some readers may find themes in this book triggering. These include, but are not limited to; Slut-shaming & tabloid style public humiliation, toxic family dynamics, mention of prior drug and alcohol usage (off-page), degrading language, antagonistic banter & sexual power dynamics, home invasion/ threat of intruder, rough sex, spanking & degrading language, verbal criticism related to academic struggle and learning disability symptoms, depression & self destructive thoughts, death of a parent & family member (off page, discussed on page), infidelity (not between mc's).